The Girl on the Promenade

By

Elizabeth Morgan

*Best wishes
Liz Morgan*

Bloomington, IN  Milton Keynes, UK

AuthorHouse™
1663 Liberty Drive, Suite 200
Bloomington, IN 47403
www.authorhouse.com
Phone: 1-800-839-8640

AuthorHouse™ UK Ltd.
500 Avebury Boulevard
Central Milton Keynes, MK9 2BE
www.authorhouse.co.uk
Phone: 08001974150

© *2006 Elizabeth Morgan. All rights reserved.*

No part of this book may be reproduced, stored in a retrieval system, or transmitted by any means without the written permission of the author.

First published by AuthorHouse 4/25/2006

ISBN: 1-4208-7982-0 (sc)

Printed in the United States of America
Bloomington, Indiana

This book is printed on acid-free paper.

Dedication

In humble gratitude to those ordinary men and women who became heroic combatants in countless secret armies; who risked, suffered, and gave, resisting the Nazi scourge

CHAPTER ONE

Lieutenant Freddy von Langdorf sat in his office at the Oberkommando in Berlin. It was very hot and still only April. The sun shone through the long window, directly into the small room. An elegant hand pushed back strands of blond hair that had fallen across his forehead. He grimaced against the glare of light that accentuated a scar under his right cheekbone, acquired during a duelling tournament at Heidelberg.

Four years of Archaeology, and here he was, little more than a clerk for the Fuhrer. He rose from the desk without removing his headphones, leant over a cumbersome radio receiver, and gave the Venetian blinds a twist, diffusing the brightness.

Freddy was in the Abwehr department of the OKW. It was his responsibility to listen to French broadcasts, military and civilian, and translate everything into German, scribbling the transcript on the fat notepad beside the apparatus. Each day he presented neatly typed information packs to the secret service for scrutiny.

Having monitored the midday news from Paris, he stretched his long legs, mopped his forehead and with a furtive glance at the door, undid the top button of his uniform jacket.

The telephone rang.

'Lieutenant von Langdorf?' asked a female voice.

'Yes.'

'I have General Count von Langdorf for you, one moment please.'

Freddy smiled with relief. His uncle had been at the Polish front for months.

'Freddy! How are you my boy?'

'Welcome back, uncle. Your secretary thinks you are a full general.'

'I am,' he chuckled.

'Really? When? Was it in Poland? Do my parents know?'

'All questions answered over lunch. When are you off duty?'

'In five minutes.'

'Good. We'll go to my favourite Italian restaurant.'

Uncle Carl had always been one of Freddy's heroes. Seeing them together no one could have doubted the strong family resemblance.

The "Roma" was at the far end of the Kurfürstendamm, and walking was the safest way to exchange confidences. Freddy was anxious to have the answer to the one question they had all been asking.

'How long is this Sitzkrieg going to last, and why isn't he going into France?'

'Lack of resources. Poland is fully occupied, and now, with Denmark and Norway pretty well subdued we shall need a large army of occupation.'

'What about France and the British?'

'Soon. Soon. The British Expeditionary Force is hardly going to put up much resistance. Mostly last war veterans,' he sighed. 'The Fuhrer feels more than confident.'

'But when?'

Carl's jaw tensed. 'After Belgium, the Netherlands and Luxembourg.'

'Jesus! The rumours are true then?'

Carl nodded.

'But that could take a year.'

'No. A matter of weeks.'

'Crazy! And France?'

'Next month.'

'God! He can't march all over Europe!'

'He'll try. But keep those thoughts to yourself lad, or you'll be shot.'

The young man shrugged. Lowering his voice he continued. 'Look uncle, I believe in Germany in Socialism; I believe we should be able to hold our heads high again.Taking Sudentenland was maybe different, but Europe? It'll never work! We'll be spread so thinly resistance will consolidate. Bound to. Like Napoleon and the Roman Empire.'

His uncle nodded. 'You are not wrong. But try telling him.'

Over lunch at a secluded table, Carl explained why he had been made a general in Poland. He looked down into his coffee, and putting his hand to his temples said, 'The Jews. I was responsible for issuing those compulsory identity stars. Massive job, going through all those papers in dozens of town halls all over the country. Ironic isn't it?'

For several moments they looked at each other in silence.

'I'm glad Aunt Sophie doesn't know.'

Carl smiled sadly. 'I miss that woman more each day'. He drained his coffee cup. 'Why didn't I go with her?'

Sophie Hoffman, a celebrity and a brilliant journalist, had been Carl's adored companion for ten years. Knowing Emmy Goering had enabled her to remain in Berlin a little longer than most Jews, who had either been taken off to labour camps, or in the case of a number of celebrities and dissenters, had suddenly 'committed suicide'. These orchestrated assassinations were becoming uncomfortably commonplace, and Carl knew Sophie was somewhere on that celebrity list. Though dreading being parted from her, he had facilitated the purchase of passport and papers, and just two months before the outbreak of war they bade a tearful farewell at a bleak dockside in Hamburg.

The very thought of his beloved Sophie touched him as always. He dabbed his mouth and his eyes. 'You know, there were fewer Jews in Poland than any of us imagined. Many hundreds of papers must have been lost, don't you think?'

Freddy said nothing. It was clear his uncle had taken a risk, and in the present climate that made him a hero.

'Now my boy, how about Intelligence in France?'

They were on their way back to the Oberkommmando offices.

'With the army?'

'Not necessarily. Ahead of it perhaps. They tell me your French is perfect.'

Freddy stared at his uncle. 'You mean a spy? In the Abwehr Police, with the Gestapo for a boss? Never! They're maniacs - I hate them!'

'In your case it wouldn't have been with the Abwehr Police. So, we have to decide. They won't want to waste you here in Berlin. I take it you'd like to go to France?'

Freddy snorted. 'A war isn't the best time to visit my favourite country, but yes, of course I'll go.'

'Very well, I'll see you stay in radio intelligence.' Carl smiled. 'They'll treat you well. Linguists are never in the firing line.'

Freddy laughed. 'That will make Mama happy.'

It made him happy too. He didn't want his uncle to think him a coward, but there were better ways to die, than for Adolf Hitler.

As though picking up his thoughts, Carl chuckled. 'And I don't think the Fuhrer would want to lose his perfect Nordic specimen either.'

Freddy grinned sheepishly at the memory of that spectacular reception at the Reich Chancellery last year. The great concert hall had been decorated with vast murals depicting scenes from Wagner's operas, and crystal chandeliers glinted from elaborate ceiling roses. Brown and black uniforms, party arm bands, even on old royalty, mingled with couturier ball-gowns as guests ate their way round a long table decked in a pink tablecloth edged with gold swastikas, and laden with gourmet delicacies.

Lined up for the Fuhrer's customary greeting, Freddy had stood next to Anna his mother. Herr Hitler, a small man molesting a crumpled handkerchief, a lump of greasy hair clinging to his forehead, approached. He stood before Freddy, carefully and silently looking the young man up and down. Suddenly he beamed, turned to Anna, his strident voice ringing through the hall, 'Frau von Langdorf,' he declaimed, 'you have produced a perfect example of our own special race. Pure Nordic! Congratulations!' and walked on, leaving Freddy immobile and mortified, aware that every head had turned to look at the Fuhrer's Nordic specimen.

Irritated by the memory, Freddy glared at his uncle. 'The worst moment of my life. Thanks for reminding me. I hope to God no one else knows I'm a specimen for the Fuhrer!'

By May the war in mainland Western Europe was gathering a grim momentum. In a matter of days, the victorious forces of the Wehrmacht had overrun Holland. Brussels had fallen, and the army with a three-pronged attack, was pushing towards the Pas de Calais, and south towards Sedan, and the Maginot Line. The British, no match for the German offensive, had a new leader, Winston Churchill, who looked quite formidable, with jowls like a bulldog. The very reason why he was chosen, it was said.

Anna was lonely these days at Schloss Langdorf. The von Langdorfs had been owners of the castle and its farm estates for two hundred years. Anna had loved her beautiful home since first coming here as a young bride, but these days most of its rooms and certainly its bedrooms, were empty and unused. She missed her adored son, and Friedrich her husband. He was obliged to spend the week at the family factory in Meissen, now directed into war production, making utensils for the Wehrmacht instead of delicate Dresden chinaware. Left alone to run Schloss Langdorf's estates she was having difficulty in finding labour for the land, as all able-bodied men had gone into the forces. It was equally difficult to find cleaning staff. Gretchen, their buxom kitchen maid, ready to have babies at any time for the Fatherland, was somewhere behind the front lines now, comforting her beloved Fuhrer's troops in a most traditional way, and probably already pregnant. The thought that Freddy could be sent to one of these baby farms she had heard about, and be forced to couple with the likes of Gretchen, made her feel sick.

When Freddy was given a sudden forty-eight hours home leave, Anna was overjoyed. The schloss had been so oppressively silent. She missed family musical evenings: Carl singing, Friedrich on violin and Freddy on piano. Once Freddy arrived she knew the Bechstein would again spring to life, just like old times.

Freddy thought his mother looked pale. 'She's alright?'

'Of course! Usual war worry.'

Friedrich didn't tell his son about Anna's angina.

At breakfast on the last morning of his leave, Anna suddenly said.

'I'm so frightened, Freddy. What's going to happen to us - to Germany?'

'Nothing so far Mama- the madman seems to be conquering everything.'

Anna shook her head. 'It can't last. D'you think it can last?'

'No Empire lasts.'

'France will surely be next, and they'll send you, darling, I know.'

He laughed. 'Not me! I like France too much to be an attacking soldier. I'd be too much of a risk!'

'Erich was wise to go to Switzerland.'

'He's in London now. I telephoned his relations in Berne.'

Anna sighed. 'Good. Even better.'

Erich, Freddy's Jewish friend from university days at Heidelberg, had been like a brother. Both studying Archaeology, they had been inseparable. But when Erich's parents' shop on Berlin's *Kurfürstendamm* had been torched, the family left Germany quickly. Once again it had been Uncle Carl who had facilitated passport and papers.

Bidding goodbye to her son this time was almost too much for Anna; her pretty round face was drawn and damp with tears. At the railway station the family stood together in silence. As the train approached the platform father and son clasped each other in farewell. When Freddy hugged his mother she pulled back to look at him, and gently ran her finger down his cheek. How she loved this son of hers, and how like a Greek god he was. 'The ring darling,' she said quietly. 'Don't forget to wear it.

See!' She turned her hand. 'I always wear mine. I think it will help God keep you safe.'

Feeling his eyes begin to smart, Freddy quickly boarded the train and waved to his parents until they were out of sight. He felt the peacock ring in his breast pocket, and recalled old Josef Feldmann the village jeweller crumpled in the corner of his shop, trays rifled of their contents by young uniformed thugs, windows smashed and anti-Jewish slogans scrawled on the walls. Out of gratitude for coming to his rescue the old man had given Anna and Freddy two identical rings made by his grandfather in the shape of peacocks, their plumes studded with gems. He had been found the next day hanging from a rafter, his son's posthumous Iron Cross from the last war tied loosely round his wrist.

Standing alone at the open window of the train Freddy pulled the ring out of his breast pocket, and placed it on his little finger.

The day was warm like high summer, and the rolling landscape of field and forest exuded a calm serenity, freakishly at odds with the rest of Europe.

He wished he had the courage to leap from the train and hide in the woods until this hideous war was over. A year-long dig in Crete had been the plan, not a wanton waste of life and learning.

A surge of tears that he could no longer contain fell from his eyes.

CHAPTER TWO

Catherine de Lazarin returned to Montpellier and a much-depleted medical school with half its lecturing staff and student body in the armed forces. Her life at the school usually filled with study and lectures had changed. Now students were left to study on their own for much of the time.

At twenty, Catherine was a slim long-legged beauty, and although she had an intense passion for medicine, her first year in medical school had been a catharsis and brought her face to face with poverty and disease. It was then she realised she was one of the world's fortunates. Had it not been for an iron determination to succeed she might well have run home after the first term.

She had been born and raised in the seventeenth century Chateau de Lazarin, one of the most beautiful and historically prestigious chateaux in southern France, standing in an estate of rolling hectares of vineyards and olive groves, near Uzès. She was an only child now, her older brother Robert having been tragically killed in a car crash three years before.

Max, Catherine's cousin in Paris and physically very like Robert, had recently qualified as a doctor. He was Catherine's mentor on life, on politics and on medicine. It was at Max's graduation party last year in Paris she had met his close friend Philippe de Brincourt, another young doctor. Catherine, with her green almond-shaped eyes and skin that never seemed to lose its bloom even in December, was already beginning to turn heads and Philippe's had been no exception.

But war changed everything, and Max and Philippe were in the army now. Max wrote to Catherine, '*Quite frankly, little cousin, I am bored out of my mind doing so little. Here I am in the army but like a village doctor, treating only men and for minor ailments. Perhaps something will happen soon. This waiting is making us uneasy. I have not heard from Philippe, but I don't think he can be too far away.'*

She received a post card from Philippe: *'I miss you. If I close my eyes, I imagine I am holding your hand, walking through the vineyards, taking you in my arms, and looking into your lovely eyes again - just like New Year. Life was so different then. Remember what I said about fate? Work hard. Thinking of you.'*

He had spent last New Year at the chateau, when there was no war, their only meeting since Paris. He told her then that despite many attempts, he had failed to find a hospital appointment either near Montpellier or Nimes, therefore they must both believe in fate. As she had several more student years before qualifying how could he expect her to promise anything? Again fate would decide. He had a girl friend; that, she knew, another doctor. But Catherine could not be sure if he was being thoroughly honest about fate and their possible relationship or was avoiding the inherent difficulties of making a commitment. Now she would never know because she believed she would never see him again. She felt no tears, simply an overwhelming sadness. They were destined not to be. Catherine slept with his card under her pillow for a week, and then threw it away.

At the chateau, with no young men about, Jacques and Mathilde, the handyman and housekeeper, organised shifts of local women and boys to gather the grapes. Four times a day, Mathilde and Marianne, Catherine's elegant bourgeois mother, delivered refreshments to perspiring grape-pickers. Days were so crowded with perpetual physical effort no one had time to think about the war. But what war? So far not even a stray shell had burst upon French soil. There was more turmoil on the streets of Paris.

Catherine was at home for the weekend when it was announced the German army had crossed the Meuse, and was pushing south towards Sedan and the Maginot Line.

'Do you think the Dutch will capitulate, Papa?'

Georges de Lazarin, a handsome middle-aged man with the natural charm of a Frenchman, smiled sadly at his daughter.

'Well darling, tulip growers don't necessarily make good soldiers. We shall see.'

'And Belgium?'

'They've only just got over the last one.'

'So what are you saying?'

'That our army will need more help from the British if we are to survive.'

'Survive?' Marianne rebuked. 'Surely the Maginot line is impregnable?'

Georges shrugged. 'Five hundred metres may not be quite enough.'

'Well, thank heavens Max was sent back to Paris.'

She turned to Catherine. 'Is his friend Philippe with him?' Marianne had liked the young doctor who had so obviously fallen for her beautiful daughter. He came from a good family, and would therefore be a worthy match, very important if you were a de Lazarin. And of course, just like the last war there would be a shortage of suitable men when it was all over.

Marianne liked to plan ahead.

Catherine cut into a wedge of cheese. 'I have no idea Maman. I believe he's still somewhere in the Maginot Line, according to Max,' she replied tartly.

How she hated her mother's unsubtle interfering.

Georges shot a warning glance at his wife. 'If there is any real danger, troops will be evacuated. They're more sensible now, unlike the last time.'

Reluctantly Georges allowed his daughter to return to Montpellier, but it was difficult to study these days. Lectures on the central nervous system seemed of little importance compared with the fate of the country.

When the Wehrmacht took Holland, occupied Brussels, and thousands of British and French troops massed on the beaches of Dunkirk waiting for any craft to take them to England, Georges telephoned his daughter.

'Catherine, we think you should come home.'

'Why?'

'Because - because the Boche are coming south. I have just heard on the radio.'

'South? You mean Lyon, Papa?'

'No of course not,' he snapped. 'But they have broken the Somme defences and thousands of their paratroops have been dropped on our side of the Maginot!'

She said nothing.

'You understand, Catherine?' He sounded impatient.

She understood too well. Thousands would be cut off. Philippe would undoubtedly be one of them. 'Yes, Papa.'

'So, you are to return immediately: no arguments if you please.'

She knew nothing would change his mind this time.

'I have just about enough petrol in the car to come to fetch you. Make sure all your belongings are packed up, because you will not be returning until this business is over.'

It was not a request. It was a command.

At the chateau they received an unexpected visit from Max. He had been sent from Paris on behalf of the military to organise casualty wards in Nimes hospital. Acutely depressed at having to abandon medicine, Catherine talked to her cousin. 'Max, it's like failing.'

'Rubbish! A national crisis is outside everyone's control. Look, I was in the middle of important research. I had patients critically ill, needing constant care. How d'you think I felt leaving them to join up?'

'At least you are a doctor.'

'Qualify when it's over. You've got three years training behind you, and some practical experience. You could work in a military hospital.'

'Nimes?'

'Sure.' he said. 'I can arrange it.'

'When?'

'When I come back, in a couple of weeks, so study hard, and don't worry'.

He laughed, and tousled her hair. 'Determined little thing aren't you?'

But the news was bad. The Maginot Line was about to collapse, and a fierce battle was raging around Sedan.

Max looked grim.'They are surrounded, poor devils. Hundreds have got away so I've heard. I only hope Philippe is one of them.' He paused. 'And there's Jeannine too.'

Catherine caught her breath. 'You mean his girl friend from medical school? Is he still-?'

'They got married. Very quickly - suddenly. In Sedan.'

Max rose and crossed to the range to refill his coffee cup.

'It was so that she could be near him. She was posted to a civilian hospital outside the town.' Catherine froze, stunned both by the news and its casual delivery.

'I'm sorry little cousin,' he faltered. 'I know it's come as a shock, but war makes people do bloody stupid things. Jeannine was very persistent.'

He put down his cup and patted her shoulder. 'I'm sure you will always have a special place in Philippe's heart, if he is still alive.'

Hadn't Philippe told her he would wait for her to finish medical school? Hadn't he been the one to pursue their friendship, their dizzy flirtation? He had mentioned Jeannine almost in passing and had seemed very cool about the relationship, as being one more of convenience, of habit, of proximity even.

But married? Now Philippe might just as well be dead. She would have to put him out of her mind.

Max returned to Paris, and Catherine, with dozens of medical books, notebooks and lecture notes, now neatly arranged on shelves in her study, put aside three hours a day to work. She was anxious to cram as much as possible before Nimes hospital beckoned.

A few mornings later, Marianne ran into the kitchen white and agitated, on the verge of hysteria.'Catherine! They're approaching Paris, the Boche! Papa is on the telephone to Simone and Louis. They must get out - they must! Louis will be killed because he's a Jew, and those barbarians are only one hundred kilometres away! Oh God!'

Simone, Marianne's younger sister, and Louis, a highly successful banker, were Max's parents. Catherine handed her trembling mother a glass of water, which she gulped down. 'My darling girl. What are we going to do, all of us?'

Max telephoned. Louis had been transferred to the bank in Vichy, so he would drive his parents south to their new apartment. They were packing the car as full as possible, although Max was having a problem with his mother. Difficult as always, she was reluctant to leave anything behind in the Chantilly house. 'I'm having to be very tough with Maman. Rapid decisions are not her forte, and we must leave as soon as possible.'

Roads from the capital were turning into grim battlefields.

They were about to join the combatants.

Georges sat down wearily and broke off a piece of baguette.

Head bent low, he meticulously pulled the bread into neat sections. There was nothing to say. Paris, their city of light, their gem, would inevitably fall to the Boche. It was like plucking out the very heart of France.

Marianne, dazed with worry, dabbed her eyes. 'And after Paris, Georges? What then? Surely the army will stop them?'

He patted his wife's hand. 'Nothing is irreversible, my sweet.'

And although he smiled reassuringly and with seeming confidence, in his heart he knew the situation was hopeless.

They were done for.

CHAPTER THREE

Returning to Berlin after home leave did little to alleviate Freddy's depression. He hated large cities, and Berlin in a heat wave was becoming unbearable. The office was like a sauna, and his lean body longed to be free of the uniform that bound him, sweating, like a straitjacket. He thought of the Mediterranean, of Cannes, of the Croisette, and desperately wished for last year. From time to time several junior Nazi officers would crash into the office whooping over another Wehrmacht victory. On June 4th when Dunkirk was captured, bells rang for three days, and beer Kellers overflowed. Freddy made a point of avoiding these areas of national celebration. Carl had given him the key of his apartment to use during his frequent absences. It was a refuge of calm, where Freddy could listen to music.

Lieutenant von Langdorf was bored with the army, bored with Berlin, and bored with waiting.

Back from France, where he had been visiting Erwin Rommel, Carl invited his nephew to dine with him at his apartment.

Refilling the champagne glasses, he said, 'Erwin's a gentleman, and a real soldier, unlike those of us who just push paper around.' Leaning over the grape dish he carefully cut a small cluster. 'Now young man, how about France?'

'Are you serious Uncle?'

Carl smiled.'But of course. We anticipate taking Paris - no force by order of the Fuhrer - in a couple of days. The French will have to agree the armistice terms, which naturally have already been drafted.'

'What are they?'

'Top secret! But I think I can tell you. France will be divided unequally, leaving one third for them.'

'And the line?'

'Most of the South from about Moulins, will remain French, except for a wide coastal strip on the west.'

Freddy huffed. 'Now I shan't be able to visit Cannes.'

'Why not?' Carl raised an eyebrow.. 'You don't seriously think the Fuhrer would leave the French completely to themselves, without a German presence do you? I'm proposing you should be sent to Paris a few days after the army moves in. You will be given an apartment and be attached to the Kommandantur as interpreter. Would you like that?'

Freddy broke into his familiar crooked grin, teeth gleaming white against tanned skin. 'Does a duck love water?'

On the morning of June 10th, Max, in civilian clothes, and his parents, left Paris for Vichy, their car packed to capacity with jewellery and family heirlooms, brought from Russia by Louis' grandfather.

Max did not tell his parents about those long discussions with others like himself who opposed the expected sell-out armistice with the Boche. Some were about to join the exodus to England along with several high ranking army officers, and a few government officials. For those who remained, there would be organised resistance to the enemy. Max was to be a part of this resistance, and his first contact would be Chartre's young prefect, Jean Moulin.

Having cleared the British from Dunkirk, radio bulletins told anxious citizens that roads leading south from Paris were packed solid with vehicles and that the Luftwaffe was strafing refugees. A longer route avoiding main roads wherever possible would now be essential.

In Chartres on June 12th they found Jean Moulin distributing food and car fuel. His boyish face was pale and exhausted, but his eyes lit with pleasure when Max gave him messages from mutual friends in Paris. That night they slept in Moulin's house, the two younger men parleying into the early hours about their country's future, conjecturing how the Government's dotards were going to deal with Hitler.

Moulin knew that groups of resisters would be springing up throughout France. 'We shan't all be resisting the Boche for the same reasons. Some will fight just for themselves. In a crisis, they'll betray. That's why resistance has to be under one flag. Everyone will have to feel a collective responsibility.' Tapping the ash from his cigarette he smiled. 'And that, my friend, is the greatest burden we shall all have to undertake. Courage is relative, and I've heard about the persuasive methods of the Gestapo.'

A network of escape routes from Paris down to Lisbon for British agents, airmen, and French saboteurs, anyone on the run from German interrogation, was already being planned. Both men sensed they would be working together and perhaps sooner than anticipated.

On the road to Blois speed was limited to ten kilometres per hour. The weather was hot, the atmosphere tense. There was no way to turn, neither back, nor laterally, for only unmade farm tracks intersected the main road. Simone, pale with fear, whimpered in Louis' arms. 'We're sitting ducks! No chance if they decide to bomb us - no chance at all. We shall all be killed!' Dapper, immaculate Louis looked very different now, with two days growth of beard; his director's suit crumpled, starched collar undone, his tie loose about his neck. In his pocket he carried the address of the bank's apartment waiting for him in Vichy.

Towards early evening, as they made a crawling approach to a village, Max noticed a deep ditch running alongside their tree-lined road and a small copse. 'I think we should try to find something to eat.'

'What about the car? We can't leave it,' said Louis.

'I'll hide it in that copse.'

Simone shook her head. 'No Max! It could be stolen'.

'The Luftwaffe is the problem mother, not theft. They destroy transport. You and Papa walk to the village. I'll wait till you come back. Should the planes arrive, jump in that ditch for cover. Lie flat in the undergrowth. Remember, get off the road.'

Light-headed with hunger, Simone clung to her husband as they pushed slowly through the long column of refugees. They found a back street cafe, where the owner made them an omelette. Just as he was opening a bottle of wine, the familiar throb of Nazi planes was heard overhead. He opened the door.

'Bastards! They are going to gun down all those poor sods. They dropped a few bombs round our Mairie last week. Lucky you're in here.'

'Max - Max!' Simone screamed and leapt to the door. She would have run back into the column had both men not restrained her.

Max had been parking the car in the copse when the planes flew over. As the trees were dense with summer foliage, both he and the car were invisible. The Messerschmitts dived repeatedly, engines shrieking. Reckless rounds of bullets were fired into stampeding humanity. Babies cried, children screamed, women shouted, some in terror, some in pain. Ten minutes later the planes sped away, leaving in their wake scenes of devastation and horror. Almost every vehicle on the road had been damaged or destroyed. Mothers wept over the bodies of their children, men over their wives. Max gave what medical help he could to the wounded nearby, and carried those for whom it was too late to the side of the road, while anguished relatives looked on, frozen with shock. There could be no dignified burial for these corpses.

Max convinced his mother the Luftwaffe was more likely to spread its favours in other directions rather than return to an old battleground. The notion was sufficient to calm Simone, who, since leaving Paris, had been on the edge of hysteria. The two men made her comfortable for the night with blankets in the back seat of the car, and for themselves erected a small army tent.

The need to reach the south was never so urgent. Abandoned vehicles, pushchairs, children's prams gashed with bullets, lined the roads and the homeless pushed carts piled with possessions.

In Vendome, Max inched the Citroen into the town centre. The restaurant across the square was already so crowded clients were spilling onto the pavement. Louis pushed his way into a large group of people and become engaged in animated discussion with several of them, returning minutes later. He spread his hands across his ashen face and slowly drew them down.

'Paris has fallen. It has just been announced on the radio. The Boche are in Paris! The swastika is flying from our Arche de Triomphe!'

No one could speak; fear lodged in the throat like a paralysis. How could any of them have been prepared for jackboots goose-stepping up the Champs Elysees?

On the seventeenth of June Freddy left Berlin by air for Paris.

His new apartment was large, and in a prime position in the Avenue de l'Opera, close to the newly set up Kommandantur in the Hotel Majestic.

He was immediately summoned to a briefing in a luxurious suite of offices occupied by the commanding officer of the radio and communications unit. The Kommandant, short and round, with a twinkling humour, read out a message of congratulations from the Fuhrer, which was somewhat embarrassing as none of them had seen active service.

'Now, words of warning,' the Kommandant continued. 'For all troops in France, from our Fuhrer. "*I do not wish my troops to behave in France the way the French behaved in the Rhineland after the last war. Anyone found looting will be shot on the spot. Through you, I want to come to a real understanding with France.*" Understood?' They understood.

'Now,' he said, 'words from me. At all times you are to be quiet, respectful and courteous. Especially to the pretty French girls!' He leant over his desk and held up a large poster, which showed a child in the arms of a German soldier. The caption read; *'Frenchmen! Trust the German soldier.'*

'This,' he said,'is to be upheld. Always, at any time and any place.'

Already the French in England were calling themselves the Free French and it was expected they would establish radio communication with their compatriots via the BBC in London. As Freddy listened that afternoon he heard the voice of a General de Gaulle, telling the French people they had lost a battle but not a war.'The flame of French resistance cannot go out,' he proclaimed.

From his apartment window, Freddy looked down on the deserted streets of Paris. A city with no heart. Millions had left. The German army had taken over seamlessly. This did not look like resistance. If he were French he would be a resister. Maybe it was simply a matter of waiting for the heart to be revived.

On the 22nd Carl telephoned from Compiègne to say he would be coming to Paris for a few days and to expect an imminent invitation from the Chancellor to a reception at a manor in the Bois de Boulogne.

Adolf Hitler, flushed with contained triumph, was talking to his two architects Speer and Giesler. He broke away when Carl and Freddy arrived. With a greasy lump of hair falling on his forehead, and a clammy palm, he welcomed them, beaming at Freddy. 'Your nephew is still our archetypal Aryan, Herr General.'

Carl agreed courteously, smiling more at Freddy's blushing discomfiture than the Fuhrer's remark.

During dinner the young man sat between his uncle and handsome Albert Speer, Hitler's architect, to whom the Fuhrer addressed his command. 'Paris is beautiful, but you must make Berlin more beautiful. Now your work begins!'

When the company had left the table to charge their cognac glasses, the Chancellor, who of course was not drinking, took Freddy by the arm. 'Are you glad to be here in Paris, Lieutenant?'

'Yes, I am sir.'

'Good! Good! You know, I have seen buildings today in this City of Light with which I have been only theoretically familiar for so many years. Tell me what do you think of the Opera House?'

'Wonderful, sir.'

'Wonderful? It is the most beautiful theatre in the world, Lieutenant!'

Suddenly his eyes flashed, and his voice rose with a passion of public rally decibels. When Carl heard the strident voice level, he strolled over to join them. Hitler, mopping his perspiring face with a crumpled handkerchief, smiled. 'I would have studied here you know, if Fate had not pushed me into politics. The magical atmosphere of this city has always fascinated me. That is why my troops have avoided combat here'. Freddy hesitated not knowing quite if Hitler expected a comment from a relatively junior officer. He took the plunge.

'And - and - if I may be allowed to say so, in my opinion, you made the right decision, Reichschancellor.'

Hitler beamed at Carl, and with damp palms, clasped Freddy's shoulders.

'Your elegant Nordic nephew approves. Good!'

Fortunately at that moment someone called for three *'Hochs',* to the Fuhrer. Glasses were raised and the toast drunk.

The object of the toast however had suddenly walked away and slumped in a chair, head bowed. The Fuhrer was asleep.

The following evening, Carl confirmed that Hitler had forbidden the Gestapo to take any part in the administration of occupied France.

Freddy raised his eyebrows. 'How did you do it?'

'I suggested there would be instant insurrection. I saw Gestapo methods in Poland remember.'

'And what will he do with England?'

'He says he will force her to accept his friendship, but she will have to drive out all her Jews.'

'He's mad.'

Carl sighed. 'If it weren't so serious, it could be almost risible.'

He picked up his cap. 'Come on my lad, let's sample some night life.'

Unlike his Fuhrer, Freddy knew Paris. In truth he was far happier here than in Berlin.

Disquieting rumours began floating round the Kommandantur about the Gestapo in Paris. The Army always found their presence irksome, as they interfered with administration and established protocol, accounting to no one. What was more they could disturb this delicate velvet glove occupation. The rumours appeared to be well founded in the ugly shape of a certain Otto Muller, who purported to be in the German Military Police, the GFP. In this role he began swaggering through each department, asking questions about personnel working in the building. Muller was built like a heavyweight boxer, but gluttony had turned muscle to flab. He didn't smile; he leered, with thick fleshy lips, displaying yellow teeth spattered with gold fillings. Freddy hated him on sight. He was crude, uncultured and a Nazi rabble-rouser to his podgy fingertips.

It was at the end of July he barged into Freddy's office, carrying under his arm a red dossier which he slammed down on the desk.

'So,' he leered. 'You are Lieutenant Friedrich von Langdorf?'

'Yes. What d' you want?'

Leaning over the dossier, he began to flick the pages. 'Aha! One of our aristos. Schloss Langdorf; French governess.' He looked up. 'Accounts for your perfect French so they tell me. Weren't you a lucky little boy?'

Freddy's cheeks burned, furious at the fellow's insolence.

'Heidelberg too. And - well well! nephew and heir to General Count von Langdorf, chief legal advisor to the Fuhrer himself. And you, lieutenant, not even a Party member - naturally.'

The lieutenant rose from his chair. He stood taller than the sergeant but would have been no match for the latter's strength.

'What is it you actually want?' Glancing at Muller's uniform, he added 'Hauptwachtmeister.'

'Muller! My name is Muller! Hauptwachtmeister Muller!' retorted the sergeant, eyes flashing. Muller was a man used to being obeyed.

'Very well, Hauptwachtmeister Muller,' the lieutenant repeated, completely taken aback by this extraordinary insubordination. His fat fingers adorned with gold rings, Muller thumbed through the remaining pages of the file with another leer. 'Just checking on the personnel. That's what the GFP does you know. Or didn't they teach you that at Heidelberg, lieutenant?'

With a click of heels and a 'Heil Hitler' he marched out of the office.

Freddy had not been singled out for this pseudo investigation. Several young officers working in the Kommandantur, with similar privileged backgrounds, and non Party, had received a visit. Taking dossiers without first consulting the Kommandant had the unmistakable thumbprint of either Gestapo, or the Intelligence branch of the S.S.

A few days later, Freddy found an angry proprietor in his favourite café reporting that two plain clothes Germans had seized files on Jews, Communists, Freemasons, and German refugees, from the local Prefecture.

'But your Boche friends didn't get all the files,' the proprietor chuckled. 'The gendarmes chucked them in the Seine, didn't they?' He rolled his eyes and roared with laughter.

At the beginning of August Freddy was given a week's home leave.

Over dinner, on the first evening, Friedrich said. 'We're thinking of shutting this place up; for the time being anyway.'

Anna patted Freddy's hand. 'Well, darling I hardly see Papa these days. And you know how I love Dresden. The villa is much easier to run. But when you are on leave we'll come back here.'

Carl arrived at the schloss quite unexpectedly, from Berlin. Freddy lost no time telling him in private about Muller, the

Kommandantur dossiers, and the plain-clothes men at the prefecture. He was not surprised.

'That corroborates intelligence from OKH.'

'So the Fuhrer was actually disobeyed?'

Carl gave a derisive snort. 'Himmler was so furious with Hitler's decision, arrogant little bastard, he apparently asked Heydrich to circumvent it.'

Carl shook his head. 'He used cars with false plates, and dressed up twenty Gestapo men in GFP uniforms. I don't trust any of them but my feeling is they'll be far too busy dispatching French and immigrant undesirables to be bothering with you chaps again.'

He was right, for slowly the purges started, and gnawed uncomfortably at the tacit peace that the Kommandantur had attempted to establish. The next time Freddy saw Muller, was at a distance on the Avenue de l'Opera. The rat had come out of his corner.

He was wearing the uniform of an Untersturmfuhrer in the SS.

At the end of August when Carl visited Paris again, French anger was taking its revenge in the occasional pot shot at German soldiers, particularly after dark. Therefore, for safety, uncle and nephew met in the apartment of a friend of Carl's, another army lawyer stationed in Paris.

Colonel Kurt Bergen was as tall as Freddy, and despite thickening middle aged girth, he was attractive with dark eyes and hair, which he attributed to his Italian grandmother. Over dinner Carl explained, 'Kurt is not only a lawyer. He once played violin in the Berlin Philharmonic.'

'Come on Carl don't embarrass me. A five minute substitute for a sick violinist!' he laughed.

'I know quality when I hear it!' Carl replied.

A few days later, the von Langdorfs were walking through the sunlit Tuileries gardens.

'I've received a report from the Kommandantur about you.'

'Why - what have I done?' Freddy asked cautiously.

'You apparently charm birds off trees, work hard, and you are an excellent liaison man with the French. Therefore,' Carl stopped and turned to his nephew. 'You have been recommended for promotion.'

This was completely unexpected. Promotion was something Freddy had never contemplated. They sat on a garden seat, the perfume of summer blooms scenting the air.

'You will be leaving Paris at the end of September,for the unoccupied zone.' Carl was amused at the look of complete astonishment on his nephew's face. 'You will be part of a hand-picked group of two officers, and fourteen men. Your remit, to be good liaison personnel, primarily through music, and to safeguard the passage of food, armaments and troops that will pass through in transit.'

'The area?'

'Somewhere between Nimes and Alès. Of course there are slim military establishments in that zone already - Nimes, Montpellier, Avignon, a few in Uzès. You could be called upon to assist in any way within the zone, but predominantly you will create a friendly presence. It is after all ostensibly unoccupied.'

'Gestapo?'

'There will be absolutely no Gestapo. Kurt was adamant about that.'

'Kurt? Colonel Kurt Bergen?'

His uncle grinned. 'I was coming to that. Kurt will be your commanding officer, and as for the rest.' He pulled out a typed list from his jacket pocket.

'Sergeant Thomas Hoffmeyer - oboeist in the Vienna Philharmonic, Corporal Rudy Schmidt - clarinetist with the Berlin!'

'I can't believe this! You did say hand - picked, didn't you?'

They talked late into the night, about the politics of Vichy France, of the Nazis and Hitler's grand plan for Europe. Draining his glass of cognac, Carl said sombrely, 'but what does it matter? What does anything matter, when the person you love isn't beside you?'

CHAPTER FOUR

The Beckers were a kilometre outside Bourges, nose to bumper in lines of vehicles of every description, when Max noticed refugees running in all directions on the road ahead. The unmistakable drone of approaching planes was all too clear.

He pulled up sharply. 'Quick, out! Down there,' he shouted, pointing to a ditch. 'Hurry Papa!' Louis lumbered, dazed, into the refuge.' Maman! ' Max dragged his terrified mother out of the back seat, and pushed her face - down alongside her husband. He threw himself under a bush, buried deep in rotting vegetation, and only just in time. Bullets rained on the road and grass verges, ripping, tearing, piercing. This was worse than the last time. After several minutes of silence, Simone shouted 'Have they gone? I'm soaked.'

She began to clamber out of the soggy undergrowth.

'Stay where you are!' Max yelled. 'Get down!'

A lone Messerschmitt could be heard returning. It discharged a monsoon of bullets over their side of the road. The noise was deafening.

In the aftermath of silence, Max called, ' you can get up now. They've had their fun for a while.' But Simone lay quite still. Blood was flowing copiously from her side. Louis cried out, and began to shake. The doctor in Max took care of his own panic. Two bullets had pierced her side, just above the hipbone, and lodged in the soft stomach tissue. She was bleeding so badly, immediate binding was imperative.

They were tearing a linen sheet into strips when a voice in halting French asked.'Would you like any help?'

A tall, dishevelled young man with pale blue eyes and a shock of auburn hair stood behind them.

'You could cut this up for me. Quickly please.'

Simone was safely laid in the back of the car, and despite assurances to his father Max knew the bullets would have to be removed as quickly as possible. Although the car had no windows left and bullets had transformed the roof into a colander, the engine was intact. The young man with auburn hair cleared the interior of glass and splinters. Max offered him a lift into Bourges.

Richard Browning was 22, a Flight Lieutenant in the R.A.F. shot down during the Dunkirk evacuation, and had baled into a Norman farm. Two days later he moved south, picking up scraps of food and lifts wherever he could. With rolled up sleeves, a grubby shirt, a week's growth of red beard and his uniform jacket over his arm, he bore little resemblance to an officer in his country's air force.

Progress into the town was slow, and Max knew his mother's life depended upon extracting the bullets, before a main artery ruptured. Already she was drifting in and out of consciousness. Bourges hospital had been hit but they were given the name of a retired doctor near the centre.

Grey bearded Dr Guillaume walked slowly with the aid of stick. He inspected Simone's bound wounds and congratulated his young colleague.

'A very good job there my boy - well done.'

The old man felt Simone's abdomen. 'However, I'm glad you didn't do more. The second bullet is so close to the aorta, it will have to be extracted with great care, or we shall have an unstoppable haemorrhage. Right, to work.'

Instruments, chloroform, ether, coats, masks, gloves, and quantities of cloths to absorb blood, were quickly assembled. The second bullet was where the doctor had predicted. Carefully he chipped away at the flesh embedding the steel, while Max, holding the anaesthetic mask over his mother's face with one hand, monitored the temporal pulse with the other. The Englishman thankfully took care of her trembling husband.

Visiting his patient the following morning, the old doctor declared firmly, 'You will be obliged to stay here for several days Madame.'

Simone nodded weakly. Max took Dr Guillaume aside.

'We need to press on - to our relatives near Uzès. My mother will be able to recuperate with her sister.'

'My dear young man, I cannot possibly allow her to travel today, even tomorrow. I appreciate your wish to get to your family, but a bad road could rupture her internal sutures.' Max could not argue with that. 'Besides, you all look as though you could do with a rest and a few square meals,' he added with clipped authority.

Richard Browning cornered Max. 'Er - thanks for taking me along, old chap, but it would be better if I went on alone. I can't risk coming face to face with Jerry.' He grinned. 'Couldn't bear to be a prisoner. I want to get back up there, to shoot the bastards down'.

With a small parcel of baguettes and cheese, he took his leave of the family. His cap pushed to the back of his head, and looking cleaner than when they had first met, he squeezed Max's elbow. 'Your mother is going to be absolutely fine.'

Pale eyes squinting from the sharp sunlight of June, he mumbled, 'thanks so much old chap-for the helping hand. Pity there was no time to talk.'

'Perhaps we will, one day. Take care English friend. If you meet any Boche, just make sure they see your uniform.'

Max watched the young Englishman until he was lost in the crowd, and wondered how on earth he would survive knowing so little of the language.

Over lunch, Dr Guillaume reproached. 'If only the English had sent more troops, not their worn out Expeditionary Force; the army of old men, little better than I. And now we have an even older man to lead us.'

Eighty-four-year-old Marshall Petain had been appointed the new premier. Broadcasting to the people that day, he announced that an armistice with Germany was being drawn up. Dr Guillaume, his eyes moist with tears peered out of the windows overlooking the square. Max stared blankly at the scene. A stunning blow had been dealt the country. Townsfolk gathered in the square, some alone, some in groups, some with bowed heads, some mouthing private prayers, some openly weeping, but all bewildered. Restaurateurs, chefs, housewives, came out of their kitchens and salons, joining the silent hundreds. It was important not to be alone, to hold the hand of another citizen of France - for comfort.

Two days after leaving Dr Guillaume's makeshift hospital, Simone, propped and wedged against the soft leather sides of the back seat, developed a fever despite cloths soaked in cold water, which Louis pressed to her face. Approaching the town of Moulins the traffic suddenly came to a complete halt. Half a kilometre ahead they could see a road block manned by French police, two German army motorcyclists, and several foot soldiers carrying machine guns. Papers were being checked, and not everyone was being allowed to continue. Max could see his mother needed sulphonamide to curb infection, but how could he expose his Jewish father to Nazis?

'That lying old goat must have signed the armistice.'

'My God - do you suppose we are in occupied territory?' Louis croaked.

'Your guess is as good as mine. We'll have to go back - turn off somewhere.'

Max swung the car round, following a narrow country road to a group of villages. Simone's temperature was rising, and blood was oozing from her abdominal wounds. Louis was in a complete panic. 'Max. I don't care if I am arrested, do you hear? It's Maman's life! There will be barricades all round the town, so for God's sake let's go back in and face them.'

It was early evening. Max stopped the car in the last village on the west side of town. At the Bureau de Poste he was told there was a doctor visiting a sick child.

Dr Julian Lebor was in his thirties, Jewish, and from Moulins, as worried as Louis about his future under the Nazis. Immediately he perceived Simone's medical condition. The reason for the barricade was apparently in the interests of

The Girl on the Promenade

the new demarcation line of the occupied zone. Moulins was going to be a border town, but as yet no one knew the precise position. It would take effect as from tomorrow.

Louis wrung his hands in despair. 'We are done for, Max. Let me go, please! Then you can drive Maman somewhere safe - anywhere. I cannot let you suffer because of me.'

'But you are the one person mother needs to recover.'

'Don't worry monsieur, we will find a solution,' the young doctor encouraged. His forehead creased into a dozen lines. His black eyes ringed with dark shadows, half closed as he thought a plan through.

'I have it,' and he clapped his bony hands.

'I shall drive your car because mine has broken down. You see?'

He opened the bonnet of his car and removed a plug. A smile broke on his thin patrician features. 'The police know me. They know I visit outside the town, so I can take you straight to my surgery.'

Max was worried.'Our papers? They'll want to see them surely.'

'Not if we are stopped by a friendly gendarme. I shall tell them the patient is having a difficult labour and I may have to take her into hospital for a section.'

'Shouldn't I hide in the boot?'

'Why? You are their doctor, coming with me. And that's not a lie.'

The thin young man was very persuasive.

As they approached the barricade on the outskirts of the town Max glanced at his terrified father, and prayed he would not surrender to an emotional outburst. But no papers were asked for. The gendarme knew the doctor, and wished poor Madame a bouncing baby.

Just as they were driving off, a tall German army officer leapt out, He spoke to Dr Lebor in heavily accented French. 'You are a doctor?'

'Yes, and I must get this woman to my surgery quickly. She is in need of a section.'

'I know the story. Your papers?'

He looked at them carefully. 'Lebor. Jewish name' He peered at Max. 'And yours!'

Dr Lebor interrupted. 'The woman is about to haemorrhage officer - I really must ask you to let us pass.'

'Your name please!' he insisted.

'Dr Becker.'

'Becker! Another Jew. And another doctor.'

He pushed his head through the window. 'You, doctor Jew Lebor, come with me.'

Max could see Julian Lebor's taut facial muscles. With remarkable sang-froid he replied, 'I cannot. Dr Becker is a country doctor. He doesn't know the route to my surgery. I have to get him there with his patient.'

In the moment's silence Simone moaned. 'I'm afraid she's starting labour.'

The officer, despite his uniform and blustering swagger was one male who had no intention of witnessing childbirth. 'Please go!' he said quickly. 'You have fifteen minutes, and then you must return here. One of my men has a bad stomach pain. A nurse is with him at the moment. Jew Becker can deliver the child.' He smirked, 'you Jews are supposed to be good doctors. Prove it! Quickly!' he barked.

As soon as the officer was out of earshot, the gendarme whispered.

'I've just got the demarcation map doctor. Here it is. Take it.' He thrust the map through the open car window.'The boundary's half way across your orchard. Wire goes up tomorrow, six o clock.'

By midnight, Julian Lebor had successfully removed an appendix from a German soldier. Simone was improving after a massive dose of the sulphonamide, and whilst a petrified Louis slept fitfully by her side, the two young men sat up talking. Tomorrow Max would drive his parents onto a road that would take them to Vichy, the new seat of Petain's government. They studied the map of the new occupied zone. The boundary was, as predicted, through the doctor's orchard. It ran across France to the west, and plunged south, leaving a band of coastal strip to Spain, another bonus for the occupiers.

Max looked at it carefully. 'D'you want to come with us?'

Julian Lebor shrugged. 'I have patients and,' his lugubrious face broke into a smile, 'and a girl friend. She is a teacher - lives on a farm, and she's not a Jew, so I imagine she will be all right. And you?'

'In a week or two, when mother is stronger I'll take them to Vichy, to their apartment. Then I shall try to get back to Paris.'

'How?'

'I shall be told. Contacts.'

'I understand.' Julian Lebor smiled 'Perhaps you should add this house. The position will be perfect for crossing.'

'Thanks, but don't forget the risk.'

'Everything's a risk when we are occupied by Fascists.'

The thin young man rose, and took another bottle of wine from the buffet. He stood for a moment. 'So Max, what will you do?'

'Work in Nimes hospital, and organise resistance. That will be our war, resistance.'

'You be careful.'

'Naturally.'

Julian shook his head.' No, what I mean is, be sure of whom you can trust. Not every Frenchman will be a patriot. This division of our country is going to change people. Citizens, whom we know, could sell us to the highest bidder. Jews, communists, gypsies, resistance, we are all the same to traitors.'

Max smiled thinly. He had heard similar words before. 'Thank you for reminding me.' He refilled his glass. 'What did you feel operating on that Nazi? Didn't you want to kill him?'

'And have them kill me?' Julian Lebor crossed back to his armchair.

'I forgot he was an enemy actually. He was just an ordinary German boy, polite, not like his officer, and grateful. Anyway medicine has to be outside politics.'

Max stared at the floor. 'I have always believed that, but - if - if I had been asked to remove the appendix of that pig officer, my hand could well have slipped a little.'

Julian Lebor was clearly surprised. 'No! Please. That way you are playing their game of political selection. We have to be trusted, by everyone. We must retain our medical integrity if nothing else.'

Max huffed. 'You could be right. See how morality is already on its head? Don't be alarmed, I shall not forget the oath, even with traitors and Germans.'

'You mean Nazis.'

'All Germans are Nazis.'

'Don't be ridiculous!' Julian Lebor lit a cigarette. 'My grandparents were German. Came first to Alsace, from Berlin, then to Bourges. I have - I had - relatives in Berlin, conscripted in the last war to fight for the Fatherland.'

'But not this war surely?'

'Oh no. A few rich cousins bought their way to England last year I believe. The rest - have - disappeared - camps certainly.'

He drew on his cigarette, and inhaled deeply. 'All good Germans, Max.'

'They were Jews.'

'Maybe, but most of their friends were not, neither were they Nazis. Just ordinary people. I know. I spent many holidays in Berlin.'

'Do you speak German?'

'Of course.'

'And your grandparents, where are they?'

'Dead fortunately, else they would have been taken to an internment camp as enemies of France.' Julian Lebor had been pulling nervously at his cigarette packet. He rose quickly from the chair.

'You see how stupid it all is? How dangerous are extremists, of any affiliation, any flag?'

Just after dawn the Beckers drove across Julian Lebor's orchard to a country road in the unoccupied zone, heading towards Vichy, and the south. When the road surface was bad, Louis could see Simone's face contort with pain, and wished with all his heart the Nazi bullet had chosen him. Gestures of love were all he could give, as she lay propped by pillows.

They drove through rich farming country and stopped outside Varennes where Max opened up a large map on the grass, searching for a route through the Auvergne. But Simone had set her heart on seeing Vichy, so in the absence of German air attacks, Max and Louis relented.

Clutching at a crumpled sheet of paper, on which was drawn a map of the town, Louis craned his neck out of the car looking for street names. The bank and their new apartment were situated on the Rue Petite, near Vichy's central Parc des Sources. As they turned into the wide tree lined boulevard leading to the town's centre, Louis whistled between his teeth. 'My God, what's this?'

Tricolours and bunting were flying from every window, and lampost. Bodies were huddled together, simmering with contained excitement from open balconies. It was like Bastille Day.

Max felt his eyes sting. 'Jesus! I can't believe what I'm seeing. We have lost, you idiots! Those flags should be black!'

'But it's the end of the war, Max!'

'Don't be fooled Maman. Give it a few months.'

They joined a slow stream of assorted traffic heading in the same direction. Pavements were crowded with more refugees carrying babies, children and possessions. Suddenly, the discordant scream of sirens rent the air. Dozens of police cars descended upon the boulevard bursting out of side streets. Darting across lines of traffic, they herded cars together like sheep, blocking exits, and finally bringing vehicles to a complete halt. Within seconds armed gendarmes were spilling out of their black Citroens, swarming like hornets around their beleaguered prey. A well-built sergeant strode towards the car. 'Madame, messieurs. You are just four?'

Max nodded.

The sergeant scrutinised their papers, and for several moments looked carefully at Simone. 'My mother was wounded by the Nazi pigs. Their bombardments are very efficient when there is no retaliation.'

Max attempted a sardonic smile. 'And as a Frenchman', he continued, 'I am delighted the Marshall is now lodging with them, in the same sty. Aren't you?'

There was an uncomfortable silence. Louis wished to God his son had kept his mouth shut. The sergeant grunted and walked away with the identity papers towards a melée of dark blue uniforms.

Max called out to a group of young local girls. 'D'you know what's going on?' Flushed with excitement, one of them chirruped, 'It's our Marshall. He is arriving any time now, with the new government. There is to be a big ceremony at the Hotel du Parc'.

'Do you know rue Petite?'

'It's right by Hotel du Parc. You'll have a good view from there, if they let you through.' She laughed delightedly, and ran off with her friends.

Max was angry. 'France has turned its traitors into heroes.'

'But he has stopped the killing.' Louis sighed. 'To half the nation he is a hero.'

The sergeant returned to the car with a lieutenant, an unpleasant looking individual, thick set with heavy jowls. 'Get out, if you please,' he bellowed.

Max opened the car door. 'My mother is sick, she can't move.'

The lieutenant made an impatient gesture. 'Is she also a Jew?'

'My mother is a loyal French citizen monsieur, which is more than I would say for most of this crowd.'

The lieutenant smiled icily. 'Really, Dr Becker?'

Furious with his son for such a provocative remark, Louis interjected.

The Girl on the Promenade

'My wife is not a Jew monsieur, neither is my son.'

Max glared at the lieutenant. 'Has Vichy started to count the Jews? Had its orders from the Fuhrer so soon?'

The officer said nothing. He scrutinised their papers, asking questions about their work, and destination. He dismissed the sergeant with a perfunctory wave, and handing the papers back he took a crumpled pack of cigarettes out of his pocket. 'Take,' he ordered, and thrust the packet into Louis hand.

'If you want my advice Monsieur Becker forget about the bank, forget about this town. Go to your family in Uzès.'

Turning to go he added, 'and stay there!' It was a disturbing comment.

Despite the first intimations of southern heat during the day, the evening was pleasantly cool. They found rooms in a village inn near Le Puy, and after dinner Max strolled into the square's only café. There was no room inside, and conversation from groups crouched over tables was low-key. In a corner by the bar, an old man strummed gnarled fingers over an accordion and played familiar melodies. The nostalgia and memory evoked was too much for some. Tears from eyes still in shock fell for absent loved ones, for themselves and for their country's future. Max sat at the only empty table outside on the pavement. He was thinking about Julian Lebor's prediction that trust was no longer a commodity to be taken for granted.

Light spilling from the bar and a street lamp diffused the evening dusk forming blurred images of faces and bodies. Head tilted to take up his glass of cognac, Max became aware of a piece of paper that somehow had landed on his table. Scrawled on it were two words.'Max. Richard.'

He looked round slowly not wanting to attract attention. Standing a few yards away, outside the arc of light he recognised the tall and now heavily bearded figure of Richard Browning.

At the auberge the patron asking no questions about the uniformed Englishman, took up a tray of food to Max's room. When offered payment, he shook his head. 'I can see who and what you are young man. To take money from an ally, would be spitting on the memory of our republique - a republique that is no more.' The portly figure hung his head in sorrow, and shuffled to the door where he stopped, drew himself to attention, saluted, and whispered hoarsely, 'Vive La France.'

Richard Browning had become gaunt, his shoulders stooped, his face prematurely lined. He had survived on scraps, and whatever he could beg from restaurants. He fell upon the tray of food, and consumed all that was set before him, abandoning any pretence of good manners.

Max laughed. 'I must say you look better already.'

'Thanks old boy! Great stuff! Well, I must be off.'

' Where?'

'I travel at night, Max, it's safer. This may be Vichy France but there are still roadblocks, manned by French police. I met someone who was convinced some would be worse than the Nazis.'

'He may be right, but if you think you can walk your way to Portugal on starvation rations, you'll be taken home in a box not a plane. You'll have to come with us.'

'God no, old chap, I'm lethal. Get caught with me on board, and we've all bought it. Thanks all the same but I'm a solo act Max.'

The lank airman walked to the door. Max raised his hand.

'Now listen. We'll get some civvy clothes. I'll bandage your head to look like a severe injury; severe enough to render you unconscious if we're stopped.'

'I.D.papers?'

'You muttered something about Avignon when we found you half dead on the roadside. Since then you've been unconscious, papers stolen. I'm taking you to Nimes hospital, where I work. D'accord?'

Richard smiled, not without some relief at the ingenious if improbable plan.

With Richard gagged and bound, propped in the front seat, they traversed empty mountain roads, and villages where they bought farm produce in abundance. After a hasty picnic lunch beside a mountain stream, Max took Richard aside. 'You will stay with my delightful cousin and her family in the Chateau, while I go to Nimes, get papers for you; then we'll go together as far as the Pyrenees.'

'No. This time I'm going alone', Richard mumbled through his bandages.

'Listen my English friend, how do you possibly think you can cross France, with your pathetic French, without arousing suspicion?'

Richard shrugged. 'True!'

'You will be my idiot brother, who doesn't speak. As the Nazis have the coastal strip you will cross through Andorra, where I shall leave you.'

Max laughed and slapped the walking wounded on the back. 'Meanwhile, I suggest you eat, drink and be merry at the chateau, while you have the chance!'

'How can you be sure the south won't be crawling with Jerries?' Richard mumbled through his gag.

'I can't, but logic tells me two things. They have to establish themselves in their own occupied zone, and they will also want to play along with the treaty they signed with the old bastard, for a while at any rate, until the ink has dried. But it may be long enough to get you out, and bombing again!'

Richard sat down on the fresh green mountain grass, pulled at a blade, and put it in the un-bandaged corner of his mouth. He stretched out in the hot sun and blinked at the cloudless blue sky. The very thought of war seemed utterly unreal.

He sighed. 'Let's hope you're right old chap.'

CHAPTER FIVE

Approaching Pont St Esprit, Simone had fitful bouts of animated conversation, which seemed to indicate that seeing her sister would be the best medication. When the chateau's towers came into view outside Uzès, she held Louis' hand, and sobbed quietly. 'Thank God! Thank God.'

Hearing the long awaited crunch of gravel on the drive, the de Lazarins, their nerves frayed with waiting, rushed out to the portico. Marianne nearly fainted from shock at seeing her injured sister, and almost passed out a second time at the sight of the heavily bandaged young man. A brief introduction, and Richard Browning was ushered, unobserved by any of the chateau's staff, into a room on the first floor, to which he would have to be consigned for the moment.

'I say Max, can't I shed this bloody Tutunkhamun outfit?' he mumbled.

'So long as you stay in your room.'

Unoccupied France was in thrall to the Third Reich, despite the implication of the treaty, and the English airman was in effect an enemy. Whilst the family knew the Englishman would have to get back to England, they hadn't the faintest idea how, nor at this moment did they care. Too much was happening in their own lives. When the horrifying details of the Becker family's experiences were recounted, no one mentioned a return journey.

One blisteringly hot afternoon, a few days later, Max invited Catherine to take a walk through the vineyards. Grapes hanging in abundance from the branches were almost ripe. They needed rain now to make them plump and succulent. The two cousins walked in silence along hard sun–baked paths, until they were well out of earshot of family snoozing in the conservatory.

'Is there anyone about?'

Catherine giggled. 'It's siesta time! This is the lazy south remember'.

'We can't be overheard?'

'Max, there are no Nazis here.'

'It's not the Nazis I'm worried about'.

'Who then?'

'Some of our own compatriots, little cousin. Be careful. There will be several Judases before this war is over.'

'The war is over. Papa says Hitler will invade Britain, and as they have lost everything there's not much hope.'

Anger flashed briefly across his face. 'The war, Catherine, is not over! The war will go on here! D'you understand?' He lowered his voice as though the vines had ears. 'The Nazis are going to use the south for communications, transport of arms, munitions, personnel, food, information. Listen to me.' He gripped her arm. 'Resistance groups are springing up all over France - our aim, to get the Fritzies out of the country, to disrupt and destroy them at every possible opportunity. Nimes will be the centre of one network of resisters.' He stopped. 'Will you be one of them?'

'Of course I will, but - but what I can do? I have to stay here with Maman and Papa.'

'I know that, but if you observe, and listen, you will find plenty of opportunities. Distribute our leaflets, pass on information.'

'To whom?'

'You will be told in due course. Tomorrow I shall go to Marseilles to meet other members of my cell.'

'Cell?'

'My group. There are six of us. We are all Socialist.'

'No Communists?'

'Good God, no! Party members are Boche bedfellows now.' he snarled.

'What are you going to do with the Englishman?'

'Get him to Lisbon.'

'Are you going with him?'

'Only to Andorra.'

They walked along the old bridle path that took them past the stables and the hectares of vegetable gardens.

'Max, you remember Mathilde's son Gaston?'

'Very well.'

'She thinks he's in Marseilles, in the garrison hospital, wounded. Could you try to find him?'

'Maybe,' he mumbled. They walked on in silence into the olive grove.

'Now listen,' he said sharply. 'I'll be back in two days. When we leave, the parents must think I am taking the English chap to Nimes. You are to tell no one the truth. Is that clear?'

She was taken aback both at the force of his tone, and that he should question her loyalty.

'One slip of the tongue, Catherine, that's all it will take for lives to be lost. This is a very different world now. Never forget that!'

Richard showed Catherine photographs of his mother and father, one of him with his bomber crew, and his last letter from home.

'Ma and Pa are going to have such a shock when I walk in,' he laughed shuffling the photographs nervously in his hands. 'You've got to be an optimist, when there's nothing else.'

She gave his arm a reassuring pat. 'You'll be all right. Max says the route is well organised.' She pointed to the letter and photographs. 'But they are too dangerous.'

Without a word, he slowly replaced them in his wallet. 'You are right. Stupid of me.' He handed it to her. 'After the war then, O.K.?'

The chateau's elders were unaware of this new civilian war strategy. The emphasis of control had suddenly switched. It would be the young who would now shape the destinies of their countries, while Europe struggled for a future.

In the early hours, tiptoeing down to the kitchen's vestibule, with a pannier of food, Catherine found Richard alone waiting for Max and the car. Already there were orange and gold boas of light in the sky, thrown off carelessly by an awakening sun. Through the open door came the mingled scents of summer heat, foliage and flowers.

Richard, dressed in the clothes of a field worker, took the food.

'It's such a glorious morning. Makes you feel lucky to be alive.'

Catherine smiled. 'The disguise is great. Do you feel alright?'

'Er – Catherine – would you –,' he hesitated. 'Look I want to ask you something, and please believe me it is only the circumstances that give me the courage.'

'What is it?'

'I may not survive this jamboree, and before I die I should like to hold a girl in my arms, and -and - and kiss her, if she'd let me – Catherine.'

His lean face was so creased with worry she raised her hand and touched his cheek. Without another word, his lips brushed hers, and he planted a light, chaste kiss, just for the briefest moment.

Then he enveloped her in his arms, clinging to her slender body as if to life itself.

'Good luck, English airman,' she said.

'Thanks a million. I'd have been six feet under without you all. One day, you never know, I could come back.' With a wan smile and little salute he joined Max in the car.

Back in her room Catherine picked up Richard's wallet, and looked at the photograph of the young bomber crew, all of them dead or missing. She thought of Philippe. Sitting on the bed, tears trickled down her cheeks. It simply wasn't fair. They were all of them too young. But she was determined to be part of the new resistance.

'Catherine dear, do you have a telephone number for Max?'

Aunt Simone was sitting in the conservatory. She raised a languid suntanned arm to brush a lock of hair off her face. These days she was physically much improved, although nothing would ever change the spoilt child inside. She took off her sunglasses. 'He's been gone over a week.'

Catherine looked unconcerned. 'You know Max, auntie. He's probably working very long hours.'

Simone sighed with characteristic petulance. Simone and Marianne had been brought up in a well to-do Parisian bourgeois milieu, and whilst Marianne had beauty and dignity, Simone, her young sister, amusing and pretty, had been hopelessly indulged by her parents, a feature of life she continued to expect.

Georges de Lazarin received an unexpected telephone call from Police Inspector Reynaud in Uzès. Reynaud's basso - profundo voice boomed down the line. 'A delicate matter, Monsieur de Lazarin, which I should like to discuss with you as soon as possible. May we say five o'clock this afternoon?'

As he replaced the receiver, Georges felt uneasy.

Inspector Reynaud was an unusually tall, thin man with a drooping moustache, and ungainly gait. When he laughed, which was rare, several of his upper teeth had such sharp points they resembled fangs. His disposition generally was lugubrious; his heavy lidded brown eyes, lifeless. After greetings had been exchanged and aperitifs taken Georges asked,

'Well now inspector, the delicate matter if you please?'

The inspector took a paper out of his pocket, and coughed.

'Monsieur de Lazarin, part of your chateau - is - um - is wanted'.

Georges raised his eyebrows. 'For what - a hospital?'

'No. For the army, monsieur.'

'French?'

'No - er German, monsieur.'

Georges' bronzed cheeks paled. After minutes of mute silence, he rose, and walked round the salon, his strong features transformed into an angry scowl.

The Girl on the Promenade

'German army?' He muttered the words several times as if trying to comprehend, and turned sharply to the Inspector who was now sitting awkwardly on the edge of a settee.

'But we are unoccupied, inspector?'

'Yes monsieur we are, officially, but this is termed a military presence - that's all. They - the German Government has a right -'

'Correct terminology if you please, inspector,' Georges exploded. 'These are Nazis!'

Reprimanded, the inspector hung his head to avert Georges de Lazarin's eyes, but continued. 'As you say, monsieur. The Nazis have a - right - within the treaty to establish -er - centres. They wish to encourage good relations and I believe cultural activities.'

Reynaud took out a large white handkerchief from his pocket and mopped the perspiration from his brow. Another minute's silence followed.

'Culture, eh? Do they suppose we have no culture? German culture I accept, enjoy, - the world enjoys, but these Nazis are pigs! Why are they here in the south? Tell me.'

The inspector raised his hands and his eyebrows heavenwards.

'Arms, airfields, Monsieur de Lazarin. All over the south, and they have to be guarded, partly by us, partly by their own men.'

Georges sat down heavily. 'And if we refuse to open the chateau to these Nazis?'

The inspector's toe traced a pattern in the carpet. He wished he were anywhere but here. He sighed deeply, and gesticulated with his bony hands.

'You cannot, monsieur.'

Georges sat quite still for a moment. 'How many?'

'Er - fifteen in all - officers and men – handpicked.'

'By whom? Hitler?'

The inspector shrugged his narrow shoulders.

'Apparently they are - er - civilised men. Must be. They are calling them 'emissaries' to the new zone.'

The chateau's west wing, the original fifteenth century building with its own tower, completely separate from the rest, had a very large reception hall, salon and kitchens, as well as a dozen bedrooms.

This would be the German HQ.

The family was stunned with the news. It appeared to be both a violation of the new treaty, and sending them to Chateau de Lazarin, a deliberate affront to their country's history and heritage. Catherine was speechless with anger. Remembering that pig of a Nazi officer sent poor Louis trembling in search of the cognac. Had Max been there, they would have left immediately. French Vichy was going to be safer for a Jew than living cheek by jowl with Nazis in the chateau.

Just before she slid into bed, Catherine looked out over the gravel courtyard and drive. A full moon shone out of a velvet blue sky, casting long shadows along the avenue of plane trees. In the distance, shafts of moonlight turned the vines into intricate stone carvings, for there was no breeze to displace even a leaf, and no sound save the chattering of tree frogs. She imagined grey uniforms and swastikas desecrating such beauty. The very thought knotted her stomach, the consequences too awful to contemplate.

At dawn, two days later, Max returned. By lunchtime Simone and Louis were ready to be driven back to Vichy. Max meanwhile recounted to Catherine how they had met a German patrol, and Richard had literally played dumb.

'Did you find out anything about Gaston?'

'He escaped.'

'So where's he gone?'

'No idea. Look, I'm going back to Paris. People I must see.'

'How will you cross the border?'

'Contacts.'

'But Max, what'll I do if anything happens to you?'

He grinned, 'Nothing will.'

'But we are going to be prisoners here, surrounded by Nazi pigs. I hate them - hate them! How can I ever help you now?'

The Girl on the Promenade

Gently he eased back her shoulders, and dabbed dry the tears drenching her long black lashes. 'Now look here - none of that defeatist talk mademoiselle! Did you really believe those bastards would stay within the treaty lines? Your presence here is even more vital now, because you are in a perfect position to obtain information. When I next visit you, should the Fritzies be curious, I am simply your doctor working in Nimes Hospital. So keep quiet, keep out of their way, ignore them, but listen and learn. Understand?'

The Beckers' car stood ready for the journey to Vichy, in a corner of the gravel courtyard, windows repaired, packed as it was when they arrived with the addition of boxes of fruit and farm produce that Marianne had collected. They had barely risen from the dining table when the screaming drone of motorbikes, their red and black swastika pennants flapping, tore into the silence and up the long drive, skidding to a standstill in front of the chateau's imposing portico. Four young German soldiers alighted and made their way up the entrance steps.

'My God,' Georges whispered. 'They're here!'

Without a word Max gathered his terrified parents. 'Quickly! We mustn't be seen.'

Catherine followed them out of the dining room. 'Get down to the cellar and wait for us to call you,' she whispered. Marianne, deathly pale, clung to the buffet to control her shaking hands and legs.

The soldiers were polite, clicking their heels, bowing to the ladies, and speaking in passable French. Their leader, a corporal, gave Catherine a smirk and a once over with his closely set eyes. She glared at him, and turned her back.

They needed to be shown the new quarters and to make a plan drawing of the site and accommodation. Georges accompanied the uninvited guests to the west wing's private entrance at the far end of the chateau's large back courtyard, and showed them its separate drive and gate entrance off the Alès road.

Catherine summoned the Beckers from the cellar. In almost total silence, mother and daughter bade farewell to their family, and stood on the steps until the car disappeared into the road. Marianne was on the verge of tears. Catherine gripped her arm. 'Don't ever let those swine see you cry, Maman.'

Two hours later the soldiers left. Georges had already taken the precaution of locking the interconnecting door on the first floor landing. There would be no access to the de Lazarin's private quarters, and the rest of the chateau.

As the motorbikes were revved into action, their tasks completed, the German corporal suddenly turned to the others. There followed what seemed to be a discussion. He walked briskly back to Georges standing with his family on the portico steps.

'Excuse me monsieur. We have omitted to ask. Do you have a pianoforte?'

'Yes, and we use it.'

'Then you will not object if the German army supplies its own?'

'None whatsoever.'

Tearing into the drive's gravel, they left.

Georges scratched his head. Why a pianoforte? It was not generally part of the German army's arsenal.

A few days later Georges and Marianne received their first communication from Simone and Louis in Vichy. They were safe and well, and Max had returned to Nimes.

Catherine said nothing. She was learning.

CHAPTER SIX

The chill winds of autumn subdued Paris even more. Streets were bleak and empty. Activity was confined to military displays of strength, to be seen marching in formation every day up the Champs Elysees, accompanied by blaring brass. The sound of German voices and laughter could be heard in restaurants, on sidewalk cafés, and in the best shops, which appeared to be of endless fascination to the dozens of grey uniforms that darted in and out of their elegant portals. Politically there was an uneasy calm, and the Kommandantur sensed it was only a matter of time.

Early in November Freddy intercepted a BBC message to high school and University students in Paris urging them to demonstrate. The Kommandant read the report several times. Taking off his glasses, he rubbed his eyes wearily, rose from his desk and looked out over the Place de l'Opera. The sun shone from a blue Paris sky, igniting the gold leaf on cupolas.

'It was too good to last - this detente. Now my dear major, the trouble will start.'

'Perhaps it will just be a simple student demonstration, sir?'

'The date, major, is the eleventh of November, therefore it cannot be simple.' The stocky little man turned abruptly from the window.

'The Champs Elysées, or Place de la Republique? Which one?'

He took a coin out of his pocket and flicked it into the air catching it on the back of his hand. 'Champs Elysées. Hm! A calculated risk. Major, see the north side is covered. I want troops posted every thirty metres. French police every ten metres. Let them deal with their own. Hope to God the location is correct', he muttered. 'Return here, major, to monitor broadcasts from London. Now I must call the General.'

The Kommandant had guessed correctly.

From early afternoon on the eleventh young people filled pavements, cafés, and avenues. All roads leading to the Champs Elysées were impassable to traffic. The occupying forces could do nothing. Up the impressive boulevard students marched in their thousands, and the air exploded with the Marseillaise, and shouted slogans. Freddy was back at the Kommandantur when the trouble started.

Hundreds were arrested.

The following day the Kommandant received an order to close the Sorbonne.

'I am sending you, Major von Langdorf.'

Freddy's heart sank.

'You seem to understand French people, as well as their language, therefore you are most suited to this rather - er - sensitive operation.'

Dozens of students were gathered silently in the tree-lined Sorbonne square, as Freddy arrived with a group of armed men. He walked to the entrance of the stately building while a sergeant hammered the official notice of closure to the ancient door. No one stirred. Silence hung like a black cloud. Freddy caught the eyes of a young girl student standing near the portico. Her bewildered expression asked questions. Questions he too was asking.

During the last week of November when Freddy and Colonel Kurt Bergen, were making final preparations to leave Paris, Kurt was summoned to the office of General von Stulpnagel, the military commander of occupied France, and ordered to defend a young Frenchman in a court case.

Later Freddy met Kurt for a beer.

'It's on the fifth – this trial.'

'How many days?'

'Just one.'

'Something serious?'

Kurt gave a dismissive chortle. 'No! Just a scuffle. The defendant merely intervened between his chums and our inebriated privates.'

Freddy drained his beer glass. 'Bit of a waste of time surely, all this formality for something so trivial.'

'It was the demonstration. Stulpnagel's got to put his foot down. He could be in big trouble with Berlin.'

'Will he get off, your Frenchman?'

'I damn well hope so my lad,' Kurt guffawed, 'as I'm defending! Six months maximum I reckon.'

When not involved with radio reconnaissance Freddy's free time was spent playing the Steinway, temporarily lodged in his apartment while waiting transportation to the south. The date of departure from Paris for Colonel Bergen and his men was now to be sometime before Christmas. They would be leaving Paris with relief not regret. The city had a muffled malaise; it was an incubator of unrest; a tinderbox waiting for a spark.

When Untersturmfuhrer Otto Muller of the SS heard about Lieutenant von Langdorf's promotion and new posting, he marched into Freddy's office, without even a perfunctory knock, slammed the door, and threw his heavy bulk on a corner of the desk, sending papers and documents flying in all directions. His ill manners were stupefying. Muller leered, his mouthful of gold fillings caked with the residue of his last meal.

'So, Major von Langdorf,' he shouted. 'Major, eh? And so soon! Amazing how you aristos always know the right strings and the right people.'

Freddy rose from his chair, and eyed the intruder coldly. 'Would you mind leaving my office, Untersturmfuhrer? I am rather busy.'

Muller thrust his evil face near Freddy's. 'I am just curious to know whether we are fighting a war, or just playing pretty music to the enemy. Eh? Tell me!'

Waves of rancid breath wafted across the young major's face.

Though burning with anger, he knew it was not wise to brush with the SS. This ruthless bunch worked with the Gestapo as spies, informers and liquidators. In Berlin, respected army officers had been removed from office, only to disappear without trace. The army represented everything the SS hated: privilege class and tradition.

'As you please, Untersturmfuhrer,' he hissed.

Muller jumped to his feet, and thumped the desk with a knuckle-breaking fist. 'You know what I'd like to know? Whose idea it was to send a bunch of string scrapers into the enemy camp? How d'you kill them? With a flute maybe?' He threw back his head and laughed.

Freddy longed to aim a punch into that foul face.

'Please remember, Untersturmfuhrer even musicians can behave like soldiers when required!'

The fat man swaggered to the door. Fixing Freddy with his rat - like eyes, he replied, 'we shall have to wait and see. And on that point, you may rest assured Major von Langdorf.'

He gave a half bow in mock subservience. 'We shall be watching you with great interest. Heil Hitler.'

On the evening of December 5th Kurt sat white - faced in Freddy's apartment. 'I can't understand it. A death sentence! It's crazy.'

'But you'll appeal?'

'I've already lodged it'

'To the Fuhrer?'

Kurt nodded.

'Then don't worry. He likes France so much he'll agree.'

'That's exactly what I told him, Bonsergeant. It's a pro forma sentence, nothing more.' Kurt put his glass on the table. 'He's a nice lad - 28 - an engineer, straight. Remarkably calm under the circumstances. No trouble maker.'

There had been rumours since Dunkirk about an invasion of Britain, but on his last visit to Paris Carl told Freddy that Hitler had changed his mind again.

'But the British have no arms, and no money. This has to be the best time.'

'Absolutely right, but,' Carl paused. 'Hitler doesn't listen to his generals, only to his astrologer.'

A smile of incredulity crossed the young man's face. 'That's crazy!'

'It's more serious than that my boy. He's crazy.'

Jean Bonsergeant's appeal was turned down. He was to be executed. Paris was stunned when posters appeared advertising the event.

Kurt was deeply shocked, both professionally and emotionally.

'The SS are little more than pigs with power. To think an innocent young chap must be shot, and for nothing! It's bloody monstrous!'

Kurt leant on the table, looked down into his cup and muttered,'he reminded me of my wife's young brother'.

They were sitting at a quiet café table, in a darkened corner.

Freddy stirred his coffee. 'We've given the French their first martyr, haven't we?'

Kurt, scowling, unwrapped a sugar lump. 'Sure! Can you think of a better way to start all-out resistance?'

Freddy gathered up the clots of creamy froth clinging to the inside of his coffee cup in his spoon. 'And the Gestapo have set up an official HQ. Avenue Foch.'

'So, Prinz Albrechtstrasse has finally come to Paris has it? Who has the power, eh?' Kurt muttered bitterly.

Freddy spooned the sugary dregs from his cup. 'Thank God we're going south. Out of it!'

The tinderbox had been ignited.

CHAPTER SEVEN

At the beginning of December Inspector Reynaud hurled his black Citroen up the chateau's gravel drive, and with brakes protesting, crunched to a halt by the colonnaded portico. Frowning, he elevated his ungainly body out of the driving seat, slammed the car door, ploughed through gravel, to the semi - circular steps and tugged on the ancient bell rope. The sun was still warm; the sky a brilliant blue, while a few boas of wispy cloud stretched and undulated delicately across the horizon. Although most of the plane trees lining the drive had lost their leaves, there was no hint of approaching winter. The briefest flicker of pleasure crossed the Inspector's solemn features at the thought of Christmas dinner on his new patio.

Sitting uncomfortably in Georges de Lazarin's office, whilst running a bony finger round the rim of a glass of cognac, he attempted to explain the reason for this second visit. Georges, enveloped in the soft folds of a leather armchair, a cigarette in a mother of pearl holder, listened, quite relaxed; a characteristic of the true aristocrat's *sang froid* under pressure.

'They want to prepare, to get it ready you see, Monsieur de Lazarin, for the sixteen men. You - er- you have some furniture there already I believe?'

'Of course! Family things.'

The Inspector spread his spider hands in a gesture. 'Too late to remove them now monsieur. Requisitioned you see. It will all be requisitioned. And of course they have to install cupboards, beds, kitchen equipment, dining area, officers' quarters.'

'Yes, yes,' Georges, muttered impatiently. 'So when are they coming, the Nazis?'

The Inspector cleared his throat and uncrossed his feet. 'Er – tomorrow, Monsieur de Lazarin. Prisoners of war - with a handful of Germans directing operations, - so I believe.'

'Tomorrow?' Georges stared blankly into the Inspector's heavy expressionless eyes and growled. There was nothing more to say.

Relieved the afternoon's errand had been easier than he had dared hope, the Inspector tipped back his lantern jaw and drained the glass of cognac, leaving thick drops clinging to his black moustache.

'You will be accompanying them I take it, inspector?'

'Of course, monsieur - well, just to bring them here you understand.'

'Good, then please see to it personnel and equipment are brought in via the back driveway. Neither myself nor my family wish to be disturbed.'

Standing in the portico, about to take his leave, Inspector Reynaud turned his bony frame to Georges. 'A bad time for us all, Monsieur de Lazarin.' He sighed, and gestured with his hands, his eyes half closed. 'Never mind! Soon be Christmas.'

The Inspector's thin lips parted into a smile. With yellow teeth bared contentedly at the thought, the tall thin figure folded itself into the driving seat, scraped into gear, and drove off.

Georges, right from his student days at the Polytechnique in Paris, had been an accomplished cellist, and had performed with the best amateur quartets and ensembles. Music was his personal antidote to stress.

It seemed to him that the only joy left now was in family and music.

Catherine awoke with a start. And switched on the light. Heavy vehicles were lumbering over the west wing's back courtyard. She grabbed her dressing gown and padded across the stone landing to a window just above the scene of activity. In this dim morning light she could see several trucks spilling headlights onto a dozen German NCOs, standing at the back of the largest vehicle, and carrying an intimidating assortment of weapons. At a command, men spilled out from the trucks' black interiors. Those who stumbled were helped on their feet by bayonet prods or rifle butts. They were clad in ill - fitting shirts and trousers, and every head had been shorn. Catherine wiped away the mist from her breath on the window. Another rasped command from the officer in charge, and the dejected group shuffled in silence, heads bowed, towards the west wing entrance. These were no military prisoners. They were political prisoners, maybe Jewish deportees, from a labour camp. She leant back against the cold stone wall, and prayed that Max would make contact soon.

During the next few days, despite constant noise from carpentry, furniture moving and barked Germanic commands, the de Lazarins kept very much to themselves. Catherine described her observations to her father, who, having drawn the same conclusion, closed eyes and ears, spending his leisure time either reading or playing the cello. They decided not to relay their conclusions to Marianne, and Georges, for reasons of safety, removed the radio transmitting BBC broadcasts to the cellar. Catherine found it difficult to study. Her mind was restless, her body impatient for action.

Marianne was fretful. 'Couldn't we go and talk to those poor French soldiers? Perhaps give them a few bottles, or some fruit. They can't be eating properly.' Georges put down his knife and fork in mild exasperation. Her naiveté astounded him at times.

'After all, we are not fighting the Germans now are we?' she chirped. 'It's over. We are free.'

Catherine glanced at her father. What was the point in disabusing her mother's comfortable ignorance? She wondered how many others in Vichy France believed similarly.

Five days later, the German army's building force left. But not without leaving their calling card. On the back drive's iron gate, and over the west wing door flew the symbols of France's defeat, two red and black swastikas.

Furious, Catherine ran into her father's office.

'We have to tear them down, Papa. Our chateau isn't a Nazi Prefecture!'

Georges leant back in his chair. 'My dear child, in time of war individual acts of heroism are straws in the wind. National pride has to take second place.'

Catherine exploded. 'Surely you don't intend to accept it, and do nothing?' She threw herself into the big leather armchair.

Calmly Georges said, 'First of all remember nothing lasts - that is a fact of history. Therefore it would be foolish to risk the possibility of imprisonment when France will need every able bodied young person to rebuild when the Nazis have gone.'

Catherine shot him a look, and burst into angry tears.

'I want to kill them,' she sobbed. 'I hate them - I hate all Germans!'

Soothing his daughter's distress, he knelt beside her, and hoped that these so-called emissaries of the Third Reich would do nothing to arouse further antagonism. His nephew was a little too close for comfort. Max, always an extremist, and likely to be involved in subversive activity, had a powerful influence over Catherine, and it would be imperative for their own security to maintain a balance of co-existence with the Third Reich.

'You must keep a cool head, Catherine - no impulsive actions d'you hear?'

Far too dangerous, and,' he cupped her chin, 'you are all we have Maman and I. Always remember you are Catherine de Lazarin. Be dignified, be polite, even to the Nazis for all our sakes'.

Georges, trusting his advice had been heeded, took out a large handkerchief from his pocket and dried his daughter's eyes.

On the afternoon of December 16th, Major Freddy von Langdorf and Colonel Kurt Bergen sat in the back of the black Mercedes as it sped along the R.N.7 to Avignon. Keeping the lowest of profiles, they had removed the swastika pennant from the car's bonnet. Their driver was Corporal Rudy Schmidt, clarinet and oboe, short and thick set with dark hair, and a warm easy-going personality. But under those twinkling eyes and the jokes, Rudy Schmidt was lonely. He hated the army, missed his music and most of all, his bubbly wife and his children in Berlin. He adored his two little girls and Liesel was coming up to five months pregnant with their third. He thanked his lucky stars he had been selected to come south; he'd had enough of Paris. Six years before the war, Liesel had joined the Berlin Philharmonic as a violinist. He smiled, remembering that first day of rehearsal in Paris, when he saw his beautiful girl for the first time.

The road to Uzès was almost deserted. Had it not been for their uniforms, no one could have guessed Freddy and Kurt were involved in a war. The scents and vistas of the south were a heady mixture for the young major, rekindling memories of life before the war. Every summer since he could remember the von Langdorfs had taken the same suite at the Hotel Carlton in Cannes. The balcony of his room had overlooked the Croisette where on countless occasions he had sat mesmerised by the beauty of the sea and coast. Reddening sky over Uzès threw dappled shafts of pink light into the car. They reminded him of one particular sunset in Cannes during the summer of '38, when a blood red fireball balanced on the horizon. Gold tipped palm trees stood still as stone, while every window of the hotel dazzled the eye like a hundred bobbing lanterns. He remembered the slim girl with dark hair leaning on the balustrade of the promenade below. Only for the briefest moment did he glimpse a lovely profile as she turned to survey the sweep of the bay. He smiled to himself remembering with what determined zeal he had scoured the promenade and streets of Cannes searching for this elusive beauty, to no avail.

They approached Chateau de Lazarin by the long main drive. Food supplies and thirteen NCOs including a very competent chef had already arrived at the west wing. The

Mercedes pulled up on the gravel and Kurt gathered his leather gloves.

'The de Lazarins are as old as the von Langdorfs I'm told.'

Freddy grinned ' How many are there?'

'Three. Come on. I need your impeccable French, young man.'

The chateau's vast entrance hall was supported front and rear by four stone columns, thereby repeating the architectural detail of the colonnaded portico. Priceless tapestries hung from smooth stone walls, and the floor's eighteenth century flag-stones,had been buffed over the years to a golden patina. Around the walls at regular intervals marble busts sat in niches. In the centre, a stone staircase, with an intricate wrought iron balustrade rose in a majestic sweep to a minstrels' gallery. Suspended from a domed ceiling, hung an exquisite chandelier. It reminded Freddy of the schloss. He hoped the west wing would prove as interesting.

Mathilde still trembling from the initial shock of seeing uniformed enemy soldiers, returned to the visitors. 'Monsieur and Madame de Lazarin, will see you in the salon,' she mumbled. 'Follow me if you please.'

The salon was dominated on one side by an old Provencal chimneypiece, carved from the local honey coloured stone, above which hung a rococo gilt mirror. The walls were hung with exquisite paintings, and the marble floor was partly covered by one of the most beautiful Aubusson carpets Freddy had ever seen. Georges and Marianne rose from a sofa as their visitors entered. Coming face to face with French aristocracy was a difficult moment for foreign occupiers, both parties being fully aware of social status and class. They shook hands formally but it was Freddy's perfect French that broke the ice. Marianne muttered a polite if nervous appreciation, while Kurt stumbled along with his passable linguistic skill. Taking in the rest of the room Freddy noticed several Boule chests with their decorative gilt, but when his eyes lit upon a Bechstein, placed in front of one of the tall windows, he caught his breath.

With her back to the room, standing by the window and ignoring the company, was a young woman. The major looked at the curve of the back, the hair falling on her shoulders, the slant of a hip. Had he seen it before? Or was time playing tricks? Monsieur de Lazarin called her to join them. When she turned, he caught her profile. His heart almost stopped. There was no doubt in his mind; this was the girl on the promenade. He took one look at Catherine's lovely face, her olive skin, large green almond - shaped eyes, her black hair, and his head reeled. She walked towards the group. He was speechless.

Mademoiselle Catherine de Lazarin was introduced to Major von Langdorf and Colonel Kurt Bergen. Catherine withdrew her hand quickly while exchanging a few perfunctory words congratulating the major on his excellent French.

Taking the initiative Kurt opened his gold cigarette case and with his own functional French, politely passed cigarettes round the group. Georges and Marianne accepted gratefully. It was a timely moment of composure in this delicate situation.

Marianne was privately pleased at the obvious touch of 'breeding' when Kurt clicked his heels, and with a deferential bow took out a large box from his greatcoat pocket. 'Monsieur, Madame de Lazarin, and Mademoiselle, for you.' It was an elaborately decorated box containing five hundred top quality Turkish cigarettes.

Over Georges' cognacs, the colonel and his major described their small makeshift orchestra, and the concerts they were hoping to give. Catherine glared at her father, daring him to say anything about his cello playing. Georges of course understood it would be quite insensitive to offer his services- not yet anyway.

Several more cognacs followed. They talked music, composers, quartets, and how the major had learnt his French. Freddy told them about his annual family holiday at the Hotel Carlton in Cannes. A smiling Marianne told them about their villa, and frequent dinners at the Carlton. 'We probably saw you. There were lots of Germans there', she chirruped brightly.

Catherine was sickened by her mother's vacuous banter.

'Will you also be requisitioning the Cannes villa, major, for your holiday breaks perhaps?'

Freddy smiled unsteadily. Just looking at her was unnerving quite apart from the scorn in her voice.

'Requisitioning is not part of our job mademoiselle. And I do assure you, the beauty of everything here, your home, your furniture, is appreciated.'

His manner remained courteous. A ploy, she thought, and glared at him. She saw him tall, and arrogant, strutting as they all did, grey peacocks in boots. She saw the haughty tilt of his chin - an archetypal blond haired, blue-eyed Hun and conqueror. She hated him, and all he represented. Yet, when she looked at him her heart raced, and a strange weakness enveloped her limbs.

It was Kurt who asked permission for his major to play the Bechstein. Freddy looked at Madame de Lazarin. 'May I?' he asked diffidently. Delighted with such refinement, Marianne waved a manicured hand in the direction of the piano. The young man caressed the fine wood, before lifting the lid, then sat down played a few scales and fulsome chords, and stopped. He shot a delighted boyish smile at Marianne. 'It's beautiful madame - really beautiful.'

Marianne could not help observing how handsome he was. The sort of face they would have sculpted in Ancient Greece. That square jaw, the blond hair, unusual eyes. He reminded her a little of Robert.

He began to play Debussy's 'Clair de Lune.' His talent was obvious, but his choice of music surprising. In the occupied zone there was a ban on all French works. Georges put everything down to background. He was after all a 'Von,' a titled aristocrat. Liquid notes floated high into the rapt silence of the salon, reverberating delicately against walls and ceiling, soothing away tensions, melting hostilities. Colonel Kurt Bergen sitting stiffly in a formal chair tipped his head back, relaxing his tightly clasped hands.

Catherine noticed the major's eyes were half closed, as his hands spanned the keys. A cheap trick she thought. How could her parents put on such a staggering show of welcome to these barbarians?

There was a moment's silence after the final chords died away. Marianne's eyelashes were damp, the Colonel smiled, and Georges applauded. 'Bravo! Bravo!' The young musician modestly thanked his small audience. He observed Catherine's hostile glare, despite applauding his playing. He knew instinctively, getting to know Mademoiselle de Lazarin was not going to be easy. He hated the war, and not for the first time, his uniform.

That night Catherine thought about the young major. He had extraordinary eyes; pale blue irises, dark rimmed. Though handsome, and talented, and possibly civilised, he was as arrogant as the rest of his dreadful race. She was ready now to listen, observe and report back to Max.

Closing her eyes, she could not help thinking she had seen Major von Langdorf somewhere before.

CHAPTER EIGHT

Within twenty-four hours of the musical introduction to the enemy, the two hideous swastikas had been removed from the west wing gate.

Following Max's instructions, Catherine kept a constant vigil over the occupied zone's courtyard. Apart from a couple of black Mercedes and larger army trucks, there were no sentry boxes, although there was a soldier on guard duty outside the west wing door.

The chateau's west wing had always been used for official functions, while the east wing housed guest and nursery suites, plus the family's summer salon, which opened onto the conservatory, offering a cooling respite from the scorching sun. Both wings adjoined the wide three storeyed central facade at right angles, forming a rear square courtyard. The west wing was hidden from the main drive by a barrier of poplar trees and exuberant bushes of mimosa and winter jasmine, which ran like an outstretched arm from the centre block's corner. At a distance this arm of trees appeared to sprout from the bricks themselves, but was in fact separated from the house by a narrow footpath that led into a most beautiful garden, with high walls on three sides. The only windows opening onto this private area were those of the west wing salon, and the room above. It was here, in this secret garden, that Catherine, Robert and Max had played as children. They knew every corner, every bush, each piece of crumbling wall. They had dislodged old bricks to make hiding places for childish messages, written in their own code, and had replaced the bricks so carefully that no adult was ever able to discover their whereabouts. After Robert was killed, the garden evoked far too much pain for Catherine, and so it remained an undisturbed shrine to their childhood.

No longer undisturbed, it was now part of the west wing occupation.

Marianne's nervousness at having the German army on her doorstep calmed through lack of incident. On the contrary, the promise of a musical presence in the chateau, irrespective of who was to provide it, lightened Georges' spirits considerably, an attitude that angered his daughter.

'How can you possibly consider listening to music made by pigs?'

Georges put down his bow, and sighed. 'First, they have not invited me to listen, and second, did you think those two men were pigs, behaved like pigs? Did you think 'Clair de Lune' was played by a pig? Have any of the other soldiers behaved like pigs? Offended you in some way?'

'They are the enemies of France, Papa.'

'Very well, but at the moment we have to co-exist with them.'

'Why?'

'Catherine, I have seen war in the trenches. I have fought against good friends. Maybe I killed them with my own bullets! Friends who solely because of politics and the political egos of their leaders became my enemies. Millions died then. And for what? So that millions more may die now?'

'These are Nazis, Papa.'

'Not all! Some are, some are not.'

'Then tell me the difference between co-existence and co-operation?'

Exasperated, Georges turned sharply to his daughter. 'Look! I have already played the hero, the patriot, in one war. And what has it solved? Nothing! War is primitive. It's animal.'

'But you said yourself the Nazis are pigs.'

'The Nazis yes! And sooner or later the German people would have realised this, and risen up against that despot. There have already been indications that - '

Angry now, Catherine interrupted.'So you think we should forget about deportations and labour camps?'

The Girl on the Promenade

'Nothing to do with us. *Laissez faire!* Do we care what our neighbours in the village do in their own homes? Tell me?'

Catherine shook her head, and walked to the door. Georges picked up his bow.'William Shakespeare said,"If music be the food of love play on" did he not? I say,"If music be the food of peace, play on." So, if you don't mind, I shall do just that. Play on.' He gave a little smile.'My contribution you understand.'

He returned to his cello and his transpositions, at which he was particularly good. Catherine slammed the door. She was ashamed of her father's lack of patriotism, his lack of fight.

As Freddy and Kurt were the only officers, two rooms on the first floor had been selected. One room faced the courtyard and the west wing's gate, the other was over the large salon, which they had already designated their concert auditorium.

Kurt took the room facing the courtyard. 'At least I shall see what's coming in and going out. That's the theory anyway.'

Freddy's room overlooked the secret garden.

With the blazing log fire in the ancient hearth, he was delighted to find a four poster bed, a Louis XV sofa, and a comfortable soft leather armchair which slouched in a far corner. In the window recess an army desk with reading lamp, typewriter, radio transmitting and receiving equipment, was a reminder of the continuity of war. A wide shelf unit held books, gramophone and records. The walls and doors were so completely covered with a faded blue Toile de Jouy that it was with some difficulty he found the door leading to his bathroom.

Just before the meeting for all personnel, called by the Colonel, he looked out of the window overlooking the garden, now striped with the moon's rays. Beyond were the vineyards. It was all so still, so serene, he wished with all his heart that this war were a fearful nightmare that would disappear at dawn. There was absolutely no doubt in his mind, it was Mademoiselle de Lazarin he had seen leaning on the promenade rail. His girl on the promenade, for whom he had so desperately searched through the small streets of Cannes. Their villa was only a hundred metres from the Carlton.

If only he had met her then. If only he could tell her now.

Of the fourteen NCOs and ratings, there were two cooks, three orderlies, and two batmen. The rest, with the two officers, were to form the makeshift chamber ensemble. Kurt had already decided to run his station along egalitarian principles, so there would be no separate Officers' Mess, merely a high table set aside for Freddy and himself, over which was hung a large photograph of the Fuhrer, flanked by two equally large swastika flags.

After supper Kurt outlined a general working schedule for the following six months, and stressed the importance of impeccable behaviour at all times. He felt embarrassed at having to role-play with so many highly respected musicians in his group, but his words were for the most part directed to the others. Apart from regular concert performances, which were designed to encourage an *entente cordiale,* there would be local relief guard duties undertaken by all. 'Naturally, you will be particularly courteous and polite to our hosts in this exquisite chateau. Our presence here is aimed to appease, not to irritate, and as we have not been invited here, make it your business to talk to local French. You will probably make friends, very good friends.' He paused and smiled. 'Only the unmarried of course.' There was a wave of laughter as he added. 'And if you get a little too close we shall point you in the direction of Major Doctor Gebhardt in Uzès.'

Spirits were remarkably high. What an agreeable way of spending a war.

As a goodwill gesture to the family, restoration of the wing's public areas would begin immediately.

In Kurt's quarters, Freddy scanned the personnel list.

'Aha! We have two members of the Party, orderlies, Hanke and Remer.'

Kurt drew on his cigarette. 'With only two we should have no problems.'

He poured a glass of schnapps.

'Look at these.' Freddy handed him their dossiers.

The Girl on the Promenade

Kurt frowned as he flicked through the pages. 'S.S.too? That means they have friends in high places. Interesting.'

'Can't we get them transferred?'

'I doubt it. Party representation and all that.'

Freddy whistled in amazement. 'I say! It's very impressive! Berlin Philharmonic, Vienna Philharmonic, Josef Hahn Stuttgart Opera. I can't wait to get started! You do realise of course that we are the only non-professionals!'

'This is war, don't worry. Anyway, you could grace a concert platform any day. Maybe after the war, eh? You should think about it seriously.'

The younger man shrugged dismissively. 'D'you think we'll get audiences?'

'Sure, if we invite the Mayor, Chief of Police, local bigwigs, their families.

The rest will follow.'

'Do we play only classical music? Why not jazz, swing? Dieter Frank plays saxophone and trumpet, Heinz Blanke viola and double bass.'

'Why not? How about jazz for Christmas, a celebration for just ourselves hm?'

The young major was pleased. He crossed to Kurt's small electric hotplate, installed specially to appease the colonel's passion for good coffee, and helped himself. 'We could perhaps invite the de Lazarins? To eat, drink, Christmas Day maybe?'

Kurt chuckled. 'Ah! I was wondering when you'd ask. Very well. You are officially ordered to invite the ravishing mademoiselle, and her family. And what is more, you may do it now! But don't get too close to her. She may have a guillotine in her bedroom.'

Protesting with a satisfied grin, Freddy walked to the door.

Kurt put up a hand. 'Another request; ask Monsieur de Lazarin if he would like to play the cello for us? I've heard him several times on my post-prandial walks. Excellent musician.'

Alone, the colonel lit up a last cigarette. It had been plain to see from the moment of introduction, young Freddy had been bowled over, and he had caught mademoiselle gazing at his handsome major with those astonishing eyes of hers. He did not relish having a lovelorn second in command, but there was nothing he could do at this stage. Contact with the family had to be made, and it had to be Freddy who made it. Running his fingers through his dark hair, he remembered his own ardent pursuit of Erika. He picked up her photograph with the three children, and kissed it. Five days to Christmas. This time last year they were deciding where to hide the children's presents.

'Crazy bloody war', he muttered.

At breakfast on December 22nd Catherine received a telephone call from Max. He said cryptically he would be coming to see them during the afternoon, for Monsieur de Lazarin's 'routine check-up'.

He arrived in a battered Citroen, and like any visiting doctor carried his black bag into the chateau. They talked about Louis and Simone, in Vichy, where already Jews in public office had been dismissed, and there were rumours of more measures on the way.

Max snorted.'Those toads will be marching with the Third Reich soon. Wait and see.' He strode to one of the salon's windows.

'Do you ever see them here on the forecourt?'
Never. They always use the west wing back courtyard.'
'Guards?'
'Only one, at the west wing door.'
'And the outside gate?'
'I haven't seen one.'
'Find out.'

Catherine detailed to Max the first meeting with the enemy, and their reasons for being there. Max shook his head in disbelief. 'That's what they tell you. Did you know there are small military stations all over the south, arms dumps, supply and equipment centres, ostensibly for their North African campaign?' He stopped suddenly.

The Girl on the Promenade

'Look, can we go up to your room, play some music. I need to talk, and I'd feel safer there.'

The radiogram was in the study adjoining Catherine's bedroom. He pushed it against the wall nearest the west wing, turned the volume to maximum, and beckoned her to sit with him on the opposite side of the room. Keeping his voice low, he said. 'Resistance groups against Vichy and the Boche, have started. There is a group at the hospital in Nimes. At some point we'll set up a field hospital near Anduze, but we are desperately short of weapons, so we have to steal anything we can lay our hands on. We'll be targeting small groups when they're out on patrol.'

'So what can I do?'

'Listen to the Free French broadcasts from the BBC, specifically for us, you understand? They give information about new Nazi locations, and new hazards. They can even get coded messages to some resistance cells.'

'Will I be the only one listening to these broadcasts for you?'

'Of course not, but no one can listen for twenty-four hours. In Paris the Fritzies have equipment that picks up radio signals and they do random house searches.'

'Naturally. They're occupied.'

He looked at her patronisingly. 'Do you actually think we can carry on as normal down here? Just wait. A year from now it will be very different. Listen to London only in the cellar, and don't forget to watch and observe everything that goes on with your new neighbours.'

'Difficult, as I never see them.'

'Then talk to them. Let them think you are not hostile. Make friendly overtures.'

'I want to work at Nimes hospital,' she said irritably. 'I want to be involved, to be a real part of the resistance!'

'Stop being obtuse! You are of more help here. For God's sake don't you see, you are in a fantastic position? They couldn't possibly suspect you, a beautiful French girl. Just get to know them. Find out if they go out on guard duty, and where. That's an order,' he added sternly.

'And when I have information. What then?'

'We'll meet in Nimes, Café Vert, the square in front of the Arena. You will be told.'

'By you?'

'By Gaston. He's working at the Hotel Terminus in Uzès now. Linked with several groups. He has new papers, and a thick beard. Even the police don't recognise him. He's also got a bad leg injury, so he limps.'

'Gaston? Does Mathilde know he's back?'

Max shrugged. 'If she does, she's going to be the last person to turn him over.'

Rising from the chair he said quietly, 'Philippe is alive Catherine. He's working in my old hospital in Paris.'

'Oh - thank God for that. I'm so - so very glad for you.'

She paused. 'His wife?'

'No idea. But I'll see him soon.'

'Where?'

'Paris.'

'How will you cross the border?'

For the first time that afternoon, his face relaxed into a smile.

'We leave nothing to chance.' As he approached the door he lowered his voice.

'That traitor Flandin is going to be visiting Nimes. The man's a fool, unless he likes courting danger.'

'But he's French.'

He huffed with exasperation. 'Don't you remember our conversation out in the vineyard? French does not necessarily imply patriot. Already there are pro-Vichy semi-military groups forming in every city in the south. How many times must I tell you? This is total war Catherine, as involved and as dangerous as a battlefield.'

Just before dinner, the chateau's ancient bell rope clanged.

Mathilde ran into the dining room, where Catherine was laying the table.

'It's a Boche soldier, mademoiselle Catherine. Don't know which one. They all look the same to me. Pigs.'

Freddy stood in the hall, cap under arm, tall, elegant, and smiling.

Remembering Max's instructions, she too smiled. Major von Langdorf clicked his heels, and bowed.

'What can we do for you, major?'

For a moment Freddy wondered if this was the same ice maiden he had already met. Why question the change? His heart was already in her hands.

Sitting in the salon Freddy invited the family to join them for a Christmas supper.

'Well, it's very generous of you, but - but - we may have family guests.'

'Mademoiselle the invitation is for all, you and your guests.'

'That's most kind. I shall discuss it with my parents and let you know.'

'We shall wait for your answer, mademoiselle.' He sipped the aperitif that she had handed him, but his eyes remained on her. He wanted so much to talk about the girl on the promenade. Instead he said, 'I have an invitation to your father from my colonel. We should be delighted if he would care to join our orchestra.'

Catherine's smiles faded.

'They are all excellent musicians, you know. All professionals, not like me. We shall ask your father personally of course, but meanwhile – er – if –'

'I shall mention it to him,' she interrupted sharply.

The purpose of the visit seemed to be concluded, but during the silence that followed, neither moved. Max was right. She was being seduced into thinking these vile Nazis were charming, honest, and harmless. This group had been sent here for a specific purpose. The family could be deported. The Nazis could bring a garrison to the chateau. All too simple.

Freddy's eyes were on Catherine. He wanted to sit beside her on the sofa, touch her, caress her, and desperately searched for a reason to linger.

'May I show you some photographs of my family and home?' He pulled out a wallet from inside his jacket.

She wanted his blue eyes, his blond hair, his tall body in that hideous uniform, to go. But a wild exciting desire, gripping the pit of her stomach, wanted to run her finger along the scar on his cheek, feel his arms around her, touch his lips.

'No', she said firmly. 'I'm so sorry. I have things I must do.'

Registering his crestfallen face, and remembering Max's advice, she added.

'But - I'd like to, when I'm more prepared.'

He rose from his chair, quickly searching for another excuse to remain.

His eyes fell upon the Bechstein. 'That instrument really has a beautiful sound.'

Catherine saw the hungry look in his eyes, and capitulated.

'Would you like to play?'

He breathed an inner sigh of relief.

'But I am keeping you, mademoiselle.'

'No. Please - do play,' she invited archly, and followed him to the piano.

She hated him for his ridiculous charm, yet -yet she longed to hear him play again. He ran his fingers up and down the keyboard. She noticed his hands, tanned and strong. His fingers, long and sinewy, tripped delicately along chromatic scales.

'Do you like Beethoven?'

'Of course.'

'Do you have a favourite?'

'Many,' she replied dismissively.

'Mademoiselle de Lazarin, would you accept "Fur Elise"?'

He suddenly took his hands off the keyboard. Looking at her, he asked softly,'what is your first name, Mademoiselle de Lazarin?'

Annoyed that he should ask, and angry with herself that she was succumbing to Max's seduction theory, she replied with a voice as brittle as she felt. 'Catherine. Why do you wish to know?'

He gave her a brief smile and shrugged. 'Nothing – only, had I been Beethoven, I would have called it "Fur Catherine".'

With half closed eyes his fingers began to stroke the keys and he was soon lost in the music. Fascinated by his hands as they coaxed and shaped sublime sounds out of the instrument, she could feel his long elegant fingers stroking her skin, rippling over the hidden untrammelled parts of her body. His playing was so beautiful, it was only the recollection of Max's words of warning that brought her back to reality.

The Major was nothing more than a Pied Piper in Nazi uniform. How stupid could she be!

In the hall, he thanked her for her hospitality, took her hand and raised it to his lips. 'Goodnight, Mademoiselle Catherine.'

Taken by surprise, she quickly pulled her hand away.'Goodnight, major.'

He smiled and shook his head. 'My name is Freddy von Langdorf, apprentice archaeologist. "Major" is only a temporary title, you know.'

When he had gone, she leant against the closed door.

'Bastards - all of you.'

Catherine telephoned Max regarding the Christmas invitations. He was doing a ward round.

'Well done! You must have charmed them silly.'

'Will you come?'

He exploded. 'Jesus Christ! No! You must realise that.' He paused. 'What have you told them?'

'Nothing!'

'Do they know you have a male doctor cousin in Nimes?'

'No!'

'Sure? Think! Think!'

She was irritated now. 'I've told you, they know nothing!'

'No one saw me when I visited you?'

'No! No! No!'

He stopped abruptly. 'So I shall write you a letter, before leaving to spend Christmas with the parents. I must go. 'Bye'.

The telephone was slammed down.

Max was certainly learning the art of interrogation very quickly.

A delighted Georges accepted the orchestra's invitation.

'It will be so good for him', Marianne confided.

'Good to play with the enemy?'

A frosty Marianne put two hands on her daughter's shoulders. 'Listen carefully young lady, your father would never do anything that would endanger neither his family, those he loved, and certainly not his country. Treachery is not in your father's make-up. It is going to be difficult enough in the next few months, possibly years. The vines need pruning, grafting, replanting. And the *vendange?* Who is here? You, me, and a handful of women from the village. For all those hectares? We have to produce and sell wine, or we do not survive. As for family money, Papa withdrew all we had. There are no investments we can draw on, so we are living on capital. Those German soldiers are already doing internal repairs that we wouldn't have a hope of seeing to, and if they wish to invite us to share their Christmas dinner with them, why not?'

Catherine was staring at the tiled floor.

She could not look her mother in the eye, knowing from childhood experience, when Maman adopted a certain tone of voice, the subject was not even open to argument, it was closed. But Marianne had not quite finished. 'And if Papa wishes to ease his mind, and bring a little happiness into both our lives with some first class music making,' she paused. 'I reiterate. Why not?'

The case was closed.

Lying in her bed between cool crisp linen sheets, Catherine switched off the electric lamp, and whispered to the enveloping darkness, 'Major von Langdorf, do not imagine I have fallen under the spell of your Nazi seduction. I shall not be duped by your charm nor by your talent. You are a Nazi, an enemy of France, a Pied Piper, and if I can ever destroy you, I shall do so.'

Closing her eyes, Catherine hoped she would now know how to deal with Major von Langdorf, however temporary his title.

CHAPTER NINE

Six days before Christmas, Nimes was surprisingly busy, though there was not very much to buy, and little choice.

By noon, Catherine and her mother had queued for ration cards, and were laden with as much food as they could find plus a few small presents. With enemy troops actually living in the chateau, it would be impossible for Louis and Simone to visit, even with enough petrol, and a travel pass.

Mother and daughter walked through back streets to the Boulevard Victor Hugo. 'Come on Maman, 'Restaurant Mimi', your favourite.'

'It used to be,' sighed Marianne. 'Anyway, I'm past caring. I simply want to sit down.'

The deep interior of Restaurant Mimi was made up of high backed cubicle seating, with small café tables spread across the wide open front and pavement. They found a table placed conveniently between the two areas. Marianne sighed with relief. 'We might just as well have this glorious sunshine before the winter really sets in.'

It was just before two p.m., as the coffee was being served, that Catherine noticed a thin line of pedestrians lining the pavement outside. Opposite, on the other side of the wide boulevard, there was a similar straggling line. Some bystanders were already craning their necks scanning the length of the sinuous street.

Marianne laughed. 'Perhaps it's for Father Xmas.'

The head-waiter joined in. 'It's some big wig from Vichy, madame, coming to take a look at us.'

Catherine remembered what Max had said. 'Is it Flandin?'

An elderly man sitting at the next table chuckled. 'My money's on Darlan mademoiselle, come to inspect the Pont du Gard!'

A large lady with a poodle piped up. 'I've heard it's Petain himself. It's an honour if you ask me, a visit from the marshall.'

'Of course it is dear lady. And what are you going to give him?' The old man teased. 'Your poodle? He likes poodles. Has them for dinner. Only French ones of course.'

Ripples of laughter followed this gentle jibe and the large lady grabbed her bewildered dog, clutching it fiercely to her cushioned bosom.

A motorcade approached and the old man's smiles faded. Catherine noticed the Croix de Guerre pinned to his jacket.

Outriders on motorbikes appeared. Marianne huffed. 'A complete waste of time and money. Ego, that's all it is.'

When an open armoured car with police appeared, their rifles poised, Catherine rose from the table, with most of the other clients. The old man edged his way to the pavement. Two more armoured cars, a dozen or more heavily armed foot police, then came a closed black Citroen, flying the tricolor. The shape of a solitary figure sitting in the rear seat was just visible. Suddenly a volley of shots ripped along the length of the car, tearing the metal. They seemed to come from somewhere above the restaurant. There were screams. Plates and chairs went flying as those near the front tried to find some refuge.

Catherine grabbed her mother and pushed her under the table. Several volleys were fired, this time from the other side of the boulevard. The motorcade stopped, police leapt out of cars and opened fire, wild, reckless, indiscriminate. Pedestrians screamed, some running into cafes and kiosks, others lying flat on the pavement, some hammering on the doors of closed shops. Foot police ran along both sides of the boulevard, firing at upper storeys. From under his table, next to theirs, the old man shouted to Catherine. 'It's the resistance, mademoiselle. At last the resistance.'

Quietly singing the opening bars of the Marseillaise he crawled out and stood up, still singing. Catherine tugged at his coat.

'Please monsieur, get back, it's too dangerous!' But the old man continued to stand and sing. The motorcade began to move on with all speed, and in one final effort, armed police ran up and down pavements firing last rounds of bullets into the first floor storeys. They tore past the restaurant firing above the awning. Glass could be heard crashing onto the pavement. Police shouted instructions to each other. A stray volley of shots from the other side of the road skirted the entrance of the restaurant. There were shouts and the firing stopped. The old man dropped to his knees; the large lady screamed hysterically, for her little poodle lay still and bloody in her arms. Catherine scrambled to the old man's side. He was bleeding badly, from the shoulder and leg, where she suspected an artery had been severed. She grabbed coats to keep the old soldier warm.

'Are you a doctor, mademoiselle,' the waiter asked.

'I was in my third year - but I'll be going back.'

She stopped the bleeding but she had nothing for pain. His grey face was tinged with blue. She moistened his lips with water.' The resistance will fight for us now mademoiselle - you'll see,' he whispered. Catherine was near to tears when the ambulance arrived. With the two stretcher - bearers was a doctor. It was Max. A number of police stood by. Marianne was trying to comfort the poor demented dog owner, and, before she could call out to her nephew, Catherine stopped her with a sharp,'be quiet! Say nothing!'

Max examined the old man, and Catherine's dressings. 'Well done mademoiselle, you may have saved his life. We need to get him to hospital quickly.'

'And that poor woman - I had nothing to give her.'

Max glanced at the large lady, piteously clutching her bloodstained poodle, and weeping hysterically.

'We'll take her in for a couple of hours. She needs a strong sedative.'

A police sergeant ambled up to Max.

'The old fool was standing up singing the Marseillaise, doctor.'

'So is he an old fool for singing the Marseillaise, sergeant?'

Lost for a reply, the sergeant walked off.

On Christmas Eve Catherine and her mother, recovering from the shocking event in Nimes, for French against French was hard to take, prepared for midnight mass in the old village church, which had been built and endowed by the de Lazarin family in the seventeenth century. They arrived early and as they walked down the aisle to the reserved family seats in the front, Catherine had another shock. Half a dozen at least of the chateau's soldiers were sitting across the aisle, and, what was more Major von Langdorf was having a convivial chat with the priest. For Fascist troops, surely this was taking seduction of the local population too far. Georges greeted the handful of soldiers with a polite smile, and discreet nod. Catherine looked reproachfully at her father,

'Just members of the orchestra, Catherine. All Catholic.'

As Major von Langdorf took his seat, he looked across and smiled at her. She wished he hadn't caught her eye. Towards the end of the service the priest announced to his overflowing congregation that a well-known singer from the Stuttgart Opera would sing a carol. The congregation sat in sullen silence, as Freddy rose to take his place at the organ. Kurt with his violin stood near the choir stalls. Corporal Joseph Hahn, serious and squat, with round pebble glasses, looking totally out of place in uniform, stood on a wooden box on the chancel steps to enable the congregation to see him. His lyric tenor voice poured out 'Silent Night', accompanied by Kurt and Freddy. The purity of his voice floated sweet and strong. He sang in French, then invited everyone to sing. There were few men in the congregation, but the uniformed musicians sang lustily with full-throated harmony. When it was over there was total silence. A few throats were cleared, a few noses blown, a few little gasps as tears were dried. Sitting between her parents, Catherine thought about Robert. Instinctively her hands found theirs, and she clasped them tightly.

There was to be no high table formality in the west wing on Christmas night. It would have been humiliating for the de Lazarins to sit with Freddy and Kurt under the Fuhrer's portrait. A fir tree decorated with baubles and cards stood in a corner of the flagstone dining hall. The long serving table was already groaning with food, wine and beer. Earlier in the day, as a privilege to officers only, Kurt and Freddy had telephoned their families. When three year old Annaliese told Kurt she had asked Santa Klaus 'to bring my Papa home, but he didn't,' and began to sob, it was more than he could bear.

At six o clock Freddy was brushing his hair and putting on his uniform jacket, ready to escort the de Lazarins to their Christmas dinner. He picked up the box of chocolate marzipans still lying in the wrapping paper, sent by his mother. Looking at her photograph he whispered, 'Mama, if you knew her, you'd approve, I promise.' Humming to himself, and with the jaunty step of a young man in pursuit, he left for the chateau's main entrance.

As chocolate was now unobtainable, Catherine thanked her beaming suitor graciously, if with some reserve.

In the dining hall Freddy whispered to Marianne, 'All the food is from Germany, Madame de Lazarin, even the cheeses. The wine however, is yours.'

Marianne smiled condescendingly at the handsome young man. 'But naturally major. We do have the best.'

Kurt called everyone to charge their glasses. With dread Catherine wondered what, or who, they were going to toast.

'Let us drink to Christmas - the sweet spirit of Christmas,' he said wistfully.

'To our loved ones: mothers, fathers, sweethearts, wives and children. Our hearts are with them.' There was a solemn murmur of agreement.

'A happy Christmas everyone.'

In a spirit of camaraderie, and of human need, the men hugged each other continuing the wish for *'Fröhliche Weihnachten'*.

Freddy politely shook the hands of the older guests. He took Catherine's hand and kissed it.

After a heavy dinner, Marianne and Georges chatted, as far as language would allow, to various members of the orchestra, while Major von Langdorf made quite sure their daughter talked only to him. Marianne was soon admiring photographs of Rudy Schmidt's wife and children while he, in a French which amused them both, told Marianne of his wife's imminent confinement. Freddy remarked, 'Your mother seems to be having a pleasant conversation.'

'Families are important to her. She hates it when they are split.'

'She's right.' His pale blue eyes gazed at Catherine. 'If I had a wife and children, separation would be like a death.'

'Like your war,' she said coldly, anger rising in her throat.

He paused. 'Everybody likes Rudy, a brilliant musician, a complete clown, and a very fine man. He reminds me of my closest friend.'

'Really? Is he in the army too?' she asked with complete disinterest.

'No. He - he left. He - he had to leave Germany, unfortunately.'

Those pale blue eyes locked into hers again.

'Why?' she provoked.

'His-his religion, mademoiselle.'

No further words were necessary.

The jazz that followed in the salon was a revelation as much to the small German audience as their French guests. 'They are brilliant,' Georges beamed, as the audience clamoured for more. But when Freddy played "Night and Day", Catherine noticed the two orderlies who had been waiting at table, whispering together. One of them strode up to Kurt and gabbled something. Both left the room and returned as Freddy's applause drew to a close. Immediately one stood on a chair, turned to the Fuhrer's portrait, and raised his glass and his voice. 'Heil Hitler. *Fröhliche Weihnachten* to our great Fuhrer!'

It was only seeing the acute embarrassment of the major and colonel that prevented Catherine from storming out. She leant over to her mother.

'They're all damned Nazis! We should never have come here!'

The evening was effectively over.

Freddy stammered apologies. 'I'm so sorry. There should be no politics at Xmas.'

Georges shrugged philosophically.'The nature of war major. You never know when it is going to raise its ugly head.'

As soon as the de Lazarins left, the two orderlies, Hanke and Remer, demanded to speak to Major von Langdorf in his quarters. Kurt insisted on being present.

'Tonight,' pugnacious Hanke accused, ' you, major, have disgraced our Fuhrer, by playing Jew music.'

'What?' The young major looked at his equally stupefied colonel.

Hanke read from a piece of paper.'Listen please. "The Jew music of George Gershwin an American Jew, and Cole Porter, another American Jew is forbidden."'

Speechless, Freddy put his head in his hands. 'This is absurd! Absurd! Does this mean we eliminate all Jewish composers from our concerts?'

'Of course.' They spoke in unison.

'But we can't do it. We are here for a purpose. Do you understand that?' Freddy felt his voice rising at these Party half–wits.

Kurt seethed. 'You do realise this reduces our repertoire to half. Or do you?'

Impervious to their colonel's sarcasm, they were Party men, posted there to keep the army in line. 'You were also playing the jazz music of American black savages. This too is against the Party line. In a few days you will receive the official list of composers who may be played. Goodnight Colonel Bergen. Good night, Major von Langdorf. Heil Hitler!'

Quivering with rage, Freddy poured out two glasses of schnapps and handed one to Kurt. 'This is bloody monstrous.

What are the idiots trying to do? Kill off Germany's musical heritage, starve us of black jazz? I can understand Socialism, it's good, opportunities available to all, make Germany a nation to be counted again. Fine! But this racial purity is lunacy, and if those two are an example of it, God help us. We had a maid like that. Thick, and stupid!'

He threw back his head and despatched his drink.

Kurt sat solemn faced. He inhaled deeply on his cigarette. 'It's all bollocks my lad. Nazi racial theories are complete and utter bollocks, and put us back in the dark ages.'

Freddy was relieved to know that his commanding officer felt as strongly. Speaking one's mind was a rare privilege these days. Kurt stubbed out his cigarette, his strong fingers pushing angrily on the embers. 'It'll kill us in the end you know.'

'I'll contact my uncle. He could speak directly to Hitler.'

Kurt lit another cigarette, and shook his head. 'Carl may have to go through that peculiar little chap Goebbels this time. Wouldn't hold out much chance for special treatment there. He's as fanatical as Hitler.'

'But this changes everything.'

'I'm afraid so my boy.'

They sat in silence, each trying to think of a solution. Then the younger man began to smile. 'I've just had a thought. Do you really suppose those bloody fools could tell the difference between an Aryan and a non -Aryan composer?'

Kurt laughed. 'You mean can a pig read?'

'It's worth a try, surely. They're not going to know whether it's Schubert or Mendelssohn.'

Kurt poured himself a coffee. 'Quite right, those two bloody fools won't know, but the others will.'

'No one else is in the Party.'

Kurt sat down with his coffee. 'You don't have to be in the Party to be a sympathiser.'

'But surely none of our group?'

'When sons denounce fathers for political reasons, it's hardly a chance we can take. Sympathisers can be informers, remember that.'

Kurt balanced his cigarette on the ashtray. 'These days, old son, trust is a commodity to be reserved for only a select few. We have to play by the book, I'm afraid.' Picking up his empty cigarette packet, he screwed it into a ball and flicked it angrily into the fireplace.

'Sod them!' he growled.

As the de Lazarins walked into their salon the telephone rang.

It was Max for Catherine.

'Cafe Terminus, Uzès. Next Monday eleven o'clock. Be there! And Merry Xmas.'

The 'phone was snapped down.

CHAPTER TEN

Catherine cycled through the bitingly cold wind to the Hotel Terminus in Uzès. She found a corner table and, with her head lowered to peruse the menu, took stock of the clientele. There had been a marked change over the past few months. In a far corner sat a predominantly Jewish group, dressed in Paris chic, faces drawn with anxiety, voices barely audible. Shrill northern and Parisian accents from tables lining the walls, rose to subdue high -spirited children still on holiday. A waiter delivered coffee to the Jewish group, and came towards her. It was Gaston, limping badly as Max had warned, disguised by his thick beard. They gave each other no hint of recognition.

'Yes, mademoiselle?'

'Coffee please.'

Suddenly conversation stopped. Two German officers strode in, and placed themselves at a table near Catherine's. No one responded to their perfunctory 'Bonjour.' The children stared silently, mesmerised by their uniforms and shining regalia. The daring ones inched nearer to take a closer look, but the Jewish group froze, paid, and slid out noiselessly.

When Gaston arrived with the coffee tray, his back to the Germans, he placed a note under the cup. It read.*'We need your help. I shall come to the chateau at five, delivering something.'*

Just after five on a small table inside the chateau's entrance hall, stood a wooden tray of root vegetables.

In an ante-room, Gaston in white overall, right leg stretched out, said, 'our information tells us there will be supplies and arms coming down, and most of it via Nimes.'

'Why Nimes?'

'Perfect centre, mademoiselle; through Spain for North Africa, and the new air strips in the Italian zone round Nice.'

'How can I help?'

'You've got troops here in the chateau. Right? Now if ever you saw them leave *en masse,* you could take a bet they'd be off to guard something. And the only thing worth guarding round here would be the army's own supplies and munitions. Right? As there aren't any close by, not yet anyway, they'd have to be brought in by train, and in the south where do you find railway sidings big enough?'

She could guess the answer, but felt Gaston wanted to say it.

'Nimes!' he grunted. 'Right?'

'But there are troops already in Nimes surely?'

He threw up his hands in a dismissive gesture. 'A handful mademoiselle. Not enough to guard trainloads of ammo and stuff - not against our boys.'

'How can I possibly find out?'

'Talk to them mademoiselle. You do talk to them I know, Max told me. You were at their Xmas party weren't you?'

There was an edge of accusation in his voice.

'So?' she answered curtly. 'How else do I get information?'

'Sure sure!' he said. 'I'm not blaming you. And get a good bellyful while you're about it.' He grinned and rose stiffly from the chair. 'As soon as you find out something - anything - call me at the Terminus. If you know something definite, say to me "I'll meet you tonight, or tomorrow," or whenever it is. If you don't know anything definite, but you have some information, you will say "I'll meet you sometime". Got it?' He limped to the door. 'Then you can expect another delivery of pig food.'

Collecting the tray of root vegetables he said quietly,

'I hope that is quite clear, mademoiselle. Remember, we need all the arms we can lay our hands on, and we'll slaughter them bastards for you at the same time.'

Only two years ago Gaston was a lanky deferential youth, helping his parents in the vineyards. Now he was broad shouldered and thick set, with authority and more than enough officiousness.

Kurt and Freddy revised the programme for their first classical concert, announcing the changes as being a simple change of programme. The real reason was known but never discussed. It was now to be Brahms' Sextet, part of Beethoven's Violin Concerto, and a Corelli Oboe concerto chosen by Rudy Schmidt. Freddy had been practising the Grieg Piano Concerto, so it was surreptitiously included in the programme. Kurt chortled. 'So what can those idiots say? He wasn't Jewish and he wasn't black was he?'

Georges transposed everything for the chamber ensemble, and was as happy as he had ever been. Each day, from the chateau's west wing music wafted over vineyards and courtyard, and of such quality, it was difficult to accept the notion that a fierce cacophony of slaughter was raging in the real world.

Freddy received a parcel from home containing the latest collection of jazz records, most of it American. He could not play them in the west wing any more but mademoiselle Catherine could. Kurt gave the would - be suitor every encouragement. It was a perfect excuse for him to see the lovely young woman again. Fate was playing into both pairs of hands.

'I believe you like jazz, mademoiselle, so I wondered if I may bring over some very good recordings my mother has just sent me.'

Her initial shy hesitation was a deliberate ploy. It was essential now to be with him on her own, to pursue Gaston's request. Freddy, on the other hand could not believe his luck.

In her study, she plied him with their own Cartagena, a deceptively strong dessert wine. She took the armchair, while he sat against the wall, his long legs stretching across half the width of the small room.

Each time she tried to refill his glass the Major refused. 'Thank you, no. It's wonderful, really, but technically, I'm still on duty.' He laughed.'You'll get me shot!'

His words sent a shiver up her spine.

'How are rehearsals going, Major?'

'Very well. Your father's transpositions are brilliant you know.'

'Papa is not in touch with the real world anymore. It doesn't exist. There is no war.'

'And is that bad, do you think?'

Catherine twisted a small signet ring on her little finger. 'Depends which side you're on,' she answered pointedly. His pale blue eyes looked at her. They were so unusual, those irises ringed with deep blue.

After a moment or two he picked up his last record, and crossed to the radiogram. 'Do you mind? It's Tchaikovsky.'

They listened in silence to the 'Romeo and Juliet' Overture.

When it was over, Catherine could feel her eyes smart, and her throat felt thick and hoarse. 'One of my brother's favourites,' she whispered. 'He's dead, killed three years ago.'

Somewhat taken aback, he apologised. 'I'm so sorry – so sorry if it has upset you, mademoiselle.'

Catherine shrugged and smiled thinly. 'When exactly is your concert?'

'In ten days. The trouble is, we've got some silly army things to do that get in the way of rehearsals.'

'Really? What?'

He smiled, and she noticed what an attractive mouth he had. One corner seemed to turn upwards. 'Guarding the statue of Caesar Augustus, probably!' Gathering up his records from the radiogram, he added. 'But it's only for one night.'

'Nimes?'

'Uh – huh.' He took the Tchaikovsky off the turntable. 'Would you like me to leave this with you, mademoiselle? Maybe you should listen to it on your own. Get used to hearing it again.'

Major von Langdorf took his leave politely, thanking her with a kiss on the hand. For the briefest moment their bodies touched. When she looked into those pale blue eyes, an overpowering sensation, like an electric charge surged through her limbs. She had never experienced anything so wildly powerful, not even with Philippe.

'You are a very beautiful young woman, and I have enjoyed your company very much.'

A smile flickered on her lips. 'Thank you,' she replied primly.

She wanted him to go. She wanted him to stay. She wanted to touch his body under that revolting uniform. What was there about this man, this enemy soldier; tall, handsome, arrogant charming? She hated him with a patriot's passion, yet she knew instinctively how close she was to a dangerous capitulation of her own. He strode back to his quarters on a cushion of air. He had at last removed the first veil.

Catherine was aware of the moral dilemma that now confronted her. 'Slaughter the bastards.' had been Gaston's promise. Should they all be killed, what would happen to the de Lazarins? If she did nothing, the ammunition in the trucks would be used against the British in North Africa, and what about Major von Langdorf? He was an enemy. One soldier more or less mattered little. She crept downstairs to the cellar to listen to the BBC to give her the courage and resolve she needed. As enemies of France, these Germans had to die. Kill or be killed surely?

Major von Langdorf was in his room listening to the same broadcast.

It was nearly eleven o' clock when she telephoned the Terminus. 'Gaston, I shall meet you sometime within the next ten days.'

At breakfast two days later, Georges suggested to his wife, as he would not be required for rehearsal that evening, they should drive into Uzès for a meal, while he still had some gasoline.

'So why aren't you rehearsing Papa?'

'Some small army manoeuvre in Nimes apparently. They're all complaining about it.' He laughed. 'Threatening to take their instruments with them.'

Catherine was dizzy with excitement, the drug thrill of danger. She crept into Georges' office, and telephoned.

'Gaston? I shall meet you tonight.'

It had been snowing all day. At 6 p.m., when Catherine heard the rumbling of diesel motors in the courtyard, she ran across the stone landing to the window. The men were grouped informally in the snow-filled yard, playfully picking up handfuls. The major and his colonel climbed into their black Mercedes, and they all left.

She paced her bedroom for most of the night. It was far worse having a passive role. She avoided the Tchaikovsky record and tried to read, but could not. She went into the cellar to listen to London; she lay on her bed, head in pillow, heart thumping, while her imagination raced with ghoulish scenes of bodies, blood,and cries of agony. She heard the rumble of returning vehicles. at six a.m. when she was in the kitchen making coffee. Catherine ran up to the landing window, counted the men as they filed into the west wing. She saw Freddy's long legs climb out of the driving seat of the Mercedes. What had happened to Gaston's promise of slaughter?

While Georges was rehearsing that evening, Max telephoned and spoke first to Marianne. To Catherine he said very little.

'Have you got enough gas to get to the Café Vert?'

'Yes - I think so.'

'Tomorrow. Two p.m.'

The Café was hardly busy, because of the snow and ice. Its marble tables lay clean and bare waiting for patrons. Mothers, with babies in pushchairs, were trying to scrounge milk from the proprietor while at the far end a few old men propped up the bar. Max stood waiting near the door. 'Come on, let's go for a walk around the Arena.'

They walked arm in arm under Max's umbrella. 'You did well, little cousin. Just as we thought, truck loads of arms and building materials.'

'What happened?'

'First of all your chateau Fritzies, supposedly guarding, seemed to be more interested in singing, and playing flutes. A complete joke! We must have taken a dozen rifles, several machine guns, and boxes of ammunition,' he chuckled. 'From right under their noses.'

'And the slaughter Gaston promised?'

'The bloody detonators failed to work. Timed for three a.m., under the arms trucks. Perfect. We'd have got rid of the damn lot.' He patted her arm. 'Never mind, next time.'

'Where are the trucks now?'

'They left this morning, travelling west.'

It had stopped snowing. Catherine brushed away the flakes that clung to her eyebrows and lashes. 'So, what next?'

'Continue to observe, and don't forget, talk to them!'

'I'd be far more useful in Nimes hospital.'

'Stop complaining girl. Do what I ask.'

Turning back in the direction of the Café Vert, a young man came running towards them, ploughing through the snow, arms flailing, slipping and sliding in his haste. As he approached, tears were running down his cheeks and he spluttered breathlessly.

'They exploded Max! Outside Perpignan station! They exploded! The whole bloody lot exploded! Nothing left! We did it! We did it! We bloody did it!'

Grabbing Max and Catherine he pulled them round in a crazy sliding dance.

They laughed. They cried. They hugged each other. Finally Max managed to introduce the young man to Catherine.

'This is Etienne. He's a scientist really, but lacks precise experience in certain areas!'

Etienne wiped his soulful brown eyes, and regained his breath. He took them both by the hand.'Come on. I'll treat you to a cup of Café Vert's lousy coffee.'

That night Catherine felt a euphoric sense of elation. She had done something for France. It was her information that had made the explosion possible. Her troubled conscience was at peace, until the next time.

For now, the concert could go on as planned.

CHAPTER ELEVEN

The day of the concert Georges was nervous, fussing over his breakfast, while Marianne fussed over his dinner suit.

'You're not really going to wear a formal dinner suit, Papa?'

'Of course. No uniforms tonight.'

'Who's been invited?'

'A few Germans, officers stationed nearby. But most of the audience will be French from Uzès, Alès, and Nimes.'

'I really didn't think chamber music was quite so popular,' said Marianne.

'D'you think that bunch of toadies would refuse the Wehrmacht?' Catherine snapped.

'While you ladies deliberate upon the quality of the audience, I must get along to rehearsal.' He left humming happily to himself.

In the salon turned concert hall, the two officers supervised seating arrangements, Freddy placing his girl on the promenade in the front row, in direct line of vision to the piano.

Catherine and her mother decided to dress as if for a function, partly for Georges' sake, but at the same time because they were de Lazarins.

The daughter wore a dark green velvet dress, bought from Coco Chanel last year, a perfect colour for her eyes. The mother, elegant as always, was in crimson silk, one of Georges' favourites.

At half past seven, an audience of about thirty trickled into the dining area, happy to feel the warmth of log fires burning in the west wing's large stone fireplaces. Freddy looked so incredibly handsome in his dinner jacket, Catherine wished she had never set eyes on him. He politely kissed their hands, but to Catherine he said. 'You look very beautiful tonight mademoiselle. Maybe you will be my inspiration.' She withdrew her hand quickly and glared coldly at him.

Although there was not a whiff of army about the orchestra's attire, drinks dispensed by the two Nazi party members in full uniform with swastika armbands, plus the Fuhrer's portrait, were the reminders that this was no ordinary chamber concert. There were mayoral dignitaries from the nearby towns, officials of town councils, a few officers from the remaining handful of French army, and a minister from the marshall's Vichy cabinet, who addressed guests and orchestra, praising the exercise as the best possible example of co-operation between their two great nations. Catherine felt nauseated at this slimy Judas, who was prepared to kiss the backside of the Third Reich, and in public.

A three-minute bell rang. 'My God! Just like the Opera!' Marianne opined *sotto voce*. The salon, barely recognisable, had been transformed with large potted palms and enormous bouquets of flowers. Into the window recess a podium had been built, with a conductor's stand placed centre stage, the baton and music scores resting on a table along with a book rest. The piano stood at one side, and seven places with music stands were arranged in a semi circle. The atmosphere was so seductive Catherine momentarily forgot she was here to listen to the enemies of France.

When Freddy began the Grieg Piano Concerto she felt her heart beat a little faster. During the lovely andante, she caught his pale blue eyes fixed on her, and immediately dropped her gaze into her lap, where her fingers wove themselves into nervous knots. Georges played the cello passages with great style and emotion, his head bowed with concentration. There were tears in Marianne's eyes, and Catherine gave her mother's hand an affectionate squeeze. But it was Rudy Schmidt who probably stole the evening with a Marcello Oboe concerto. Catherine had never heard anything quite as breathtaking as those bell-like sounds, piercing the velvet silence like starbursts. When he took his applause, dark hair flopping on his damp forehead, everyone stood, even the orchestra.

After the concert Freddy, weaving his way through congratulatory handshakes, eventually reached Catherine.

He kissed her hand. 'Thank you for your inspiration, mademoiselle.'

'Inspiration?' She raised an eyebrow. 'Surely a Nazi officer has no need for inspiration, certainly not from a French woman!'

He gave her a thin smile. 'Let us be clear, mademoiselle. Temporarily I am a German officer, and if a lovely French woman inspires me when I play, then under the circumstances that is obviously my misfortune. *N'est ce pas*?' he asked with a hint of sarcasm.

Later, alone in her room, playing the Tschaikovsky she was glad the concert had been staged, that no one had been killed, and that included the major.

Sitting, brushing her hair, Marianne turned to Georges. 'You know darling they really are, apart from those two horrible Nazis, a very nice bunch, polite, charming, and as for little Rudy Schmidt,' she smiled,' what a delightful person, and brilliant musician too. He just wants to be with his wife and his two adorable little girls. I do hope the colonel will let him go home for his wife's confinement.'

Georges was taking off his shoes, and gave his wife a perfunctory nod of agreement. Marianne suddenly rose from the dressing table. 'Georges, you will just have to speak to him.'

'Who?'

'The colonel, and tell him he should allow Rudy Schmidt to go home.'

Georges was nonplussed. 'What? You want me to tell a colonel of the Third Reich how to treat a soldier? To send him home because his wife is having a baby? Marianne, sometimes I think you live in another world!'

At the end of January Freddy had a telephone call from Carl.

The Girl on the Promenade

'I think your mother would like me to visit you, see the squalid conditions she seems convinced you are living under.'

Freddy laughed. 'That's not the reason you are coming.'

'Actually I may have a friend visiting.'

'Anyone I know?'

'Perhaps.'

Carl had been driven from Paris, and was tired. After a private lunch with Kurt and Freddy, the general and his nephew retired to Freddy's quarters where a log fire blazed in welcome. They exchanged news, concerning Anna's health, and Friedrich's problems having to employ undernourished forced labour deportees and prisoners of war at the factory.

These days Carl was in Berlin working in the Abwehr. 'The Fuhrer believes he is surrounded by enemies, and I am there supposedly to advise him on legalities.' He sighed. 'A hopeless task, because he always does precisely what he wants.'

'It's better than being in Poland, surely?'

'My God yes! Now the Einsatzgruppen have been let loose. But for you,' he smiled, 'an enjoyable musical vacation, eh?'

'For how long, Uncle? Supplies wagons were blown sky-high outside Perpignan by a resistance group. At the moment, opposition is too fragmented to be a real danger, but once it is organised, our musical vacation as you call it is over - we're sitting ducks.'

'When are they likely to organise?'

'Who knows? London is constantly urging action. Thank God the communists aren't actively involved. Better for us to keep them as passive collaborators.'

Carl said nothing but looked grim.

'So when is your friend arriving?'

'Erwin Rommel will arrive this evening, in time for dinner with Kurt and me.'

Freddy beamed. 'Erwin Rommel here? Why?'

'We are all such old friends. Our meeting is to be private. He is travelling incognito. No soldier here must know who is visiting, you understand?

He and I will leave together early tomorrow.'

'Shall I meet him?'

'Provided you take breakfast with us here at six. He will be leaving for North Africa in ten days, where there are a few problems.'

Carl placed another log on the flames. 'Natives friendly are they?'

Freddy raised his eyebrows. 'Perfectly. Why?'

Imitating Freddy's raised eyebrow nonchalance he replied, 'I've heard they are very beautiful too'.

While Freddy applied himself to monitoring foreign broadcasts, and transmitting back to Berlin, in another room in the west wing three men sat discussing their Fuhrer. It was rumoured he was about to take over the role of Supreme Commander and Minister of War, thus taking decisive power from the Wehrmacht. At the same time in Berlin, a number of other high-ranking officers of the armed forces were holding similar secret meetings. Dissatisfaction with their leader was growing, each malcontent having his own reasons for deposing the Reichschancellor. Erwin Rommel disapproved of his war strategy, Kurt hated Nazism and absolute power, Carl detested Hitler's racial policies, and the rabble of henchmen who aided him. But they all knew the strength of Hitler's support, and how quickly and silently any individual opposition was being cut down and disposed of. Each of those men knew of someone, or some family, that had disappeared. There had been a few generals who had stepped out of line, and been given public trials, mere charades, where justice and legal procedure were ignored.

They were embarking upon the dangerous game of resistance, and it would take time to gather the support they needed.

Marianne had kept in touch with Simone and Louis by telephone, because impersonal postcards, newly introduced, permitted only thirteen lines and were already partly printed. The Vichy government had lately been passing more anti-Semitic legislation, so when suddenly the line of communication with Simone ceased, Marianne was in a panic.

Catherine had a rendezvous with Max at the Café Vert.

Strolling past the Arena he said, 'Father's been dismissed from the bank.'

'Why? He fought in the last war!'

'Both sets of grandparents were Russian Jews. Because of the last war he's been allowed to live at home. For all the other foreign Jews it's detention centres, then Drancey and deportations to Deutschland.'

Drancey, the prison outside Paris, had an evil reputation for subhuman living conditions and torture.

Catherine shuddered. 'Oh God! Max. Are you safe?'

'Sure - I haven't more than two Jewish grandparents and mother's a non-Jew. That's the distinction.'

'Supposing the legislation changes?'

'I'll join a group up in the Cevennes, near Anduze. But we are making progress,' he grinned. 'Etienne's made contact with a British agent in Nice, and we've got hold of a few transmitters. And that's not all.' His face became animated with excitement. 'I'm going to Marseilles to meet Jean Moulin; I told you about him, remember? And Henri Frenay, ex-army chap who's started a network in Lyons.'

Catherine was looking so disconsolate, Max stopped. 'What's the matter?'

'The matter is, Max, you are not involving me. If it hadn't been for my information those trucks would never have exploded.'

He placed an arm round her shoulder. 'Look, if we have a field hospital in the Cevennes, you will be part of the team. How's that? But meanwhile you have this unique role to play in the chateau. You must see that.'

Max delved into his pocket. 'Here we are. Here's some involvement.'

He pulled out a bundle of printed leaflets, urging the population to resist, and telling young men how to avoid being labour deportees.

'How did you get these printed?'

'The network. Drop them in shops leave them on corners, cafés, anywhere. But don't get caught.'

Planning the next public concert was not easy. Rehearsal time was now severely reduced because of extra guard duties around local supply depots. Consequently, army training exercise and shooting practice had to take priority over music. Already several resistance cells in Paris had been uncovered and their leaders shot. In the unoccupied zone Perpignan had been a warning salvo to all German troops, and they could take no chances. The concert would be sometime in April, and if each musician chose an adagio, rehearsal time could be reduced. Every day, from her window Catherine watched them disappear into the garrigue and duly reported back to Max at the Café Vert.

They were sitting at a corner table. Catherine pulled a face at her so-called black coffee, lining the cup, thick and heavy, like tar.

'Come on, don't be a spoilt brat! Drink up. At least it's hot,' Max chided.

She started on her report, her cousin questioning like a military debriefing.

'Which part of the garrigue?'

'Close-by. Has to be. I can hear the gunfire.'

'We'll have to be careful. We don't want the Boche walking into any of our hideouts.'

'Do you have men up there?'

'Mostly equipment – guns, ammo, foodstuffs, medical supplies.'

She sipped the brew. 'Do you think the Americans will join the war?'

'Why should they?'

'Well - they're going to send aid to the British.'

'Catherine, lorry loads of well-intentioned American women are about to descend upon French cities in the zone, with food and dried milk for babies. Doesn't mean a thing.'

Max took a thirsty swig of his coffee. 'You're right. It is revolting. You can still get good coffee on the black market - at a price.'

'I know.'

'Are you in it yet?'

'Not really. Mathilde organises barter arrangements for Maman, with our wine, and Jacques has dug a small family vegetable garden which mother adores.'

'And your Boche? How does their food arrive?'

'Provisions, every Friday without fail.'

Max frowned, and tapped the saucer gently with his spoon. 'Tell me, do they unload everything immediately?'

'I don't know.'

His frown deepened. 'Catherine, it is your duty to watch, and report. Food is becoming as precious as arms.'

'I -I'm sorry.'

'How many lorries?'

'I'm not sure. I haven't counted - maybe - two.'

'What time do they arrive?'

'Er-about eight or nine p.m. I think. I-I'm not absolutely sure.'

He drained his cup, and replaced it noisily on the saucer. With folded arms on the table he leant towards her. His voice, though barely more than a loud whisper, was angry and clipped. 'Now listen! You will find out the following. One; what time the lorries arrive. Two; how many vehicles. Three; how many men are used for unloading. Four; how long it takes. Five; do the vehicles remain in the courtyard overnight? Got it?' he snapped, with the ferocity of a drill sergeant. 'We could do with the vehicles, if not the food. You say there's only one guard on duty by the west wing gate. Right?'

Catherine was furious. Her eyes glared angrily as she grabbed his forearm, resting on the table. 'No. Absolutely No! We live at the chateau too. Mother and father would die of shock, quite apart from the danger you'd be inflicting upon them. If you want their lorries, their food, intercept them en route, not at the chateau. Got it?' she retorted.

Though surprised at his cousin's outburst he found it hard not to suppress a smile. 'Point taken, mademoiselle; so please find out from which direction they approach.'

She nodded. They were silent for a moment or two while tempers calmed.

'How did your meeting go in Marseilles?'

'Jean Moulin is trying to get us all together - some groups are holding out because objectives are different. All rather petty.'

He took out a cigarette from a crumpled packet, and tapped it several times on the marble topped table. 'Moulin's working under de Gaulle, that's the problem. De Gaulle isn't particularly popular because he's in London and not here, and left of centre are wary of his politics.'

Max lit the cigarette, and blew out a couple of smoke rings. 'Anyway, when Moulin said, "But gentlemen, think of France", the bickering simmered down.'

'Will they ever unite?'

'Eventually. Maybe something momentous has to happen. Who knows?'

CHAPTER TWELVE

The Wehrmacht was sweeping across a dazed Europe.

'There's no stopping them, Papa.'

Georges was distracted. He had been looking through a few of his favourite adagios. 'All empires come to an end. That is a fact.'

'It may be fact Papa, but if the Roman Empire lasted four hundred years, the Nazis have promised a thousand, so God help us.'

Georges put down his sheets of music. 'The Roman Empire failed because it expanded more than its manpower would allow. Hitler hasn't enough German labour left to operate factories, so he too has slave labour, Jews and prisoners. The RAF has blown the Luftwaffe out of British skies, therefore invading Britain is unlikely. Soon, like the Romans he will also fail.'

'I'd like to believe you, Papa.'

'Papa has a nose for politics, Catherine.' Marianne intoned smugly. 'Meanwhile, may I suggest a cup of real coffee?'

'Fantastic!' Catherine shrieked. 'Did Mathilde get it for us?'

'No dear, it was the handsome young major. He said we could have as much as we wanted, any time.'

The following week, Catherine worked in the vineyards alongside a few dozen village women gathering up dead leaves and branches after extensive pruning. On Friday evening, as promised, she stood at the landing window, watching and waiting. Just before eight p.m., a large army truck arrived from the direction of Alès, and drew up at the west wing's entrance. The canvas flap was pulled up and two armed soldiers jumped out. Orderlies from the chateau, carrying lamps, began to unload the packed interior. Sides of beef, pork, boxes of dairy produce, coffee, chocolate, sausages, sacks of dried milk, flour, and crates of beer were carried inside.

The following day Catherine cycled to see Gaston at the Hotel Terminus in Uzès. They strolled across the Esplanade during his five-minute break.

'Direction Alès, you think?'

'There's no other way.'

'Good. One stretch of that road is very narrow with trees overhanging - like a tunnel.' He grinned. 'Perfect, mademoiselle - just perfect.'

The concert audience was like the previous one, with local dignitaries, police, a sprinkling of attractive young women, some of whom Catherine recognised from the village, plus a large number of army personnel. As before, mother and daughter dressed for the occasion. Marianne felt it lifted one's spirits. Catherine wore a long black velvet skirt with a cream organdie blouse, its wide high collar framing her face. With her hair coiled in a chignon, she could have stepped out of a Renaissance painting.

The music was perfection, but this time it was Freddy who received the accolade with Rachmaninoff's Second Piano Concerto. In the sensuous andante, he looked at Catherine, carefully positioned in exactly the same seat. This time, her eyelids flickered and for a brief moment she held his gaze. It was all he needed.

When he kissed her hand afterwards, he apololgised. 'I am sorry, but you really were my inspiration, mademoiselle.'

She averted his gaze, and replied coolly. 'I really can't think why you needed any. You are a superb pianist.' She hated his nation. She hated him looking so elegant in his evening dress. She should wish him a thousand miles away, yet his body was like a magnet to hers, and her stomach trembled with a thousand butterflies each time their eyes met.

The following day at breakfast, a beaming Georges announced he had been given several barrels of gasoline.

'From whom, Papa?'

'Our neighbours.'

'So, we are being bought now, are we?' Catherine replied acidly.

Marianne slammed the bread knife down. 'Don't speak to Papa like that. The gasoline is for all his work with the orchestra. He's spent hours transposing for them.'

'He didn't have to,' she snarled.

Georges was irritated. 'No, young lady, I don't have to accept the gasoline, either. Therefore the next time you wish to drive off to Nimes in your car, you won't be able to.'

Catherine suddenly realised the irony of the situation. She would be using Nazi gas to meet and to give information to the resistance.

'No Papa. You are right. I'm sorry,' she recanted graciously.

The second concert had been so successful they had received a letter of congratulation signed by the Reichschancellor no less, on their ambassadorial efforts on behalf of the Third Reich. Hanke and Remer were delighted. 'You see colonel, how easy it is to avoid all Jew and black savage music.'

A few days later Freddy and Kurt were having a quiet after dinner schnapps in Kurt's quarters. Usually in good spirits and full of optimism, tonight the commanding officer was in a very sombre state of mind.

'Something worrying you?'

The colonel downed his gin. 'I heard from Carl today. Hitler has started a build-up on the Russian front.'

Freddy absentmindedly picked up a pencil. 'It's probably just a precaution, a warning; defensive, not offensive.'

Kurt poured himself another. 'In that case, I'm curious to know what a non-aggression pact means to our Fuhrer.'

'So long as the idiot remembers what happened to Napoleon.'

'Fat chance,' Kurt snorted.

They left these grim prospects for a lighter subject, and discussed taking a weekly box of provisions to de Lazarins, as food was becoming a real hardship for the locals. If madame seemed offended, they would suggest barter for wine. The following morning Freddy filled a large wooden box with coffee, butter, dried milk, oil, meat, dried vegetables, chocolate, plus a number of assorted tinned foods. As expected, Madame de Lazarin suggested an exchange with the chateau's wine. The deal done, both parties happy, Freddy asked if he could speak with her daughter.

Catherine had just washed her hair. It hung in thick dark curls around her face. Usually she tied it back, but the major's visit had taken her by surprise. She was wearing a black jumper and trousers because she was going out to work with Jacques in the vineyards. He asked if she would care to listen to more of his records. She gave a nonchalant shrug, but her heart raced.

'If you like.'

'Tonight perhaps?'

He could barely wait. The young man was more in love with her each time they met.

Sitting in her study, they listened, and she relaxed enough to laugh a little, as they talked about college days, recounting stories of quirky professors, and quirky students. He told her about their family holidays in Cannes, about his small apartment, rather like hers, at the schloss. This time she told him about Robert, and their holiday villa near the Carlton in Cannes.

'Have you time to see some photographs of my home and family now, mademoiselle?'

This time she could not refuse. Sitting on the floor at her feet, he showed her photographs of his mother and father, the schloss, his uncle, and their farms.

'When I was a boy, I loved working on the land. Riding on tractors especially. I remember once — '.

His stories continued. Most were perfectly ordinary and homespun. It was odd how similar their backgrounds were. Sitting so close, his arm occasionally brushing her knee, defocused her mind, disturbingly. Then she would think of France and intellectually freeze him out of her head. But still they talked. He asked about Montpellier, and her abandoned medical studies. He told her about Heidelberg, and his abandoned archaeology plans.

'So, why aren't you going to Crete?'

He looked puzzled. 'Why do you ask?'

'You Nazis have occupied the island, and you said you wanted to work there.'

His face clouded. He rose from the floor, leant on the mantelpiece, his head bent. After a moment he turned to face her.

'Mademoiselle de Lazarin, if you please!' His voice was sharp. 'I must clarify one point with you. I am a German. I am not a Nazi. I am not a member of the Nazi Party. I was not influential enough to prevent my country from going to war. That does not mean I cannot be held responsible for the collective action of my country. But I will never be held responsible for the actions of individuals with whom I have nothing in common! Of course I want to work in Crete, but as an archaeologist and with my own wardrobe.' He flicked at his jacket.

She could see a raw nerve had been touched. In a kinder voice she said.

'I'm sure you'll go there - after - well, when there is no war.'

'Of course. If there is anything left,' he retorted.

He stepped back to the only other chair in the room his forehead glistening with perspiration, and asked permission to remove his jacket. As he did so, two photographs fell out of an inner pocket at Catherine's feet. She instinctively bent to pick them up. He took them from her quite slowly, his hands trembling, knowing she had for the briefest moment glanced at them. 'Mademoiselle,' he began, 'I'd like to tell you about these two very dear people. No one else, outside my family, has seen these photographs.'

He paused. 'They are both Jews. This is Erich, my dear old friend. I may have mentioned him. He had to go to Switzerland - wanted me to go with him. I was foolish not to. I miss him enormously, like a brother. The Nazis burnt down their shop in

Berlin, so the family went to relatives in London. I do not know whether they are still alive after all the bombing.'

He handed her Sophie's photograph. 'My aunt Sophie - a wonderful, warm, lovely woman; journalist, from one of the best families in Berlin. She went to America. I don't suppose we shall ever see her again. So please, mademoiselle, don't ever call me a Nazi.'

Catherine was silent, smarting with mortification.

Slowly he put on his jacket, and replaced the photographs carefully in an inside pocket. He took her hand and brushed it with his lips. She did not withdraw it, but kept it there long enough to say falteringly, 'I'm so sorry - really so sorry, Major von Langdorf. We all suffer in a crazy war.'

Their eyes held each other, both knowing, sensing, the power of the attraction that flowed between them. Gazing at her, Freddy drew both her hands to his mouth, and held them to his lips. Catherine's legs felt weak, her cheeks burned and her heart beat faster. He bade her a quiet goodnight, and left.

When he had gone she felt depressed. Fuelling the mood she put on the Tchaikovsky and lay on the bed. She understood the considerable risk Major von Langdorf had taken by telling her of his Jewish connections, and his anti-Nazi sentiments. The question remained, why? This could all be part of Max's seduction theory, but what political mileage was there in it for him, and why put himself in such a dangerous position? Committing such trust in her, could she ever again put him intentionally in the way of danger?

Back in his room Freddy pondered over what his beloved mademoiselle now knew about him. All too late. He would have to trust her with his life. Those green eyes held him captive. He loved her, of that there was no doubt.

But what about her? She was inscrutable, giving nothing away, and would have been a difficult beauty to pursue, war or no war.

Freddy had left his gramophone records in Catherine's room. Apart from giving him a reason to see her again, he did

The Girl on the Promenade

not relish keeping such a volume of 'subversive' music in his quarters with two Party idiots around.

The following evening, he called again at the chateau. Catherine was catching up on medical revision in her study, and was in no mood for interruption. However, the moment her eyes met those of Major von Langdorf standing in the hall, her heart beat a little faster. She wondered if he was already regretting having disclosed so much about himself. Was he about to recant?

He smiled amiably. 'I wanted to play some music. My records are with you, mademoiselle.'

She blushed. 'Do you – er, do you want to listen to them here?' she blurted impulsively, immediately regretting the invitation. What was she thinking about? Actually inviting this enemy soldier into her room? But, a small voice of placating rationale told her she was doing this for France, for the resistance; that there was no better way to glean information.

They listened, they talked, but no mention was made of last night's conversation. He picked up one of her medical books strewn across the desk. 'I am sure you will make a fine doctor, mademoiselle.'

'If I ever have the chance to finish,' she rejoined.

He knelt in front of her, and placing his hands around hers, said,

'Nothing lasts forever, mademoiselle Catherine. Everything changes, remember that.'

Their eyes locked, neither saying a word. Her body and heart yearned for his arms to be around her. She wanted to melt into his lean frame. The desire in him would have taken her, possessed her. But the protocol of war, of occupation, would always have its own rules.

He crossed to the gramophone. 'Is there anything you'd like to hear now, before I go, mademoiselle?'

'The Tchaikovsky.'

When the overture was approaching the finale, Freddy, once again knelt before her took her hands, held them to his lips, and kissed them.

Crossing the hall after he had left, Catharine was summoned by her mother in the salon. She was sitting on the sofa reading, and seeing her daughter, removed her pince-nez. There was a look of displeasure on her face.

'The major here again, Catherine?'

'He'd left his records in my study.'

'How careless. Is he going to make a habit of this?'

'I really have no idea. Why?'

'Because my dear he is a Nazi, and tongues will wag. Mathilde could merely mention it in the boulangerie, and all France would know.'

Catherine now had a problem. Quite apart from her own feelings, how could she possibly tell her mother that Max had asked her to ferret out information?

'First of all Maman, he is not a Nazi, and I really can't see the difference between me and Papa, who transposes, rehearses and plays with them.'

Marianne did not like opposition.

'Utterly different! You are a young woman and the major an extremely handsome young man. He may be well bred, of good stock, and charming. He may not be a Nazi, though how you can tell heaven knows, but he is nevertheless a German, and a male! Haven't you medical studies to pursue?' The war had no influence upon Marianne's acid tongue.

Catherine was angered by her mother's capricious standards, created to suit her own prejudices. 'Well then, may I suggest in future you do not accept boxes of Nazi food, supplied by courtesy of the Fuhrer's pantry.'

Flushed with temper, she stormed out of the salon, slamming the door.

On the morning of June 21, Kurt came into Freddy's quarters, pulled out a cigarette from his case and for a few seconds slowly rolled it in his fingers.

'Tomorrow the German army will invade the Soviet Union.'

'Jesus!' Freddy gasped.

The colonel drew hungrily on his cigarette.'I've just spoken to Carl. Our Fuhrer has refused both dialogue and advice. He is hell bent on going his own way, and tragically we must follow.'

Catherine received a telephone call from Max, cryptic as ever.

'Café Vert tomorrow at two p.m. Enough gas?'

'Plenty.'

'Good. See you there.'

The sun was hotter than usual for June. These days she worked in the vineyards and in their vegetable garden. Already her face was bronzed to a golden olive. Max was sitting relaxed in shorts at one of the cafe's tables spread across the broad pavement, and appeared more animated than of late, because he had met Frenay again and would now be heading a Combat group in Nimes. The invasion of the Soviet Union had swelled the ranks of the resistance with dozens of communist party members. To avoid capture and deportation, they were hiding up in the Cevennes.

'Some of them are so damned undisciplined. They just want to shoot every bloody Boche in sight. Asking for trouble!'

The proprietor, a chubby little man, appeared with two cups of coffee. As he placed them on the marble topped table, he whispered. 'Real coffee. Keep it to yourselves. I haven't enough for everybody.'

Max winked at him. 'You'll go to heaven, Jean!' The proprietor's several chins quivered with glee.

Catherine savoured the taste of the coffee.'Mmm superb! Well, what's the news?'

'The Gestapo has moved into Vichy, rue Comely.'

'Oh no!'

'Now they'll be squeezing out information about communists and Jews. And they pay for it apparently.'

'Who gives the info?'

Max gave a sardonic smile. 'My dear Catherine, we are crawling with anti-Semites and anti-communists, only too happy to run to the Boche. By the way, Gaston has joined the Communist Party, officially.'

'What for?'

'He sees the war as an anti - Imperialist struggle.'

'But the British are Imperialists.'

'Not the British working class.'

'Is he with Combat?'

Max rocked his hand in a gesture. 'The communists largely follow their own agenda.'

They walked into a small grassy square where a statue of Caesar Augustus looked down benignly, and trees offered cool shade. They sat on a bench well out of earshot of anyone.

'Look, we 've got horses, but we need saddles for the chaps in the Cevennes.' Catherine smiled. 'We've got eight.'

'And they are where?'

'In the hay loft above the east wing garages - our garages.'

'Gaston will be dropped at the top of your drive at ten-thirty. He'll take four tonight, and four tomorrow night. Could he be seen by a sentry on duty?'

'Unlikely. I'll show you.' She took out a pencil and a piece of paper from her handbag. 'Here, there's a line of cypresses and trellis that runs down to the garage block from the end of the east wing,our part of the chateau. It's completely screened from the west wing courtyard.'

'And the saddles?'

'Hanging on the wall in the hayloft.'

'How do you get into the hayloft?'

'An old ladder. Look, why don't I deliver them? Just say where.'

'Gaston thinks it's safer if he collects them.'

Just before ten-thirty Catherine left her room, checked her parents had retired for the night, and went quietly downstairs to sit in the conservatory. Its tall half-glazed walls interspersed with French windows opened on to the driveway which led to the garage block. Though the sun-blinds were drawn across the roof and sides, there was just enough fitful moonlight filtering

The Girl on the Promenade

through to see without switching on the lamp. The night sky was cloudy and seemed to be building up into one of the region's momentous summer storms. Catherine looked at her watch. It was now just after ten-thirty. She was about to pull up one of the blinds when she perceived a fleeting shadow cross it. She counted three more. Why four men for four saddles? Perhaps he intended to collect all eight. She would wait until she saw the shadows flit back up the drive again. She waited; twenty minutes passed. Uneasy, she quietly opened the conservatory door. A loud noise of breaking wood from the garage block echoed in the silence of the night. She raced down the gravel drive and stepped into the black interior of the open garage, where her car was parked. From somewhere above, deep inside the hay-loft Gaston's voice rasped down.'Go away, mademoiselle. We have a date with the Boche.'

She heard the click of cocked rifles. 'Go on! Get away! For God's sake woman, go!' hissed another.

The truth dawned. Collecting saddles had been a pretext, the noise deliberate, intended to draw the enemy.

'Don't be so damn stupid Gaston,' she hissed back. 'They are too many.'

Suddenly, out of the silence a babble of German voices and shouted commands from the west wing courtyard came closer, bringing with them the sound of boots clattering across cobblestones.

'For Christ's sake woman go!'

Her heart pounded. Hesitation now could mean death. 'Get out through the window, Gaston. Hurry! Please! Please!' she pleaded.

'We're staying, rich bitch!' 'Fuck off, you silly cow!' Voices snarled.

Several armed soldiers came running toward the block squeezing through a gap in the row of cypresses.

Desperate to hide her fear, she went out to meet them. One was Rudy Schmidt. 'Are you alright, mademoiselle?'

'Yes, of course,' she smiled. 'I'm so sorry if I disturbed you. I'd left something in my car.'

Hanke was shining his torch around the garage, and saw the electric light switch. 'Why is there no light in this garage?'

She was thankful she could tell the truth. 'The bulb has gone.'

Rudi saw the broken ladder. 'Was this the noise we heard mademoiselle?'

'Yes. I'm afraid I stumbled on it. The ladder has been broken for a long time.'

Hanke looked at her in total disbelief. 'No, mademoiselle, it was more than just a stumble we heard. Open your car, please.'

She had not locked the car doors when she returned from Nimes.

'Help yourself,' she replied graciously, knowing that there was absolutely nothing they could find. It was too late now. She knew Gaston and his team were trapped in the hay-loft. But could they refrain from shooting the enemy soldiers just because she was there, a class enemy, an exploiter, and completely expendable? She knew all the jargon. If Gaston remained hell bent, they could pop her off first, an easy target.

Whilst the two Nazis were flashing torches all over the car and garage, Freddy appeared. Her heart sank. He was the last person she wanted to involve. Her hands trembled with fear. How could she draw them away, before Gaston registered Freddy's rank? Immediately, the major ordered the two Nazis to stop searching, and shut the car doors. 'I'm sorry if we have disturbed you, Mademoiselle de Lazarin.'

'What about this hay loft, major?' Hanke asked.

'What about it?' Freddy replied.

'Do you want us to search it?'

Hanke flicked the torch into the hayloft.

Catherine's heart pounded. Would Gaston and his men shoot it out?

'I'm sure Mademoiselle de Lazarin will tell you what's in it.'

'Just hay and saddles.'

Freddy looked at Hanke. 'Now you know.'

Major von Langdorf dismissed the men. 'Everything alright, mademoiselle?'

She nodded and gave him a wan smile. In truth she felt quite ill with fear. He touched her arm; she was trembling.

'I'm sorry if my men have been over-zealous.'

He put a hand under her elbow. 'Come along, mademoiselle. I'll see you to the door.'

She felt an overwhelming sense of relief to be walking away from the garage. It was too terrible to contemplate what could have happened.

Freddy took her back to the open conservatory door. He watched as she steadied herself against the back of a chair. 'Thank you. Would you like a drink of something?'

'I'm on duty,' he smiled. 'But you should have some Cartagena; help you to sleep.'

Freddy did not return to his quarters. He ran across the front of the chateau, through the secret garden and into the west wing. With six men he searched the garages, and scoured the area of garrigue behind the chateau. When Hanke had flicked his torch into the hayloft, Freddy had noticed what could have been the glint of a rifle barrel. It could equally have been the metal on a saddle, but no chances could be taken, not now the communists had joined the resistance.

The army patrol found nothing, except eight saddles, which were hung on the wall of the hayloft.

Kurt read Freddy's typed report, and signed it.

'Caution at all times. Good. Incident closed'.

CHAPTER THIRTEEN

Max was furious.

'The little bastard lied to me! Asshole! We need to keep your Fritzies sweet and quiet at the moment. He bloody well knew that!'

They were sitting as usual at one of the Café Vert's outside tables, drinking citron pressé. An afternoon in mid August was too hot and heavy for anything else. Catherine had just left the vineyard in answer to Max's telephone call. Her hands were cut and swollen with heat and work, her nails broken.

'I knew I was expendable,' she sighed.

Max patted her hand perfunctorily. 'He's had a bollocking, but,' he shrugged 'he's one of the Communist Party's young militants now. And guess what?' he guffawed.'The central committee met last week in Paris. Dressed as boy scouts, sitting round a camp fire, middle of Paris, and the old sods got away with it!'

'But you'll still work together, you and the communists?'

'Sure. We steal equipment and arms, and if deaths result, so be it. They go for the jugular first.'

'Vichy radio says hundreds of anti-communists have joined the German army in Russia, true?'

Max drained his citron pressé. 'Needs more sugar! No. Relatively few. It's backfired. Not so other illustrious compatriots.' He took out a cigarette from his familiar crumpled packet, and tapped it on the table. 'In Paris, rue Lauriston.'

He delved into a pocket for a box of matches, pulled one out, and struck it. He watched the flame grow larger. 'Rue Lauriston is now the centre of the French Gestapo.'

' French? French torturing French?'

'Yep! Ex-convicts mostly. Vermin!'

The Girl on the Promenade

Catherine looked down her tall glass, and idly stirred the bits of lemon at the bottom. 'I find this difficult to understand.'

'Does a criminal care about the nationality of his victim?'

As they walked up the Victor Hugo to her car he said, 'Gaston tells me you appeared to be friendly with the Fritz major. Gave you his arm. True?'

' Because I was shivering: terrified frankly. My instructions were to be pleasant not hostile, remember?'

'Uh - huh! Nice chap, the major?'

'Alright.'

'Remember he's a Fritz, Catherine, so must never be too "alright".' 'What d'you take me for?' she snapped crossly.

She wondered what she had to do to please any of them.

The following week, no box of provisions was presented to the de Lazarins because the food transport did not arrive. It was Major von Langdorf and a group from the chateau who had gone in search of the lost truck. On a narrow stretch of the road from Alès, near a dense overhang of foliage, they found four dead soldiers lying in a ditch, and no trace of the vehicle, except skid marks. The victualling centre in Vichy promised an armed escort in future.

As Max explained later to Catherine, 'we shan't try it again. Not worth being cut to pieces for a tin of anchovies.' He grinned. 'No matter, the lads in the garrigue are still living off Hitler!'

The *vendange* was going to be a problem this year. Marianne and Catherine drove into every nearby village recruiting help, but too many had already promised their local vineyards. Kurt suggested a solution. 'You can have six of my men every day, for three weeks. They'll enjoy a break from routine. Anyway, they all like the sun!'

The atmosphere between village women and six Boche soldiers in army dungarees, picking grapes alongside them, was generally strained.

Rudi Schmidt's terrible French, and his antics, broke through most barriers. But the women who had lost loved ones kept their distance, and their silence.

At the end of September, the colonel and his major were holding one of their regular confabs. Kurt laid out his cigarette case on the table, his lighter neatly alongside.

The younger man waited for this habitual opening routine.

The colonel lit up, sat back in his leather chair, and, as little trails of smoke curled out of his nostrils, he began.

'So, Schaumberg and Stulpnagel are furious. I don't blame them - they have to protect their men.'

Freddy picked up his report and read. '"*Since cadet Moser was shot in the Metro, there have been dozens more individual assassinations of German soldiers, at Metro stations, hotel foyers, and on the streets. Retaliation will mean the shooting of hostages. All Frenchmen arrested and currently serving sentences will be regarded as hostages*"'.

'How many hostages for one soldier?'

'Two to one apparently.'

'And the Frenchmen? Who are they? Felons?'

'Mostly communists.'

'And the thugs who are waging this street war?'

'Young communist militants.'

'Who are obviously content to see their own murdered too. What's the attitude of the resistance groups?'

'They don't approve of shooting people in the back.'

'That's something. And Vichy?'

'They don't want us interfering in the legal process.'

'So the French will arrest the French, and presumably shoot them.'

Kurt held his glass up to the light. 'What crass idiots.'

To Max's relief Gaston left Nimes for occupied Brittany where he said he had contacts. In October, the Feldkommandant of Nantes was shot in the back. The next day fifty hostages were taken from a Breton prison.

Max and Etienne met Catherine at the Café Vert. All three were depressed. Even the fat proprietor's black market beer did little to lift their spirits. Max, cigarette perched on his lower lip, slowly and methodically tore his empty cigarette packet into small strips.

'It was Gaston. He shot the Boche brass.' Carefully Max collected the small strips together. 'Shoot brass you pay, *Ipso facto*. Bloody idiots. Gaston's back here now.'

Catherine looked anxious. 'Nowhere near us I hope.'

'Don't worry, he'll have gone to ground with the *sanglier*.' He threw the strips up in the air. 'If the commies get themselves some sort of framework then maybe we'll be able to talk, before the Boche has emptied all of our prisons.'

'Can't your friend Moulin help?' Catherine asked.

'He's in London, but he'll be back.'

Despite everything, the war, conscience, guilt, and Marianne's beady eye, Catherine and Freddy were meeting for a record evening fairly regularly. From time to time, he sensed a cool formality on her part, but inevitably, barriers were being lifted. In private they were using first names. They were simply two lonely young people aware of a powerful mutual attraction. They discussed families, incidents, but never the war. She avoided criticism of the regime's treatment of Jews, knowing he had been affected. He avoided mention of the resistance, remembering the hay-loft incident.

A few days after the meeting with Max, Catherine was sitting with Freddy in her study listening to banned music. Prepared to cross into the taboo area, Catherine said, 'these - hostage reprisals, one hundred for one. Sickening, don't you think?'

Unperturbed, he replied, 'Catherine I think war is sickening. I think taking a life is sickening, but war changes the whole concept of morality. I'm not responsible for innocent hostages, neither are you responsible for young thugs that shoot unarmed soldiers in the back.'

Observing him carefully for a reaction Catherine opined, 'If I were an army commander I'd say, an eye for an eye no more.'

'Then you can be my army commander any time.'

He cupped her face in his hands and kissed her lightly several times. Taken by surprise she made no move to avoid his touch. Her face burned. Her stomach leapt. Breathlessly she gripped the arms of the chair, to hang on to reality. Freddy's kisses, though delicate and almost chaste, belied his own desperate desire for this woman he so loved. With his hands still cupping her face, he planted a long lingering kiss on her lips, while their hearts pounded, and burning cheek met burning cheek. Their fuse of passion was so near to exploding that the merest move from either would have sent them hurtling onto their own planet. But cautionary bells again reminded them of who they were and what they were.

Marianne was in the kitchen making soup out of pea pods and potatoes. Catherine ran in. ' Maman! De Gaulle has just commanded young militants to stop killing Germans openly, because it's too easy for them to retaliate.' She had been listening to the BBC in the cellar.

'Yes dear, but the General is in London. Papa says that's the problem. They need someone to shake some sense into them, here, in France, and get them organised.' She picked up the paring knife. 'Your father 's never wrong about politics.'

Without replying but thinking of Max, Catherine began peeling the cooked chestnuts lying in a large mound at the other end of the table. After a minute of silent activity, Marianne asked.

'What time did the German major leave your room?'

Catherine knew from her mother's tone she was ready to provoke an argument.

'Not late: about ten,' she replied casually.

'He's here far too often. I've nothing against him, as you know. Charming boy, pity he's German, but we have to be careful. Mathilde and Jacques have seen him here several times. The villagers will think you are fraternising, and I remember very well what they thought of girls who did that in the last war, and you are a de Lazarin for heavens' sake.'

There was only one way to stop her mother launching into one of her tirades. 'Maman, listen - please listen.' She lowered her voice conspiratorially.

'Max has asked me to find out as much as possible. He says I am in a prime position to observe and report back. Which I do.'

Marianne slumped into a chair, pale with shock. 'What? Oh my God! Surely, surely, that political hothead of a cousin hasn't got you involved with the resistance?' she murmured, hardly daring to utter the word.

'No! No! Of course not, Maman. But if I can help Max with snippets of information about our next-door neighbours, so what? I'm not in any danger. I'm not shooting soldiers am I?'

'Thank God for something,' she muttered.

'So that's why I'm being civilised to the major. Do you understand?' Marianne nodded. 'But it has to be a secret Maman. Between us. If anyone outside found out, I could be arrested. So, sssh!'

Madame de Lazarin returned silently to her culinary efforts, shaking her head, and sighing.

Catherine knew this was the only way to prevent her mother confiding in Mathilde, and to prevent her monitoring evenings spent with the major.

Whilst the de Lazarins continued to receive weekly provisions of luxuries like coffee and dried milk from the Germans, the day-to-day essentials were more difficult to come by. Chestnuts were fast becoming a substitute for almost anything; vegetables, coffee, and now bread.

Marianne's cooking could never have been termed successful, even with pre-war ingredients. Now, it was even worse.

In early December the major and his colonel held their last concert for the year. The programme chose itself, Mozart and Bach: Freddy playing a Mozart Piano Concerto. This time Catherine allowed her eyes to glance at him for the briefest moment. It would have been too humiliating to be taken for a collaborator. She watched as the oleaginous government ministers directed their greased compliments to the colonel.

Marianne confided caustically. 'Half of them wouldn't be able to tell the difference between a Mozart symphony and the Mairie's clock.'

Afterwards, Freddy graciously kissed the hands of mother and daughter, and continued to hold Catherine's for several minutes, whilst talking to her. It did not go unnoticed by the Party members. 'Mademoiselle Catherine, I would like photographs of yourself, the chateau, and the family.'

'Why?'

'I've been given ten days leave for New Year, and I want my mother to meet you.'

December was cold. Catherine was in the warm kitchen attempting to control her mother's supper preparations, when Georges burst in white-faced from the cellar, where he had been listening to the BBC.

'Papa! What's the matter?' Catherine pulled out a kitchen chair and guided him into it.

Georges mopped his brow. 'America is in the war. The Japanese have bombed their fleet in Hawaii.' The two women stood momentarily stunned. 'So, Hitler will have to declare war on America, because Japan's part of the Axis.'

Marianne smiled. 'That's wonderful! They'll help the British now. They'll land in Normandy again!'

Georges rose impatiently 'No! The British are going to have to split their resources. They have colonies in the Far East, Marianne.'

Catherine cracked two eggs into a basin. 'So they'll forget about us.'

'Of course! America is strong enough to support two war zones. But - the question is, can the British survive?'

He looked at the two women in his life, dejected and anxious. 'Come along, we have to believe that maybe in a year or two the British, and perhaps the Americans, will be on Dunkirk beach again, but this time marching straight to Paris.' Marianne began to cry.

'Now now!' he chided. 'You've always said I had a nose for politics!'

'But Georges, d'you realise the whole world is now at war?'

Kurt went off on home leave for Christmas, leaving Freddy in charge, and once again the family was invited to Christmas dinner in the west wing. Catherine said she had no intention of listening to Nazis toasting Hitler again. But Georges asked Marianne what they were going to eat.

'My chestnut purée, dear.' They accepted the invitation forthwith.

As last year at midnight mass, Josef Hahn, Freddy and Rudy Schmidt provided seasonal music. The congregation now accepted German soldiers with a degree of tolerance, and the presence of a few young women in the congregation indicated that some of them were already making forays into French life.

After their Christmas dinner, Freddy invited Catherine to the dance that had been arranged. 'You will stay, won't you?'

'Of course not!' she answered firmly.

'Why?'

'Major, as a de Lazarin, and a French woman, I will not be taken for a collaborator by every little gossiping tart your soldiers choose to invite.'

She smiled sweetly. 'Goodnight major, and thank you so much for dinner!' Freddy was speechless.

By nine o clock the de Lazarins were back in the east wing, and Catherine was ensconced in her study, pleased she had turned him down. She was nevertheless angry that the blight of war was destroying the potential of their relationship, but tonight she thought of her country, not of herself.

After ten miserable minutes watching the cavortings of his men, Freddy stole out of the west wing to the chateau's door, and pulled the bell chain.

'I - I - have a present for Mademoiselle Catherine,' Freddy stammered to a mildly astonished Georges. Marianne who had followed her husband into the hall, said icily, 'I'll fetch Catherine. Wait there if you please, Major von Langdorf.'

Freddy was beginning to regret his impetuosity, but Catherine arrived at the foot of the stairs and, without a glance to her parents, invited him up to her study.

'I thought your mother was going to throw me out.'

'Maman can be frosty when she chooses. So, why didn't you stay to dance?'

He grinned. 'Because I'd prefer to dance with you! Anyway, I have something for you.' He took out a small packet from his inner pocket. 'At home we give presents on Christmas night.'

It was a bottle of her favourite Guerlain perfume, which was fast becoming unobtainable.

'Freddy,' she gasped. 'Oh, Freddy, this is so generous of you. How did you know?' she giggled.

'I managed to read the label on your bottle when you weren't looking.'

She kissed his cheeks lightly. 'Thank you so much.'

He took the box of perfume out of her hand, and put it on the chair, and found a record of "Night and Day."

'May I have this dance, mademoiselle?'

It felt so right and so comfortable dancing together. They moved slowly, Freddy holding her close for the first time, she, slender and pliant, glided rhythmically against his strong limbs. He put his arms around her, and planted a chaste kiss on her lips, and another, that lingered. They stopped dancing. Suddenly the attraction, which had been such a potent force between them, was unleashed, and their lips touched gently at first, but then the fierce passion, which had been denied for a year, broke through barriers of guilt, of responsibility, of patriotism. Their tongues met, lips stimulated, excited. Mouths hungry for each other searched and found again and again. Heads reeled, intoxicated with a desire that could not be, should not be fulfilled. Out of breath, they stopped, and held hands tightly half expecting the other to run away. Tracing his elegant fingers around Catherine's face, Freddy whispered, 'Dearest girl, please don't think I have taken advantage of you.'

She looked at him, with a softness and tenderness he had not seen before. 'Ssh,' she murmured, putting her finger on his mouth.

A few days later he went home to Germany on two weeks leave.
She knew she would miss him.
He knew she was the one who made the war bearable.

CHAPTER FOURTEEN

The von Langdorf Christmas celebrations at the schloss were to be delayed until New Year's Day, when Carl would be joining them.

Anna's increasingly frequent attacks of angina were only made tolerable by living in Dresden as much as possible. The city buzzed with social activity, and showed little indication that the country was at war.

However, for Friedrich the war was causing major problems.

'It's the physical condition of the labour they send me. Undernourished, and dropping with fatigue most of them.'

Freddy and his father were sliding through the woods, on their narrow langlauf skis, a thick crisp layer of snow beneath them. With pink cheeks and slightly out of breath, Friedrich stopped for a moment's rest.

'What do you do with them?' Freddy asked.

'Take them into the canteen and give them bread and soup.'

He smiled at the change in his fence-sitting father. 'You could be court-martialled, Papa.'

Freidrich took a swig from a hip flask. 'I got rid of those little uniformed thugs, thank God! D'you know,' he said sombrely, 'they would actually kick and beat anyone who even slowed down.'

Freddy thought of Muller. 'I'll bet they did.'

'Anyway,' said Freidrich laughing, ' I told them if we couldn't produce the required daily quota, because my workers were fearful of being kicked, I would report the little shits for encouraging lower production levels.'

They started to ski slowly along a familiar bridle path. 'Then I ordered them to get the hell out of my factory.'

They reached a large hut in a clearing. One of their tenant farmers had lit the stove that stood in the centre. It was a cosy place with thick rugs on the wooden floor and at the two small windows hung bright red and white gingham curtains made by Anna when Freddy was a child. This was where his French governess would bring him for lessons in the summer, where his mother and he would have their picnics. Later it would be his secret hideout, to observe small animals and the bird life of the forest. As a student the solitude of the hut was an ideal retreat for study, with a mountain stream nearby surrounded by pools and waterfalls. An assortment of comfortable seating had been pushed against the walls and in one corner stood a pine table and chairs. He noticed a pack of playing cards, and remembered the last time he and Erich were here.

Freddy heated up his mother's homemade sweet lemon tea in a saucepan on top of the stove, and laced it with a few drops of plum brandy, a taste they had acquired from a Romanian count. Flicking idly through the playing cards, Freidrich remarked, 'It's quite appalling you know. There I have been, explaining some simple mechanical assembly line task to a prisoner only to find he's a professor of chemistry, or a doctor, or a teacher of philosophy - even a surgeon!' He rubbed his hands together to warm them. 'Loathsome situation.'

Skiing back to the Schloss, Freddy's thoughts were on Catherine. He wanted to show her their hut, the forest, ski with her, touch her, catch the fragrance of her perfumed skin, hold her in his arms again.

At breakfast on New Year's Eve, Anna watched her son with motherly concern as he helped himself to ham and cheese. 'You are getting enough to eat at your chateau, darling?'

Freddy laughed. 'Of course not, Mama! They starve us. Only bread and water.' He patted her hand. 'We have plenty.'

'What about the chateau family? Are they short of food?'

'We have an arrangement of wine for food. Works well. In fact I've brought you two bottles of their vintage.'

'Carl told me the chateau was absolutely magnificent, and you were living in great style!'

He dabbed his mouth with his napkin. 'After breakfast I'll tell you everything.'

Sitting beside him on the soft cushioned sofa Freddy showed his mother photographs of the chateau, and told her about Georges and Marianne de Lazarin, and about the concerts.

'Uncle Carl tells me they have a beautiful daughter.' She turned to him with a wicked gleam. 'True?'

'Absolutely. See for yourself.' He took out Catherine's photograph and Anna looked at it for some moments. 'So this is Catherine. What a lovely young woman. Funny, but there is something about her face - I don't know, I feel I have seen her before, but of course I couldn't have, could I?'

When Freddy told her where the de Lazarins had their villa, and how they used to eat at the Carlton, she said, 'well, there we go. We must have seen them.'

He described the evening he saw the girl on the promenade in Cannes and how he saw that very same back in the de Lazarins' salon the moment they arrived. Anna's blue eyes sparkled. 'It's fate, my love.'

'It's more than that, Mama. I'm in love with her.'

Anna touched his cheek. 'The war makes us all feel a little desperate and lonely.'

'I want to marry her.'

Anna's round blue eyes widened.' Have you asked her?'

'Not yet.'

He put the photographs back into his wallet. 'Anyway, even if she agreed, we couldn't marry until this idiotic war is over. And there's another obstacle. She has to finish her medical degree at Montpellier.'

'Darling, if two people want to marry, finishing a medical degree is no obstacle.' She laughed, 'and as you are almost a Frenchman now, you can live in Montpellier too!'

Anna knew she was simply cheering him up. They were facing many years of they knew not what, but she understood how important it was to have someone to love. She ruffled his hair.'I think you'd better ask her first, before you start worrying about the future.'

Carl arrived handsome and distinguished in his general's uniform. He wore a Nazi party armband these days. For Hitler's chief legal advisor party membership was obligatory. Although Anna insisted her men wore lounge suits for these family occasions, just like old times to take minds off the war, the conversation returned ineluctably to the political situation.

Carl was downcast. 'America has resources. We do not.'

Friedrich attempted to lighten the mood. 'And how is our Fuhrer? Still searching for the perfect Aryan?'

He winked at his brother who grinned slyly.

'The Fuhrer sends you his warmest embraces, Freddy. How warm he wouldn't say!'

The two brothers burst into laughter.

'Just shut up, you two!' Freddy remonstrated, blushing.

'You can tell the Fuhrer my boy is in love with a beautiful French girl, so there,' Anna piped. Freidrich raised his eyebrows, but thought it more diplomatic to make no comment.

Carl had received half a dozen letters from Sophie, his lost love, at first via the American Embassy, but now the Swedish. 'She has met other émigrés, but is very lonely. She still finds the language difficult.'

'How is she living uncle?'

'She's a house-cleaner to some rich Americans; Jewish, and she says they treat her well.'

It was shocking to imagine that beautiful, sophisticated Sophie, the cream of Berlin society, and a top journalist, was now a house-cleaner. Carl walked over to the piano. 'Come on young Freddy, let's have some music, before I jump on a plane to New York.'

'Carl, I know how you must miss her - we all do, but just imagine what would have happened had she stayed. My God!' Anna slipped her arm through Carl's, with a comforting squeeze. 'I often think of that horrendous dinner.'

Carl nodded. 'That manic maid.'

It had been a dangerous moment for the family when Gretchen the maid, in full Deutsche Mädel uniform, had tipped a plate of scalding dinner into poor Sophie's lap, declaiming loudly that Germans did not serve Jews.

Fortunately Sophie was leaving for Hamburg and America two days later, while Gretchen was told Carl was taking her to a labour camp; a story she believed completely coming from Herr General.

Later that night as they were getting into bed Friedrich asked his wife about Freddy's French girl. Anna giggled. 'Our son is in love, darling. Don't you remember how we were, or rather how you were in the last War?' Friedrich chuckled. 'How could I forget?'

She went to the bookshelf and pulled out the Almanac de Gotha, a tome listing all European aristocracy. Turning pages muttering to herself, she suddenly whooped triumphantly. 'They're here! Listen to this. *"The de Lazarin family of Chateau de Lazarin, southern France. Landowners since the fifteenth century. At the time of the Revolution, Comte de Lazarin voluntarily gave up the title."* Well, what do you think of that, eh?'

Friedrich was already asleep.

Just before Freddy returned to France, Anna said. 'Look darling I don't want you to think I am a morbid old mother, but we must be sensible. Papi has told you about my heart problem, so – so I want you to have my peacock ring and then you will have both.'

'Why Mama?'

'I want you,' she said, giving him a maternal pat on the cheek, 'to give this to the girl you intend to marry. Don't argue. It's important to me. It's a way of keeping them both safely in the family.'

'Suppose something happens to me?'

'If anything happened to you my precious, what would I care about rings? Here. Take it, for me – please.'

In the early hours of January the first, while the de Lazarins and the von Langdorfs were sleeping, Max was waiting in a farmhouse near Arles for Jean Moulin, who had been dropped by parachute from a British plane, with orders from de Gaulle in London to unite the resistance under one banner.

CHAPTER FIFTEEN

Freddy could hardly wait to see Catherine.

They stood for moments, their arms about each other

Then, quite abruptly she broke away from him and stared at the floor. 'Look - I - I - don't think this – er - friendship of ours can continue.'

He was stunned.'Why? But why?'

Catherine tried to explain to her stupefied suitor that she did not wish to be publicly associated with anyone, or anything, that would imply disloyalty to France. In his absence she had had hours of heart-searching.

Face to face, her feelings were more difficult to explain, her resolve weaker.

'Freddy I shall be called a collaborator. My family is one of the oldest in France.It is a name I am proud of. I have no right to dishonour it.'

He looked anxiously into her eyes.

'I understand about the family - of course I do. I would never never wish to be the cause of any malevolence or danger to you from your own people.'

He stroked her hair.'Dearest girl, I would rather die first. You must believe that.'

He took her hand. 'Come here.'

They sat in front of the study's log fire. He knew he would have to choose his words carefully. To lose her now would be unbearable. 'Catherine, there is something I have wanted to tell you ever since we met. The first time I saw you, there was no war. You and I were in Cannes, just two people on holiday.' She was completely nonplussed when he recalled the evening he saw the girl on the promenade, and described what she was wearing. It was true she did remember a spectacular sunset, somewhere in front of the Carlton, and feeling very unhappy.

She also recognised her clothes, which he could describe in careful detail.

'But are you sure it was me?'

'Never more sure of anything. My mother said it was Fate.'

'You told her?'

'Of course. So, my dear Catherine, how can you be a collaborator with someone who knew you before the war?'

She smiled ruefully. 'Semantics, Freddy! In any case only we know that.'

'But darling, we are pawns in the war game, thoroughly expendable, and spending time together does not make us enemies of our countries.'

She thought for a moment. 'Who else knows?'

'Only Kurt. Look, until this mess is over, one way or the other, why can't our friendship be our secret.' He tilted her chin. 'You don't really want us to end, do you? Please say you don't?'

She put her hand up to his face affectionately, and smiled with that same tenderness he had seen once before. In her heart she did not want to break the bond that was growing between them.

'Very well. Our secret, Major von Langdorf'.

Rumours that the Fuhrer would be relieving General Brauchitsch of his Wehrmacht command were now a fact. 'He is so influenced by that bastard Himmler, God knows what they could push us into.'

The two men were eating late in Kurt's quarters. Freddy had returned tired after a very long day of garrigue manoeuvres. On the makeshift dining table stood a bottle of Chateau de Lazarin, from which both poured liberal servings. Freddy broke off another chunk of baguette.

'Do you think it could affect us?'

'Well, Himmler and that musical fiend Reinhardt Heydrich are ambitious, keen to extend their power. So, who knows?'

Freddy grinned. 'My uncle told me Heydrich's father's real name was Suss.'

Kurt snorted. 'Therein lies the man's problem. He screams with anger if it's mentioned.' The colonel peeled an apple, excused himself from the table and slumped into his favourite leather armchair by the log fire, a dark lock falling onto his forehead, which he pushed back impatiently.

'So, young Freddy, the manoeuvres threw up nothing of importance?'

'Nothing. The men are getting to know the territory. It's full of small ravines and ditches, perfect for -'

'Resisters?'

Freddy began to chuckle. 'We did have a moment of suspense. We were all a bit tired, when we heard this rustling noise and froze for action. Hanke and two others crawled closer to the sound. I thought it was an ambush, so we circled the area to cover them. This wild boar jumped out straight at Hanke who fell backwards, his rifle went flying, and he let out a yell that could have alerted every resistance group for miles. Idiot!'

'Tick him off?'

'You bet! Bloody fool.'

'What happened to the pig?'

'Got away.'

'Didn't anyone try to shoot it?'

'Sure.' Freddy guffawed. 'They missed!'

When Catherine met Max in Nimes at the Café Vert in March, she was surprised at how pale and thin he appeared. Unshaven, with dark circles under his eyes, he looked as though he hadn't slept for weeks. He had visited his parents at Christmas, but had no idea when he would see them again. 'It's too dangerous .The more people who know me, the more are implicated if I am caught.' He took out his crumpled pack of cigarettes, and lit up. 'Jean Moulin has been trying to convert Vichy bureaucrats to the resistance.'

'Any success?'

The Girl on the Promenade

'Huge', he smiled. 'We've had information and intelligence that we've passed on to our boys and to the British. We've also got a list of collaborators.'

'What do you do to them? '

'Neutralize them.' Illustrating the point he picked up a matchstick and snapped it in two. 'Some people have left their jobs in order to work full time with us.'

'Where d'you get the money from?'

'London, but it's not enough.'

She pulled her coat around her legs against the cold. 'Who organized this latest crop of railway sabotage?'

'Successful don 't you think?'

'Fantastic! Any losses?'

He drew on his cigarette and scratched his chin. 'Yep.Too many.'

'And injuries?'

He gave his cousin a thin smile. 'OK - I know why you are asking. The trouble is our immediate problems are more important than a field hospital.'

He put his half - smoked cigarette on the ashtray. 'First of all we have to organise a secret army, send out agents, and get information about our own Gendarmerie. We've already sent round a circular asking them to slow down sabotage investigations, even to follow false trails.'

'The response?'

' Good, but there's a new set-up, the STO. Anti-communist, anti-de Gaulle, and pro-Vichy. They are the bastards that would murder us all.'

She tied her scarf about her neck, and drained her cup of hot chocolate.

'I'd better go. Papa has orchestra practice tonight.'

'Still playing with the Fritzies, Uncle Georges?'

'He loves the cello,' she replied curtly.

'And his fellow musicians too, eh?'

'Very funny!'

'No need to get tetchy. War changes people.'

'Not my father!' She spat the words out, and rose noisily from the table.

Max finished his drink and wiped his mouth with a paper serviette.

'I've seen Philippe,' he said casually.

'Oh really? And his wife?'

'Dead.'

'Dead?' She sat down again. 'What —?'

'Tragic, really. Complicated prem. birth; seven months. No hospital available.' Max looked down at the table and began twisting the serviette into a tight ball. 'Both died. Baby girl. He couldn't get there — in time.'

He picked up his smouldering cigarette. 'Poor chap was quite distraught. But he'll recover. Everyone has to.'

She knew it must have been a terrible blow for Philippe, but the fact he had fathered a child within that marriage, somehow created an even greater distance between herself and the Philippe she had once known.

He was now irretrievably in the past.

One morning in early May, Freddy was sitting at his desk, typing up radio reports from OKH Berlin. The sun was already hot and the colours of Provence were beginning to burst through green foliage. He looked at the small red box with velvet lining sitting on his desk, containing his mother's ring, and wondered when he could ask Catherine to be his wife. Whilst momentarily lost in this daydream, the door to his quarters was perfunctorily tapped, and Kurt, livid with rage, stormed in holding a piece of paper and paced over to the window. He grabbed at a cigarette and lit it, holding his lighter with trembling hands. A couple of deep inhalations later and he was able to speak.

'I've just heard from Carl. Oberg has been appointed head of the SS and Gestapo in France! Remember what I said about Himmler? The bastard has been desperate to reduce the power of the army's occupational command, since the outbreak of war. Well, now he's bloody well done it!'

The colonel's well - built frame sat heavily on the antique settee.

'What'll be the overall effect on the army?'

'Sheer bloody impotence!' he growled. 'Listen to this. He will have *"absolute power over all police matters, and reprisals against criminals, Jews, and communists implicated in attacks against the Third Reich or the citizens of the Reich".'*

'So, is he not under the army's control in any area?'

Karl gave one of his familiar snorts. 'There's more.

"All disputes between the two services will be settled by the Fuhrer himself."'

Angrily he flipped his fingers across the sheet of paper, throwing it down on the settee. 'And that, young Freddy, means Himmler.'

He found the ashtray which was always kept on the table for him. 'Bloody eunuchs in a harem, that's what we are, nothing more!'

'What about us, our posting here?'

'Oberg won't give a damn between occupied and un-occupied zones, my old son. The same goes for our posting.' Kurt squeezed the life out of his cigarette, and took another. 'And I have to go to Paris for the sodding ceremony. Next week!'

'Will Himmler be there?'

Kurt shook his head.'Heydrich. Herr Suss!' he snarled. 'Never mind, Carl will be coming, thank God. A good excuse for us to talk again - in private.

Stulpnagel is speechless, apparently.'

There were two in the chateau's garrison who were also speechless, but with delight. Remer and Hanke had heard the advance news from Party HQ in Paris.

Kurt arrived back from Paris, in a state of despondency, largely over the future of the army. He had spent most of the two days with Carl, in a heavily guarded hotel, and had not ventured out. Despite the number of hostages being shot, sniping soldiers irrespective of rank or of what they were doing was becoming a national pastime.

'This is a haven compared with those poor buggers in Paris,' he said, stirring his coffee. 'If the Paris street battles start down here, God help the resisters, with Oberg's bully boys at the top.'

'I've had some intelligence from an agent in Vichy.'

Kurt's brown Italian eyes opened with interest. 'Yes?'

'A certain ex - prefect of Chartres, who comes from Arles, has been charged by de Gaulle to unite the resistance.'

The colonel picked up a copy of 'Signal', a war reportage picture magazine, lying in Freddy's file. He flicked through a few pages. 'What 's the name of de Gaulle's man?'

'Jean Moulin, and he has an assistant, a Doctor Max Becker.'

'Where's he from?'

'Paris, but works in the south.'

Kurt replaced the magazine and rose wearily from the armchair.

'No doubt Herr Oberg looks forward to meeting them.'

There was more unwelcome news to come. A representative of the Supreme Head of the SS and Gestapo in France, Karl Albrecht Oberg, would be visiting to make detailed reports on each military establishment and on personnel, and would have the right to scrutinise all papers and files.

Kurt ran fingers through his thick dark hair. 'I knew it couldn't be long before that bloody banana importer pushed his pink snout into every army garrison.'

Freddy was ready to leave for a day in the garrigue.

'Do I cancel manoeuvres for this representative?'

'Certainly not! We are army. We don't stop for anyone. Sod them!'

When Major von Langdorf returned, quite naturally he reported to his colonel. A large thick-set figure in a black uniform with his back to the door, sat facing a grim faced Kurt. As Freddy entered, the figure rose, and turned to him.

'Good afternoon Major von Langdorf.'

Freddy's heart sank. Thick fleshy lips parted, and gold fillings covered in food particles exposed themselves in what was supposedly a smile.

It was none other than Otto Muller, wearing the uniform of a Hauptsturmfuhrer, one S.S. rank below major. He came towards Freddy, who stood frozen at the door. 'Major von Langdorf and I already know each other, do we not?'

He extended a podgy, bejewelled hand. Muller's grip was crushing.

'To what do we owe this honour, Hauptsturmfuhrer Muller?' Freddy asked, deliberately exaggerating his title, remembering the last occasion.

'Your colonel will explain. Meanwhile I am glad to see you are soldiers, with guns.' He pointed to Freddy's holster.'We thought you would be fiddling and fluting, while Rome burned!' He cackled at his own joke.

'Do you think Rome is burning?' The colonel asked sardonically.

The fleshy lips snapped. 'Fires are beginning here in the south, but we shall stamp them out, smother them, you'll see.'

He turned quickly to the door. 'I shall go to my quarters, and see you gentlemen in the morning. Heil Hitler!' The door slammed.

A shaken major quickly relayed his previous encounters with Muller.

'He's a bastard an absolute bastard – the worst there is.'

'Great! Muller and co. are our new bosses, and God help the resistance.

Oberg intends to put us all under the SS microscope, old son', Kurt added solemnly.

'But surely resistance will be Vichy's problem.'

Kurt took out his cigarette case. 'Want a bet? I have a feeling things are about to change.'

On Muller's desk, in his suite next door to Freddy's quarters, were the dossiers of every soldier in the chateau. Rudi treated it all as a bit of a joke. 'He's a crackpot fanatic. Wants information about everyone, including the de Lazarins.'

At the end of the day, Muller sent word that he would like to see the major and the colonel separately, in his office.

'The impertinent turd!' Kurt raged. 'If he wants to see me, he comes here, to my quarters, and you likewise. Jesus! There are limits!'

Freddy sat behind his desk when Muller came in, carrying a dossier. The SS man lowered himself into a chair and his prize-fighter hands opened a page. 'I shall come straight to the point, Major von Langdorf. A report from one of your men says you failed to protect them adequately when a garage was being searched.'

Freddy looked puzzled.

Muller's lips parted and flashed his gold fillings. 'Let me explain. You refused to search the hayloft, where members of the French Resistance could have been hiding. Instead you dismissed your men, put your arms round the French woman who lives in the chateau, saying you would take her home.'

Freddy fists tightened. 'Did your informer also advise you of the patrol I took out immediately after the event, to comb the garage, hay-loft, and the surrounding area?'

Muller thumped the desk. 'Why, major, did you bother to take this woman back to her door? Why did you waste time? Who were you trying to protect? Or is she your little French fuck?' he leered.

The major rose, and looked coldly down his patrician nose at the gross peasant. 'Hauptsturmfuhrer Muller, allow me to explain something to you. First, how dare you have the impudence to accuse me, and so crudely, of something that is totally untrue, and even if it were, my private life is no concern of yours. Second, I am a soldier, and the killing of innocent civilians is not within my remit. Had any resisters been located while the lady was present, she would have been killed.'

Muller slapped the table hard with the palm of his hand, heaved his bulk out of the chair, and stood with his head upturned attempting to match Freddy's height. 'So what Herr

Major von Langdorf? Just because the woman is a rich bitch and lives in a chateau, like your schloss, so what? She's French. Let her die! How do you know she's not part of the resistance, eh?'

'We would have found that out long ago.'

'How do you know it wasn't she who arranged your provisions transport to be attacked, eh?'

'The French police are dealing with that. It would not require a bursting intelligence to follow the route of a provisions transport and ambush it. I daresay even you and your men could have done that, Hauptsturmfuhrer Muller.'

Freddy walked to the door, and opened it. 'Now, if you don't mind, I have several broadcasts to listen to.'

As he went out of the door, Muller leered. 'Major von Langdorf, I leave you with this thought. The army is like a large jellyfish and we are going to push a spine into you.' He cackled. 'It could be painful! Heil Hitler!'

CHAPTER SIXTEEN

July was hot as always.

Catherine spent her days working in the vineyard with her father, Jacques, and any other labour they could find.

She was to meet Max again in Nimes at the Café Vert, and waited for him on the forecourt, awash with mothers and babies. The only men about were either old, wounded, or tradesmen who had opted to work for the Boche three days a week to avoid being drafted to Germany. Shop windows were practically empty, but, despite privations, there was a sense of being better off than those up north.

Max arrived looking rested and clean apart from the dark stubble of a growing beard. Jean the proprietor brought them a tray with a full coffee jug. As always with special treats, his chins danced for joy. 'It's real! Wait till you try it!'

Max stirred sugar beet sweetener into his coffee and leant closer to his cousin. 'I shall be having new identity papers soon before going to London to meet de Gaulle,' he whispered. 'Working for the resistance full time now with Moulin. My new identity is safer for everyone, you included.'

He noticed the scratches and cuts on her rough hands. 'You do know about Oberg's new Family Hostage Law, don't you?'

Catherine held the cup to her mouth, and inhaled the delicious aroma. 'I think so.'

He was irritated, and rattled his spoon. 'You have to know for sure, not think you know! Now listen, if I were caught they would shoot my father and your father and send my mother, your mother and you to a labour camp in Germany. It would be a miracle if any of you came out alive. Got it?'

'But Max, not here in the south.'

The Girl on the Promenade

He took out another crumpled packet of cigarettes. 'It applies to anyone who plots against the Boche.' He sighed with exasperation. 'You could live in Timbuktu.' He lit a cigarette. 'To think you are safe anywhere in France is stupidity! Anything to report?'

She could only describe the regular garrigue patrols.

'Have you seen or heard of any collaborators?'

'No.'

He blew out a couple of smoke rings and narrowed his eyes.

'We're having some problems. Keep your ears open.'

He rose from the marble topped table. 'Come on! Let's walk.'

The Roman Fountain Gardens, one of the city's major landmarks, was large enough to find privacy. At the gardens' entrance was a canal with miniature waterfalls down which ducks and mallards slid happily. A vast park with broad gravel walkways, lined with trees, white Roman statuary and stone benches, most of it Roman in origin, led to steps and terraces of varying levels. Below the elaborate balustrade terraces decorated with impressive classical deities, acolytes and nymphs, were the sunken Roman baths with preserved stone seating. In the rock face behind, hundreds of steps had been cut winding upwards through thick foliage, and in the several arbours and landings on the long climb to the Roman watchtower at the top of the hill, were benches set inside the rock's natural concave spaces, so private as to all but conceal any incumbents: a perfect place for a clandestine rendezvous. There were a few German soldiers in the gardens, some sitting on benches writing letters, some taking photographs. Keeping his head down, Max put an arm about his cousin's shoulder as they climbed the steps and found an empty seat tucked inside the rock. They talked about the money being offered for information on Jews, the reason why so many of them had been shot whilst in hiding.

'Could you get your father into the Italian zone? He'll be safer surely?'

'We'd never get him out of Vichy, even if we paid for a travel pass.'

'What's happened to your doctor friend in Moulins?'

'Julian. Fantastic fellow.' He picked at a fingernail. 'Betrayed, not because he was a Jew, but because he helped resisters. By a patient whose life he had saved, too. He's in Dachau now. That's the end of him, poor devil.'

Catherine was one of the few people Max could open his heart to without fear of her being caught and 'turned around' by the Gestapo, a situation that was on the increase. The Gestapo were experts in finding the breaking point. Once someone had been 'turned around', they became not only useless to the movement, but also dangerous, and had to be eliminated. This was his reason for keeping Catherine out of any active role, for the present.

When she was in her car about to leave, Max said, 'I don't know when we shall meet again, but Etienne will be in charge here. Any info to pass on, make contact through the Bengali café in Uzès. All the waiters work for us. Be there every Saturday morning. Market day, you won't be noticed.'

'Will do. Be careful won't you?'

He pecked her on the cheeks. 'Sure. And don't trust anyone, remember.'

Driving away she felt an overwhelming sadness. What a way to live.

Would it ever again be the world they used to know?

The *vendange* went on, as before, Kurt supplying daily labour, without which they could never have managed. The crop was greatly reduced, as many vines had neither been pruned nor grafted during the spring. Nevertheless, there were sufficient bottles for the bartering of food to continue.

At the beginning of November Georges brought news from the cellar that the Americans and British had landed on the coast of north-west Africa.

He was so excited there were tears in his eyes. Catherine and her mother threw their arms about him, as though he had done it single-handed.

'But darling, the British are already in North Africa, aren't they?'

'Of course Marianne,' Georges beamed. 'But on the eastern side, so now they'll meet up and cut Rommel off completely.'

'Africa does seem a long way from us, Papa.'

Georges put his arm around his daughter. 'Don't look so gloomy little one. It's a start. They've got to clear that hornet's nest first.'

Kurt was worried about the American landings in North Africa, and for his friend Erwin Rommel. However, the news he received the two days later from Carl in Berlin was worse. ' Hitler expects Petain to declare war on the Americans just because Algiers happens to be a French colony. He's mad! Can a rat fight a tiger?'

'D'you think Laval will let him use the Tunisian airfields?'

'You never know with that old arse licker.' Kurt looked at his watch. 'Laval must still be in conference with him.'

An hour later Kurt returned to Freddy's quarters. 'Laval's refused. Hitler's purple with rage. Your uncle thinks he is going to do something radical to intimidate Vichy. You are going to have to listen to the radio, my lad - all night if necessary.' He grinned. 'You have permission to wake me up! Goodnight.'

Just after two o clock, Freddy was rousing his slumbering colonel. The German army was about to invade unoccupied France, and two SS battalions would be making their way to Nimes. Freddy and Kurt sat talking and drinking coffee in Freddy's quarters, throughout that long night. On his umpteenth cigarette Kurt said suddenly, 'What the hell's going to happen to the French army? Join us?'

Freddy, earphones slung round his neck, picked up a transcript. 'Listen to this, *"Scores of soldiers have left garrisons and gone into the hills"'*.

Kurt was stretched out in stockinged feet, on Freddy's settee. He inhaled, and narrowed his eyes as smoke filled them. 'That's more like it. That's what I'd do! Trouble is they'll join the bloody resistance.' Kurt pushed worried fingers through his hair. 'And there's our problem old son.'

Absent-mindedly shuffling the reports into some order Freddy huffed quietly. 'So how much longer our low profile? That was our brief wasn't it?'

Cigarette between his fingers, Kurt stared at the ceiling. 'Yes Freddy, that was our brief, but in answer to your question, Christ knows.'

Catherine and her father felt the new situation could not be so different from the current one. Marianne was convinced they would be deported. Freddy tried to placate her. 'Madame, this invasion - a surprise to us all - will make absolutely no difference to you, nor to us. My colonel has already spoken to Berlin. We are to carry on as normal, giving concerts.'

Marianne's long fingers were nervously twisting the fringe on one of the settee's cushions. 'Will we be seeing hundreds of soldiers at every turn, and will there be curfews, and more food shortages? I mean, we don' t know, do we, major?'

She was right, no one knew, but he had no intention of alarming her.

'There will be a larger force in Uzès and a couple of divisions in Nimes.'

He did not tell her they were to be SS divisions.

'But', he smiled, 'life for us here will go on just as before.'

The following day Sturmbannfuhrer Muller of the S.S. in Nimes arrived at the chateau's west wing, and marched into Major von Langdorf's quarters where Freddy was at his desk. Muller's lips parted into something resembling a smile. 'Partly a social visit, you know.' As he leaned across the desk, Freddy turned his head fractionally to avoid the full onslaught of Muller's halitosis. 'Congratulations on your promotion, Sturmbannfuhrer.'

'Yes, we are now exactly the same, aren't we. And I'm not even a 'von'.'

He cackled at his quip. Each gap between his gold fillings was stuck with grey gobbets of food. Freddy smiled icily.'How true. But of course you are a Party man, aren't you?'

'Very much.' He leered, as he sat in the chair opposite. 'All you aristocrats need people like us to fight for you.'

'I can see you know nothing of our history, Sturmbannfuhrer.'

Muller slapped the table with the palm of his hand.'History is now, Major. We make it.' He rose from the chair. 'Not your lot. Not anymore.'

When he reached the door Muller turned. 'By the way Herr Major, as they say you are the French expert in these parts, I have asked for you to be my interpreter when I interrogate criminals.'

'What criminals?'

'Resisters to the Third Reich of course! Oh, and another thing. Where can I find a clean French whore? A man needs a fuck away from home, as you well know. Perhaps you could lend me yours?' Muller leered again 'Heil Hitler!'

With great control, the major kept his white knuckles firmly on the desk.

Two days later there was a massive explosion at a railway depot outside Nimes. Several trucks containing arms, explosives and equipment were detonated. Six guards, plus a dozen members of the resistance, were killed. Kurt received a telephone call from Muller in Nimes. Freddy was to report to the Hotel Silhol, Gestapo H.Q.

'The bastard! Plenty of chaps know the language. This is quite deliberate'.

Kurt shrugged. 'Probably, but you'll have to go today. I'll think of something for next time.'

Hotel Silhol was a large building, with red black and white swastika flags draped over its portals. The marble floor and colonnade of the reception hall was cold and austere, made more so by the numbers of black uniforms to be seen. Freddy was taken to the reception area of a suite of offices, by a pretty young French woman, where he was given coffee and asked to wait. The name on the door facing him was Muller's. Rich looking brocade curtains hung from the ceiling to floor windows. Freddy guessed it was the managing director's offices, in better days. Twenty minutes later an SS Unterscharfuhrer asked the major to take the lift with him to the basement.

He was taken into what could have been a storage room, large, cold and dank, a windowless room, with grey walls. One electric light bulb hung from the ceiling, and a dirty one-bar electric fire was plugged into a wall socket. Adjoining was a second room, with a door in the glass partition wall. When opened, he saw Muller in full flight, interrogating a dark haired French youth of about seventeen. The lad was thin, exhausted, and terrified. About his forehead and eyes he had dark blue weals. His mouth was cut open at the corner, and blood ran from his nose. The Unterscharfuhrer picked up a leather whip lying on a small table, and stood waiting for orders. Muller carried a short wooden truncheon in his hand.

He bared his teeth to Freddy. 'Well, Herr Major, you see how difficult my work is? All I'm trying to do is get information about this boy's fucking boss. The one who organised the raid on the trucks?'

Freddy glowered. 'I can't help you.'

Still leering, Muller replied.'Oh but you can Herr Major. Tell him if he gives the name of the village his leader comes from, we will let him go. If he doesn't, we shall shoot his mother and his father and fuck his sister. And all will be done before his eyes.'

With stomach turning Freddy quietly put Muller's proposals to the young Frenchman who seemed thankful to hear his own language again.

'I don't know - I don't know,' he gasped.

Freddy translated for Muller, who gave the boy several heavy blows with the truncheon about the head. The boy keeled over onto the floor, half conscious. Freddy knelt down to pick him up, muttering angrily. 'You've half killed the boy. What the hell d'you expect to get out of him now?'

Muller's neck swelled with rage, both at his own failure to elicit information and at interference with his methods. He pushed Freddy away from the crumpled heap, pulled the body flat on the floor, and with his heavy boots kicked him in his groin. The young man screamed in agony, but Muller's eyes were glazed with sadistic pleasure. Freddy took a step to stand between Muller and the boy on the floor. He had no idea what he was going to do. This was a situation well outside his experience.'Why don't you leave him for a while. You'll never get information out of him now.'

Perspiring heavily, Muller shouted. 'Get out of my way, Major von Langdorf! Remember who we are. We are in charge! You and your toy soldiers can fuck off! Only the Fuhrer tells us what to do. Leave, or I'll put you under arrest for aiding a member of the French Resistance! Get out!'

Muller started on the young man again, kicking him repeatedly, his screams reverberating through that rat hole. Freddy walked into the other room, closed his eyes, and held on to the back of the chair.

In the brief silence that followed, Muller shouted. 'Come and ask him where his fucking boss comes from!'

Freddy knelt by the young man, who was sobbing in pain.

'Montaren,' the boy whispered.

Montaren was the village within walking distance of the chateau.

Freddy pretended he couldn't understand. But Muller wasn't going to give up. 'Very well we'll try again! - and again - and again!'

The boy reached his breaking point.

'M0NTAREN!' he sobbed.

Returning to his quarters at the chateau, the young major felt ill. How many more times was Muller going to ask him to witness his appalling brutality, and for how long was he, a von Langdorf, going to stand by and watch what was being done in the name of Germans everywhere? They were the traitors. His own mother hadn't stood by when old Jakob was attacked. Hadn't he complained about his father's passivity while Hitler was gradually inching out power for the Nazi party? How could he live with himself if he did nothing, turned a blind eye? Physical intervention was never going to work. He would end up in prison, or being shot, which would be pointless. Supposing he found Muller's lists of possible suspects for interrogation? Muller had lists. He had caught a glimpse of one on his desk. Maybe that was the way, to forewarn victims. Who could he give their names to?

There was only one person. If she refused, there had to be someone else. He would have to find his own personal agenda of conscience for Erich, for Aunt Sophie, and thousands like them.

One morning, two days later, an army vehicle with SS machine gunners placed fore and aft raced up and down through the village of Montaren, killing several animals, women and children.

One of those shot dead was Mathilde.

CHAPTER SEVENTEEN

Montaren was in turmoil, with debris, glass, blood, and screams.

Georges transported the more seriously injured to hospital while Marianne and Catherine hurried to Jacques' house. He was weeping piteously in the bedroom where Mathilde's body lay. A neighbour had placed a white sheet over her to cover up what was left of her shattered body.

Rumours were flying as to why and how the village had been singled out for attack. No one admitted to knowing anyone in the resistance, and no one, not even his parents, had seen Gaston for months. But it was known that an officer from the chateau was at the interrogation of a young resister in Nimes, who had been shot later when already half dead from torture.

Catherine was distraught.Could it have been Freddy? Surely he wouldn't have tortured anyone? If the dead resister had implicated Gaston, which was the most likely explanation, Gaston, wherever he was, would know by now that his mother was dead. News travelled quickly into the garrigue.

Marianne was angry through her tears. 'They're just animals. Killing innocent people, and next door it's Brahms and Beethoven. Two nations!'

Freddy came over later that evening for a pre-arranged musical session. She could barely look at him. He thought it was the effects of Mathilde's death, but when she relayed the rumours circulating about him in the village, he stared out of the tall window, wondering just how much he could tell her.

'I trust you to tell me the truth,' she said quietly.

'Whatever I tell you, Catherine, will be the truth. Let's sit down.'

He explained about Muller and the SS in Nimes, assuming the resistance would be well aware of his presence, mentioning briefly his personal brush with Muller in Paris. 'As a direct result of that, Muller has demanded I should be his interpreter.'

'So, you saw - you actually saw the torture?'

'Yes.' he said quietly.

'Well for God's sake, why didn't you stop him?'

'I tried. I tried to reason, but it had no effect.'

'So you just stood there and watched. How disgusting!'

'I was ordered out by Muller, who threatened to have me arrested as a traitor had I continued.'

Her face crumpled with misery.

'Even in Germany, Catherine, it happens.' He related the Jakob Mendel incident. 'Afterwards my mother wept in sorrow and in anger as you are doing, which is how I feel after Nimes.'

'If you really did try – I must believe you,' she murmured.

'I want to do more than try, Catherine. My choice is limited, but maybe you will help me?'

She frowned. 'How?'

He leant his back against the marble edge of the mantelpiece.

'Catherine, I'm not going to ask you if you have ever worked for, or even know anyone involved in a resistance group.'

Her large eyes looked unflinchingly into his, even though her heart beat rapidly with fear, not of Freddy, but remembering the Family Hostage Law, she feared for Max, Uncle Louis, her parents,herself.

'With half the country involved in one way or another, it would be difficult to find anyone who did not know of somebody, somewhere,' she answered with as much sang-froid as she dared.

'I told you; I'm not asking you to tell me. I don't want to know. I only know I have made up my mind to do all I can to help the resistance.'

She was so stunned she could barely utter.

'Why?'

The Girl on the Promenade

With the proud bearing of old Prussian aristocracy he replied, 'because the war being fought by the SS is dishonourable, degrading and inhuman. I am ashamed they are German. I cannot stand by and see my heritage, my family name, the Germany I love, thrown into the cesspits of world history by these thugs.'

Still unable to fully grasp what he had just said, 'Freddy - Do you mean this? I mean - it's - it's not a trick - a ploy -?' she faltered.

His eyes momentarily flashed with anger. 'Do you honestly think I would put myself into this situation for a trick? For what I propose doing I could be shot as a traitor! Catherine! For God's sake, it's no trick.'

Deep furrows of anxiety creased his face. 'This will put us both in danger, you know that don't you?'

She said nothing, simply gazed at him in disbelief. Here was a German officer, willing and wanting to help the enemy camp.

'You are an honourable man,' she whispered.

'It's nothing to do with honour. It's a question of morality.'

'But what can you do?'

'Listen. Muller brags about his lists. These are the lists of victims to be rounded up for interrogation. He keeps these lists in his pockets, in files, and drawers. He's not organised enough to be careful about storing information. He is so carried away by the physicality of his venom, the intellectual side of secrecy eludes him completely. I shall copy down whatever lists I can find, and give them to you.'

'Thank you,' she whispered. 'And I shall – I shall - place them.'

This would have to be an exercise in mutual trust.

Berlin announced to the chateau's troops they would have a Christmas concert, with no Vichy representative, and the programme of non-Jewish and non-enemy music must include some Wagner. The stupidity of the government was staggering. On the telephone to Berlin, Kurt asked,

'Is the music of a country we occupy also classed as enemy music?'

'Yes!' was the short answer.

'Austria too, in that case.'

The voice in Berlin spluttered.'Of course not! Austria is part of Germany, colonel.'

'But we took it over didn't we?'

'We WALKED in colonel, that's the difference.'

'So Mozart's acceptable. Good. And Mahler?'

' Jew!'

'Became Catholic. Friend of Wagner's wife?'

'No. Born Jew. But I'll let you know when I find the list.'

'What about Brahms?'

The voice from Berlin said gleefully. 'Of course Brahms. German.'

'Ah! But what about Brahms' Hungarian Dances? Hungary is an enemy country isn't it?'

'Yes, of course. I'm glad you mentioned that, colonel. Clearly it has been overlooked. I shall have the list completely revised.'

'Good. And could you check out our former East African colonies? We've a chap who's good on native drums.'

'Immediately colonel.'

Kurt put down the telephone and threw up his hands in mock horror.

Freddy exploded. 'Where do these arseholes in Berlin come from?'

'Berlin's crawling with them. Ignorant Party pricks, who wouldn't know a note of music from a fart.'

Muller had been promoted to Obersturmbannfuhrer, one rank higher than Freddy, therefore when the SS demanded the major's presence he had to be there. Interrogations followed the same pattern of brutal physical assault. Freddy was sent into the next room, and called back, usually when it was too late to elicit a coherent response from the battered victim. The breaking point for some was quite early in the interrogation, and information was divulged in return for freedom. But, by and large, Freddy observed the quality of brain cells possessed by these S.S. bully boys was limited, therefore it was not unknown for a clever man to give just a few truthful facts, weave them into a pack of lies, and be set free.

One morning he was summoned to be interpreter to a young woman prisoner of about twenty-three, courageously withstanding Muller's hard slaps. She had been pulled in for so little, Freddy wondered what Muller's real motives were. They were soon made plain. Through a very embarrassed major, Muller told her to take her clothes off. She was assisted in this by his henchman. Freddy was repulsed by Muller's lewd remarks, which he asked him to translate. He found them so disgusting he invented alternatives.

'Now explain to her what she will do for me and my Unterscharfuhrer! I'm looking forward to this. I haven't had a fuck in a long time,' he cackled. 'Go on tell her!'

Scarlet with embarrassment and anger the young major whispered to the anguished young woman. 'I apologise for this, but he wants to - to have sex with you. You may find it easier than another beating.'

She nodded and began to cry. Muller and his Unterscharfuhrer had already unbuttoned their trousers and stood in front of the girl taking it in turns to feel her breasts and maul her thighs, making her wince. Muller dropped his trousers to his ankles.

'Tell her to kneel in front of me!'

'Now open your fucking mouth, you stupid bitch. How am I going to get my cock in?' he yelled.

'Go on Major von Langdorf, tell her!'

Freddy whispered. 'There's no need for me to tell you what he wants to do.'

Tears rolled from the girl's eyes. The Unterscharfuhrer stood behind her grabbing her jaw and holding it open in a vice-like grip, while his boss pushed his erect penis hard into her mouth. Immediately she gagged and Muller's penis and testicles were covered in vomit. His assistant leapt out of the way suppressing a snigger.

Muller, raging, slapped the girl hard, furious that an army major had not seen him achieve a climax of sexual pleasure. Instead the major had seen his manhood covered with the contents of a French stomach; humiliating even to one as insensitive as Muller.

The interrogation over, the girl sent away, Muller and his Unterscharfuhrer went off to clean themselves up, giving Freddy the opportunity to search.

In the desk drawer was a list of about twenty French names that he assumed would be Muller's next trawl, and copied them quickly into his pocket book, ready for delivery into appropriate hands.

The evening of the concert was cold and wet, so Catherine and her mother let themselves out through the kitchen door into the courtyard and walked across to the west wing's entrance. The eating hall was warm with a blazing log fire, and the drinks table displayed no shortage of anything. This time there were more black uniforms in evidence. During Freddy's solo piece, part of a Brahms piano concerto, he avoided a glance from his muse, aware of SS eyes. Afterwards, kissing Catherine's hand very formally, he whispered,

'Here comes the pig Muller. Be polite, but go soon. I'll come to see you later.'

Muller strutted up to them, his gold fillings dazzling.

'And who is your beautiful friend Major von Langdorf? Please introduce me.'

With set jaw Freddy muttered. 'Mademoiselle de Lazarin.' 'Obersturmbannfuhrer Muller, mademoiselle.' The fat man clicked his heels, picked up Catherine's hand, on which he placed two wet fleshy lips. She shuddered. It was the touch of a slug. He could make no conversation, only leered and breathed out, which was enough to make Catherine excuse herself hastily.

The family returned to their part of the chateau, talking about the concert and praising Georges for his beautiful interpretation of the only Wagner piece. Marianne was shocked at seeing so many black uniforms.

'If only they were all like Rudi, Freddy, and Kurt.'

'Well they are not, Maman. The SS are swine.'

As Catherine carried cups of coffee into the dining room,

Georges said, 'may I say, how very proud I was of the two women in my life. You looked lovely, both of you.'

Marianne was about to reply playfully, when there was a deafening sound of an almighty explosion. It came from somewhere in the west wing courtyard. Every window shook with force, followed by shattering glass. After a split second of shocked silence, there were shouted commands, and the sounds of boots on the cobbled courtyard.

Then the firing started. It seemed to be coming from the bank of garrigue behind the stable block. Georges ran into the kitchen, to the back door that led into the courtyard. Catherine shouted to her father.

'No Papa! No! It's a battlefield.'

Marianne, white-faced, clutched her daughter's hand, as they both chased after Georges.

The firing was gathering momentum. Catherine, pushing her father out of the way, made sure all the bolts were in place on the heavy old oak door.

'We can't stay here. Let's go into the salon.'

'No! Stay there, Marianne. Don't move! We'll put out the lights.'

In the dark they climbed the stone stairs to the landing window. Rain clouds had cleared and a bright moon shed a cold light over a shocking scene.

Three black Mercedes, and an army truck, were twisted into unrecognisable heaps.

The explosion had occurred just as the main body of guests were taking their leave through the narrow vestibule leading to the west wing's entrance. The force of the explosion had blasted into the building, throwing many waiting personnel on the floor. Immediately, armed troops had been marshalled to surround the near vicinity.

Kurt sought out the two doctors in the evening's audience, but apart from swabbing a few grazes, their services were miraculously not required. Muller, in a fury, and vowing vengeance, put a call through to Nimes for a replacement car.

The de Lazarins could see a solid line of German soldiers advance into the distant garrigue, shooting at an unseen enemy. One group ran towards the east wing's garage and hay-loft, shouting and taking pot shots at anything. Suddenly a volley from several machine guns rained down on the group from the raised rocky scrub behind the garages. Black shapes ran, crouching behind rocks, firing, leaping across open ground to vantage points. The German posse clambered, giving chase into the dark scrub-dotted landscape. The de Lazarins stood mesmerised at the window, hardly daring to move lest they should attract a bullet. Gradually the firing around the chateau subsided. The battle had been drawn away into the garrigue. No one knew the terrain like the resisters. They would all be safe now.

'Come along my dears. Take Maman into the study, Catherine. Let's try to calm down a little.' Georges slipped away briefly to inspect the windows. He came downstairs, checked the dining room and salon, and then crossed the large entrance hall. Such was the sound-proofing of the chateau's walls, he was completely unaware that the chase was returning to the chateau, and armed resisters pursued by German military were already running up the gravel towards the front entrance intent upon killing each other. Bullets in their dozens were spewing from weapons as Georges opened the chateau's massive door. Suddenly there was crossfire within metres of the portico. Bullets struck stone, and ricocheted. Georges shouted as he fell. His cry brought Catherine running from the study.

She and her hysterical mother pulled his crumpled body into the hall and shut the heavy door. He was still alive, but bleeding badly from his leg and chest. Medical help was needed quickly. She grabbed cushions, and plugged the bleeding with kitchen cloths. No doctor could possibly be called from Uzès with a battle still raging outside. Marianne sat on the floor by her husband holding his hand against her cheek. Her hysteria had now evaporated into cold shock.

Catherine wasted no time. 'I'm going through to the west wing - through the connecting door. I know where the key is. I'll find Freddy. Stay there!'

Marianne nodded her head, marmoreal, cold, staring.

Unlocking her way into the west wing, Catherine tore along the landing corridor and down the staircase into the enemy quarters, shouting,

'Major von Langdorf!'

He was outside supervising the removal of wrecked vehicles from the courtyard. She had almost reached the west wing's ground floor before he heard her. When he saw Catherine's flushed face, her neat chignon tumbling onto her shoulders, her cream dress heavily stained with blood, and her bloodstained arms, his heart almost missed a beat.

'Quick! It's Papa!'

Dr Gebhardt from the Uzès garrison was in Kurt's quarters. The short, stocky doctor grabbed his medical bag and ran with Freddy and Catherine down into the entrance hall, where Marianne sat cradling her husband's head. Georges was cold, and drifting in and out of consciousness.

Dr Gebhardt examined Georges' chest.

'Is it the lung, doctor?'

'I'm afraid so, mademoiselle.'

The doctor probed gently. A copious amount of blood flowed from Georges' wounds. More sinister was the ugly trickle that oozed from the corner of his mouth. Freddy fetched bowls of water to swab, and mop up blood. The doctor took off his jacket. 'He should really be in hospital. The bullet has gone through his left lung. It has to be removed.'

Marianne pleaded. 'Please doctor won't you do it – please.'

Dr Gebhardt looked at Freddy and Catherine. 'If you can help me, mademoiselle.'

They carried Georges into the kitchen on an army stretcher, and laid him on the table. Marianne insisted on remaining, so

Freddy persuaded her into a chair, where she sat silent and shivering.

Catherine held the chloroform cap, and Freddy boiled water to sterilise instruments. Once the artery clamp had stopped some of the bleeding, the doctor carefully extracted the bullet from the lung. The leg was seriously damaged, the fibula shattered just below the knee. Georges' pulse was weak, his skin the colour of yellow parchment.

'We shall have to hurry if your father is to stay alive, mademoiselle.'

Catherine was too dazed to speak. Freddy gave her arm a reassuring squeeze. The second bullet was embedded in the shattered bone, and extraction was more difficult. When all was over, they covered Georges in a blanket, on the makeshift operating table.

Dr Gebhardt sat down exhausted on a kitchen chair.

'Well mademoiselle, if your father survives, he will still have his leg, but only one lung. I'm afraid he needs a transfusion. He's lost too much.'

The doctor took off his glasses and rubbed his eyes.' Do you know your blood groups, mademoiselle?'

Catherine put her hand to her forehead. 'Papa is A, we are B.'

Rolling up his sleeve Freddy said.' I'm A, doctor. Take it.'

As the syringe needle punctured his arm, Catherine grasped Freddy's hand tightly. They waited in silence while his blood passed into the dying man. Georges was carried on the stretcher into the study. Freddy lit a log fire and helped Catherine make up comfortable chairs for mother and daughter's night vigil.

The doctor shook his head. 'We can do no more. He is a very sick man. I'll call tomorrow, and we shall take him to hospital.' He paused. 'You must be prepared. He may not survive.' Looking at Freddy he added. 'And you major, must rest now, that is an order. I shall see your colonel on the way out.'

When she hugged him goodnight, by the connecting door, Catherine noticed bloodstains on Freddy's uniform jacket and began to tremble.

He held her tighter. 'Do you want me to stay?' he whispered.

'No. You must rest.' She kissed his cheek. 'Dear Freddy - you have done so much .You may have saved his life. Thank you.'

Georges survived the night, but his pulse became weaker. Catherine knew her father was slipping away. At six a.m., Freddy arrived.

'We have a car to take your father to Uzès. Dr Gebhardt has already spoken to them.'

Rudi had volunteered to drive, and was waiting outside with the car. When he saw Marianne he said nothing but gently patted her hands. In the study, just as Catherine and Freddy prepared to ease Georges on to the stretcher, Catherine suddenly gasped. 'Oh God! Papa! No! No!'

A guttural sound was vibrating in his throat. She dropped to her knees beside him. There was terror in her eyes as the guttural sounds increased, only to be silenced by a long exhalation of breath. Catherine stared at her father's lifeless body, with wide eyes and disbelief. Her tense trembling fingers touched Georges' yellow cheek. She listened to his heart, felt his pulse again and again. She gazed at Freddy in bewilderment. 'He's dead! Papa! - He's dead! He's dead!'

Vulnerable and afraid, her hands grasped his shoulders, as if to shake life back. She shouted through her tears, 'Papa. Don't leave us! Not now! Please! Come back! Don't die, Papa! Come back!' She buried her head next to his lifeless face, and sobbed her breaking heart away.

Freddy, eyes stinging, kissed her tear-stained cheek. 'I'll fetch your mother.' Moved and perplexed, the young major stood outside the study and took a deep breath. This was his first real encounter with death. Catherine followed, dark circles under red-rimmed eyes, her dress a blood stained rag, she half stumbled towards her mother, who stood waiting to take her sick husband to Uzès.

There was no need for words. For minutes the two women stood clasping each other tightly.

Rudi took Marianne into the study, and stood outside while the grief-stricken woman bade farewell to her husband of thirty years. What a waste of a great fellow were Rudi's thoughts, but then war was a total waste.

Outside, the portico still bearing traces of Georges' blood, Catherine stood, a forlorn figure. Freddy took her hand. 'Come and take some air.' They stepped down into the gravel drive and walked through Georges' rose beds. She shook her head. 'It's a nightmare Freddy. Tell me it will all go away.' He put his arm around her shoulders as once more tears shook the slender body.

When they returned to the steps of the portico they saw it.

On the lintel, scrawled in large black letters was the ugly word:

'COLLABORATOR'.

CHAPTER EIGHTEEN

The word COLLABORATOR scrawled on the portico realised Catherine's worst nightmare, but one that had to be put aside for the living nightmare of organising her father's funeral. Marianne under sedation spent hours talking to Monseigneur Dufort, the parish priest, but his words of comfort did nothing, and could not touch her broken heart.

Catherine was her rock now.

Catherine had taken on the yoke of chatelaine.

When Georges' body lay in the chateau's private chapel, surrounded by four large candles in impressive ancient candlesticks, their flickering flames bouncing on yellow stone walls, Catherine would kneel beside her beloved parent, stroke his hands and weep that they would never more make beautiful music, that the children she would one day have would never know him.

Georges de Lazarin was buried on the estate, in a piece of consecrated ground used by the de Lazarins for generations. The orchestra sent flowers, and a concert to commemorate Georges was planned for some time in the future.

Through a local resister's family, a sympathetic and consoling letter from Max was handed in secret to the grieving mother and daughter.

Evidence suggested Georges' death had been a terrible accident, for although the bullets extracted had been German, the resistance used stolen German weaponry. The scrawled word on the portico was far more disturbing.

'Catherine, why would your father have been called a collaborator? Any ideas?' Freddy stretched out to put another log on the fire.

'The orchestra. Nothing else. The raid was probably a retaliation for Montaren.'

'Muller thinks there is another link.'

She felt a little stab of alarm in the pit of her stomach. Catherine was convinced it was Gaston who had organised the raid and Gaston who had scrawled on the portico.

Freddy returned to the floor cushion placed next to hers. 'Muller's looking for a close, even a family link. God help the chap he finds.'

He put his arm round her. 'My lovely Catherine,' he whispered. 'Promise me you will never get in Muller's way.'

'Why on earth should I?' She tried to sound confident.

One late evening, a few months after Georges' death, Freddy returned from Nimes, and stood in the chateau's hall, cap in hand, grim faced.

'We have to speak, Catherine!'

He shut the study door and slowly, without a word, took off his greatcoat and ran his fingers through thick blond hair.

'What's happened? It's Muller isn't it?'

He gathered her in his arms. 'He's arrested a prominent member of the resistance, Gaston Martin.'

Catherine caught her breath.

'It gets worse. Muller already knows he and his family used to work here. I didn't realise he was Mathilde's son.'

She sat down, her legs trembling. 'Has he been - interrogated?'

'Tomorrow. And -'. He punched the palm of his hand for emphasis. 'The bastard wants me as interpreter.' Freddy leant on the mantelpiece. 'Muller is salivating like a hungry wolf.'

'Is Gaston so important?'

He shook his head dismissively. 'Don't you see? Muller hates me as much as the French Resistance, therefore will try to get at me through you.'

' How?' Catherine's throat tensed with fear.

'Look, he has caught someone who used to work here, so he'll stop at nothing. He could force Martin into confessing any rubbish and use it. Forget about truth. It's dead, murdered like Muller's victims.'

They stared at each other in silence. 'If only his name had been on that last list.'

'I've known Gaston since he was a little boy,' she said pointlessly.

'It's your safety I care about. Muller knows more I'm certain.'

'Surely, if I've been accused of being a collaborator?'

'No no! Muller is convinced the word and the bullets were meant only for your father.'

The next morning Major von Langdorf reported for duty in the interrogation rooms at the Hotel Silhol in Nimes, where Muller was already at work screaming shrilly. Shortly the glass door was kicked open and the Unterscharfuhrer beckoned Freddy inside. Gaston was sitting on a chair, under a bright lamp, long legs sprawled out, arms hanging limply. Across his cheeks Muller had already left his trademark, deep weals, raw red. With matted beard and his face unshaven, Freddy perceived fear and defiance in the young man's eyes. It was hard to believe this was Mathilde's son, whom Catherine had known all her life. It was as if a de Lazarin were sitting there. Gaston recognised Freddy immediately as the officer in the garage. In a far corner, a younger officer saluted when Freddy entered.

'He also speaks this language,' said Muller dismissively 'and I want to make sure your translations are not lies!'

He picked up a truncheon, and struck his prisoner across the cheek, splitting skin down to the bone, as the Unterscharfuhrer grabbed Gaston's hands. 'Who else is involved Martin? We want names, names, names!' Muller screamed. Freddy translated through the young man's groans as blood poured from the wound.

Gaston thought of his dead mother, and in his head he vowed on her memory that whatever they did to him, he would never disclose Mademoiselle Catherine's involvement with her cousin and the resistance.

By the end of the day, as Gaston lay in a bruised, bloody heap, he managed to utter ten names. Muller wrote them on a sheet of paper which he placed in the desk drawer. But Gaston's names were either of dead comrades, or inventions. Not satisfied, Muller, purple with rage, his tie loosely knotted around his thick neck, shirt collar unbuttoned, face running with sweat, ordered his Unterscharfuhrer to take the prisoner back to the cells.

'If you have given false information, tomorrow you will have such surprises, today will seem like a holiday!' he snarled.

As Gaston staggered out of the room, manacled, bruised and swollen, Muller straightened his tie, and addressed Freddy.

'I want you here by seven thirty tomorrow morning Herr Major. You too.' he barked to the young Lieutenant. 'Tomorrow you toy soldiers will see how real soldiers deal with lying enemies. Tomorrow we shall have real information.'

He smiled, fleshy lips parting to reveal, as usual, details of his diet.

'It should be of great interest to you, major. Personally,' he added, with an evil simper.

It was seven a.m.and only one bleary eyed guard to check Freddy's I.D. at the HQ's back entrance. He went straight to Muller's desk and found several pages of names and hideout locations, copying into his pocket book as many as he could before leaving and re-entering via the front entrance.

Gaston was stripped completely naked for the morning's interrogation, which began by a dozen lashes to his back. As he lay with his face on the floor, arms tied behind him, barely moving, Muller turned him over with a kick, and shouted in his ear.

'That's how we say 'Good morning' to those who lie to the Fatherland!

You swine! Every name you gave us was false, a lie! So today we shall twist the truth out of you.'

The Unterscharfuhrer approached with what looked like a large pair of forceps with two metal half cups set wide apart. Vicious-looking serrations of small steel teeth formed the cups' outer edge, which could be drawn together by closing the scissor handles. Muller laughed.'We call this the little nut cracker!' Gaston's feet and then his hands were tied together, the cups placed around the young man's testicles, and grasping the scissor handles together, Muller's henchman began to twist them - slowly.

The two interpreters looked at each other in horror. Gaston began to groan as the twisting increased, until Muller yelled, 'Halt!'

His victim lay rigid, unable to move, perspiration pouring down his agonised face. Freddy turned away. Muller cackled,

'Too much for you, toy soldier? he yelled. 'I need you to interpret, if you please. Ask him how well he knew the de Lazarin girl?'

Freddy stood frozen. Muller laughing, took a large swig of water out of the glass on his table, gargled, and spat it out over Gaston's face. 'Ask him if he was fucking her?'

The young major had never wanted to kill anyone until now. The fat man grinned. 'Why do you hesitate? Have you both been fucking her? Is that how she gets her information? Ask him!' he thundered.

Gaston's face puckered into a gasping denial. 'No! No! No! De Lazarins my bosses. No! No! No!'

A particularly vicious twist, and Gaston's back arched in agony. Muller knelt down and screamed into his prisoner's ear.

'Then why did Catherine de Lazarin visit you when you worked at the Hotel Terminus?' Freddy closed his eyes and prayed that Gaston could hold out.

'To get news of my mother - she worked for them,' the young man panted. Muller stomped around the room like a petulant child. 'I don't believe him! And your father, Jacques Martin, still works for the girl doesn't he?'

'I - I don't know. I don't know!'

That was absolutely true. Gaston did not know.

Muller pulled the prisoner's face up to his own.

'She gives your father information, which he passes on to you. Right?'

The scenario had turned into a nightmare. 'Tell me!' Muller roared.

The same questions were repeated, the twisting increasing as the prisoner screamed out the same explanations and denials. How long could the man endure such agony before he confessed to something, anything, true or false. Gaston admitted he scrawled on the portico, but he insisted Georges de Lazarin's death was an accident. No Frenchman would have shot him. For Muller, it was unimportant, one Frenchman less. He nodded to his Unterscharfuhrer who twisted the forceps, stretching the delicate skin to bursting point tighter and tighter until it split and bled profusely, leaving angry gashes cut by a dozen sharp steel teeth. Gaston lost consciousness.

The lieutenant interpreter rushed from the room, and into the lavatories in the corridor. Freddy followed him out and leant against the wall of the windowless storeroom, and pressing his forehead against the damp surface for a little cool comfort, whispered, 'God, if you are in Heaven, help me. Help me. Help me.'

When Gaston had been shaken back to life, the interpreters were recalled.

Muller was going to try another route. A deep bath of urine was brought in. He now wanted the name of a local resistance leader, and by way of encouragement Gaston's head was plunged into the stinking liquid and held down for increasing lengths of time, Muller giving him just long enough before starting again. Finally with his lungs almost bursting, Gaston's body and spirit had reached breaking point. His head swam, but his thoughts were coherent enough to recall questions and answers. The Boche knew nothing about Mademoiselle Catherine. They knew nothing about his trip to Nantes. He would give them Max Becker's name. No harm in that, because Max had already changed his name anyway and was working with Jean Moulin, and de Gaulle, probably in London now. 'Max Becker,' he gasped finally.

Muller shrieked for joy. 'And a Jew, too!'

The Girl on the Promenade

Freddy was astonished at Muller's ignorance. How could he not have known the name of Moulin's second in command? The courageous man had in fact given nothing away.

Major von Langdorf shouted to the Unterscharfuhrer, 'Can't you see your methods have finished him, you fool?' The lieutenant, white and trembling, rallied to Freddy's side, and together they pushed Muller's henchman out of the way, laying Gaston down on his stomach, Freddy attempted artificial resuscitation while the lieutenant massaged his lifeless limbs.

Muller was apoplectic.

'How dare you! If you do not stop interfering with the work of the police department, I shall have you both arrested for insubordination, and charged with treason!' he screamed.

The henchman stood transfixed, watching his superior officers actually defy someone as important as Muller. Urine and blood poured out of Gaston's lungs. Cracked ribs and pressure had been too much. There was no life left in his broken body. Freddy glared at Muller. 'He's dead.'

'Sod him! I've got what I wanted, a name.'

The patrician looked down his nose at the peasant, and said quietly.

'One name, after two obscene days. Only one name?'

'This is only the beginning Herr Major,' Muller intoned, parting his fleshy lips.

'I can promise you that.'

Freddy did not disclose to Catherine what took place in that torture room, but simply expressed his admiration for Gaston's courage. The two young people sat silently holding hands, in the firelight.

'Oh God, poor Jacques!' Catherine said suddenly. 'What will happen now? The family hostage law?'

'My guess is Muller will do nothing, hoping to catch the next resister who tries to make contact. What's the phrase - a sprat to catch a mackerel?'

'Supposing there are no mackerels?'

'He'll focus his attention elsewhere.'

He took out of his jacket pocket the lists he had copied that morning.

'Take it, and for God's sake hide it. Perhaps the mackerel will be on it.'

Catherine put the lists in her secret drawer while Freddy reflected upon Muller's unhealthy interest in the de Lazarins, and his lewd questioning.

Putting his arms round Catherine as she sat gazing at the logs burning in the grate, he kissed her cheek warm from the firelight, and whispered,

'I would want to die if Muller ever - '

She put two fingers to his lips. 'Forget about dying, Major von Langdorf.

We have had quite enough of it here.'

Resistance activity in the south was increasing; therefore the French Milice was inaugurated in Nimes at the end of January, with pomp and ceremony, their role, to aid the SS in the destruction of the French Resistance.

On a Saturday morning, in Uzès, at the beginning of March, Catherine sat at a table in the Bengali drinking coffee, waiting for an exchange of information. Tables of grey uniformed German troops pointedly ignored conspiratorial clutches of black uniformed SS sitting on the outer edges. When she had finished, her bill read, *Monday 2 p.m. Fountain Gardens.* She carefully wrapped Freddy's lists inside a paper note, for payment, and stuffed the bill in her pocket.

It was a brisk March day as Catherine walked through the iron gates of the gardens. The sun shone warm, with summer promise, chilled by a sharp breeze that lapped around foliage and trees.

Max was sitting reading a newspaper on one of the stone benches, and beckoned to her. She would hardly have recognised him, for a thick black beard enveloped the lower part of his face. They hugged like a pair of old friends, while grey uniforms strolled by taking the afternoon air.

'It's been so awful Max. Papa,' she sobbed.

'I know - I know. Terrible for you little cousin.'

They strolled arm in arm towards the stone steps that wound around the foliaged hillside. Catherine recounted details surrounding Georges' death, even to a German soldier giving his blood.

'You are lucky you've met the one good German. By the way, the last list you passed to Etienne was brilliant. We managed to get at least half into hiding.'

He gave her a sidelong glance. 'Who gives you the info?'

'My secret,' she replied.

Max knew Gaston was dead. 'And your officer, Catherine - the major. What's his role?'

'I - I only know he has to be an interpreter,' she mumbled.

'Of course. He has his orders. The war is full of people who are only carrying out their orders,' he snapped.

'Disobey the SS, and your life is over; so why waste it when you could be of help?'

'Help? Do you honestly believe your major would help you and your mother?'

She shrugged dismissively.

They talked about the family in Vichy. Simone was not well and apparently had aged considerably. The general deprivations of life, a small apartment, food shortages, no domestic staff, no son, were for her the intolerable components of her new existence. Max, his name now changed to Jean Pierre Soulas, had been on a month's visit in February to London with Jean Moulin, and met de Gaulle. He was appalled at the extent of the Luftwaffe's destruction of the city, but surprised there appeared to be no real shortages. They were working on the formation of a National Council of the Resistance. The General was insistent upon breaking up the various factions.

'By May we'll have our first meeting, in Paris.'

'Under the Boche's nose?'

Max grinned. 'Where else?'

The war in North Africa was not going well for the Fatherland. Soon after Erwin Rommel was recalled to Germany, the British and American forces linked up in Tunisia. Futhermore, an attempt on Hitler's life, organised by officers of the Wehrmacht, had failed.

Carl telephoned his nephew.' I need a break from stuffy Berlin.'

Freddy laughed. 'Then come to the sunny south - immediately.'

'Can you fix me up with a couple of rooms?'

'Of course.' Freddy paused. 'You'll be two?'

'Yes,' Carl replied curtly. 'Be seeing you,' and put the receiver down.

Carl was not his usual jovial self. He was quiet and reflective, and spent several hours incarcerated with Kurt in the latter's quarters. On the second day of his visit the other guest arrived, a Major General, of the old Prussian school. Carl proudly introduced his nephew. 'Major General Henning von Trescow, Major von Langdorf'.

No one heiled Hitler.

At dinner in Kurt's quarters, to which Freddy had been invited, conversation ranged over a number of topics. Von Trescow was a gentle, serious man with a conscience. At one time he had been a farmer, so immediately he launched into common farm experiences with Freddy.

After the meal, with Freddy tactfully dismissed, the three men sat heads down over the table, caressing brandy glasses. Conversation had to be low and muted. Von Tresco sat between Carl and Kurt as they talked about the failed assassination plot. The Major General put his head in his hands and sighed. 'It was perfect - everything according to plan. At Smolensk, just before Hitler took off, I took the package, squeezed the detonator, and gave it to Brandt who put it with the luggage. The damn thing froze up. Had to get rid of it in Berlin. Thank God it was harmless.'

They drank, smoked, and thought in silence, for some time.

'It's uncanny,' said Carl eventually. 'That monster seems to have the devil's luck. Or else he is beginning to be suspicious.

Have you noticed how many times he changes his plans at the last minute, changes cars, or takes another route?'

'And how many carefully planned attempts has he thwarted?' Kurt growled. 'By the way, has either of you seen Erwin since he's been recalled from North Africa? Is he one of us yet?'

Carl waved his hand in a gesture that conveyed uncertainty. 'Let's say Erwin's sympathies are with us, but it is unlikely he will ever be pressed into action.'

Henning von Trescow cut some grapes off the bunch lying on an elaborate plate. 'He has had several stand-up rows with Hitler over strategy, so I suggest, my friends, we wait and see on that score.'

Carl rose from the table, and refilled glasses. 'A toast! Gentlemen, let us drink to the success of our ongoing attempts to rid our nation of a devil incarnate, and bring Germany back to sense, and dignity.'

They talked into the early hours not only of the assassination of Hitler, but for the overthrow of the regime, and an immediate government replacement. While the Allies had so far dismissed overtures for peace, they felt sure that once Hitler was dead, terms could be negotiated.

One evening towards the end of March, Freddy arrived to spend the evening with Catherine. It was a regular practice now to give Catherine any names he found scrawled on bits of paper, in Muller's desk or his coat pockets. Leaning against her chair, she ran her fingers across his forehead and gently massaged his temples in the soporific firelight. She loved this man, despite his uniform, which branded him as an enemy. Briefly she wondered what it would be like meeting him after the war. But it was unwise to speculate on the future. Expect too much, and you could die of despair.

Freddy stirred and turned over to face her. He kissed her hands.

'That was great - soothing. I needed it.'

Uncharacteristically, he rose to turn off Brahms, and stood looking into the fire. 'Eleven young men are to be guillotined next month. I don't have their names, but in any case it's too late to do anything about them. They are already imprisoned. Condemned by your Milice and our Gestapo.'

Catherine was horrified. 'It's barbaric! Can't we do anything?'

'No.'

Her eyes filled up. 'What a world!'

'Come here', he said drawing her down on the cushion beside him.'Do you realise how lucky we are, that despite all these horrors, we can still share moments of calm and happiness?' He took her hand and pressed it to his cheek. 'I want to share more than that with you Mademoiselle Catherine, because I love you so much - so much.'

Leaning over her, their mouths met hot and passionate. They clung together, arms entwining. His hands moved down to her breasts, and, loosening the buttons of her blouse, he stroked and kissed her. Delicately he caressed her thighs, but when his hungry kisses followed, burning into her golden skin, their passion began to reach a point of no return.

'No, Freddy!' she gasped. 'No! - We can't. I'm so afraid.'

His face was hot and flushed. 'Afraid? Why?'

She gently pushed his hair off his forehead. 'Freddy, I want you more than anything in the world. It's an aching need for you. But I'm afraid.'

Kissing him lightly on the mouth, she said, 'I'm afraid because it could be taken away - in an instant.'

'I know, I know. But I want to be part of you - you to be part of me.'

He traced her profile with his finger.'The thought of being without you - ever - drives me crazy,' he sighed. 'But maybe you are right - maybe we shouldn't just snatch at happiness. We have the rest of our lives.'

He leant over and fumbled in his jacket pocket. He pulled out a little leather ring box, and opened it. With his familiar crooked grin he said.

'You will marry me won't you, Catherine?'

He explained how he and his mother were given the pair of rings and of his mother's wishes. Although Catherine had sensed how they felt about each other, here was a real commitment from Major von Langdorf, heir to the Langdorf estates, and in the midst of such turmoil.

'Yes, I will marry you Freddy, but -we make no plans. Plans mean pain.'

'That you will marry me is all I ask.'

She held the ring up to the light. 'It is so beautiful.'

He stroked her hair. 'Like my future wife,' he said placing the ring on her finger.

'May I wear it?'

'Only when we are alone. Muller's already spotted mine, and we don't want him jumping to the right conclusions'.

When German forces in North Africa surrendered to the Allies, Kurt was in a foul mood as he poured out coffees in his quarters. 'Spread out all over bloody Europe we were no match for the combined forces. Erwin warned him.'

Freddy looked out of the window on to the courtyard, hands in pocket.

'The Roman Empire! Does history teach dictators nothing?' He turned to Kurt. 'Is this the beginning of the end?'

The colonel began to 'doodle ' on a piece of paper. 'I - think it could be, old son, and God help us all. Unless.' He paused. 'Unless something can rescue our country'.

'Just tell me, I'll do it.'

The older man smiled. 'Who knows? Maybe a miracle will happen.'

Without thinking, Kurt had drawn Hitler's face with moustache and lump of hair, which at least made them laugh.

To lighten their gloom still further, Freddy told him he had asked Catherine to marry him. The colonel was naturally delighted. She was a plucky little thing, and beautiful. He was also grateful to her for keeping his young officer sane. A bottle of champagne was found and they drank to the future.

When Freddy left, Kurt wondered what future? He picked up the photograph of Erika and the children. 'At least I've loved, made a home, and had my wonderful kids.' He kissed the photograph, and sat down heavily with a glass of schnapps.

'Damn sight more than the Freddys of this nation - God bless them.'

His eyes were damp as he drained the glass.

CHAPTER NINETEEN

Since the invasion of the South, and Georges' death, Catherine and Freddy were even more aware they should not be seen together. The balmy days of early summer had to be confined to the conservatory, which for a couple of hours each afternoon, played host to the Provencal sun, with the advantages of a cool marble floor. Open windows facing east were shrouded in fine muslin, and allowed complete privacy from any prying eyes.

Catherine, though acknowledging her feelings towards Freddy, felt the commitment to sharing a future was no more than a surreal dream. In a perfect world, she would already have met his parents, and a date would have been set for the wedding, with all the attendant paraphernalia. Now it was little more than a temporary anchorage, but dreams of the future, however unreal, gave their relationship a flimsy stability.

'Will you wait for me if I'm a prisoner of war?'

They were sitting on deck chairs in the conservatory, sipping fresh lemonade. Catherine stretched languidly. 'Of course I will.'

He rose from the deck chair, and walked slowly across the marble floor. In the doorway, he stopped to gaze at nature's glorious palette. Fields of poppies cut boas of flaming red across a golden dazzle of sunflowers, cooled by lavender blue. Beyond, Roman tiled rooftops of village houses clustered in groups, dissolved into the heat hazed distance, and the foothills of the Cevennes. Who could ever doubt this land was a painter's Mecca; a Mecca that could hold you in thrall for the rest of your life. That this would remain to enchant and inspire when the Mullers of Europe had been destroyed, was a consolation. Freddy was feeling tired, but was enjoying this rare afternoon break. For weeks he had been cooped up with Muller in Nimes, and watched a sickening procession of victims.

He thought about Erich, his old friend, dark curls flopping on his forehead, singing high soprano at college reviews amidst helpless laughter. Would he ever see him again? He leant his head against the cool doorframe.

Each day there were new Allied victories. Kurt was right, there would have to be a miracle.

'Supposing - supposing there will be nothing left to go back to?'

Catherine propped herself up on an elbow. 'How do you mean? Where?'

'Germany. Schloss Langdorf - everything?'

'Then you stay here, and become a lecturer in archaeology at Montpellier, just until I've finished my medical degree. Then we'll go off to Crete, where you can dig, and I'll be the medical officer to the team. How's that?'

'Suits me fine,' he said, kissing her hand and the tip of her nose. However far-fetched, the very idea was sustaining.

In early August at the Bengali café in Uzès, pushed under her coffee cup, Catherine received a note on which was scribbled an address, together with date and time of a rendezvous, in the rue Jean Jaurès, in Nimes. She guessed it was Etienne's apartment.

It was on the top floor of an imposing nineteenth century block built in the grand Parisian Haussman tradition, with high ceilings heavily decorated with plaster mouldings. Most of the doors were double, and tall floor to ceiling windows overlooked the broad avenue, with a corner view of the Roman Gardens. She had always had a romantic notion of large city apartments. There was a certain *élan,* in having elegant balconies and a secluded tree lined square, particularly if the Faubourg St Honoré were only a step away.

Etienne's apartment was a total mess, despite its elegant shape. However, rectifying the flat's interior was a peacetime activity, and certainly not Catherine's objective today.

The young scientist was in a state of suppressed agitation. Max was due at the flat for their rendezvous and he was late. Etienne said very little, pacing backwards and forwards

The Girl on the Promenade

between two tall windows, looking at his wristwatch, never exposing himself completely, because there were rumours that members of the Gestapo, with binoculars, were permanently seated at the windows opposite. By the time Catherine had brewed a jug of coffee Max had arrived. His hair and thick beard were grey. 'My God! Max what's happened to you?'

'Don't worry little cousin,' he laughed. 'We have a resister who was a make-up artist in films. Tomorrow I shall be black again!'

Max and Etienne had been involved in a raid the night before, which had not gone according to plan. In the disarray that followed, a number of French had been killed and too many had been captured.

There was a reason for this meeting with Catherine, but first Max gave her the big news. The French Resistance had been officially and successfully united following a meeting in Paris, and two weeks later Max had accompanied Jean Moulin to Lyon. While Max went on to a pre-arranged meeting, Jean Moulin had an important rendezvous with prominent resistance leaders in the city.

The young doctor paused for a moment of recall staring vacantly at his slim delicate fingers as he locked them tightly into a cat's cradle.

'There was a tip off - God knows how, or who. Jean had only been at his rendezvous minutes when the Gestapo stormed in - took them all.'

'Oh no!' Catherine looked at her cousin's taut jaw, and the furrows across his forehead. Etienne poured a large cup of coffee for him, spilling drops of the hot brown liquid in the saucer then crossed to the curtains, peering out through a small gap. 'It's O.K. Don't worry,' he whispered. There's a fire escape through the corridor.'

Max patted his cousin's arm. 'They aren't as clued up here as they are in Lyons. Barbie 'the butcher' and his men are a special breed.'

Catherine spooned dried milk into her coffee, thinking of another similar breed. 'And Jean Moulin, Max? What happened?'

'He's dead. Tortured to death.'

No one said a word.

Max lit a cigarette and silently watched his smoke rings as they floated high over the table, dissolve into thin grey wisps.

'He told them nothing,' he said quietly. 'Not even his name until the end - the very end.'

He spread out his hand across his face and with thumb and forefinger, dabbed his eyes. 'Jean was a wanted man, and he was afraid they would continue to torture others - anyone - until they found him. So finally, he had to tell them.'

With his cigarette end Max pushed the ash in the saucer set beside him into abstract patterns. 'One of our chaps was sent in to shave him. It was he who told us. Jean was barely alive. Blue weals on his temples, broken bones. Christ knows what they did. He asked for water. Fortunately the guard wasn't S.S. so he got it.'

Max lowered his head and, puckered his eyelids. 'They put him on a train for Germany - what a catch, eh? The leader of the French Resistance. But it was Jean's victory in the end, not theirs. He died on the way.'

Once more they sat in silence. There were no words to alleviate the loss. Max, now officially co-ordinator for the south, had learnt to put aside personal feelings and get on with the business in hand.

'Now little cousin, the reason why you are here; a road convoy of several large vehicles transporting tanks, plus heavy supplies of ammo, will be leaving the outskirts of Paris.' He looked at Etienne. 'When?'

'Beginning of September.'

'It will be coming south to Marseilles via Nimes.'

'That's a long way round,' said Catherine.

Etienne took a cigarette from Max's packet that lay on the table. 'They'll be dumping some off in Nimes.'

Catherine looked from one to the other. 'Why?'

'They're afraid of a south coast invasion, little cousin. But we want to get the convoy before it reaches Nimes. And this is where you come in. They will marshal every soldier stationed in the vicinity to guard this little number. We have the route so we know it will be crossing the bridge in Collias.'

Etienne grinned. 'And it won't get to the other side because we'll be blowing it up as it crosses.'

'So, d'you want me to set the charges?'

Max laughed at the note of alarm in her voice. 'No Catherine! We just want you to tell us the moment you see the chateau Fritzies setting off for some collective duty.'

'But how will I know where they're going?'

'You'll ask,' he grinned. 'You have the makings of a very good spy, young lady. Look at those fantastic lists you give us! So I have every confidence you can wheedle information out of your young major, at least!'

Etienne chuckled. 'We'll blow the damn lot up this time, Fritzies and tanks. You'll see.'

Catherine smiled uneasily. 'Supposing I can't get the information.'

'No problem. We have reconnaissance groups posted all along the route. You'll simply be providing back-up intelligence to be passed on in the normal way.'

'I have some good news for you,' said Max just as she was preparing to leave.'By the end of September we shall have a field hospital just behind Anduze, up in the garrigue.' Putting a hand on her shoulder and smiling broadly, he said, 'We'll need you!'

Catherine threw her arms round her cousin. 'At last! Thank you, thank you, Maxi! Shall I see you there?'

He shrugged. 'Perhaps. Two months is a long time. Anything could happen. When we're ready you'll be contacted.'

Driving back to the chateau she thought about war and greed; about Max, and Freddy. She felt sure they could have been friends, and longed to be able to tell Freddy about the hospital and of Jean Moulin's death at the hands of another set of Mullers. The prospect of actually working at last in a field hospital was exhilarating, but to ferret out intelligence about Collias bridge activities, was not. The problem nagged and worried. Finally she stopped the car, pulling up in an isolated lay - by.

'*I am merely a back-up intelligence*', she told herself. '*The resistance will know exactly when the convoy will be crossing the bridge because the explosives will be placed the night before. Therefore what will be the point in telling them something they already know?*

Good! She had absolved herself from a Mata Hari role, but what if Freddy were to be posted to the bridge?

She prayed it would be a Muller day for him.

One hot evening at the beginning of September, Freddy and Catherine were sitting in the conservatory playing a game of cards, a game it seemed they had both played as children. It was Catherine's turn to deal. Freddy stifled a yawn. 'I hope it's like this tomorrow.'

'Why?'

'Some exercise down at Collias. I'm going to take my swimming trunks, just in case.'

Her stomach turned over.

Hiding behind the hand of cards, she asked lightly. 'What about your usual rendezvous with Muller?'

Freddy laughed. 'He can't have me, thank God. Kurt's orders, and he's my colonel!'

She thought desperately of reasons, something, anything to stop him.

Still appearing engrossed in the cards her mind stumbled into a half-formed idea.

'What a coincidence. I'm going to Collias tomorrow, to make sure Sylvie, Jeannine, Hortense, Madame Dufours, and anyone else I can find, will be available for the *vendange*.' She threw a card down.

'Be careful. The bridge will be closed to civilians for a while, maybe a few hours.'

'I'll have to chance it, won't I?' she smiled. 'Anyway, I can also take a swim.'

In her room later, panic set in. How could she find out the expected time of the convoy's arrival? How could she warn Freddy? Would he leave his post the moment he saw her car?

Unlikely. Unless something was amiss.

She paced her room, and sat at her desk, thinking. She remembered the story Max told when he and his parents were fleeing from Paris. Something about immobilising the car. That was it! She would immobilise the car on the bridge, hold up the convoy, and if Freddy saw her he would surely come running. But with so many 'ifs', the idea was crazy and fraught with danger. She found the driver's manual for her little Citroen. Robert had been an automobile fanatic, and had always used his sister as junior mechanic whenever he tinkered with the family's cars. She would have to stall the car on the bridge, jump out quickly and immobilise the engine before grey uniforms surrounded her. There was always the grim prospect of being shot at first.

The diagram of the engine showed a small nut holding the ignition wire on the coil. If she loosened the nut just enough before starting out, she could twist it off with her fingers in a couple of seconds on the bridge, and lose it in the engine. It was going to be a frightening chance to take, but Freddy's life depended upon it. She lay awake that night turning over and over in her head the precise sequence of events that had to happen in the dangerous scenario she was planning.

The next morning, within five minutes of the chateau's troops leaving the west gate in lumbering army trucks, Catherine raced into the garage, opened the car bonnet, made sure the nut was loose enough, and set off through local back roads to Collias some twenty minutes away. She parked the car in a small copse on a secondary road that joined the main highway leading to the bridge. Several troop carrying vehicles had already arrived and had parked up on the bank clear of the road. She spotted the chateau's trucks on the opposite side of the road closer to the bridge. Civilian cars were still crossing without a problem, for this was an important link route to Nimes. Catherine ran through the thickets and peered along the main road to the bridge. As yet no barricades had been set up. An officer looked at his wristwatch. Orders were shouted and foot soldiers began to assemble at both ends of the narrow bridge. There was no sign of Freddy, though he had to be there, somewhere. Two civilian cars were now approaching the area. When she saw them halted by armed guards, and their papers checked, there was no time to lose. Quickly she drove the Citroen towards the check-point, pulling up as a corporal approached. 'Papers, mademoiselle.'

Her heart thumped as she passed her documentation to the grey uniform, trying to smile sweetly. Someone from the bank barked a command.

'Yes sir,' the corporal replied. 'Sorry mademoiselle, you will have to turn back.'

A blast of icy terror gripped her body. She had to try wiles, anything, to get on that bridge. 'Please officer, it's for the *vendange*, you have my permits. The workers are waiting for me. I'll be very quick.'

He threw her papers back. 'You'll have to wait.'

Through the mirror she could see the car behind her had already been turned away and a solid phalanx of armed troops had appeared, lining the route, all the way back to the road junction. Just then she saw Rudi, and called to him,

'Can't you let me cross, Rudi - please?'

The car in front had now just reached the other side of the bridge.

'Sure,' he replied.'If you're quick.' Rudi addressed the corporal. 'Let her through. We know her. We've got five minutes anyway.'

To Catherine he whispered,'the major's down on the bank somewhere. I'll tell him you're here.'

Trembling, she began the drive across the bridge. Her damp hands slipped on the driving wheel. Where was Freddy? If he were anywhere near the river bank, the explosion would kill him.

With no other vehicle on the bridge Catherine was surrounded and watched by dozens of armed men. Weapons were poised, waiting, silent, suspended in ice-cold tension. Only a few metres underneath tons of dynamite were waiting to be detonated by resisters secreted somewhere in the pitted rock face and thick copses flanking the river. There were no troops on the bridge, suggesting the convoy was expected to be too wide for guarding personnel. Catherine took a deep breath to calm her quivering body and pounding heart. The halfway point had been reached. *'This is it! Here we go'*, she muttered to herself. In three seconds she had stalled the engine, leapt out, and pushed up the bonnet. Just as her shaking fingers had lost the nut, and pulled away the connecting wire, a dozen feet came running. *'Schnell.!...Dummkopf Fraulein!'*

A bewildering assortment of ranks ran noisily towards her. She looked round frantically for Freddy. A soldier shoved her away from the raised bonnet and inspected the engine. He found the loose connecting wire.

'Ein minuten,' he snarled, and began twisting the ends of the wire, but to little effect. Another inserted the handle and tried to crank the engine. Another jumped into the driver's seat, and attempted to pull the starter button. She heard Freddy's voice. He came running towards her, followed by Rudi. Showing no outward sign of acquaintance, he ushered her into the driving seat, and shut the door. Lowering his head through the open window and giving a mere flick of a wink, he said, 'Steer your car if you please, mademoiselle. We'll push you to the other side.' He turned to the armed group. 'Two of you will assist Sergeant Schmidt and me to push the car. The rest return to your posts and quickly!' he barked.

Steering across the empty bridge Catherine felt like crying for joy. Her crazy plan was working. Freddy would be safe on the other side. The fact that Rudi could also survive was a bonus.

South of the bridge the river sliced through a deep ravine, which climbed on both sides, to meet vast expanses of garrigue spreading as far as the eye could see. Etienne crouched with three resisters behind a rock, overlooking the scene. At that distance all they could see were Boche soldiers gathered round a stationary car driven by a woman.

'For Christ's sake hurry up you silly cow,' muttered one of them through his bush of a beard. Etienne laughed. 'Patience Henri. The Boche also want her off that bridge pronto. Concentrate on Michel.'

Michel was their vital lookout, positioned dangerously near the underbelly of the bridge. As soon as he gave the signal, the sticks of dynamite, hidden in foliage on the twin banks, and secreted in the bridge's iron arches, would be detonated by resisters hiding in a copse lower down the slope. Throughout the night they had buried fuses in dry river gravel and soil, the water level being no more than half a centimetre. During the morning from their lofty eyrie, they had watched the Boche inspecting the site. They were lucky.

It had been a cursory inspection.

The perspiring uniformed troupe pushed the Citroen to the other side of the bridge where the village street with houses, café, church, and more troops, twisted and climbed out of sight. Catherine realised that Freddy could quite easily run back to his men, once she was safely pushed off the road but finding a suitable parking even for her small car took longer than anticipated. Finally Freddy spotted a small alley at the side of the café.

'In here. Quickly! We must get back.' He poked his head into the open window. 'Put your break on, mademoiselle. I will see what our mechanics can do later. Meanwhile stay here.'

Frantically she wondered how she could delay him a little longer. With another sly wink, he turned to go. Just then, Rudi who had stepped out to view the scene shouted. 'Too late. The convoy has already reached the bridge.'

Freddy shrugged. 'Then we stay here.' And they joined a thin line of armed guards along the village street. The pounding in her chest had perceptibly eased, so Catherine walked a little way into the road along with patrons of the café, to see what all the fuss was about. An impressive procession of tanks on open trailers, and sealed trucks which presumably contained munitions, rumbled slowly towards the bridge centre.

Behind the rock Etienne and his comrades watched and waited for Michel's signal. 'Jesus! Four- five- six tanks! What's he waiting for? Come on!'

Etienne turned to his bearded companion. 'He's waiting for the sixth tank to reach the middle. Orders.' Three men watched in tense silence as the rolling fleet of weaponry crunched across the bridge.

Michel signalled.

Etienne whispered excitedly.'That's it! Go on lads! Vive la France!'

Somewhere below them, hands poised on plungers, pushed and prayed.

Freddy and Rudi were half way down the village street. Freddy turned to search out Catherine, and they exchanged brief smiles.

At that moment, both earth and sky were suddenly rent apart, again and again and again, split, blown into a million pieces, shattering bodies, limbs, heads. It was deafening, terrifying, like a vast aerial bombardment. Debris, pieces of machinery flew into the air and landed on troops, crushing and maiming. Above the noise of explosions human screams and shouts struggled to be heard. Twisted metal cascaded over the village street. Civilians and soldiers alike threw themselves on the ground. Some lay, pinned down under vehicles upturned by the blast.

Minutes after the series of earth splitting roars Freddy and Rudi lay on the road, covered in dust. Freddy's first thoughts were of Catherine. He looked up the street and could not see her. He felt his scalp tingle as he staggered up the hill to the café. Around the entrance a few bodies lay on the ground, with grazes and cuts, too dazed to move. Others had been hit by large pieces of shrapnel. Some who had remained inside were bleeding from shards of flying glass, and all were in a state of numb shock. The sun which minutes before had shone so brightly in an azure sky had been eclipsed by dust and smoke, turning day into night. The acrid smell of cordite stung nostrils and throat. Catherine's car lay on its side. A few yards away, thrown against the wall, she was lying quite still, bleeding from a gash in her head. He ran to her side, and cradled her in his arms, angry that she had been wounded by her own people. 'Catherine, Catherine darling,' he whispered.

She stirred, opening her eyes. 'It's - it's just my head.'

She drifted into a hazy semi-consciousness, while he made her comfortable, and arranged with the café to gather up as many local doctors as possible for the wounded. Down the hill he and Rudi assisted in clearing the havoc, while smaller explosions continued relentlessly as more ammunition ignited. Army patrols combed the hillsides and dozens clambered down on to the river-bed to rescue injured men. Finally the old bridge gave way, plunging its mangled cargo deep into the dry gravel.

A quiet summer afternoon had now become an inferno. Flames from the explosion spread over dry bracken coating the river's steep banks. Underneath the bridge lay the body of Michel.

The Gestapo would force no secrets out of him.

A French doctor drove Catherine back to the château, rallying a stunned Marianne to the task of caring for her daughter.The incident provided the catalyst to shake the widow out of her solitary confinement that was becoming rather more self-indulgent than recuperative.

Hours later Freddy arrived at the chateau, his uniform torn and grimy. Catherine was in bed with her head bandaged. He marvelled at her remarkably high spirits. 'It's nothing,' she smiled. 'Just a bit of a headache.'

'Sorry I'm so dirty. Even the river hadn't enough water.'

'Who cares? You're safe, Freddy. That's what matters.'

She sank back on the pillow her dark curls peeping out of the turban bandage.

He touched her cheek. 'I must go. I haven't seen Kurt yet. There will be sheaves of Army reports.' At the door he stopped.

'Thank you for saving my life, Catherine.'

She opened her green eyes wide. 'Did I?' She smiled ingenuously. 'It was just chance Freddy, my car; just chance'.

'We're going to be crawling with bloody SS and Gestapo after this.' Kurt poured out another glass of wine. The colonel and his major were having dinner privately in the senior officer's quarters. Freddy had already written up the report to be sent to Berlin. 'I suppose you saw Muller?'

'And hundreds of his garrison. They combed those hills like an army of ants, I watched them.'

Kurt cut a slice of cheese. 'Did they find anybody?'

'Apparently - three or four resisters, connected with the sabotage.'

Freddy broke off a piece of crispy baguette. 'Better if their own had dispatched them.'

'Their own? Is that something new?'

'Seems to be. Resisters are likely to be shot by their own chaps before they are summoned a second time to Gestapo HQ. They certainly can't risk a third visit.'

Kurt replenished his glass of wine. 'Drastic don't you think?'

Freddy shook his head. 'I'd rather be shot cleanly by a partisan than endure Muller's slow death.' He spread a thin covering of margarine on his bread, and picked an olive from a bowl on the table.

Kurt gazed thoughtfully into his dark red wine. 'I suppose everyone gives something away, eventually. The Gestapo's powers of persuasion are particularly innovative, aren't they?'

'Yep! That's why the important chaps carry cyanide pills.'

'Who doesn't?' Kurt dabbed his mouth with a napkin. 'So how many men killed?'

'About fifty in all. Our chaps were particularly lucky. The trees shielded them from blast and most of the debris.'

'And Remer?'

'He wandered down on to the bank, against orders I should add.'

'Serves him bloody right then.' Kurt rose, and stretched his legs.

'Isn't that where you would have been - the bank?'

Freddy nodded.

'Then you're damn lucky your good fairy came along in her car at that precise moment, aren't you?'

'Very.'

'And that her car just happened to break down as she was crossing the bridge. Good timing don't you think?'

'Chance,' he replied with exaggerated nonchalance. 'A lucky chance.'

Reflecting on the unlikely odds of Catherine's car breaking down at that precise moment, it was obvious she knew in advance. Saving his life was brave of her, but she was playing a dangerous game.

Freddy hoped to God no one else would draw similar conclusions.

CHAPTER TWENTY

In October, Fascist Italy surrendered and changed sides.

In the east, Kiev had been recaptured and the Soviet Army was liberating Mother Russia.

Kurt seemed to be spending more time in Berlin, apparently dining with Carl.

The truth was far more perilous.

Kurt, Carl, von Trescow, and a dozen more conspirators were painstakingly piecing together a plot to assassinate Hitler which von Stauffenberg, an officer from an old titled family, and lately severely wounded, had volunteered to carry out. Although the common denominator amongst the conspirators was a detestation of the regime, and their leader's megalomanic bungling of military strategy, a number of the Prussian hierarchy had problems with conscience and sworn oaths of loyalty to the Fuhrer. The realists had no qualms. The crucial step was orchestrating both time and opportunity.

During one of Kurt's Berlin trips, the French Resistance blew up a section of Nimes barracks and badly gashed Milice HQ. Muller was out for blood. Arrests were made on mere pretexts, followed by pummelling interrogations, at which Freddy had to be present.

One evening, after a brutish day in Muller's company, a weary major sat in his colonel's office and gratefully accepted, 'A restorative glass old son! So what's that bastard been up to now?'

Freddy grimaced. 'He gets worse. Two weeks of interrogation and all his victims are innocent. He's beating up old men and women - armed guards mounted round the room. The man's a lunatic!'

Kurt sighed. 'Berlin is crawling with them.' He pushed a fresh baguette and some cheese across the table. 'Eat! You look like you need it.'

'After two shameful weeks Muller's had only one tip off. That was from a Belgian, a plant.'

'Will that keep his blood lust assuaged for a while, d'you think?'

Freddy raised his glass and shrugged. 'There's a new armed group of resisters in the Cevennes; a massive raid last night. Several Frenchmen killed or wounded. Prisoners are being sent to Germany. So in answer to your question, yes, that will probably satisfy him until the next time.'

Kurt sliced into an apple. 'Can't ever rely on a madman.'

The following morning at SS HQ in Nimes, Muller greeted Freddy with an unusually affable leer. He was sitting, sprawled at his office desk, bejewelled fists clenched on the desktop. 'Now major, I shall not be requiring your services for the next few weeks, at least.'

As Freddy turned to leave, the overweight black uniform rose from his chair.

'Just one thing major, I know very well you disapprove of the methods I use to obtain the truth out of these peasants.' Freddy was stony faced.

'But they work, and very successfully too.'

The patrician regarded the lout with utter contempt. 'Do they?'

'You remember that little bastard Gaston Martin, worked for your French bitch at the chateau? He gave me the name of a resistance leader.'

He looked down at a paper lying on the desk. Freddy feigning interest peered at the piece of paper, but there was only one name.

'Max Becker – Jew.'

'So?' Freddy snapped.

The leer spread wider. 'So Herr Major, we have traced his family. For the moment, he, of course, has disappeared.'

The Girl on the Promenade

'How do you know he isn't dead?'

Muller's small eyes narrowed. 'Dead? Don't be naïve Herr Major. He's in the mountains somewhere - new identity - new papers. But we shall find him.'

He thumped the desk so hard, pencils rolled off and fell on the floor, paper clips danced in the air. The leer on the face of the fat Obersturmbannfuhrer, returned. 'And you know what? You are going to help me. Heil Hitler!'

Marianne had retreated into a state of neurotic anxiety. They had not heard from Simone for weeks and since Vichy was now sending a percentage of its own French born Jews to camps in Germany, Catherine was anxiously waiting for a rendezvous with Max.

One warm Saturday morning at the end of October a note was scribbled on her coffee bill at the Bengali.

'Monday evening, Anduze-Nimes crossroads nine o clock. Leave bike in ditch. Wait for ambulance.'

This had to be the hospital.

Her body tingled with nervous exhilaration.

Fortunately Marianne retired early to her room now the nights were drawing in, therefore Catherine would also retire early to her room, to pursue medical revision. Freddy would be told likewise. It would be the only way she could leave the chateau unobserved.

She carried her bicycle and a small medical bag through the rose gardens, treading the crunching gravel with care in the silent evening. Cycling to the rendezvous, she hid the bike in a ditch as instructed, and waited. When a lumbering German Army Red Cross ambulance appeared, she thought it was an ambush, until the young man in the passenger seat called,

'Get in the back, mademoiselle. If we get stopped lie on the floor.'

In his late twenties, he wore a white coat, and on his lap sat a large medical bag.

From somewhere inside the van another man, a *maquisard* she assumed, with a gun slung across his shoulder, shuffled over to give her a helping hand over stretchers and boxes of equipment. The young man in front turned round, and smiled.

'I'm Francois Gerard, an old friend of Jean-Pierre, like you I believe.'

It took her a moment, to remember Jean-Pierre Soulas was Max's new name. 'Oh yes! Catherine de Lazarin.' She leant over and shook his hand.

'Are you a doctor?'

'Uh - Huh. Uzès hospital. And you?'

She felt embarrassed. 'Well - not yet. I was in my third year. So maybe I won't be much use to you.'

'Of course you will be,' he said reassuringly. 'Jean-Pierre speaks very highly of you. Says you'll be Surgeon-General one day.'

Almost into Anduze, the driver took a sharp turning, completely hidden from the road. They climbed steeply through rocky garrigue, the ambulance frequently teetering on the edge of sharp precipices. The so-called road was no more than a stony path for hikers. The other passenger took out a packet of cigarettes. 'Mademoiselle?' His voice was gentle.

'No thanks monsieur,' she smiled.

'Henri,' he grinned, *'maquisard,'* confirming he was also a resistance fighter.

He held out his hand politely and shook hers. 'We need you, mademoiselle.'

'Catherine,' she prompted.

'Good.' He seemed pleased with this immediate informality.

Under normal circumstances Catherine's upbringing would never have allowed her to drop the strict formalities of social etiquette. But circumstances were not normal. 'Where are we going Henri?'

He paused and pointed a finger. 'Up there,' and chuckled. It was a smoker's gurgle, throaty and rasping. By now the pale moon was shedding its light over the stunningly beautiful terrain, sliding stealthy shafts that bobbed like searchlights into the van's interior. Catherine could see Henri quite clearly now.

His hair was short and grey, and around his chin several days' stubble was combining into a beard. He looked about fifty, older than the average age of a *maquisard*. Deep clefts lined his face, and his toughened hands fondled his gun as they would a pet dog. In the moonlight Henri's foxy pale green eyes shone as they darted over the landscape, missing nothing.

The ambulance pulled up in a small clearing on one of the many plateaux. Henri jumped out. 'We must walk the rest, Mademoiselle Catherine.'

The driver shook hands with them, got back in the driving seat turned the vehicle round and leant out of the window. 'See you here at four o'clock.' And drove off, shuddering down the rock-strewn path.

Catherine walked between Henri and Francois Gerard. 'Don't the patrols come up here?'

'So far, no,' Henri rasped.

'You're always safe with him, Catherine,' Francois assured. 'Henri knows every rock, every bush, cave, tree and pathway between here and the Auvergne. And what's more he knows every *sanglier* personally and by name.'

Henri chuckled. 'I have all their calling cards.'

Wild boars, the *sangliers* could be a dangerous hazard in this terrain.

They climbed still higher, over rough garrigue. Finally they stopped, and Henri pointed to what appeared to be a solid piece of rock face.

'Welcome to the palace!'

Leaving him sitting on a flat piece of stone, on guard, Dr Francois Gerard pushed aside some bracken that Catherine had taken for a natural bush, and walked into the rock's interior. With the help of a pocket torch she followed Francois Gerard carefully along the shale littered ground, and around a dark corner where several kerosene lamps had been placed on various levels throwing pools of illumination over cleared areas. Beams of diffused light bounced against irregular walls, picking out runnels of moisture, which oozed sluggishly like a sepsis, and collected in pools on the cave floor, creating muddy mounds. The air was dank and fetid. Catherine shivered, and wrapped her coat tighter around her body. Walking a few paces in front, Francois Gerard stopped at an obscured opening in the cave wall, across which two thick white sheets had been securely draped. Pulling them back, he stood aside for his new colleague. Catherine blinked in amazement. The cave hospital had the dimensions of a cathedral. Electric generators had been fitted to provide plenty of light, and basic heating. The walls had been white-washed as far as was necessary, and indeed possible, for they seemed to climb upwards to a black infinity. Rush matting covered the floor, and a familiar hospital smell of strong antiseptic had successfully banished any other odours. Aluminium saucepans of water bubbled with instruments on a battery of electric rings, and a couple of battered glass fronted cupboards provided storage for instruments. A deep porcelain sink, served by one tap, and propped on bricks, drained into a mound of sand behind another white drape. Nearby, a dozen or more buckets were grouped. A low murmur of voices could be heard coming from an assortment of hospital screens pulled together, serving as an operating theatre. A young blond of about twenty-one, slight, small and pale, wearing a white apron, her hair tucked under a little white cap, was bent over one of the beds dressing a leg wound, and placating the unshaven young occupant who winced noiselessly. Her large blue eyes looked up as she gave her doctor colleague a brief nod of recognition. Eight men and two women, stretched out, fully clothed except for their boots, lay half covered in grey blankets. One young man, heavily bandaged across his head and one eye, was moaning quietly. Some were sitting up smoking.

'It's extraordinarily quiet,' Catherine whispered. The young doctor smiled. 'Right now maybe, but not when they're brought in after a raid. It's mayhem! But we generally try to keep as quiet as possible. You never know who could be crawling around up there.'

The screens parted. Max, in bloodstained white coat and stethoscope around his neck, walked out, and crossed briskly to them, arms outstretched. Seeing her cousin for the first time in months, Catherine was once again shocked at his appearance. He had lost a considerable amount of weight, his face was drawn, and his eyes, heavily ringed, had sunk further into their sockets.

'Welcome, Mademoiselle Catherine', he said quite formally, pecking her on the cheeks. 'It's good to see you Jean-Pierre', she responded. 'Thank you for asking me here.'

Francois Gerard donned his white coat and took over behind the screens, while Max led Catherine outside to the dank passageway.

'Uncle Louis. Anything happened? Maman is desperately worried', she whispered.

Max lit up a cigarette, leant against the cave wall and rubbed his eyes.

'They've sent Papa to Dachau.'

'Oh Max! Because he's Jewish?'

'No! Because of me. You do realise that don't you? I have sent my own father to a death camp.'

'How could they have found out about you?'

He inhaled, tensing up his eyelids into narrow grooves. 'You are quite sure your Fritzies know nothing?'

'God! No! I'd give my life! I have never, ever, used your name.'

She was becoming so agitated he put a placating arm on her shoulder.

'Calm down, little cousin. I asked, that's all. I know how easy it is. Probably tortured out of some poor devil who knows me.' He inhaled impatiently on his cigarette. 'Now you can see the importance of dispatching people before the pigs get at them a second time. Second time around, everyone cracks.'

'Then it is true. You do kill resisters.'

'Grow up Catherine! What would you prefer? Face an agonising death in the hands of the Gestapo or SS, and probably cause the death of a comrade into the bargain or- '. He pulled the cigarette from his mouth. 'Or be killed quickly by one of our bullets? Think about it, and remember it is not a decision we take lightly.'

It made cruel sense. Max had this irritating ability to make her feel completely juvenile. 'Do the SS know what you look like?'

'No. But that doesn't help Papa. Only the dead leave Dachau,' he mumbled.

He spread a palm across the bridge of his nose pressing the corners of his eyes. 'I'd so love to see mother. Try to comfort her, talk to her. It's all a bloody nightmare little cousin,' he murmured. 'What happened to those honeyed days on the Boul 'Mich, the arguments, the laughter? The promise that was ours, was everyone's?'

He tugged at his stethoscope. 'All in the past. Finito!'

For the first time Catherine saw her always positive, always in charge cousin without hope, wretched.

'No Max! No! Once the Boche is out we'll start again. And we're winning, so come on!' She put her arms around his shoulders. Damp cheeks brushed in the eerie kerosene silence, and hearts shared memories of Robert's death, of Georges' death, and now the present fear for Louis' life.

'We need you, Max. France needs you, as Jean Moulin did.'

He smiled wistfully. 'You have to be right, Catherine, and I have to believe it.'

'I am right! You can't let us down now. We shall win!' she snapped.

It was her command this time.

He put out his cigarette, smiled, and touched her cheek. 'Thanks. Personal sorrows are luxuries we cannot afford. O.K., young doc, I shall have to go very soon, so let me show you round.'

Throughout the night she swabbed wounds, changed dressings, washed bandages, tore up old sheets, prepared cups of coffee and chocolate. Each of the small medical team did what had to be done. There was no hierarchy here. The young blond nurse, Annabelle, was from Uzès. She had been trained in Montpellier, so she and Catherine immediately had acquaintances in common. Annabelle had disappeared into

The Girl on the Promenade

the hills, to help out at other medical stations, but was now the cave hospital's only full-time nurse. On days off she could walk up to the *maquisards'* hut, deeper into the garrigue, in comparative safety. She showed Catherine her small cubicle, tucked away behind an outcrop of rock. Beside the bed was a locker, on which stood an electric lamp, and a pistol. Running her fingers along the barrel, Catherine asked,

'Have you ever used it Annabelle?'

The young blonde's delicate features broke into an elfin smile, puckering her pert retroussée nose. 'No. But I would, if-'. She shrugged.

From time to time they each stopped to talk to the patients. Resisters far from home, living a life of tension and danger, needed to talk, if only to get messages through to their anxious families.

It was also a time to renew collective courage.

At four a.m., Henri appeared. Catherine and Francois followed him outside to the ambulance standing in the dim dawn light. 'Is Annabelle going to be on her own today?'

Francois nodded. 'It's safer that way. Anyway, most of the action takes place under cover of darkness, so she can get her well-earned kips in the day!'

Catherine was energised by the fact she was at last doing something practical for the resistance. She looked forward to Monday and Friday duty nights, and talking with Annabelle. The two young women had an instant rapport. Annabelle was particularly good at light-hearted banter with whichever patient was the joker, and there was always one. Laughter, telling jokes, often risqué, listening to naughty songs, all blunted the sharp edge of fear, for everyone. Sometimes Catherine and Annabelle would sit on Annabelle's bed and hold their sides with laughter recalling an incident, a story, or a salacious song. Like a couple of schoolgirls, for a brief moment their world would glow again with the irresponsibility of youth. A youth that fate had stripped away, projecting them all too abruptly into a dangerous adulthood, for which they had been unprepared.

Catherine noticed Annabelle and Francois were close.

'We met in Montpellier - in the same team. I was eighteen and Francois was in his final year. We fell in love. Been together ever since. Montpellier to mountain. Romantic isn't it?' Her pert face was radiant.

Catherine was the first to congratulate them when they quietly announced their secret marriage at an isolated village Mairie in the Cevennes.

'But when all this is over, we'll have a huge wedding in Uzès Cathedral.' Annabelle, put her arm round Catherine's waist. 'And will you be my bridesmaid, Cathy?'

'I'd be honoured, Ma'am', she replied with a curtsey, and meant it.

She wished she could have told Annabelle of the young German officer with whom she had fallen in love, who was helping the resistance, and who wanted to marry her. These days Muller kept Freddy so busy in Nimes he and Catherine could meet only when circumstances permitted, and there were stolen lists of names to pass on.

After a raid when the wounded arrived at the 'hospital', often in droves, the team worked frantically. But they could do only what their equipment allowed, and it was not a lack of expertise that caused a death.

During the early hours of one quiet Tuesday morning, Catherine espied Henri beckoning from the ward's entrance. He called her outside.

'Problem, mademoiselle Catherine. I've found a young Kraut, not much life left in him. Been on the mountain for a day or two, looks like; hardly conscious. What am I to do? Dispatch the bastard?'

'Of course not! I'll call the doctor.'

Crossing the rush matting to Francois and Annabelle in the operating theatre, Catherine reflected on the medical care her own father had received from the enemy camp.

'We cannot shoot him, Henri,' said Annabelle simply.

Catherine agreed.

The Girl on the Promenade

Henri scratched his stubble. 'Ye-es. But what if he brings the whole damn garrison back here, my loves? We'd all have had it then.'

Catherine looked at Francois, who was deep in thought.

Henri put his hands on his hips. 'How do you know he wasn't sent up here to spy on us? If he knew the way up here first time, he'll sure as hell find it second time. Shoot the bastard, begging your pardon ladies, that's what I advise.' He turned to François. 'What do you say, Doc?'

Francois threw his hands up in a gesture. 'I am bound by three things, my Hippocratic oath, the Geneva Convention, and my feelings as a human being, therefore I have to be against shooting the fellow. So -.'

He hesitated, looking from one to the other. 'We'd better have a look at him.'

Annabelle gave a half smile and a nod of approval to her new husband.

They made up a bed for the German soldier in a hidden area of subterranean rock formation leading off the main passageway. It formed a perfect ante-chamber, solving the problem of security. Ten minutes later, cigarette stuck to his lower lip, Henri appeared carrying the semi-conscious soldier over his shoulder like a sack of potatoes.

Heinz Gollner was an army corporal, of twenty-three, from Austria. Judging from the photographs they found in his pocket he had climbed and skied from an early age, along with the rest of his family. Stretched out on the hospital bed, he was of average height with a mop of brown hair. His emaciated body drifted in and out of consciousness. The one phrase he whispered in German over and over again was 'Help me! Help me!'

Catherine and Annabelle were quite shocked at the state of his shattered right leg, broken in three places, the tibia splintered as though from a heavy blow. When his coat was removed they found a bloodstained tear in his jacket, and a deep hole in his rib cage, which was bleeding profusely.

Francois examined his patient. 'He's been bleeding for some time; amazing he's still alive. A *sanglier* must have given chase, he stumbled and the animal attacked.'

Several hours later corporal Gollner was warmer, his leg set in plaster of Paris, and the hole in his rib cage sutured and clean. Sedatives were helping him sleep away the pain.

Annabelle and Catherine sat together by the young soldier's bedside, their hands warming around hot mugs of ersatz coffee.

'Do you want to get married Catherine?' Annabelle pulled a face at the coffee's bitter taste.

Catherine smiled. 'Well yes - eventually I suppose.'

'You'll finish medical school first, won't you?'

'If they'll take me back.'

The little blonde nurse picked up the jug of coffee. 'More champagne?' She giggled. Catherine held out her mug.

'You're going to be a fine doctor, Cathy.'

'Thanks. I just wish I knew more, right now.'

'So what's your prognosis on young Fritz?'

'I think he'll be standing with a crutch in a day or two, but I reckon his climbing and skiing days are over.'

Annabelle looked down at the youthful face and brown hair.

'Not fair is it? They are all so young - him - those in the ward. Hardly lived.'

Lowering her voice, she looked at Catherine, fear brightening large expressive eyes. 'Sometimes I get scared - not for me - for Francois. I love him so much, if anything happened to him, I wouldn't want to live.'

Catherine gave her new friend a reassuring hug. 'Hey! Nothing is going to happen. You'll have lots of kids and live till you are ninety.'

A smile spread across the earnest little face. 'Anything you say, Doc.' They stifled giggles like adolescent girls again.

The young German corporal was soon able to stand, with support. He had made a remarkable recovery, due largely to Annabelle's nursing, and also to being heavily smitten by his pretty little French nurse. He had found out her name, and would keep her by his bedside for as long as possible, recounting family stories in fractured French, making half serious romantic assignations with her .The fact they were on opposing sides in a bloody war did not appear to have entered his mind.

'Annabelle beautiful Annabelle, when you will come to Vienna, I will fill your room with roses, for you are like a rose, and then we will waltz. I show you how I can waltz - until dawn.'

'Annabelle, one day you meet my parents who treats you like a queen, and with great love, because you are saving my life. The whole village loves you, and I am so proud of you. Then I take you skiing, and we flies like birds across the white snow, with nothing between us and heavens.'

A perfect nurse, Annabelle could not help but respond sweetly and agree. Then she would pull the blanket over him, and he would drift into a contented sleep like a child. She knew the poor lad's waltzing and ski-ing days were over.

Late Monday evening, as the medical team and Henri gathered round a small radiator, Francois announced. 'We have to let young Heinz out soon. Already he'll be classed as a deserter.'

'Funny they haven't come looking,' said Annabelle.

Henri spat out a piece of cigarette paper stuck to his lip. 'They've only got a handful of troops in Anduze,' he rasped. 'They're not going to send a dozen men into the rocks, with the *sangliers* and our boys, are they? Not worth it for old whats-is-name.'

It made sense, but Catherine was worried. 'What's he going to tell them? They'll see he's been professionally treated.'

Annabelle put her hand to her mouth.' Oh! I'd forgotten about that.'

Francois thought for a moment. 'First of all I don't think he has any idea about what really goes on here. In any case he's always pretty well knocked out before any action starts. Don't worry, I shall find out precisely how he's going to explain away his absence.'

'So how do we get him out?' asked Catherine.

Francois poured himself a small glass of wine. 'Henri takes him down to Anduze, in the van, blindfolded.'

The following day, in the early hours before dawn, Annabelle and Francois carefully helped the corporal onto crutches. Already he could hobble a few paces. Francois warned him against carrying anything heavy until his chest had healed completely.

Heinz Gollner believed he had been injured unconscious on the outskirts of a remote mountain village, and thereafter brought for treatment to the village's primitive clinic. He remembered very little.

Just before the blindfold was put on, the young soldier whispered tearfully. 'Thank you, thank you, a million times Annabelle. I love you. I wish there is no war.'

Henri knew every rat run for miles and in a small deserted street on the opposite side of town, at the foot of an identical mountain, the soldier was carefully taken out of the vehicle. Keeping his promise and his blindfold until the ambulance pulled away he was left on a grassy mound with some bread and half a bottle of water, much to Henri's disapproval, thinking this treatment quite unnecessary for an enemy Kraut, but then, medicos were always a bit weird.

War exacted its toll from everyone. When the injured were brought in after a raid, Catherine would hear them talking about how many dead Fritzies they had left on the ground, and how many they had wounded. Although she joined in their enthusiasm over these victories, she agonized privately over the real possibility that Freddy could be one of the dead.

Major von Langdorf spent Christmas Day with his men. Morale was low. Resistance hunting had been taken over by Nimes, with Muller in charge. To be sent to the Russian front was every man's nightmare. The siege of Leningrad was about to collapse at any time, and God help the retreating army. He slipped away to Catherine's study to share a Christmas toast.

'Do you think you'll be posted, Freddy?'

He was sitting on the floor, his back against the wall. 'Well, - what use am I to the Fuhrer's war plans, hm? Muller needs me, unfortunately.'

She stretched out her hand and touched his.

'But that's fortunate, for me, isn't it?'

He looked down into his glass, and absent-mindedly swirled the brandy slowly round the sides. 'Muller brings no fortune to anyone. He is thoroughly evil, a murderer, and don't ever forget that.'

He put down his glass and held out his arms to her.'*Du bist so traurig mein Liebchen,*' he whispered. 'Which means, you seem so sad, my darling.'

She snuggled into his arms. 'Not especially, but I shall be if I have to learn German.'

'Well I think I'd like my wife to know just half a dozen words of my language.'

She turned her face up to his. 'And what will mein Herr do if I don't?'

His blue eyes locked into hers. 'Probably love you all the more. Till the day I die, Catherine de Lazarin.'

She put a finger on his lips and slowly shook her head. 'Don't talk about dying. Please! I can't bear it.'

The news on the BBC told Marianne that the invincible *Scharnhorst* had been sunk. 'I think the war must be slowly coming to an end. How this would have delighted dear Papa.' She paused for a moment, her eyes spiritless. 'I shall be sorry for one thing only, to see young Freddy go. A charming, delightful young man, impeccably mannered, but he is a German. Pity.' She gave her daughter one of those 'Don't you contradict me' looks.

'I'm quite sure you will also be sorry to see him go,' she continued. 'But you cannot afford to be inordinately sad at his departure, Catherine. You are French; you have your life to live here. He must return to his parents in Germany. Of course should fate intervene perhaps you may see him again, but generally soldiers are only too happy for a little light-hearted romance whilst away from home. Once back in familiar surroundings he'll soon find a young Marlene to brighten up his evenings, mark my words.'

Freiderich von Langdorf wrote to his son. Anna was suffering from increasing attacks of angina. For his father to bother to write implied a serious condition. He was therefore given leave for New Year. Never happy away from Catherine, this time Freddy was more concerned at having to leave her so uncomfortably close to Muller. He made arrangements to see her the evening before his early departure.

After aperitifs in the study before going down to dinner, prepared by Marianne, Catherine remembered a record she had left in her bedroom, one she wanted to play through the meal. Waiting in her study, Freddy quite naturally looked at photographs of Catherine's childhood and family dotted round the room. One photograph seemed to be wedged in the pile of books on a table. He pulled it out, and attempted to straighten it. His chest tightened with shock as he looked down at a photograph of two young men fooling around, assuming comic poses. One was Catherine's brother Robert whom Freddy recognised from other photographs. The inscription read;

'The two crazy cousins. Mad Professor Robert Einstein de Lazarin and Dotty Dr Max Freud Becker'.

He saw the name, Max Becker, and felt sick. Not because of Catherine's certain relationship with a wanted resistance leader, but what Muller could do to her, with impunity now. Quickly he stuffed the photograph into his pocket.

Later after dinner as they sat in the study, he said suddenly, 'Catherine, I don't know what you do when we are not together, and I don't want to know. I love you, and I trust you. That's enough. But please, please my darling do not take any risks. Muller needs no pretext. He grabs off the street. Should he finds a pretext, he's an animal.'

Her green eyes wide and innocent looked at him.'Why are you telling me this Freddy?'

'Because-because of who you are. Your family. You could become involved in anything, innocently, but that wouldn't worry Muller, and then - '.

He stopped, and drew her close. 'It's because I love you so much,' he whispered. 'You are my life. My reason to stay alive in this frightful war.'

She tightened her arms about his waist, and buried her head into his shoulder. Suddenly fear gripped her. 'I - I feel frightened, Freddy!' she whispered, her heart throbbing in an aching throat. 'What 's going to happen to us?'

There were no answers for either of them. There were no words of comfort. For the moment, they could merely hold on to each other, and hope for a miracle.

During the long train journey back to Germany, Freddy, awake or asleep, could see only Catherine's tear - stained face, and the fear in her eyes. The question he asked over and over again was, how much did Muller know?

By the time he reached Schloss von Langdorf, he felt his nerve ends had been shredded into a million strands.

CHAPTER TWENTY-ONE

Freddy's home leave was the perfect time for Catherine to introduce Annabelle to the chateau, and get her away, if only for a few days, from her dank underground existence.

'I take it your mother knows all about our hospital, Catherine?'

A mischievous grin spread across the pert face.

'My mother?' Catherine giggled. 'She'd faint!'

Annabelle sat down wearily. 'I love what we do here. Front line stuff and all that, but I'm really looking forward to a break.' She smiled shyly. 'I'm so grateful. So is Francois.'

'You need one. If I were your doctor I'd order it, so there!'

Annabelle tilted her head. 'Pale aren't I?' The slim blonde rose from the chair and nibbled at a piece of hard cheese, the remains of their snack. 'Actually, I look as though I've been dipped in a flour bag. All I need is a clown's costume.' Pulling a comic face, she lumbered round the bed, and puffed out her cheeks like a circus act. Annabelle would always turn a problem upside down, and laugh at it; one of the many reasons why Catherine found such joy in her company.

In the early hours, just as Catherine was about to leave the hospital, Henri burst into the ward followed by a small round middle-aged man, called Raymond. They carried guns, and were out of breath. Francois walked over to them.

'What's up?'

'Patrol,' Henri wheezed. 'Raymond's seen them.'

Raymond had a surprisingly light voice for his girth. 'Yep. Milice- on foot. Just turned off the main road, bottom of the mountain.'

'Many?'

'About twelve I think, Doctor.'

Francois looked at Henri. 'You've alerted the ambulance?'

'You bet.'

'OK. There'll be no lift tonight, Catherine. These two old foxes will take you home. Don't worry. They know every rock.'

'But what about you two and the patients?'

Francois patted her on the shoulder. 'Fear not. We have a contingency plan. Off you go. Leave your bag here. Safer.'

As they left, Raymond turned back to Francois. 'Scouts at every level. You'll have plenty of time.'

The two young women exchanged worried au revoirs.

There was no moon on the slippery garrigue paths. Only when unfamiliar sounds disturbed the silence did Henri and Raymond, with Catherine following, stop dead in their tracks.

After about half an hour, they paused in a clearing. Catherine sat on a piece of flat rock while Henri rolled a thin cigarette, burying his head in a thicket while he lit up.

'They are going to be safe up there, Henri?'

Henri chuckled. 'Don't you know about the emergency plan?'

'No.'

'Behind the hospital cave, are dozens more, identical. A labyrinth. It's a huge mountain with exits completely hidden. The tunnels and caves go on for kilometres. They've practised clearing everything out in fifteen minutes flat. Bit like a fire drill.'

'Will they get fifteen minutes?'

Henri nodded. 'Oh yeah. That's why we've got runners at every level.'

'All those tunnels and caves are well mapped out, I suppose.'

'Course they are. Don't worry.'

'What if the Boche detonated?'

Henri shrugged. 'Nothing's perfect, little one.'

Raymond was gazing intently into the semi darkness.'I think they are down there. We'll have to think of another route.'

Henri scratched his new beard. 'What about dropping to the road beyond the col?'

'Nope! There's a new Fritzy guard post just there. We'll just have to get down slowly. Come on.'

The stumbling descent continued for another half kilometre until Raymond whispered urgently, 'stop! Don't move! They are right below us. Be careful how you step. Any noise, they'll mow us flat.'

A distant babble of French voices could be heard.

'Shit', growled Henri.

'I'll draw their fire. Take them in the opposite direction.'

Catherine grabbed Raymond's arm. 'No! It's a terrible risk.'

The little man grinned, his teeth gleaming in the semi darkness. 'Mademoiselle, I know this terrain better than that lot down there. And I've done it before.'

'I've got a better idea,' Henri rasped. 'Take Catherine to one of the caves up top, and collect her when the coast is clear.'

She was beginning to feel totally useless. More than anything she wanted a gun, at least then she could feel equal to them.

'Just give me a spare pistol,' she pleaded.'I can get home alone. You have far more important things to do.'

She was ignored. Raymond's plan was put into action.

'Keep quite still while I go. Over there.' He pointed in the opposite direction. 'I'll make a noise. Animal, bird, - something like that. As soon as you hear me, run for it.'

Men could be shot for being out after hours. She took his hand. 'For God's sake be careful, Raymond.'

'Good luck, mate,' Henri mumbled.'Come on Catherine.'

She followed him up on to a flattish stone pathway, while Raymond moved off with the stealth of a panther. They waited.

A shrill animal cry, a distance away, pierced the night.

'That's him! Let's go!'

They scrambled and stumbled, Catherine following Henri like a faithful dog, while he helped her over outcrops of rock made smooth and slippery by the elements. Pausing briefly, the old *maquisard* chuckled. 'Half an hour, we'll be nearing the Uzès road. Get you home for breakfast.'

As they were about to drop down to the road, he stopped abruptly, putting his hand over his mouth. 'Jesus! Boche!'

Below them were the headlights of several armoured vehicles.

He wagged his finger to indicate silence. Catherine watched mesmerized like a rabbit as the vehicles, instead of disappearing out of sight, started to turn up an unmade road, in their direction.

' God!' he croaked. 'In a couple of minutes they'll have to stop. The road ends.'

Catherine felt her legs would give way. 'But what are we going to do?'

'Come on, follow me. There's one chance!'

Through Henri's detailed knowledge of the terrain, they gained distance between themselves and the pack of troops. He led her round the outskirts of a village to derelict buildings bordering a narrow river. Both banks were so overgrown with bramble and thicket the river was inaccessible.

'Sod it,' muttered Henri. 'Never mind, we'll go in through the barn.'

'Go in where?'

'The river.'

He did not wait for her answer, but made tracks for an old barn built across sturdy oak piles, rammed into the riverbed. The floor of the barn was covered in loose hay and heavy bales.

Henri uncovered a trap door, and lifted the iron ring to reveal the river itself. The level was high at this point, stagnant, and would undoubtedly be freezing.

'Can you swim?'

She nodded.

'Get in. Quick! Hang on to a support and get as far from the trap as possible. Hide your face. They'll flash torches. Remember to keep your nose above water. Go on. Hurry!'

Catherine lowered herself into the freezing water, and grabbed the furthest pile, slippery with algae. The water was so cold her heart almost stopped with shock. She clenched her jaw fiercely to stop her teeth from chattering, tilting face so her nose touched the underside of the barn's floor. Foul smelling detritus, sewage, and rotting vegetation floated and settled into her hair and eyes. She turned her face away from the trap door into the nightmare of fetid black. Henri not only shut the trap door after him, he cleverly managed to slide a heavy bale over the ring.

'Hold on,' he whispered from somewhere in the stinking dark. 'They'll be here soon.'

Numb with fright and cold, her fingers, nails and legs gripped the pole's wet slime, her mind focused only on staying alive.

Several shots rang through the air. Heavy boots thudded along the road outside. There were shouted commands. Footsteps approached.

The barn door swung open, and several pairs of heavily shod feet kicked hay and bales. One of them, young by the sound of him, spotted the trap door, and called to the others. Catherine clung rigid, terrified, to her slippery support. The trap lifted, and a torch played searchlights over the square of visible water. A mere ripple would have betrayed a presence.

'My God!' yelled the young soldier. 'It's the village shithouse. It stinks!'

A chorus of raucous laughter followed as he slammed the trap shut.

'Let's get out of here.' With guffaws and ribald jokes they stumbled over each other in their haste to leave. When all was silent, Catherine and Henri clambered, cold as ice, out of their sewer and ran into the dark anonymity of the garrigue.

'It's bad enough falling off your bicycle, but to fall into such a foul smelling ditch is really quite dreadful. I hope your visit to Annabelle's home was worth this disastrous result.'

Still recovering from the experience, Catherine attempted a cheerful smile. 'Oh yes Maman, they are delightful people.'

Fortunately, on this occasion, Marianne did not ask too many questions.

Intelligence revealed that both Boche and Milice patrols had been purely routine and their combined manoeuvres coincidental. It seemed safe now to arrange Annabelle's visit to the chateau. During dinner the night before Marianne suggested where Catherine's friend should sleep and, as there was no social etiquette in wartime, she accepted that the young nurse could be arriving during the early hours, as a result of her father's night shift, and petrol shortage. With Marianne safely retired to bed Catherine gathered her things together for the hospital shift. She was about to leave, via the conservatory, when the chateau's bell pealed, followed by a thunderous banging on the heavy door. Instinctively she took off her coat and threw it into an old cupboard. Heart pounding, she ran to the door.

Obersturmbannfuhrer Muller stood there. Behind him, surrounding the portico, were eight black uniforms, guns poised. Obersturmbannfuhrer Muller's lips parted in a golden leer. 'Mademoiselle Catherine de Lazarin', he whined. 'I'd like you to come with me on a little visit to Nimes. We shan't keep you long. Just a few questions.'

Fighting against paralysing terror, her voice was deliberately flat.

'Can't it wait until tomorrow?'

His florid face flushed. 'No! The Third Reich does not wait.'

'Then may I inform my mother?'

'No! You will come immediately!'

He nodded briefly to the armed men behind him who rapidly encircled her.

Muller stretched his fleshy lips into a smile. 'Get in the car, mademoiselle.'

She was sick with fear her imagination weaving horrifying images of Muller's methods.

On the route to Nimes, she tried to fathom the possible reasons for her capture. The hospital? Max? They'd never find him with his change of identity. She feared for the strength of her own courage, and said a few silent prayers.

In the interrogation room, Muller called a plain-clothes interpreter, a middle aged Frenchman, and one black uniformed guard. She was visibly trembling.

'Feeling cold, mademoiselle?' Muller intoned. 'Never mind, we'll warm you up. Get your clothes off.'

She hesitated.

'Your clothes, bitch!'

The interpreter added quietly. 'Better do what he says, mademoiselle.'

She took off her outer garments, and laid them on the floor, standing only in her underwear.

'I said undress you whore! All off! Understand?'

Mortified, she stood before the Obersturmbannfuhrer, the interpreter, and the guard, naked and terrified. The guard tied her hands behind her back, and pushed her close to the back wall of a wide alcove. In the centre of the floor was a drain. Muller swaggered up to her, and peering into her eyes, spat.

'You two-timing bitch! Fucking an officer of the Third Reich, who is too stupid to see what you are! Working for the resistance aren't you, little aristo whore?'

His spittle dribbled down her cheek, just missing her mouth. A fleshy hand touched her breasts.

'Nice tits for an upper class tart,' he laughed. 'I bet von Langdorf can't believe his luck.'

He moved in close, placed both hands on her breasts and gripped them.

'Where is Max Becker?' She remained mute. Once again he grabbed her breasts, twisting and pinching the flesh. 'I repeat, cunt, where is Max Becker?'

She spat back at him.

'Playing games are we?' he yelled, and nodded to the guard who immediately pushed her against the wall, and locked her feet into manacles, secured to an iron ring, forcing her legs apart.

'Now, whore, let me explain something to you. We know you are related to Jews! You are Max Becker's cousin,' he added triumphantly.

Catherine was flabbergasted. How much more did he know?

He picked up a short whip from the table. 'We know this Jew is a doctor, and was working in Nimes.'

He took a pace forward and placed his fleshy face within an inch of hers, his foul breath making her nostrils wince.

'We know,' he whined, 'Becker was working very closely with Moulin, de Gaulle's little puppet.'

He gave her legs a searing lash with his whip, and laughed.

'We have dealt effectively with Moulin, and shall do the same with Becker,' he leered. 'Now, would you like to hear what else we know?'

She remained mute. 'Come on, whore! Say yes or no.'

This time he lashed her hips with force. The burning pain brought tears to her eyes.

'YES or NO? ' he yelled.

'Why should I care what you tell me?' she shouted back.

He spat at her again. 'You will care, I promise you.'

He walked away, and then turned on her with manic fury in his face.

'Now listen, bitch! Games are over, understand? We know Becker has visited you at your chateau, many times, AND under the eyes of those dummkopf officers too. But WE ARE NOT DUMMKOPF OFFICERS!' he screamed.

Once more he lashed at her body. The pain was excruciating. She choked back the tears.

'You have been seen with Becker, YOUR COUSIN,' he emphasised. 'And other resistance traitors, in Nimes many times.'

He stomped around the interrogation room, tapping the whip handle in the palm of his hand. He moved in close again, grabbed her pubic hair, and intoned menacingly. 'You were also studying medicine, and your Jew doctor cousin is not only a leader of French traitors, we believe he is also providing some sort of medical aid to those few French traitors we haven't quite managed to kill.'

He leered. 'We also believe you are helping him. Now', he continued, 'I am sure you understand there is a little more we need to know.'

She turned her head away. He grabbed her chin with his pugilistic hand, and forced her face to his. 'Look at me, bitch!' he shouted.

'The Jew has changed his name. What is it? When did you last see him? Where is his medical hideout?'

She said nothing. He slapped her face hard, first one side, then the other, swinging her head round like a rag doll, the rings on his fingers cutting into her flesh. 'Answer me and you shall be taken back to your chateau.'

She stared at him, silently.

'Of course', he said, 'If you remain silent we shall have to persuade you.' He cackled. 'And that could be a little unpleasant for an aristo bitch. So! Answers please!'

Catherine trembled in anticipation of what he would do next.

'Very well', he sneered, 'this is where we have fun.'

He nodded to the guard, who strode to the door, and stood back to allow the eight black uniformed soldiers to enter. They lined up in front of her, grinning. One by one they unbuttoned their jackets and their top trouser buttons. Muller's laugh echoed in the empty room. 'You look surprised, aristo whore! You must be used to being fucked by the Third Reich by now.'

He laughed raucously, encouraging the men to join in, and made lewd comments about her body, which the interpreter did not translate.

'Now,' thundered Muller,'we must make sure you are clean. We don't want to fuck a dirty French tart do we, boys?'

'No Herr Obersturmbannfuhrer,' they chorused.

The Girl on the Promenade

The guard brought out a long hosepipe. A strong powerful jet of water gushed from the nozzle like a bullet. Catherine closed her eyes. She felt light-headed, and for a moment the situation seemed unreal, a nightmare. But the water jet confirmed this was reality. One by one the eight soldiers trained the powerful nozzle on her body, everywhere, anywhere. Her flesh was pummelled, bruised. She gasped for air, as water filled nostrils, mouth, and every orifice. She fell on her knees to the floor, unable to move her feet. She leant back and thought her ankles, strapped in as they were, would break. Muller gave the signal to stop. The guard pulled Catherine up to her feet, propping her slim frame against the wall.

'Enjoy the shower? At least she's clean,' he laughed. A peal of lewd amusement came from the men. Muller would love to have shown off in front of his men, to have her on her knees his penis down her throat. But the memory of his last attempt at taking pleasure from a French woman was too ignominious to repeat. Suddenly he shouted. 'Sorry boys, but I think the whore will enjoy this too much. She's used to fucking German soldiers. There's something we must do first before we give her fun.'

The guard pulled over a chair and small table and pushed her down into the seat.

'Comfortable?' Muller whined. 'Before you touch my boys, I just want to make sure your nails are clean. Or perhaps you'd like to tell me what I want to know?'

The interpreter translated. Even if she had wanted to tell Muller anything, Catherine could now barely open her jaw. The water jet had caused muscles to cramp. Her flesh bruised and swollen, every bone in her body throbbed with pain.

'Don't know – don't know,' she mumbled.

Muller then said something to the guard, who placed a pair of chrome pliers on the table. Untying Catherine's hands he grabbed the left one. Her arm and hand shook uncontrollably.

Muller approached. 'Keep still you bitch. We are going to save you cleaning your fingernails for a very long time, by removing them one by one,' he cackled. The interpreter translated, then very quietly whispered. 'Faint! It's the only way.'

A telephone on Muller's table rang. As he made his way back to pick it up, a black uniform gripped her trembling limbs like a vice, while the guard grabbed the forefinger of her left hand. She turned her head away. He took out a scalpel from his breast pocket, and slowly began to slice at the flesh under the nail. Catherine screamed. Unperturbed, he stabbed and sliced the flesh down to the quick. She continued screaming, ankles still manacled, held and gripped, unable to move. There was no escape from the searing pain that continued relentlessly, until the guard had separated nail from finger down to the cuticle and finally removed the nail with large tweezers. Blood gushed in pools over the table. Catherine's agonised screams continued. She could no longer see clearly. Her vision was blurred. The room started to spin. It became darker and darker. The excruciating pain began to diminish.

The French interpreter looked away. He need not have been concerned, for she had fainted naturally, falling across her bloody hand.

Muller put down the telephone. 'Stop!' he commanded the guard. 'Put her in a towel, roll up her clothes, and take the bitch to her front door.

We've got better fish to fry,' he leered.

CHAPTER TWENTY-TWO

Freddy was not enjoying a relaxing home leave at Schloss Langdorf.

His mind constantly wandered back to Catherine, and what Muller could do, and how much Muller knew.

Anna, his mother, no longer radiated rosy health, although when talking to Freddy her voice still bubbled. 'And your Catherine, is she still the woman of your life?'

'She will always be – unfortunately.'

'Unfortunately?'

'Well, it's as you have always said, life is at a premium in war.'

Anna touched his hand affectionately. 'If it is meant to be, my darling.'

He plumped up another cushion and placed it behind her head.

'How lucky we have been, you, Carl, even poor dear Sophie. All of you, alive.' She looked at him anxiously. 'You are not going to be posted, are you? God! You are not going to Russia?'

Freddy could see his mother was ready to work herself into a nervous state of palpitations, to be followed by another angina attack.

He pulled a blanket over her legs. 'No Mama, I am not going to Russia. I shall be returning to the chateau, and remain there until the end of the war.'

'Promise?'

He leant over and kissed her forehead. 'Promise'.

Freddy and his father took out their slim *Langlauf* skis for an afternoon on the estate's woodland. Later, warming themselves at the stove in the hut, Friedrich poured out steaming glasses of lemon tea and brandy.

'Papa, how productive are the farms these days?'

'Hopeless really. Machinery can't be replaced and women can't do heavy digging.' He shook his head. 'It's so ludicrous. Farms in the occupied zones have our chaps to do the work.' Freddy knew what he meant.

'Have you seen your uncle lately?'

'Sure. He came down to the chateau not long ago. Didn't he tell you?'

'Your uncle rarely tells us anything nowadays,' his father replied archly. 'Haven't seen him for over a year. We receive the occasional guarded telephone call. The war's obviously getting to him.'

Freddy rubbed his hands together and spread them on the hot tiles.

'Getting to us all, Papi.'

The older man huffed. 'If only some of our generals, Carl included, would try to steer the madman from certain defeat. An idiot can see it coming.

Germany will be flattened if the RAF continues. We shall be forced into an ignominious defeat like the last time, and like the last time, be obliged to lick the crumbs from under the feet of the British, the French, the Americans with the extra bonus of the Soviets.' He smiled thinly. 'Frankly, I don't want to be alive to see it.'

During his second week of leave Freddy felt uneasy. The photograph he had found in Catherine's bedroom was a reminder that Muller, like a bird of prey, could pounce. He decided to curtail his leave by a few days.

It was about midnight when Marianne heard the chateau's doorbell. She waited, thinking Catherine would answer it. But the pealing was continuous and urgent. Pulling on her dressing gown she padded downstairs.

What she saw almost paralysed the woman with shock. Catherine was draped in a towel, carrying a bundle of clothes. Her face was swollen and bruised, sockets so puffed her eyes were invisible. Her left hand, red and caked with blood was shaking.

'My God! Oh my God! Catherine. My darling girl! My darling girl!'

Catherine fell sobbing into her mother's arms.

Marianne bathed and bandaged. She made cold compresses for Catherine's face, and gave her sterilized milk with brandy to drink. The mutilated fingernail socket, with slivers of torn flesh hanging from the bloody crater, turned her stomach so violently, she was ready to drive to Gestapo HQ and shoot Muller herself.

For several hours Marianne sat at Catherine's bedside. Speaking slowly, with difficulty, Catherine disclosed nothing about the garrigue hospital, only that the SS thought Max was important in the resistance, and they had found out she was his cousin. How Marianne cursed her hothead nephew.

'Please my darling don't ever try to be brave. Tell them! They're going to find out anyway.'

'Maman, I have nothing to tell them – nothing at all.'

Marianne laid her cheek on the pillow beside her daughter's. 'If only Freddy had been here,' she moaned, 'this would never have happened.'

Catherine slept fitfully, frequently waking up, her whole body shaking violently with the trauma of the interrogation. Marianne kept vigil, afraid to shut her eyes; afraid of everything.

How she missed her beloved Georges.

On the Wednesday morning of his second week's leave Freddy telephoned chateau HQ. from the schloss and asked for Colonel Bergen.

'I am afraid that will not be possible,' a sharp unfamiliar voice informed.

'Why is that?'

'He has been called away to a special briefing at the coast.'

Freddy wondered why Kurt had not told him. 'So, who is in charge?'

'I am. Hauptsturmfuhrer Hoffmann SS. And who are you?'

'Major von Langdorf. Second in command at the chateau.'

'Of course, Herr Major I know. And you are on leave, returning on Saturday. Correct?'

Something was going on, and it smelled of Muller. Freddy hoped to God he wasn't going to be too late.

'Yes, Saturday,' he lied.

Freddy caught an overnight train out of Bonn. A long journey with several changes, he spent the time leaning on window rails in train corridors. His mind, focused on Muller's diabolical caprice, composed a variety of scenarios, and feverishly wondered how to counter them.

Just before ten o'clock on Thursday morning, Catherine was awakened by the sound of brusque voices and a shrill scream from her mother. She sat up in bed, dazed with sleep. Heavy footsteps up the stone stairs stomped across the landing. They stopped outside Catherine's study door, and burst in. An Unterscharfuhrer yelled downstairs, and held the door open while six SS guards searched through bookcases, throwing books papers, pens, pencils, medical diagrams, anything they could find, with unnecessary force into the middle of the floor. She heard Muller barking orders before he swaggered into her bedroom. 'Well,' he whined. 'Not quite so pretty as we used to be are we. Hm?'

Shaking, she pulled the blankets around her neck.

He bared his gold fillings. 'Don't bother, princess; I know exactly what you look like. In fact, we all do.' He turned to the men and guffawed.

He grabbed the bedclothes and pulled them away from her body.

'Get dressed. I'll give you five minutes, and don't try anything funny.'

He nodded and the uniforms filed out. At the door, Muller turned. 'You know I don't like to be kept waiting.'

Downstairs in the hall, a large soldier was holding Marianne, his hand gagging her mouth from which stifled gurgling

The Girl on the Promenade

sounds emanated. Catherine looked at her mother. Two pairs of frightened eyes exchanged more than words could express. The phalanx of black uniforms pushed the frightened young woman out into the winter sunlight. Marianne's guard threw her, stumbling and sobbing, onto the cold stone floor. 'Catherine! My little one! Catherine!' she screamed.

Muller swung round. 'Shut up old woman! We're taking your daughter to join friends in Anduze.' He laughed. 'For a special party!' An acolyte repeated the message in French.

The heavy oak door slammed. Marianne crawled into a corner of the hall and sat, crouched, wringing her hands, whimpering and moaning, like an animal torn from its newborn.

At nine forty five a.m. Major von Langdorf arrived at Uzès station. He needed a car. There were always a few staff cars with drivers waiting for some unknown bigwig. He put his head into the open window of a waiting Mercedes. 'Chateau de Lazarin. On the double, if you please.'

Freddy arrived at the chateau, via the Uzès road, moments after Catherine had left with Muller for Anduze, in the opposite direction. He pulled the old bell several times. Unusually, there seemed to be no one at home. He ran round to the back, where the kitchen door had been left open. A prepared breakfast tray sat on the table, and there were signs of interrupted activity. He walked into the corridor, and found Marianne moaning, sprawled in a corner of the hall. Quickly he extracted from her three essentials. 'Muller.' 'Anduze,' 'special party'. She wanted to tell him more, but he stopped her short. 'Madame de Lazarin, I must act quickly, I must go!'

He burst into his office in the west wing. A junior SS officer sat at his desk.

'I am Major von Langdorf,' Freddy yelled. 'This is my office. What the hell are you doing here? Get out!'

'But Herr Major-,' he began.

'Out!'

As soon as he had locked the door behind the astonished officer, Freddy dialled Carl in Berlin, his damp hands slipping on the earpiece. There was no other way to stop Muller. He had never heard him call anything a "special party" before. To "join friends in Anduze," had to mean deportation. Freddy explained briefly and rapidly to Carl, careful to avoid turning it into a personal favour.

'Is she the one you want to marry?'

'Uncle, that is academic. If anything happens to her, the resistance won't rest until we are all dead, believe me. The de Lazarins are an important family.'

'Very well. I'll try the Fuhrer's office. If he knows it's you - well, there may be a chance.'

Freddy closed his eyes muttering as he waited *'Please God. Please God, please God, please God, and please God! Don't let her go! Don't let her go!'*

'Sorry Freddy, the Fuhrer can't be disturbed. One of his moods.'

' Oh Jesus! What about Himmler?'

'Away. In any case he's hardly sympathetic to the velvet glove policy.'

Freddy could feel his throat tighten, and bit on his clenched fist. 'There has to be something you can do, Uncle. Please! If anything happens, I shall kill Muller.'

'No! No! For God's sake don't do anything stupid. It could have the direst consequences for all of us. Think of your parents. We are at war, and whoever she is, she remains technically our enemy. So calm yourself boy. I'll call the Reich minister for Culture. Hitler likes him. Could work. Where do we telephone?'

Freddy tore out of the chateau at the wheel of Catherine's car. An army Mercedes would invite the resistance. Over his uniform he threw an old coat of Robert's. Wearing a beret, no one could have guessed he was a German soldier.

As he raced towards Anduze he realised that despite his own desperation, Carl was right. This was war and one had to be strong enough to accept the terrible pain of separation.

The Girl on the Promenade

Major von Langdorf knew he would have to behave correctly, or they would all be shot.

German Army HQ. Anduze was a converted warehouse, several storeys high, with dozens of rooms on each floor. During the preceding week the barrack's army officers had been put out by the unplanned, and certainly unwanted arrival of an SS contingent from Nimes, under the command of an unpleasant Lieutenant-Colonel, Obersturmbannfuhrer Muller. The ground floor had been taken for his personal use, as offices and interrogation rooms. Anduze's Colonel, a reasonable man, who had been forced to move upstairs, declared Muller, 'an arrogant little shit.'

In the back courtyard of the HQ, Catherine was bundled from the car nudged with rifle butts across the cobbles, and pushed inside the building. Damp hair clung to her head and about her face, grown skeletally thin. No longer did her young eyes dance with life. They had sunk into their sockets luminous with fear. She leant her head against the shabby peeling wall of the corridor, unable to stop the tremor in her left hand. She heard voices and a cry from a room at the end of the corridor followed by a bellow from Muller. Her legs shook in anticipation of what he was going to do this time. Her eyes closed and she slumped fainting to the floor. A grey uniformed guard called for a bucket of water.

Catherine came to, as the last dregs from the bucket were thrown at her. Her guard, a middle-aged man, with a kindly face, knelt down beside her. 'Come on young lady get up. Better for you.'

The cries from Muller's room were uncomfortably audible. The guard shuffled his feet, and looked down at them. Suddenly the door was flung open. Muller filled the space, and barked a command.

'Come on, mademoiselle,' said the guard. 'Your turn.'

She was unsteady, so he helped her along the unevenly paved corridor. 'Leave her.' Muller shouted. 'Let the bitch fall.'

The guard ignored him. Why should he? This SS bloke was definitely out of order. He handed the prisoner over, marched back to the mess, to a table next to his mate, and took out a cigarette. 'Pretty kid that one. Looked fucking scared.'

His mate grimaced. 'With all these bloody black uniforms we're all fucking scared!'

Catherine was pushed into a chair placed on one side of a desk facing Muller. His black uniformed guards ringed the walls. The interrogation room was the makeshift barracks' gymnasium. Several 'bucks' and 'horses' had been pushed against the wooden bars attached to the back wall. Two windows provided the only daylight illumination. Despite the addition of a couple of lamps, the place was gloomy, particularly as clouds had now obliterated a pale January sun.

Catherine did not notice the bloodstains under her chair, but she recognised the same interpreter. Muller leered. 'Well, mademoiselle rich bitch, as I promised we are going to have a party, and I always keep my word. But!'

He slammed his fat gold - encrusted hand on the table, and stood up. 'Before we do, mademoiselle, would you like to tell me where your cousin is, and what name he is using? You see,' he whined, 'it might be better than going to the party. And do you know why?' He lowered his head near hers, exhaling waves of odorous breath. 'Once you go, you will not come back. DO YOU UNDERSTAND?' he bellowed.

Her ears rang and her eyes swam in dizzy focus.

'So I ask you again, where is your cousin, and what name does Jew Becker use now? Just two answers and we'll send you home.'

She shook her head. 'I don't know.'

'Very well, once more.'

He nodded to a guard who pulled her to her feet. Muller stood in front of the desk, facing his victim, and slapped her with both hands again and again with unrelenting ferocity. He would stop for a moment, then the assault would continue. Finally he stopped.

The Girl on the Promenade

Like a rag doll, her throbbing head, still bruised and cut from the last encounter, hung limply from her slender neck.

'Still sure we don't know, are we?' he shouted.

She was mute, shaking. 'Well, aristo cunt,' he hissed, 'I cannot waste any more time on you, so off to the party. Your friends are all waiting.'

His gold teeth shone in the reflected light of the lamps.

Muller led the way along a corridor leading to the back of the building. Two uniformed guards pushed her into a large parade ground. It was wet and grey now, with a fine drizzle. She looked for an army truck ready for deportation.

What she actually saw almost stopped her heart.

There were five posts set close to the far back wall. In the middle of the yard surrounded by guards, stood four victims huddled together, holding hands. Catherine approached. They turned. When Catherine saw Francois, in his white coat, Henri and Raymond, she felt her legs had been shot away. But when she saw Annabelle, still in her nurse's uniform, her face marked with several beatings, Catherine let out a howl of pain. 'No! No! No!' The guard hit her with his rifle butt, and shoved her into the silent group. No one spoke. They looked at each other in complete bewilderment, each silently asking the same question. Catherine embraced first Annabelle who whispered. 'Goodbye Cathy my dear friend. I'm so frightened.'

'So am I! Oh thank you, dearest Annabelle for all your friendship! But oh God, why, why?' They hugged each other in a last farewell.

Annabelle and Francois clung together. 'Now, my darling, we will be together for always, and I shall love you for eternity,' he said softly.

With her large blue eyes brimming, she nodded. 'And I love you so much - so very much. We could have had -.' She broke off and sobbed quietly into his white hospital jacket. Henri and Raymond said little. They clasped each other like the old comrades they were. Catherine felt desperately alone. The man she loved couldn't be here, and even if he were able to witness this, he could do nothing. A priest arrived. The little man, dabbing his eyes and nose to fight back tears, knelt in the grey drizzle. To each of them he gave last rites, and to each of them he whispered. 'You are dying for France, and God will punish these swine.'

The priest dismissed, black uniformed guards began lining up their victims to stakes. No one spoke in the terrible silence. From somewhere inside the building a telephone rang. Muller, watching the procedure from the parade podium, was summoned indoors.

It was Annabelle first, then Francois, Henri, Raymond, and lastly, Catherine. Hands were tied behind backs to stakes. They all declined the blindfold. 'Because Francois and I,' Annabelle swallowed her tears, ' want to look at each other until our very last moment on earth,' she told the guard. The guard looked grim, but even he softened as he looked into those large eyes set in such a pretty face. They stood tied, waiting for death, waiting for Muller to return to the podium.

Catherine looked up at the grey sky. She had no fear now, because she felt already dead. The trembling had stopped. Her body and mind were resigned. To what? Oblivion? Was there something else? One had to believe. She whispered into the heavens. 'Goodbye my lovely country. Papa, Robert, I shall be seeing you. Maman, try to be strong. We shall win the war – we shall. Freddy, dear Freddy I love you. Keep safe. But why God, why? This is so senseless. And please God don't let the bullets hurt too much. Let it be quick for all of us.'

A firing squad of four marched out of the building, positioning themselves in front of Francois, Henri, Raymond and Catherine. There was no one facing Annabelle. Then two SS men walked out of the barracks, half supporting a grey uniformed soldier hobbling on crutches. Henri emitted a low whistle. It was Heinz Gollner, in far worse shape than when he had left their garrigue hospital. He was placed in front of his little blond nurse. Annabelle gasped when she saw him. The young soldier was stunned speechless as he gazed at them all in turn. He mouthed her name over and over again. 'Annabelle, Annabelle'. A black uniform gave him a rifle.

Henri cleared his throat and began, '*Allons enfants de la patrie, le jour du gloire est arrivé —contre nous de la tyrranie —* '

His croaking voice somehow found the tune, and all five of them joined in, heads raised, Annabelle and Francois singing to each other.

It was the singing that brought old Professor Gabriel Becaud to his window overlooking the square. He had retired from Chair of Surgery in the medical faculty at Montpellier soon after the outbreak of war, returning to his native Anduze. With the shortage of doctors he was now offering his services as a GP. This was the first time he had witnessed an execution. He shook his white head.'Murdering swine! What have these poor children done?'

He adjusted his pince-nez.

The tall, slim, dark haired girl looked familiar. He had seen her before. But where? The two older *maquisards* as they had to be, were complete strangers, but when he saw Francois, in his white coat, he took off his pince nez rubbed his eyes and looked again. 'My God it is. Francois Gerard, and that little nurse of his!' he exclaimed. The shock was so staggering, the old man had to steady himself on a small table. 'God in heaven! A brilliant young doctor and nurse. To be murdered? Are the Boche going crazy?'

He looked back at Catherine, and thought hard. Of course, Montpellier! She had been a second or third year student in the Medical Faculty, when he retired. Dr Becaud was on formal but amicable terms with the colonel at the barracks. He reached for the telephone.

'Colonel! Do you know who these young people are, the ones you are about to murder? They were with me at Montpellier! The young doctor, brilliant. One of my best students. God in heaven man, why?'

The colonel sighed. 'Sorry Dr Becaud, it's S.S. Nothing to do with us.'

'May I ask what crimes they have committed?'

'They were running a hospital for wounded resistance fighters, I believe.'

The old doctor sat down. 'And for that, they are murdered?' he asked, his voice rising in disbelief.

'It's SS. I'm so sorry. Uh -Look, would you like to bury them for me? At least I can insist upon a decent burial.'

'Of course.' He put the telephone down, muttering to himself. 'It's all I can do. Curse the impotence of old age.'

At the window, his head high, the old doctor sang his national anthem, joining the condemned with all the energy his lungs would allow, while tears flowed copiously into the runnels of his gaunt cheeks.

From his particular vantage point overlooking the courtyard, the old professor was the only real witness to the extraordinary sequence of events, which now followed. The colonel, looking grim, came out of the barracks to stand on the podium. A moment later a fat SS officer appeared, and straddled the central position.

The grey uniformed young soldier on crutches, facing the little nurse, could not hold his rifle. The black uniforms flanking him gave their shoulders for support, but the rifle still wavered unsteadily. Then the fat officer yelled the order. 'Feuer!'

Shots rang out, each body dropped, and simultaneously the young soldier on crutches screamed. *'Nein! Nein! Gott im Himmel. Wo bist Du?"*

Jamming the rifle into his own chest, he fired and fell. There was pandemonium. Dr Becaud did not wish to see any more. The five victims, lying dead, ignored in the chaos, would have an honourable, heroic burial, so he would call the sisters in the convent next door to help him later, when all was quiet. In the meantime he would just say his prayers, hoping there was a God somewhere who wasn't still sleeping.

The colonel ran to the young soldier, who had tried to take his own life. This was unheard of. He remembered the boy. He had gone missing for a few days and had been picked up in Anduze with a badly broken leg, but obviously in good shape, having received excellent medical attention. He couldn't remember where he had been, except that he said it was a village hospital in the mountains, and he had fallen for his French nurse. The colonel intended to thank the hospital personally, when Gollner could locate it. But when Nimes SS heard the story, any attempts to make contact had been forbidden. Muller was a thorough nuisance yanking the poor chap out of sick bay for interviews, over and over again; some nonsense about an unauthorised French hospital.

Heinz Gollner now lay in a bloody heap on the wet ground. His face and blond hair streaked with splashes of blood from an artery severed by his own bullet. He was bleeding so profusely the colonel could see there was no hope. A couple of his friends placed jackets under his head. His two broken legs - broken several times during the interrogations, the colonel found out later - lay twisted in spastic angles to his body.

'How d'you feel, old chap?'

'Not good, sir.' The young soldier was gasping for breath now. 'They - they all - saved my life sir. I - I couldn't let them die and not me.' He was getting weaker, but managed to whisper.'I'm a Christian sir. Annabelle was lovely – tell my Mum-tell my Mum.' His head slumped on one side, and a final breath left his body. One of his friends asked whether he should fetch a priest, as Heinz was a devout Catholic.

'No,' said the colonel wearily. 'Too late,' and he closed the dead soldier's eyes. 'He's given his own absolution. Young Gollner has already won a place, I'm sure.' He rose from his knees and walked slowly into the barracks to his office, where he would have to begin the grisly protocol with endless forms, explaining a young soldier's suicide whilst on duty, and wished he could tell the truth.

Freddy skidded to a halt in the back courtyard of the barracks, and emerged from the car in his officer's uniform. His heart sank. There was no deportation truck. He had to find Muller. Inside the building there appeared to be a great deal of activity, with SS uniforms dotted amongst the usual grey.

'Obersturmbannfuhrer Muller?' he shouted to a grey uniformed sergeant.

'Don't know major, but he's using the 'gym' down there.' Freddy ran down the silent corridor and burst into the room. It was empty. Convinced Catherine had been deported, he hurried to the desk, and searched for a deportation order somewhere in the detritus littering the surface, itself proof of Muller's presence. Drawers yielded nothing. Then he noticed the SS greatcoat hanging behind the door. He delved into pockets, used to this routine now. They were empty, but running his hands down the coat lining, he felt the outline of a small package secreted inside a pocket stitched into a fold. The package was a sealed envelope. He ripped it open and was aghast at what he saw. It was political dynamite. Out of the envelope spilled a dozen photographs of Muller and his Unterscharfuhrer performing a variety of explicit homosexual acts with young men, who looked like prisoners, judging from the fear in their faces, and who would certainly have been shot afterwards. It was obvious the Unterscharfuhrer was involved not only to stop him squealing, but because he was a passionate amateur photographer. Homosexual activities were treasonable. To the Nazi party it was a strictly 'no tolerance' zone. The question was when were they taken? He would have to bluff Muller into believing the photographs had been in his possession for a few weeks. This piece of exceptional luck could secure, at the very least, Catherine's release. At last he had some hold over Muller.

He heard the fat man's step approach the door. He extracted two photographs from the packet, stuffing them into his outside pocket. The rest he hid inside his jacket. Standing behind the door he pulled his luger out of its holster and cocked the barrel. Muller entered. Freddy shut the door, taking the key, and stabbed the gun into the back of Muller's neck, turned him round, and grabbed the SS man's revolver before he could put his hands on it. Muller stood rigid with shock. Attempting bravado, he whined weakly.

The Girl on the Promenade

'So major, what a surprise. You have left the Fatherland a little early?'

Freddy was ice cold. 'Where is Mademoiselle de Lazarin?'

Muller tried to slip his assailant's grasp and retreat behind the desk. His lumbering bulk was no match for the nimble major, who grabbed his lapels, and forced him into a chair. 'Where is Mademoiselle de Lazarin?'

'Alive, if that's what you want to know.'

'Where?' He snapped. 'On the way to Dachau?'

Muller's flailing arms were trying to reach the emergency button on the desk's underside, but Freddy kicked the chair from under him pulling the obese man down so violently he fell onto the wooden floor, his knees juddering with the impact. 'Come, come, Herr Major', he spluttered. 'You don't think I'm going to send her away do you? For Christ's sake, she knows too much.'

' Where is she?' Freddy repeated pushing the revolver into Muller's chest.

'In our custody, Herr Major.'

'Dead or alive?' He shouted. 'Tell me!'

Muller shook. 'Alive, I swear to God!'

'Prove it! I want proof. Now!' One hand held Muller's collar chokingly tight; one hand was on the trigger. 'And I'm warning you Muller, this gun is ready to blast away whatever you substitute for brains.'

The SS man gagged for breath, his face pink and wet. 'Out of the window von Langdorf,' he gasped. 'See for yourself. Parade ground.'

Freddy dragged Muller with him to the window. A muffed cry of pain came from the young man's lips. 'You evil bastard,' he yelled, reeling with the horror of seeing Catherine's body slumped on the parade ground. 'You can start saying your prayers, murderer,' he cried. Muller made a desperate grab for Freddy's hand to pull it away from the trigger.

'She's alive! She's alive! I swear it! Don't shoot! For Christ's sake, von Langdorf! She's only stunned!'

'Prove it!' Freddy shoved Muller's face into the glass. Standing out of sight, he rammed the pistol into Muller's back. 'Open the window and tell an orderly to find out if she is alive. Do it,' he snarled. Muller had no choice. He yelled at a passing private, who brought confirmation that the woman's heart was still beating. Satisfied, Freddy pushed Muller into a cowering heap, on the floor, his boot pinning him down, the luger skewering his Adam's apple.

'You'll be shot for this, von Langdorf. No good pulling strings in Berlin next time.' Muller croaked.

'Next time Muller? Next time? There won't be a next time unless you would like Herr Himmler to see photographs of you, Obersturmbannfuhrer Muller of the SS, fucking young men?' Freddy pulled the two photographs from his pocket. Muller's head still pinned down he waved them in front of his half closed eyes. The folds of heavy flesh draped around his cheekbones began to twitch. 'Where did you get them, fucking aristo bastard?'

The revolver still trained on Muller, Freddy pulled the fat man onto his knees. 'Now listen! These photographs are my insurance that Mademoiselle de Lazarin and I stay alive. The rest of your collection is already in safe keeping in Berlin. In Berlin! Do you understand?'

Muller's jowls shook. 'Berlin?' His fleshy lips parted and a trickle of saliva ran from the corner of his mouth.

'Whatever you say, von Langdorf.' he croaked.

'Should anything happen to either of us, they will be sent immediately to Herr Himmler. Just make sure we stay alive, Muller.'

Freddy marched to the door. 'Insurance! Understood?'

He left the fat man locked in his room, a frightened lump on the floor too confused to think clearly about anything, except Herr Himmler and Berlin.

Freddy tore across the parade ground to Catherine's motionless body, His rage had for the moment been diffused into an overwhelming relief that she was still alive. He looked at the others lying there, bloodstained, and pathetic, and wondered who they were and why they were there; the blond girl in the nurse's uniform, the young man in a doctor's coat?

With Catherine's limp body in his arms he crossed the empty parade ground, and walked around the building to avoid meeting inquisitive military. As he laid her body on the back seat of her car, he saw Muller jump into his Mercedes and drive off, the fleet following him. He prayed for a resistance ambush.

On the way back to the chateau along a quiet country road he stopped the car and clambered into the back seat. He felt her pulse, and wrapping his arms about her shoulders he pressed her face to his and sobbed.

The barracks' courtyard was bleak and wet. The rain was heavy now, the mountains shrouded in mist. A chill wind blew across the empty space. Four bodies lay crumpled against their stakes, faces streaked with rain, some with blood oozing out of mouth and nostrils. Around each still figure, ribbons of dark red mingled with rainwater creating crimson pools on the grey stone.

Professor Gabriel Becaud put on his overcoat to join the two Sisters from the convent, waiting for him down below. They each carried a couple of stretchers. He noticed the dark young woman's body had been taken, family he presumed. Approaching the dead, the Sisters crossed themselves and bowed their heads. The doctor suddenly stopped.

'Just a minute.' Alone, he walked quickly to the bodies, and examined them. The old man almost ran back to the waiting Sisters, his eyes glowing with excitement. 'Quickly! Let's get them out. My surgery please, as discreetly as possible. I think one of them may still be alive!'

CHAPTER TWENTY-THREE

Catherine lay listlessly on her bed, from time to time weeping uncontrollably. So far, her responses to anything had been dismissive and incoherent.

But one evening at the end of the third week, she exclaimed angrily.

'Why am I alive? Annabelle, Francois, Henri, Raymond, are dead. Why? Why?'

Piecing together her random references to the garrigue hospital, Freddy guessed she must have been in contact with her cousin. She had already mumbled something about the young German in love with Annabelle, who had been brought out of the barracks, that awful morning, barely able to walk, to face his idol, a rifle in his hand.

Gradually she told Freddy everything, no longer aware of his uniform. She saw only a man whom she loved and who had saved her life. He held her close while she sobbed, revolted by Muller's cruelty to her to the medical team and to the young soldier. He had been told by the colonel that the boy's leg had been broken several times to extract information. 'You should know, Catherine, young Gollner did not set out to betray you. He told his friends about his beautiful young nurse. One of them was in the Party and reported him.'

'Heinz Gollner was almost walking when he left us.'

He told her of his suicide.

'Oh dear God! He shot himself for Annabelle? I believe she knows - she knows what he did. That poor, poor boy! He's with them all now! It's where I should be too, Freddy!'

She buried her head in his shoulder, torn with grief again. Being the only one alive was an intolerable burden of guilt.

He feared for her safety now as much from the resistance as from Muller.

'Do you think the resistance will know it was not I who betrayed the hospital?'

'Of course. They'll blame Gollner. They will also know of your courage.'

His assurances were merely placatory, for in truth, no one could be sure.

'Why do I have to live and they die? Why?'

'If you had died then I would also have died. At least Annabelle and Francois are together.'

Stroking her damaged hand he warned her again of Muller. 'But I don't think he'll do anything while I'm around.'

She touched his cheek tenderly. 'You have risked so much for me, Freddy.' He kissed her lightly on the mouth. 'You know that I shall kill Muller should he ever touch you again.'

Holding her hands firmly in his, he said, 'There is one thing more Catherine, I know Max Becker is your cousin, and a resistance leader.'

She stared at him mutely.

'Muller does too,' she whispered.

This was a new scenario for the major. He crossed to the window, and stood looking out over the landscape. 'Does Muller know what your cousin looks like?'

'Do you?' she asked.

'Yes', he replied, and told her about the photograph. 'I had to take it. I was terrified Muller would come here searching while I was on leave.'

Catherine stared at her fingers knotted in her lap.

He moved aimlessly round the room for several minutes. Leaning his arms on the back of the bedside chair he said. 'In that case - in that case Muller could have been telling the truth.'

'And I shall have a third interrogation?'

'No,' he said confidently, 'because – because I have the means to get back at him. But we must be prepared. Muller is never without plans.'

Freddy insisted Catherine remain at the chateau and Marianne should let it be known her daughter had been deported, just in case the resistance were 'concerned.'

Colonel Kurt Bergen was furious at the cheap way he had been set up by the SS and deliberately sent away. Freddy briefed him on everything including Muller's obscene photographs. He walked the length of Freddy's office with his usual cigarette and glass of cognac, his forehead in a tight frown.

'Do you realise just how much power these bastards have? You were bloody lucky, old son, to find those photographs. I'm all for blackmail against swine like Muller. Incidentally, how involved is young Catherine?'

'Name a true French national who isn't?'

Kurt gave a little smile.' So you'll be all right on the day of judgement then.'

'Earthly or heavenly?' Freddy quipped.

Kurt snorted. 'Earthly, need you ask? And in my opinion it's not too far ahead.'

The siege of Leningrad had been lifted, with enormous German losses, and the Allies had landed behind German lines in Italy.

Kurt was justifiably pessimistic.

Resistance activity was increasing, so another armoured SS division had been sent to Nimes with predictable results. In early March, fifteen resisters were hanged from the railway arches in Nimes, their bodies left to decompose. One of them was Etienne. A small hamlet outside Nimes was burned and the inhabitants, including children, shot as a reprisal for something. No one knew what.

Muller was having a field day.

It was a morning in mid April that the dreaded peal of the old doorbell reverberated once again through the chateau's hall. Catherine's panic returned, but Marianne took charge. 'Go through into Freddy's office. He can hide you somewhere. They will never think of looking for you in a German barracks. Go on. Quickly!'

'Look out of the window first, Maman. See how many cars there are.'

The bell pealed again. Catherine shuffled quietly behind a curtain at a first floor window overlooking the gravelled forecourt. There were no cars, only a bicycle. Whoever was pulling the bell was hidden in the portico. There was no sign of SS.

When Marianne opened the door, she was surprised to see a nun standing there. Small and petite, she smiled warmly. 'Is this the home of the de Lazarin family?' Marianne nodded nervously.

'And you are Madame de Lazarin?'

'Yes, sister.'

'Then may I speak to you, in private please?'

As soon as they were seated in the salon the unexpected guest took out a letter from her pocket. 'This is for you Madame de Lazarin. We know last January you suffered a most tragic loss. Please, do read the letter.'

With shaking hands Marianne ripped open the envelope. The letter read;

My dear Madame de Lazarin,

This will sound like a voice from the dead. I was one of those put in front of the firing squad with your daughter Catherine who was my dear sweet friend. I wish with all my heart, she were still alive. I wish with all my heart like you, that I could see her again, that she too could have shared my truly incredible fate.

You see, when the nuns and a wonderful old surgeon, who used to teach at Montpellier came to bury me, they found I was just alive. Since that time I have been looked after and almost restored to health. But alas, the pain of losing not only my darling Francois, to whom I had been married for barely a month, and Catherine my dearest friend, is sometimes more than I can bear. I knew from Catherine you too have borne enormous grief.

Do you think you could help me? I would so love to talk to you. I'm sure we could help each other.
With sympathy and love,
Annabelle.

By the time she reached the end of the letter Marianne's eyes were so blurred with tears the page swam. She looked up at her visitor who was eyeing her anxiously. The sister asked quietly, 'Would you talk to her - please? We'd be so grateful. We'd bring her to you, of course, and she would be dressed just like us, so it would place you in no real danger.'

Marianne was still numb with shock. She felt like leaping in the air for her daughter and for Annabelle. She rose from the armchair, crossed to the diminutive sister and clasped her rough red hands.

'Sister, you will never know what you have done. I think you have saved two lives, not just one.'

'With God's grace we are here to help each other in sorrow as well as joy, are we not?' the nun replied, oblivious to the facts.

'Indeed we are.' Marianne brushed away her tears. 'Please excuse me for a moment, sister.'

She flew to the foot of the stairs. 'Someone wishes to see you, Catherine,' she called. Seeing the look of alarm on her daughter's face she added, 'It's all right, it's all right my love.'

Catherine and a smiling Marianne entered the salon. 'Sister, may I present my daughter, Catherine de Lazarin.'

It was the sister's turn to reel. She sat down shaking her head in disbelief.

'This is a miracle - a miracle.'

Marianne handed her daughter Annabelle's letter, replaced in the envelope, and left the room. Catherine was completely mystified, both by her mother's behaviour and the nun's. She began to read. She choked on her breath. Her legs became numb. She tried to inhale deeply, to steady herself, and sat down, trembling. She put her hand to her head, stared at the letter. And In a voice that was just audible asked, 'This is not some sick joke is it?'

The nun smiled. 'No my dear. It's all true.'

Catherine read the letter over and over again, trying to assimilate the momentousness of the news. She stood up, the letter clutched in both shaking hands to her breast. Head thrown back, tears gushed from her closed eyes. She crossed to the dazed nun, putting her arms about the little figure.

'Annabelle! Annabelle is alive. She's alive Maman!'

Maman, quickly! Annabelle's alive. Annabelle's alive!'

The three of them stood together arms entwined, laughing and crying.

The sister took Annabelle a letter from Catherine.

My dearest Annabelle,
How I have mourned you!

I have barely stopped weeping since that terrible day in January. But we are alive. We live on! I know how you must have suffered because dear Francois has gone, but we have been spared to carry on for his sake, and for Henri and Raymond. I shall tell you, when we meet, how I survived, but so, so in despair until this moment.

Dear Annabelle, this has to be a miracle. This has to be the best moment of my life. I pinch myself to make sure I am not dreaming.

I cannot believe I shall actually be seeing you.

Do you realise this will be a real resurrection which we shall both see and experience. Come here soon soon, soon.

We have so much to talk about.

Your weeping, overjoyed, stunned, dazed and deliriously happy friend.

With all my love,
Catherine.

Freddy was as astounded as Catherine when he heard of Annabelle's incredible survival. It was clear that young Gollner had tried to avoid shooting her, and Freddy had also heard reports of his inability to hold the gun steady. Had Muller not been such a sadistic freak, he would have used someone else in Gollner's place, so for once his sadism had saved a life.

Annabelle's incredible resurrection did much to assuage the guilt that had consumed Catherine since that day in January. In her heart she hoped it had been Muller's intention to keep her alive for a third interrogation, to justify her own agony of conscience for being saved through Berlin string-pulling.

Since Muller knew of the Max Becker connection, Freddy now believed Catherine's death parade was in fact a dress rehearsal meant to frighten. Next time there would be no rehearsal, and it was becoming clear the Berlin telephone call would have had no effect had Muller really made the decision to kill her. However, the obscene photographs would remain a threat and Kurt knew exactly where to send them should the necessity arise.

The imminence of death had highlighted the importance to Catherine of family, friends and love. She could no longer talk about next year, next month, Of course there were countless ambitions in her head, but this was not the time for looking too far forward.

Three nuns in a small Citroen drove up the drive.

Catherine and Annabelle could not believe they were actually seeing each other. On that damp parade ground months before, they had said their goodbyes to each other and to life. Their reunion was just as tearful, but this time there would be a tomorrow. Annabelle's pert little face, as white as the wimple binding it, broke into elfin smiles once again, and her large blue eyes, though underlined with dark circles, shone with joy. They threw their arms about each other, and made sure they were actually embracing flesh and bone, not a cruel mirage. Up in Catherine's study they each told their stories about capture, interrogation, and Muller. Catherine made an oblique, but necessary reference to Max when she said, 'Muller had no idea I worked at the hospital. He wanted

The Girl on the Promenade

to know about a member of my family, whom he said was a resistance leader'.

Annabelle's face puckered in sympathy. 'Did you tell him anything when he pulled your nail out? I'm sure I would have.'

'I fainted - thank God!'

'We couldn't tell him much, because we didn't know the names of our doctors, except of course Jean-Pierre Soulas. But in fact we didn't.' She frowned. 'He kept asking about a Max -er - Becker, I think. Never heard of him. Anyway, Muller did it, didn't he? Destroyed the hospital and us.'

She took Catherine's hand. 'Wasn't it awful Cathy, waiting for the bullets – still gives me nightmares. I turned to my darling Francois, and he to me. There was a terrible burning pain, and then black. - It was all black.

When I opened my eyes,' she smiled wanly, 'I really thought I was in heaven. Dear Professor Becaud and the Sisters, all in white smiling down on me.'

Annabelle wept over young Heinz Gollner's torture and suicide. He had fired a bullet into her left shoulder, just glancing a chest artery. She had bled profusely, and owed her life to the professor's care. An evil red scar spread from neck to shoulder. 'But, Francois was the love of my life, Catherine. I shall never get over him. Sometimes I wish I really had died.'

'Annabelle, you have been given a second chance. Do you realise that? You have to carry on in medicine for his sake. You must.'

So far as the Nazis were concerned Annabelle was dead, and until the war was over she must remain so. Even her parents did not know she was alive. Catherine was in a far more vulnerable situation.

'Why don't you come to the convent? I'm sure the nuns would take you in'.

'I can't.'

'Why?'

'Look, if Muller comes searching he'll find out nuns have visited Maman. He'll send his men up to the convent. Oh

Annabelle! He'd find you, and God, no! You could be in terrible danger.'

'Isn't there somewhere you could hide?'

Catherine shook her head. 'No. The village thinks I have been deported.'

'You could go into the garrigue. The network could take you somewhere safe.'

'The resistance? No, I've been interrogated twice, and you know what that means.'

Annabelle nodded. 'Look, do your Germans know you are here?'

'Ye-es,' Catherine replied. Annabelle knew nothing about Freddy.

'That is, the one who rescued me from the parade ground, who tried to save me. Major von Langdorf.'

Annabelle was astonished. 'Really? He saved your life?'

'He is a German Annabelle, but he's not a Nazi. He hates them. He hates Muller. He says he's going to kill him.'

'Let's hope he does.' She sighed. 'I can still see Heinz Gollner's little white face staring at me across the barrel of his gun, mouthing my name, and weeping. So terrible,' she whispered. 'That poor boy. So terrible.' Clasping her hands together tightly in her lap, for a moment her brimming eyes focused somewhere in memory.

'This major must like you an awful lot, Cathy, to risk his life for a Muller prisoner.'

Catherine felt embarrassed as Annabelle looked at her searchingly her head to one side.

'Cathy, if you love a good person, and they love you, it doesn't matter who they are. Hold on to it for as long as you can. Nothing lasts for ever, does it?'

Catherine put her arms around the little blonde's shoulders.

'Thanks Annabelle.Thanks.'

The change in Catherine was as miraculous as Annabelle's survival. She began to relax and smile again, her old confidence

The Girl on the Promenade

returning. One fine evening in May, Freddy and Catherine were in the small study, listening to music. It was certainly warm enough to sit outside in the secret garden, but Freddy was afraid she might be seen.

'Why hasn't Muller called on me Freddy?'

'He's too busy chasing resisters in Nimes. Anyway, don't talk about him, we are much more important - you are anyway.'

She was standing at the window looking at the particularly beautiful sunset. He put his arms about her waist.

'My girl on the promenade at Cannes.'

'Are you still sure?'

'Absolutely'. He swung her round to face him.' I've loved you since that moment.'

He kissed her lightly at first, and then suddenly their arms were about each other. Kisses were breathless and passionate, tongues touched, cheeks burned.

'Freddy, Freddy', she whispered, 'I do love you'.

'I want you Catherine. I want to make you my wife – now.'

The terrifying ordeals they had both been put through of late had triggered off a need, a hunger for each other. Their lives were balancing on a fine edge. Perhaps there would be no tomorrow. She smiled at him through half closed lids, and whispered in his ear.'Will you marry me, Freddy?'

Without another word he picked her up in his arms and carried her into the bedroom. Gently he sat her on the bed while he drew the curtains of the long window. In the study, Brahms second Piano Concerto could still be heard drifting through the open door. He took off his uniform jacket, raised her up, and took her in his arms. Standing beside the bed he began to undress her. His fingers undid the buttons of her blouse, and slipped it off her shoulders. His hands slid over her soft satin petticoat, and it cascaded around her feet. He stroked the satin and lace around her thighs, and gently eased the garment away. He lifted her onto the bed, running his hands over the silk stockings, which encased her long limbs. When Catherine lay completely unclothed, he ran his hands lightly down her lovely olive - skinned body. Tracing around her breasts, her stomach, her thighs with his delicate fingers, her cheeks burned with desire and her breath quickened.

'I have been so impatient to possess you my darling, yet now, I want to savour this moment.' He kissed her breasts.'It's too important to rush.

Catherine - my Catherine, you are so beautiful - every part of you.'

He too had a beautiful body, his thighs taut, his legs long and powerful, his skin soft. Soon they were lying together, body against body, and mouth against mouth, kisses feverish with passion. The natural scent of her skin combined with traces of lingering perfume made a seductive combination. His hands stroked her long legs, and slowly climbed. Catherine ached with desire

'Freddy!' she panted. 'What's happening to me?'

His kisses became stronger, his tongue harder as it thrust into her mouth. She began to shudder. Her muscles clenched in a heady paroxysm, she clung fiercely to his shoulders.

'Darling Freddy, I want you - to be part of me.'

Finally, hot and breathless, they wrapped their arms about each other, and lay side by side.

'Happy?' she whispered.

'I have never been so happy in my life - ever. You'll have to marry me now, a good Catholic girl like you.'

'But of course!' She traced the scar on his cheek and kissed it.

'However I may have to report you to the priest for violating an innocent, Major von Langdorf.'

They spent the rest of the evening immersed in their own private universe of new sensations and intimacies, like lovers the world over.

From this time, Catherine and Freddy made love as often as was possible. One evening, Catherine said. 'I'm so glad you knew about - well, you knew what to do.'

'Sure - I knew about sex darling, but I knew nothing about love. It was a first time for me too.'

The Girl on the Promenade

Marianne noticed the way they were looking at each other, the way they touched. Catherine had taken to wearing a most unusual ring, which Freddy had given her. She could guess why, but said nothing, reasoning that there was little point in obeying the strictures of religious teaching, when God Himself seemed to have crossed morality off His omnipotent list. However she determined this relationship was a passing phase, and must certainly not continue beyond the exigency of war.

Annabelle's weekly visits to the chateau became an essential component of the healing process. Both girls were feeling the strain of being kept in hiding, but the Sisters remarked upon the change in Annabelle's disposition. She had become more optimistic, and they had heard her laugh for the first time. There was no doubt they were extremely fond of their wounded foundling.

In the third week of May Freddy received a summons to present himself in SS.Standartenfuhrer Muller's office in Nimes. 'What the hell -? ' were his first words when he saw Muller had been promoted to the SS rank of Colonel.

A young SS officer called him into the great one's presence, the first time they had come face to face since Anduze.

The new office was very large with elaborate bookshelves, one prominently displaying a signed copy of "Mein Kampf". Walls were festooned with framed photographs, several of the Fuhrer, in varying moods, and one, extra large, of Muller shaking hands with Adolf himself. Muller's desk was enormous, strewn with papers and files. He sat in a capacious button - back leather chair. Freddy noted how they suited each other, fat, overstuffed and bulging. Even the rings on Muller's hands no longer sat easily on his gross fingers. As Freddy approached, Muller hauled his bulk into a standing position. 'Heil Hitler, Herr Major.'

Freddy responded with a dismissive salute to the Fuhrer, and a carefully enunciated 'Standartenfuhrer Muller'. Promotion had done nothing for Muller's personal hygiene; his gold teeth still glistened with grey gobbets.

'Please sit down,' he whined, contorting his mouth into a smile.

'I promised you I should need your help Herr Major, some months ago. Well, the time has come, as you are no doubt aware. That is, if any news of the outside world ever penetrates the seclusion of your splendid little chateau'.

He threw his head back and cackled at his joke. 'As I was saying, we are in the process of flushing out the fucking resistance, but although we can, and are, doing this with great success, your services are now imperative.'

He walked across to the window, looked out briefly, and then began to prowl around Freddy's chair, stopping occasionally to declaim, as though addressing a prisoner. It had obviously become a habit.

'The trouble is, Major, you are the best interpreter we have. The only one who has such an excellent understanding of fucking 'Froggiesprach'.

He cackled again at his joke. 'Any moment now we shall be starting in the Cevennes outside Alès, and we shall work towards a certain chateau, not yours.'

He bared his teeth. No reference was made to the photographs. Muller's unusual civility emphasized his understanding of the power Freddy was holding in that small envelope, supposedly somewhere in Berlin.

'This chateau is up in the mountains where there may be a few large prizes.'

Leering with self-satisfaction he walked back to his desk. 'That is why Herr Major, I must,' he thumped the desk knocking over an elaborate beer mug containing an assortment of pencils and pens, 'I must', he reiterated, 'have exact and absolutely correct information from our prisoners.' Another thump sent papers flying.

'It seems we have been led on a few wild goose chases by some of our fucking Frog translators.' He spat.

'Of course you wouldn't do that, Herr Major, as an officer in the German army and an aristocrat, would you?'

'Certainly not, Standartenfuhrer.'

The Girl on the Promenade

'Even if the prisoner was -' he stopped abruptly remembering the photographs. 'You will report here the moment you have your orders. Your colonel must expect you to be away for three or four days.'

Freddy's heart sank. He hated to be away from the chateau. 'Will you be with us, Standartenfuhrer?'

'Of course! You don't think I'm going to miss any of the fun do you?'

At least Freddy would know where the bastard was.

The Allies were bombing railway depots and roads in Nimes now, consequently the resistance had redoubled their own efforts, with the help of civilians and the Gendarmerie who kept up a steady supply of false ration cards. Several viaducts had been blown apart and sabotage around railway sidings packed with Army supplies was constant.

Freddy was duly summoned to Nimes, and joined a small SS platoon of about fifty well-armed men. A stern faced SS captain, Hauptsturmfuhrer Streissmann, and Standartenfuhrer Muller were the only officers. The platoon filled several large army trucks while Freddy and the two officers followed in a smaller armoured vehicle.

'You will not be required for fighting, Major von Langdorf, but later, for interrogations. You will be left to patrol and protect vehicles and reserves.'

'Where?'

Muller smiled. 'In these woods.' He stabbed a point on a detailed map spread across his knees. 'Behind the lines.'

'And my defence if attacked?'

Muller cackled. 'Your revolver, and one Unterofficier with a machine gun.'

Muller spread his fat lips. 'Don't worry, we shall look after you.'

Freddy concluded that whilst there was too much at stake for Muller to want him dead, an incapacitating wound would be more than satisfactory.

The attack would begin at nightfall from positions as close to the chateau as possible.

'I presume you expect no opposition?' Freddy asked sardonically.

Muller laughed. 'From that lot? They've only got a few fucking toy pistols. It'll be a walk-over. They'll shit themselves when they see us, Herr Major. This time our man will be there, and we're going to fucking well get him.'

Muller cackled with glee.

As promised, Freddy was left with one soldier and the transport in a heavily wooded stretch about a hundred metres from the point of attack.

He did not intend to offer himself up as a sacrifice to a passing posse, so he took careful cover in thick bushes away from the trucks.

The chateau was in fact an old medieval fortress, and Muller was wrong about an easy surrender. As soon as the SS platoon opened fire, a barrage of shots flew from the castle, in every direction, from every level and from every window. The resistance was putting up a terrific fight and the deciding factor would almost certainly lie in the quality and quantity of arms. It took nearly two hours for the SS platoon to make any headway. An hour later the firing stopped.

Freddy waited pistol in hand. An SS staff sergeant came running towards the truck. 'We are ready, Herr Major. All prisoners are lined up.'

'The operation has been a success, I take it?' Freddy asked, emerging from cover.

'Yes, Herr Major. But we do have about two dozen casualties, some bad.'

'Can't you take them back to Nimes?'

'Not without orders, sir.'

'Has your Standartenfuhrer seen them?'

'We can't find him, sir. There's a search party out looking.'

They were now approaching the entrance to the chateau.

In the great hall were lined up about thirty prisoners. Hauptsturmfuhrer Streissman sat at a small desk. The resisters were shoved one by one in front of him, while he scrutinised their identity papers.

Freddy entered by the room next door. It had once been the kitchen, with a couple of deep sinks and plenty of water, which was just as well, for here the wounded belonging to both sides had been brought. The French had been thrown in a heap on one side, while SS personnel were laid out with as much comfort as a random collection of palliasses found on the premises could provide. An SS corporal was attempting primitive first aid on his comrades. The missing Standartenfuhrer Muller had apparently not bothered to bring a doctor, not for a simple flushing out exercise. With everyone occupied, and the initial scrutiny of papers not yet finished, Freddy volunteered to look for Muller. On his own, it would have been a perfect opportunity, but Streissman ordered a young private to accompany him. Out through the kitchen door they crossed a vegetable garden, grown wild.

'Now corporal, any ideas?'

'Well, Herr Major, I might have.'

'Really? When did you last see him?'

'Well sir, at the front of the chateau are these old wine cellars. Anyway, there was a lot of firing, and the Standartenfuhrer and a group of us were caught in the crossfire. So he sends us on, and I think he ran in - on his own sir, in there, sir.'

By now they had reached the dark vaulted ground floor storage areas, which were usually built like rabbit warrens under important establishments.

Within a couple of minutes they found Muller exactly where the soldier had indicated. He was lying quite still, his forehead badly gashed, and covered in blood. He had obviously run scared into the opening and straight into a low granite lintel. Muller lying motionless gave Freddy intense pleasure. He hoped the bastard was dead. Playing the concerned officer, he felt his pulse. He was alive. For an officer to desert his troops would not bode well for Muller. The young private left for a stretcher and strong men.

Freddy looked at the fat bulk. He would like to have killed him, but to kill an unconscious Muller would have been too kind a despatch. To make Muller's waking hours as painful as he had made them for others, was a satisfying possibility. Separating Muller's legs, he carefully positioned himself, and his right boot in line with Muller's crotch, and swinging a long leg, gathering the momentum to kick for goal, he unleashed an almighty blow into Muller's flaccid centre, and another, and another, muttering, 'this is for Gaston! This is for Catherine! This is for the hospital!' Finally summoning all his strength, he delivered the most crushing blow of all, with its special dedication. 'This is for the hundreds of poor sods you've killed, bastard!'

Freddy astounded himself by his own brutality. Never before had he wilfully injured anyone. It was a sad fact of life, he reflected, brutality bred its like. Whilst immensely satisfied that it was done, the fact he could do it was disturbing, but only momentarily.

It required four men to bring Muller alongside the others in the chateau's kitchen. A mattress was found and the corporal made futile attempts to dress the gash. Freddy approached Streissmann.

'There are over thirty wounded in there. Most of them need urgent hospital treatment, and some of them look as though they won't last the journey. I propose therefore, as senior officer here, we ask if there is a French doctor on the premises.'

Streissmann sneered. 'Amongst this rabble?'

'They weren't rabble a few years ago, were they? Use your head, man.'

The prisoners had now had their papers checked, so Freddy asked politely for a doctor. 'I promise, you have my word you will be able to attend to your own comrades as well as ours. You will be treated with respect.'

No one moved. From the kitchen, groans from both groups of wounded could be heard.

'The wounded will die if there is no help.' Freddy continued.

There was a shuffling of feet, and a man with a moustache, stepped out.

'I am a doctor. I have my bag upstairs.'

'Name?' shouted Streissman.

'Jean-Pierre Soulas,' the man replied.

Freddy stared at him. He had seen that face somewhere before. He looked at his dark eyes, and noticed his well-preserved hands.

In a remarkably short time Dr Soulas was dressing, suturing, binding dangerous bleeding, and sorting out those who were in urgent need of a hospital, and those who could make the journey back to base. The same went for the wounded resisters. They would be taken to a prison hospital, at least that is what Streissman had told them. Four resisters and five SS soldiers were dead or dying. Dr. Soulas sutured Muller's gash. 'I'm pretty sure he's cracked his skull. He will certainly need an X – ray.'

Freddy again feigned concern.

Two hours later the doctor rose from the floor and smiled briefly making some quip about Muller's girth.

That smile told Freddy all he needed to know.

He was never so thankful that the fat man lay an inert blob on the floor.

Expressing his gratitude, Freddy invited the doctor outside for a cigarette. There was enough going on in the hall not to notice absence. Without a leader the whole platoon seemed to have been thrown into confusion.

Freddy shut the kitchen door and beckoned the doctor to follow him a few paces into the wilderness. The night air was chill. A moon shone benignly over the violent landscape. He took a packet of cigarettes out of his pocket, and handed them to the doctor.'Here. I don't smoke. Take the packet.'

He came straight to the point.

'Look Dr. Soulas I'm pretty sure I know who you are, and I'm going to give you the chance to run.'

The doctor smiled, and huffed down his nose.' Really major. And of course you will shoot me in the back if I do.'

'You are Max Becker. I do not intend to shoot you as I am in love with your cousin Catherine. I'm stationed at Chateau de Lazarin, and I want to marry her when this is over. Now for God's sake go before I'm shot.'

Max grabbed Freddy's hand. 'Catherine's not dead? We heard she was.'

Freddy shook his head. 'No. She's safe.'

'Thank God. Look after her. And thanks.'

'And you make sure your chaps leave her alone.'

'They will. I promise.'

Freddy turned away.'And I haven't seen you go,' he mumbled.

Max disappeared through tangled vegetation, into the enveloping black foliage of the vineyards beyond.

The major gave another convincing performance looking for the doctor when he returned to the kitchen. Not that one less made any difference. The captured resisters were to be kept in prison until the Standartenfuhrer was fit to interrogate, and Freddy hoped that would be some time in the distant future.

Major von Langdorf returned to the chateau satisfied.

Muller had not only cracked his skull, but with luck, would never be able to reproduce in his own image.

He brought back something for Catherine: Max's medical bag.

CHAPTER TWENTY-FOUR

They were working their way through slices of heavy potato omelette; there was no meat this week. Kurt filled up his glass.

'Thank God for vino. This food is like cement.'

'Kurt, do you think a deal with the Allies is possible?'

The colonel placed his fork on the table. 'Our Generals have been suggesting it for some time, but the madman's deaf. He's even refused Erwin Rommell's request to withdraw his troops in Normandy.They're getting slaughtered! We are short of everything, manpower, arms food.'

When they had finished the meagre meal, Kurt threw his napkin down angrily, and rose from his chair. 'Christ knows, there are so few solutions left.'

Rome had fallen. The Americans and the British were pushing into Northern France, and Allied planes were systematically severing communication links with the Fatherland. The latest directive instructed that troops be confined to barracks and to be prepared to move at any time. The fight for survival was about to start.

Freddy pushed his cheese plate aside. 'So what do we do, here?'

'Sit tight. Watch the Allies advance, and you make the most of your little ladylove. I shall be off to Berlin in a week or two.'

Catherine and Annabelle laughed heartily at Muller cracking his skull, and at Freddy kicking him hard in his crotch.

'Hey, you'll probably be able to go back home soon. Have you thought about your parents when they actually see you?'

Annabelle smiled. 'The sisters will break the news to them, then I'll walk in.'

'Oh Annabelle, I feel quite goose-pimply just thinking of it.'

The little blonde had more colour in her cheeks these days, but she was thin and fragile, despite the blood transfusions she had been given in Professor Becaud's surgery in January. Her shoulder was still not completely mobile and she rose stiffly from the chair in Catherine's study, to the bookcase, running her finger along the book spines cramming the shelves.

'I'm afraid to think about it, Cathy. So many terrible things have happened to us both, I have resigned myself to being in this habit, and in this convent, till I die.' She smiled ruefully. 'Again.'

Freddy had less time to spend with Catherine. His days, and sometimes nights, were taken up with exercises, using a new issue of rifle, the *Sturmgewehr*, whilst continuing to monitor BBC radio bulletins to the French Resistance, which was now a powerful armed force, that worked with air-dropped British agents.

The weather was gloriously hot, and Catherine crept quietly from time to time into the secret garden or into the conservatory. Freddy and Catherine, in a new relationship of confident intimacy, gave each other what they most needed, comfort, support and security.

Muller was still hors de combat, and barrack room jokes about his permanently damaged appendage, and even his change of voice, were rampant and of immense satisfaction to his enemies.

Before going to Berlin Kurt had arranged to see his wife and children, now evacuated to his parents' house deep in the country. 'Can't wait to cuddle them, especially little Annelise, she's so gorgeous.'

He refused to take a letter to Carl from Freddy, but offered to give him instead a verbal report. Just after he left, news came through that Erwin Rommel had been severely wounded by RAF bullets in Normandy, and would be returning to Germany, but the momentous news which followed days later, totally eclipsed the General's injury.

On July 20th, von Stauffenberg attempted to assassinate the Fuhrer. That evening Hitler broadcast to the German

The Girl on the Promenade

people, swearing vengeance upon all traitors. Freddy, like the rest of his nation, was flabbergasted, staggered at the plot's audacity, and like many more deeply regretted its failure. He wondered what Kurt's reaction would be in Berlin, knowing his anti-Fuhrer feelings.

But Count von Stauffenberg had not been alone. The following morning a first list of conspirators was broadcast. Some had already been shot, the rest had been taken to Plotzensee prison: one of them was Colonel Kurt Bergen. Freddy was numb. Throughout the day he sat stunned. Kurt had been his close friend for four years and he had had no idea.

Military exercises were cancelled for twelve hours. Ears, anxious to catch names in new endless lists, were trained on radio sets. By the next day every soldier in the chateau knew, but no one talked about it. Kurt had been well liked by his men. Major von Langdorf was now in charge.

'Why didn't he tell me?' was Freddy's first reaction 'Did he think I couldn't be trusted? Did he think I was too juvenile to take responsibility? That's probably what it was. He thought I was too immature.'

He was pacing around Catherine's study distraught with worry.

'Come on Freddy be logical. How could he implicate you, or any of his associates? That's why he wouldn't take a letter to your uncle. Imagine the risk? Be thankful.'

His face crumpled with despair. 'Berlin seems to be rounding up anyone who has uttered a word of dissent, or has even had a passive connection. Over two hundred now. It's a blood bath! Kurt will never get out alive from Plotzensee.There is going to be a trial, but there'll be no justice with that fanatic Friesler.'

'Kurt was a brave man, Freddy. They were all brave men, honourable men. It could have worked.' There was little else she could say.

The next day Freddy heard from a mutual friend in Berlin that Kurt's wife and children had been sent to Sachsenhausen concentration camp.

Muller, still convalescing, lost no time telephoning.

'So major, your colonel was a traitor. And how much did you fucking know?'

The call was unnerving.

Four days later a new list was read out on the radio. It was a shocking double blow for Freddy, for at the top of the list was General Count Carl von Langdorf, already in Plotzensee, awaiting trial. Freddy's private grief was inconsolable. Catherine knew how deeply he loved his uncle, his mentor, and how worried he was about his parents.

'Are they arresting all families?'

'No. Seems to be quite random, capricious.'

'Brothers of conspirators?'

'In some cases, not all.'

'But not a nephew, surely not. You were here in France.'

'God knows. I'll have to wait until my uncle has been tried. It could be the end of our family.'

On the edge of tears again, his head in her lap, Catherine gently ran her fingers through his hair. 'We have to be proud of them. They tried to change history.'

'Sure! They risked everything to rescue Germany from the abyss, but I am so sickened that all these good men will have to be murdered for a madman. He can now add to his assassinations the very best and most honourable, while bastards like Muller live!'

He kissed her hand, and pressed it tightly to his cheek.

Muller wasted no time. An evil smile spread across his face, as he once again telephoned Freddy.

'I have never trusted you fucking aristocrats.' he bellowed. 'Traitors! All of you! You can be bloody lucky he was not your father, or I should have great pleasure in taking you to Plotzensee, personally. And you can tell your French fuck, I shall be inviting her to tea soon.'

But Muller did not invite Catherine to tea.

Fanaticism when edged with panic becomes totally ruthless, qualities that Muller had recently shown off admirably. He was a natural choice therefore to lead a company from the crack SS battalion 'Das Reich' to a village near Limoges, where there had been rumours of resistance activity, with orders to destroy. Accordingly, they herded women and children into the church, and set it alight. They shot the men and Muller took special delight in recounting how he shoved the miller and his family into their own bread ovens. The company then joined its battalion en route to Normandy, but Muller, still anxious about his embarrassing pelvic problems returned to Nimes, where flushing out the increasing numbers of resisters became his personal remit. Aided by air-drops, the resistance was now detonating viaducts, power stations, and blowing trucks and stores, high into the night sky.

Marianne was quite moved by the fate of the conspirators, particularly as she knew and liked Kurt. 'Pity they had to wait until they were losing the war,' was her dry comment. 'A few years ago they could have saved so many lives.'

On the wall of Kurt's old office was a map of Europe, showing the Fascist empire shaded red, ringed with a black line denoting Allied advances. It was alarming to see how the festering carbuncle of Europe was about to be squeezed on all sides. A melancholy young major picked up the few scattered photographs Kurt had left on his desk, and hoped he'd had a chance to hug his children before leaving for Berlin. He opened up his violin case, and idly plucked the strings. He felt an immeasurable sense of loss.

At the beginning of August, in Berlin, seven conspirators were hanged with piano wire from meat hooks. Kurt Bergen was one of the seven.

Freddy wept.

Directives for an imminent evacuation came through. All personnel would make for a central barracks in Lyon, before being despatched to fighting units. The problem was, how?

'How the hell are we going to get to Lyon with hardly a viaduct left standing?' Rudi, recently promoted to lieutenant, and ever the optimist replied. 'We'll have to chance the 'D' roads.'

'They'll be full.'

Rudi grinned. 'Don't forget I was a driver. I know roads that aren't even on the map. We'll get to Lyon.'

Freddy and Catherine were being carried along in the current of events. No time now for coffee and Brahms. No inclination for laughter, time was short. Catherine was rent in two. As a Frenchwoman she was overjoyed that the end to her country's occupation was in sight; that at last there could be a future. But she loved a man, an enemy no less, who at this moment had no future, no family he could contact, but who had given the resistance incalculable help.

'You could always stay here Freddy. Join our resistance. A number of Germans already have.'

He stroked her cheek. 'I know my love, but I - I need to find my parents.'

They were in Catherine's study. He put on their favourite Tschaikovsky and led her through to her bedroom where they sat side by side on the bed.

'Catherine, I may be going tomorrow, the next day, certainly very soon, and I don't want to go without saying everything that is in my heart.'

She pressed her face into his shoulder.'No Freddy - please!'

'Don't make it harder *Liebling*. Listen - if I don't come back, because I 'm pretty certain I'll be going to Normandy, it will only be because my life is over. Remember I have loved you more than anyone else in the world, but if the worst happens, you must forget about me, you will have to, because - because - I want you to be happy – always.'

Tears filled her eyes, but she tried to lighten the mood.

'You old pessimist! When it's over, you will still be alive and healthy, I know you will.'

He grinned. 'Then I'll come straight back. You are my wife. I have to marry you - officially.'

In mid - August the Americans landed on the south coast of France, and Freddy received evacuation orders. He spent his last night with Catherine, their love-making wonderful, desperate and tearful.

Catherine and Marianne stood at the kitchen door early next morning, and bade goodbye to Rudi and the few others left from the old orchestra. The trucks lumbered into action and left. Freddy took Catherine inside for a last silent embrace. There were no words left.

She watched him get into the back seat of the Mercedes with Rudi and they drove away.

At lunchtime in the kitchen a week later, after seeing her daughter grieve and refuse what food was available, Marianne, ever practical, knew she had to do something, or she would be in danger of losing her daughter too. She sat her down and placed cheese, bread, and a glass of wine before her.

'You cannot continue like this, Catherine. I know how you feel, who better - but we must try to put things in perspective. I was very fond of Freddy, a dear boy, but darling, he is going into frightful battles up north from which alas, few will survive. You cannot spend your life thinking about what might have been. You have to get on with your own life.' She put her hand on Catherine's arm. 'Darling girl, you have had some terrible experiences in this war, which I know, like little Annabelle you will be strong enough to put aside. You will have your studies to finish. And for heavens' sake, even if Freddy comes back, he will still be a German, and very unwelcome. It will take years for memories to fade.' She wagged her finger for emphasis.

Catherine knew there was some truth in her words, but they made her even more depressed. She had no desire to read, to eat, and to talk, in fact to do anything. Marianne took over. She had assumed her old dominant role again. 'It' s about time you went into the village. You haven't set foot outside the chateau since January. I've prepared a shopping list .You probably won't get half of it, but try.'

The baker's wife at the village boulangerie, Madame Martin, was a mean little creature with tiny eyes and black hair scraped into a straggly bun. She wore a flowered cross-over apron, and though her thin face rarely assumed any expression, she was startled when Catherine walked into the shop.'Good Lord! Mademoiselle de Lazarin! Haven't you been away?'

'Er – yes,' replied Catherine. 'I was deported, didn't you know?'

'Oh yes! Funny the other deportees aren't back yet. War's still going on up north.'

Catherine gave a little shrug and smiled weakly.

'Baguettes, all I've got,' she snapped.

Catherine handed the shopkeeper two ration cards, and money.

'Your friends have gone then?' she asked with a smirk.

'Friends? Who do you mean?'

The thin face broke into a smile. 'Your Boche friends of course.'

'They weren't my friends.'

'Not what I heard. Still, in your position the chateau and all that, I expect you know all the right people — on both sides.' She looked triumphant. 'That's probably why you're first home, don't you think?'

'No, I do not!'

Catherine snatched up the baguettes angrily, and strode from the shop.

She walked back to the chateau along the main road from Uzès. High summer, and hot, the foliage was thick, and carpets of sunflowers and lavender swathed across vistas in every direction. The plane trees edging the road-needed pruning, their overhanging branches forming tunnels rather than shade as Napoleon had originally intended. Apart from the grasshoppers' unceasing chatter, and her footsteps swishing softly through dry grass verges on the side of the road, it was blissfully quiet. Gradually she became aware of a ringing,

The Girl on the Promenade

like bells, in the distance. As the volume of shrill screeching tremolo increased, she recognised the sound of bicycle bells. Suddenly from around the bend in the road, hundreds of cyclists appeared. Not ordinary cyclists, these were German soldiers pedalling for their very lives.

The exodus was frantic.

She received a card from Lyon. Freddy could give nothing away, but a reference to warm socks being handed out could only mean he was going north. During the last week in August, the resistance liberated Nimes, and the Americans had come and gone.

She had a call from Annabelle who had at last been delivered home.

'We couldn't stop crying, and we still can't. Poor Maman, she keeps touching me, my face, my hands, just to make sure I really am alive.'

Catherine arranged to meet Annabelle in Uzès. Feeling the ripple of life again and looking forward to this first Saturday of freedom, she put on a favourite summer dress, and tied her hair back with some ribbon she had found in a drawer. She brushed her thick black eyebrows, put on some lipstick, and sprayed herself with Freddy's perfume.

The café Bengali was packed, buzzing with an air of celebration. Friends embraced in greeting, some not having set eyes on each other for years. Those who had no chairs sat on the pavement. Catherine found a table for two. The waiter kissed her hand. 'No more messages under the coffee cup today, mademoiselle,' he laughed 'and no bloody Boche! What a day!'

He was a large young man, and despite his girth fairly pirouetted through the tables in a state of complete euphoria. France was being won back and at last, everyone could breathe French air again.

Annabelle, prettily dressed in blue cotton, with colour back in her cheeks, laughed. 'How Maman makes me eat! You know I really appreciate both of them, maybe for the first time ever. They are my friends now, as well.'

They talked for a while, then Annabelle touched Catherine's arm, and gave one of her special grins.'I've got something to tell you. I'm going to start a medical degree at Montpellier, as soon as the war is really over. Professor Becaud has been giving me private instruction for months, since the convent days. I couldn't say anything to you until I'd talked to Maman and Papa. He says I'm well up to first year finals, and he's going to get me a place there. Maman is going to work as Papa's secretary in his tile business to save money.'

She was so excited she hardly stopped to take a breath.

'Oh! Annabelle it's wonderful, really wonderful!'

'It's for Francois really. I feel I must do it for him – well, for us both.'

'He would be so proud of you Annabelle.'

The little face creased, and a large tear fell into the saucer of the coffee cup.

'Yes I know - I know.'

Catherine reached for her hand and held on to it handing Annabelle a handkerchief. Thinking of her father and how he would have loved this time of liberation, her own eyes overflowed. They were not alone.

The war had touched everyone.

'Just think, we shall be bumping into each other every day. I'm sure I shall have to do a refresher course for a term or two. I'll probably end up with you.'

Annabelle giggled.' Bet you won't.'

They talked and drank coffee for the whole afternoon. At the end of it there was nothing Annabelle did not know about Freddy.

By the end of August, although there was no fighting German soldier left in the south, some members of the resistance began meting out their own vengeance, against collaborators, particularly the Milice. Kangaroo courts were set up to dispatch traitors. It was also known that some groups calling themselves resisters would kill for reasons of personal vendettas. Times were uneasy.

The Girl on the Promenade

In Nimes, Marianne and Catherine saw a crowd of jeering people following four young women each carrying a baby. Their heads were shaved, and swastikas had been painted on their foreheads. Around their necks they carried placards; "Horizontal Collaborators.' When the crowd had gone Marianne said tartly.'I suppose it depends who you are. I wonder if they've shaved Coco Chanel's head?'

But they could shave mine, Catherine thought to herself, if Madame Martin is still the village voice.

When they returned home, Marianne called from the kitchen table. 'Catherine, come here for a moment.'

Looking directly at her daughter who was leaning against a chair she said, 'I have been thinking, and remembering that ugly word scrawled on the portico when dear Papa - left us. It is pretty clear a great deal of gossip has been going on in the village, carried I'm quite sure via the little girls who used to keep company with the soldiers here. We cannot allow our family name to be besmirched, nor harmed, can we?'

Catherine had returned to the cooker, to boil the kettle for some lemon tea. She wondered what was coming next. 'Of course not Maman.'

'In that case Catherine,' Marianne paused. 'In that case, don't you think the sooner you find yourself a French boy friend, the better - for us all. Even if Major von Langdorf survives, which is doubtful, he is a German, and you are French. And don't you ever, ever forget that.'

When de Gaulle marched through the streets of Paris in triumph, Catherine received a telephone call from Max.

'I'm in Paris, little cousin, with the General's entourage.'

'Max! You're famous!'

'I doubt that. Look, may I come to see you in a week or two?'

'Great! What about your mother.'

'Seeing her tomorrow. Er - did that German officer tell you about - er?'

'Yes.'

'Nice guy. One of the few.'

'Yes, he was. He returned your medical bag.'

'Really? I wondered where I'd left it. Must go. See you soon.'

It was the end of September. Max was expected at any time. He was visiting his mother, who had been told that Louis was at least alive in Dachau. There were plans to empty the camp before the Allies got there, so, for that reason she could not leave Vichy. A chilly Mistral was blowing through the thin garments of the grape pickers, and dry autumn leaves were being driven into mounds. This year the *vendange* was less of a problem, with more young men available, and what was more, eager to work.

Max's car scraped to a halt on the gravel drive just before eight. Catherine was in her room, changing her clothes. Adding a brightly coloured lipstick that she had bought in Uzès, she rushed downstairs, through the hall and bounded down the steps to the gravel courtyard. Max was standing there, arms outstretched.

'Dear little cousin,' he laughed. 'Let me look at you. Mmm! Quite a woman now.' He hugged her. 'I think the little girl got lost in the war.'

Catherine grinned. 'She needed to.'

'I want to hear all about what happened at Anduze.'

She gave a thin smile, and shrugged. 'Maybe.'

'We have to talk about these things. Otherwise we never bury them. By the way, I have brought an old friend to see you.'

The rear door opened, and out stepped Philippe, bronzed, smiling and very handsome with his slightly increased weight.

He stepped towards her. She was so astonished to see him, she could find nothing to say.

He put his arms gently on her shoulders and placed three traditional kisses on her cheeks. 'You are even more beautiful, Catherine, than when I last saw you. Max has told me some of what you have been through.'

'You too,' she replied, finding her voice.

She did not feel hostile to him anymore. However she was quite convinced this scenario had been stage-managed by her mother, particularly when Marianne, registering no surprise whatsoever at his unexpected arrival, showed Philippe to his already prepared room.

CHAPTER TWENTY-FIVE

Lyon had been chaotic, swarming with German troops arriving by the hundreds, on foot, bicycle, farm trucks, army vehicles, anything that moved. Freddy was aware that his family name could put him in danger now, but thankfully the commanding officer in Lyon to whom he reported, appeared so frustrated by the general confusion, and the problem of getting himself out, names meant very little.

They were on their way north, fifty men crammed into the chateau's trucks, their destination, Holland. The standard of morale was abysmal. Each time they stopped near the Fatherland's frontier, men disappeared. Barricades were already being erected. A far cry from the joyful passage of victorious troops festooned with flowers, and showered with kisses.

They joined a regiment outside Deventer, a small town where, to Freddy's immense relief, the commanding officer was his old Kommandant from the Kommandantur in Paris. Rounder now, and with less hair, he welcomed Freddy with characteristic good humour. 'A pleasant surprise, what? And a major too! Well done. Glad to have you with us. We need a first-rate French speaker. London sends coded messages to the resistance, and British agents working behind our lines. Could be vital.'

As Freddy was about to leave, the Kommandant looking slightly embarrassed, stepped away from his desk, and took his arm.

'Look, my boy, I know about Colonel Kurt Bergen and your uncle Carl, dear old friend of mine. I hope there will be no measures taken against the family. But one never knows. Some have not been touched. Others taken immediately.'

Freddy, feeling equally ill at ease raised his eyebrows.

The Girl on the Promenade

The Kommandant answered his unspoken question. 'Nothing has come through for you, yet. Let's hope, eh?'

'Thank you sir,' Freddy faltered. ' I hold my uncle in the highest esteem as I do my colonel. Brave men.'

'Quite so. I daresay had it succeeded, there would have been many of us who would have joined them.' He gave his young officer a knowing nod.

On September 17th, an urgent SOS was put out to all serving groups in the area. British paratroopers were converging on the town of Arnhem, a short distance away. Freddy set up a field communications unit in a forest clearing just behind the front line, but it became clear that something was amiss. Freddy's platoon picked up the drops of arms, food, and medical supplies meant for the besieged paratroopers waiting on the other side of the bridge. Seven days later the British were still trying to defend themselves with no sign of reinforcements. By September 26th it was an obvious Wehrmacht victory, a shot in the arm for despairing spirits, but the piles of dead bodies were a nauseating sight; the suffering of the almost dead even more.

Plodding back with his platoon, through the slush, smoke and detritus of skewered limbs; through the grey mists of a September dawn, he would have given anything to be holding Catherine in his arms, instead of his cold lethal *Sturmgewehr.*

Philippe was to stay at the chateau, along with Max, for two weeks, during which time they received a visit from an American colonel. He was polite, tall, tanned and smoked cigars. Seeing the chateau his eyes opened in wonder. 'Say, great place you've got here. Colonel Harry Muller ma'am.' He smiled with perfect gleaming white teeth, as he shook hands with Marianne. 'Yep! It's a German name, but don't get worried. My grandfather was an immigrant piano player O.K.?'

After a few lubricating glasses of Chateau de Lazarin, Colonel Muller said, 'I'll come straight to the point Max. I need your help. It's these goddamn killings without reference to any judiciary. Kangaroo courts, family vendettas, all done in the name of resistance and retribution. This is Mafia time Max! We don't want a civil war.' He paused to light a fat cigar. 'By profession I'm a lawyer, and it's my job to get the legal system working again. I want lists of genuine resisters and genuine collaborators. Tomorrow morning, O.K.?'

The Colonel lit Marianne's Camel cigarette. 'I'm not concerned with the women,' he huffed. 'Any French broad who slept with a Kraut deserves to get her head shaved and get run out of town! Hookers, the goddam lot. Prostitutes to you!' he explained with a grin. Catherine felt her stomach tighten. Marianne observed a stony silence.

Looking directly at Marianne, the Colonel took a piece of paper from his pocket. 'I have to inform you Madame de Lazarin, and Mademoiselle de Lazarin, that I and a few fellow officers, will be taking over the part of your chateau last occupied by the Nazis, I believe.'

'But of course,' Marianne smiled sweetly, with relief.

'Sometime this afternoon, ma'am. We Americans don't waste time.'

He laughed loudly. 'We'll have to fumigate it first of course.'

'You have no need to,' Catherine smiled thinly. 'There were only three Nazi party members. The commanding officer was part of the Hitler assassination plot.

He was hanged.'

There was an awkward pause. Catherine wished she had kept her mouth shut.

By evening the sounds of laughter and loud jazz were flowing out of open windows. The following evening women's voices added to the rhythmical beat of the Jitterbug.

Catherine found the presence of investigating Americans in the west wing, frightening. Should anyone find out about Freddy, or listen to village gossip, the shame on the family would be withering. Max had stood with de Gaulle at the Paris

Liberation ceremony. How could he have a cousin dubbed collaborator?

It was obvious Philippe wanted to talk to Catherine alone, but her heart was far too involved with Freddy to allow even a spark of interest in him. He didn't exist as a man for her, just a person to pass the time of day with. But persistence on his part, and loneliness on hers, plus the combination of foursomes with Annabelle and Max, gradually began to take effect.

They were sitting round the Chateau's kitchen table, eating Philippe's spaghetti, with ingredients provided by the Americans, when Annabelle asked, 'won't you go back to Paris, Jean- er- Max?' She giggled. 'I've only just got used to calling you 'Max''.

These days she had begun to fill out, and looked prettier than ever with her blond hair cut short around her face, and her skin tanned.

'Maybe when it's all over in Europe. But if I can do Psychiatry here at Montpellier, I'll stay.'

'So we'll all be here!' said Philippe, who was in the process of negotiating a Heart Surgery Fellowship at Montpellier. Moving round the table with second helpings of cheese sauce, he stopped beside Catherine.'And you little mademoiselle? You are still going back to finish aren't you?'

All eyes turned to her. She hesitated.

'Now look here young woman,' said Max sharply. 'You of all people have a gift for medicine, and if you let these ghastly five years deprive our country of a doctor, I shall disown you, so there!'

Philippe looked at her with smiling grey eyes, a lock of hair still tumbling over his forehead. 'I remember a teenager who was so dedicated she was happy not to be in Paris, lest I took her away from her studies.'

Catherine blushed. 'Of course I'm going back.'

A month later Max and Philippe were still at the chateau.

One night, Annabelle and Catherine were sitting alone, on the floor in Catherine's study with cups of hot milk, Annabelle said quietly, 'Philippe is nuts about you, Catherine.'

'So? He had his chance once.'

'That was five years ago. He knows what he wants now. He's been married sure, but from what he's said I don't think it was a great love match. She died in childbirth didn't she, poor girl?'

Catherine nodded.

'Do you feel nothing for him, at all?'

'It's - it's Freddy, Annabelle. He's always there.'

'I know. How I know. And it's hard. But Francois would want me to live again, and perhaps -'

Catherine's swift rejoinder was confident. 'Freddy's going to come back for me.'

'And then?'

'Stay here, maybe, while I finish off medical school.'

Annabelle drained her cup, and dabbed her mouth. 'Have you thought what sort of life he'd have here? Everyone knows him as the German Major at the chateau. He's no Nazi, we know that, but they don't. They know he was involved with Muller, and he'd be ripped apart. Do you think they'd stop to ask questions?'

'Well then, I could go to Germany.'

'Cathy! How d'you finish medical school, in Germany? Anyway, what's he going back to?'

'I don't know Annabelle.'

Her eyes filled up with tears that trickled down her cheeks onto some of Freddy's records she was clutching in her arms.

'Supposing-supposing Freddy doesn't survive? You've got to think of that.'

'I do, all the time.' Catherine dabbed her eyes. 'I tell myself that he– he's dead.'

Annabelle put her arms around her friend's shoulders. 'It's the best way, honestly. The only way.'

One lunchtime when they were alone in the kitchen, Max drew up a chair. 'Little cousin, we have never really talked about that Kraut officer who saved my life.'

He cheeks reddened. 'What is there to talk about?'

'He told me he loved you and was going to marry you, that's all.'

Really?' Her eyes opened wide in total surprise.

Max gave her a pitying look. 'Catherine please! No need for games between us. Wasn't he the one who saved your life in Anduze? Who telephoned his uncle General in Berlin, one of the July plot conspirators? Who gave blood to Uncle Georges?'

She blushed. 'Who told you all this?'

'Your mother, and, what's more, he had to be the one who fed us all that fantastic info.' He paused. 'Am I right?' She said nothing.

'Who could blame you,' he said softly. 'Handsome chap, but, Catherine, he has gone, probably for ever. Don't throw away all your chances of happiness for a mirage.'

Catherine's silence continued. Max patted her hand.

'No one else knows anything of this. Neither shall they. Ever.'

'Catherine', Marianne chirped brightly,' I have suggested to Philippe he stays here until February when he starts his Heart Surgery studies. I like to have a man about the house, and he's quite a good handyman. Always useful.'

Whenever her mother attempted to sound casual, there was always a hidden agenda. This one was becoming obvious.

Despite herself, and her mother, Catherine was beginning to enjoy seeing Philippe return to the chateau at the end of the day. A subtle dependence was growing between them, and with it, a deepening friendship.

The war had changed Philippe. He was gentler, calmer, and more understanding. He thought the same of Catherine. He talked about his dead wife, and the relationship they had. He already knew in general terms about Muller, the hospital and the firing squad. Catherine considered that to be quite enough.

She had received no news from Freddy except the postcard from Lyon in mid-August. Marianne therefore pushed Philippe's candidature with renewed vigour.

'He is a very good looking young man, he has an excellent career in front of him, he comes from a good family, he's French, and you are not going to find that combination easily, not now with the shortage of men.'

Marianne picked up the coffee percolator. 'I must say it's lovely to have real coffee again.'

'The Americans are as generous as the Germans, aren't they Maman?'

Marianne scowled. 'I think the less you say, we both say, about the years of occupation the better Catherine, and the more you consider the relationship, or whatever it was with the German major, simply as a growing up experience, the better.'

This opening salvo was just the beginning..

'It was patently obvious you had a love affair with him, and that you were his mistress.'

Catherine sat mute with guilt.

'It was understandable, I suppose. But the thought of anyone finding out would be too terrible for words, particularly for the family name. You know what they said of poor Papa for only playing in that wretched orchestra!'

Catherine looked down into her cup. Marianne was unstoppable.

'You must assume the young man is dead. So take advice, think very seriously about Philippe. He loves you I know, probably far more than your major ever did, and he'd make a wonderful husband.'

Marianne's new rule - book could not have been clearer. Catherine should now resign her heart and her feelings to Philippe.

One Sunday in November when they had returned from a dinner and he gently put his hands on her shoulders and

The Girl on the Promenade

kissed her, she found herself responding. When he took her hand and led her to his room, her coy reluctance was soon overcome. Sexuality had already been awakened in Catherine and at the time, assuaged. It was ready to re-emerge.

'Dearest Catherine, I was a fool to let you go. Please forgive me.'

Philippe kissed her until desire somersaulted through her body once more. Between cool sheets as his hand gently traced the contours of her body, a rekindled passion pulsated through eager limbs, powerful enough to obliterate past loyalties and past loves, banishing them into a brief oblivion. They had both known bereavement, for Freddy's parting had been no less. To find a relationship, which no longer could be unnaturally wrenched apart, was a mutual need. War had taken its barbarous toll. It would take time to adjust.

'Remember when we were in Cannes? I was afraid to touch you. That wretched cousin of yours absolutely forbade me.'

'That's because he knew you had somebody else.'

He kissed her nose. 'Well I don't now. Do you?'

'Not any more,' she said, quite truthfully.

'Five years is a long time. We've both done a lot of growing. I don't care what you did, who you made love to. We change. And I can't rush into anything, not yet because - well we all have memories.'

'Yes, we do,' she replied simply.

'There is no one else for me, only you. I love you, and one day I want to marry you, if you'll have me.'

That night before going to bed Catherine took off Freddy's peacock ring, put it back in its box, and locked it away in her secret drawer.

Philippe was a good man. But Freddy would remain the love of her life.

In the first week of December, Freddy was summoned to his Kommandant's office. It had been a depressing few months what with Erwin Rommel's suicide, and still no news of his uncle.

The Kommandant was poring over a map, spread out on the desk, round pebble glasses balancing on the end of his nose. It was a map of the Belgian Ardennes, and the German spill over the Eifel.

'You see this line? That's the Americans, and from Monschau, up here, to the Losheim Gap down here, defence is thin. It's a weakly held position.'

He straightened himself. 'You remember the Fuhrer's brilliantly successful thrust through the Ardennes in the French campaign in 1940?'

'Of course.'

'Well, we had strength then; a good fighting army, and it was spring. The Fuhrer will not listen to anyone now, not even to Rundstedt, not even to Sepp Dietrich.'

Freddy wondered where all this was leading. The Kommandant continued.

'The objective this time is to burst through the American lines, the Ist SS Panzers taking the southerly route round here, and the 12th SS Panzers.'

He took off his glasses cleaned them with a handkerchief, and leant heavily on the desk. 'The 12th SS Panzers are Hitler Youth. Dietrich has told me they are the sweepings, inadequately trained kids. Just about hold a rifle. Anyway', he turned back to the map. 'The 12th SS will swing round to the North West, the ultimate objective is to re-take Antwerp and Brussels.'

'Impossible sir, surely!'

'Try telling the Fuhrer. 'The short stout man began to pace around his desk. He crossed to the window, and back again.

'Sit down my boy. Listen carefully. Two things. One, I have heard rumours on the Berlin grapevine that your uncle, my old friend Carl, will be up for trial imminently. The chances are strong that you too will be arrested. Two, Sepp Dietrich has asked for experienced communications officers to lead these platoons of boys in this new offensive.' He shook his head. 'Barely fifteen some of them.'

Freddy looked in silence at the Kommandant for several moments.

'Are you saying, arrest or the Ardennes, sir?'

The older man nodded 'Pretty much' he sighed. 'And if you are out of the way, not here? Follow me?' He sat at his desk. 'Well, which is it to be?'

Freddy shrugged. 'No choice. The Ardennes sir.'

'Good man!'

On the 14th of December Freddy had his marching orders. He gave Rudi another letter to post to Catherine doubting it would ever reach her.

Rudi forced a smile. 'God be with you my old orchestra partner, and take heart. Bach, Beethoven, and Brahms will still be here to rescue this insane world when the slaughter is over.'

The two men hugged. Freddy felt he was saying goodbye to Erich again.

In the early hours of Saturday December 16th, in the bitter cold and freezing mists of the Belgian Ardennes, the Panzer tanks began their ferocious attack with a devastating barrage on the American lines. The Americans, taken by surprise, panicked and fled, putting the small town to the torch. The assault troops following the Panzers ravaged the remnants. Two entire American divisions were shattered.

Major von Langdorf's platoon was, as predicted, made up of boys between fifteen and seventeen. What they lacked in experience, they made up for in characteristic zeal, some already displaying embryonic SS ruthlessness. Freddy had orders to assemble his group of boy soldiers outside the town of Buellingen ready for attack on a ridge. He found a house with three large interconnecting cellars, perfect for communication equipment and quarters. He ordered them to take a rest while they could. Observing their faces as they slumbered, they were little more than children. It was going to be a massacre.

Stumbling into the freezing night for action many of them wept, but they fought like tigers and pounded the American dugouts. The strength of American resistance was devastating. Only one Panzer tank got through. Each time they attempted to scale the ridge they were mown down by American bullets and grenades. The wounded kids, screaming and calling for their mothers, were rushed back on stretchers into one of Freddy's cellars where the field medical team had been on stand-by.

In battle terms the situation was a stalemate, which is what Freddy radioed back to HQ.

An hour later, after another wave of wounded boys had been brought in, there was a commotion and shouting outside the cellar door. The voice was unmistakable. Freddy's spirits plunged. SS.Standartenfuhrer Muller clumped awkwardly down the stone steps. His leer his teeth, his belly, were unchanged, but apart from the long scar across his forehead, there was a satisfying change in his gait. Keeping his legs well apart he walked with a crab-like limp, drawing one foot behind the other. He filled the arched doorway.

'Well! What a surprise. Major von Langdorf! Trying to make a soldier out of you, are they? Putting you in the real army now.'

Freddy's knuckles tightened. If he was going to die, he was going to take Muller with him. It was every man for himself.

'Might I suggest, under the circumstances Standartenfuhrer, we avoid personality clashes and concentrate on fighting the Americans instead?'

'I will decide what we avoid Herr Major.' he roared. 'Now where is your platoon?'

'Most of them in there, injured'. Freddy pointed to the adjacent sick-bay cellar room.

'Pathetic.' he barked, and barged in shouting about loyalty to the Fuhrer. He wanted every boy who could hold a rifle to join him and a few hundred others, to take the ridge from another position. A straggling line of dazed and mostly walking wounded youngsters followed him out into the bitter December night, which already smelt of death.

By the 20th the offensive had ground to a temporary halt. The reconnaissance boys found an abandoned food depot, containing tins of corned beef and vegetables, cans of soup, bread and apfelstrudels. Freddy suggested an early Christmas feast. He watched their child faces, as they sang Christmas carols, some laughing, some in pain, some tearful, but all finding comfort in this brief retreat into normality, while all around them American mortar fire continued incessantly day and night.

By midday on the 23rd the house had been blown to pieces, only the cellars remained, and where Freddy too remained trying to protect his radio and transmitter. The medical team had retreated to a safer building. The platoon was out there somewhere, being slaughtered. It was mad to suppose there would be a signal to retreat. "Fight to the death" had been the battle command. Fleeing from this hell had crossed his mind, but where to?

Standartenfuhrer Muller, yelling with enough power to drown the noise of mortars crabbed down the half-demolished steps, and appeared at the doorway, his face twisted with anger. Behind him were two SS personnel. 'Arrest this man!' he shouted.

Before Freddy could gather his senses, the two men had grabbed him, and were holding him like a vice.

'Now strip the fucking bastard'.

They tore off every stitch of his clothing, threw his identity disc into the rubble, pounding it with a boot, and ripped his I.D. papers into shreds.

'Traitor, fucking traitor!' he screamed. 'You don't exist anymore major! Haven't you heard the news Major von Langdorf? General Count von Langdorf was executed today, and do you know how?' Muller started to cackle. 'Piano wire, which they let down very very slowly. He was in fucking agony and quite right for fucking traitors. All of them! It's what they fucking deserve!' He was shouting so loudly the veins on his temples and neck were standing out like sinuous blue worms. Freddy knew his uncle would have to die horribly like the others, but to hear this fiend gloat over his agony doubled the pain.

Muller yelled to his acolytes,

'Strap him down and go. I have a personal score to settle.'

They threw Freddy face down onto a heavy farm table, roping his legs to the table's legs, and spread-eagling his body across the table top, binding his hands together underneath. The men left. There was a loud explosion nearby. Freddy hoped they had been killed as surely as he was going to be.

Muller stood behind Freddy and cackled. 'First time I've seen a naked aristo arse. How d'you like this?' He pushed his revolver sharply into the young man.

'Like it?' he whined. 'I hope you do because that's where I'm going to shoot you. They used to call it disembowelling in the old days didn't they?'

'For Christ's sake, bastard, get it over with.' Freddy gasped.

Muller laughed again. 'Pity there'll be no more von Langdorfs, with you and your uncle dead.'

There was no point in shouting now. No one would hear with the noise outside. Even if he could haul the heavy table up, Muller could shoot him. He thought of Catherine, and tried to focus his thoughts on her. He was still wearing his mother's ring and held it in his wet manacled hands under the table. A talisman no longer.

There was another loud explosion. Muller looked up. He had no intention of staying here. 'Now one final thing, before your bowels dance Herr Major. I have always said, fuck the aristocracy. Well now,' he cackled, 'I'm really going to do it.' Freddy shut his eyes, every muscle clenched. 'Oh God,' he whispered. 'Why do you allow these pigs to live?'

Muller positioned himself behind his spread-eagled victim.

The whine of an approaching mortar pierced the air shattering the cellar's main concrete beam. Muller ran to the entrance. The blast threw the table upside down, landing on a mattress, with Freddy pinned underneath. The table legs broke with the shower of heavy debris that tumbled down from the ceiling.

The table was saving his life, but the weight of heavy masonry was suffocating. Out of the corner of his eye he could see Muller's foot. He was lying face down in the rubble under heavy concrete lintels that had crushed the porcine body.

'Thank you God! You are there,' Freddy whispered to the acrid gloom.

He knew if the Americans took him alive he would have to be a Frenchman. There was nothing left of his German identity, Muller had seen to that. His head swam, and a black veil drew across his closing eyelids.

An American jeep carrying a colonel and his lieutenant drove slowly through the smoking ruins of the little town. It was bitterly cold and snowing lightly, the heavy fall earlier having put out fires. The Infantry were already combing the town for snipers, although with the appalling number of dead, they didn't expect to find anyone left alive. Wounded had already been taken off to a P.O.W. field hospital. As they were driving past a row of what would have been substantial houses, an American sergeant ran out.

'Excuse me sir, something a bit crazy in there.' The colonel laughed and took out a cigarette. 'As if I haven't seen enough crazy things! O.K. Lead the way.'

They followed the sergeant into the cellar where Freddy and Muller were lying. 'The SS officer's flattened, sir. Naked guy tied to a table still alive, sir - just'.

The colonel lit his cigarette, pushed his cap back, and turned to his lieutenant. 'Well what's this tell you, lieutenant?'

The lieutenant, a studious looking young man, wearing heavy rimmed spectacles, frowned. 'I would say, the SS officer from his position on the ground, was running away, leaving the naked guy to be killed sir.'

'Agreed,' replied the colonel. 'And I would also think the poor bastard under the table was about to receive some SS attention.'

'He doesn't look Jewish, sir,' opined the sergeant.

The colonel smiled. 'The SS don't reserve their little pleasures just for Jews, Sergeant Hoffman. They spread them around! Now get him out, wrap him up, and put him with our guys. Anyone the SS doesn't like is a friend of ours. Clear?'

'Merry Christmas! Merry Christmas! Merry Christmas! Come on wake up!' Somewhere at the back of Freddy's subconscious he remembered he was now a Frenchman. He opened his eyes. A pretty face hovered above his. His ribs ached. In rapid French, he whispered 'Where am I? What has happened to me?'

'Oh gee! You're French. Hank!' she called, 'C'm'ere'.

A few days later, Freddy in an American army dressing gown and sitting in a wheelchair, arms and legs tightly bandaged, rib cage bound, was with an interpreter in the M.O.'s office. Although Freddy understood English reasonably well, American was more difficult.

He told them he was Jean-Louis Soulas from Strasbourg, giving as his home address that of his old French governess. He told them he was working for the resistance in the south but had been caught by the SS, brought to the front line and was about to be assaulted then shot. All his papers had been destroyed. To be Alsatian was safer in case a slight accent was detected. They asked a few questions about the south, which he answered with absolute truth.

The M.O. found the story convincing.

'Well, Jean-Louis, you seem a regular guy. You'll have some temporary ID papers when you leave.'

'When will that be, sir?'

'Three weeks.'

By Christmas it was generally assumed that Catherine and Philippe would marry. But there were times when she would sit in her room, take out Freddy's ring and photograph from the secret drawer of the bureau, and weep. The German army's

Ardennes disaster, with thousands killed, had given emphasis to her mother's predictions.

From February Philippe would be at Montpellier, Catherine would be attending a crammer revision course in July and August, and in October Annabelle would be going into the second year at the Medical Faculty. Catherine noticed she and Max seemed to be spending evenings alone together.

'Getting on well with Max?'

Annabelle smiled.'He's very supportive Cathy; a link with Francois.'

They were sitting alone in the conservatory. Catherine was resting her head in cupped hands leaning on the table. 'Now my little friend, I'm going to say to you what you say to me. Don't throw away chances of new happiness for the sake of the past.'

'Cathy, my head is too full of Medical School at the moment. But, Max is great.' She grinned.'You want to know if I - fancy him, don't you?'

'Well, do you?'

The nose puckered as she thought for a moment and giggled. 'Of course I could. He's very attractive. But not yet. He understands exactly how I feel.'

'So he should! He' s going to be a psychiatrist isn't he? Be nice to have you as my cousin-in-law'.'

Annabelle rocked with laughter. 'Now look here, mademoiselle, don't you say anything to your mother, or she'll be straight on the phone to your aunt, and she'll want my blood sample!' She launched into an impersonation of the two sisters. At last life was more than fear, torture and death squads.

The American colonel in the west wing sent in a large hamper of food for Christmas. Philippe was cook for the festive day, and Catherine his galley slave. Marianne could not have been more content especially as Max had persuaded his mother to spend New Year at the chateau, with all of them, Annabelle included. They dressed for New Year's Eve to celebrate France's liberation. Catherine wore her green eau de nil dress, the one she had worn to Max's graduation party all those years before. Philippe looking very handsome in a dinner suit, held his arms out to her as she came downstairs. 'You are just as I remember you the first time. Loved you then. Love you much more now.'

Annabelle was in turquoise silk, the fabric found by her parents and made up as a Christmas present. The gown fitted her slender shape perfectly, the colour reflecting her blue eyes. A stiffened shawl collar framed her face and blond curls like a piece of delicate porcelain.

After dinner they danced to records in the hall, the big fireplace flaming bright with logs. Catherine took particular note of the way Max was looking at Annabelle. So was Simone. Through the open door she imagined she could see Freddy sitting at the Bechstein in the salon. She had to stop herself remembering. Annabelle too had to stop remembering last Christmas with Francois. During a war a year can be a lifetime.

Out in the leafless vineyards, the two sisters took a brisk winter walk,

'Tell me Marianne dear, Annabelle, sweet pretty little thing. D' you think Max is keen?'

Marianne smiled. 'Haven't an idea about Max. They all seem very jolly together. But why not? I'm deeply fond of darling Annabelle. Lovely child, plucky too. Been through hell.'

'And her family, Marianne. Would we know them from Paris?'

'Heavens no! They're trades people from this region. Father has his own business. Large house, I believe.'

'Oh! No money then.'

'Shouldn't think so. Does it matter these days?'

'I suppose not,' Simone replied petulantly.

On the fifteenth of January despite snow and bitter weather, Max drove Philippe back to his Norman family home via Vichy, where Simone intended to remain until her husband returned from Dachau.

Around midnight on the night of the nineteenth of January, Catherine had just put out her light, when there was a noise of gravel being thrown up at the window. She got out of bed, and pushed back the shutters. The moon was casting violet shadows on the snow. She looked down into the front courtyard. Someone was standing there.

'Catherine! Catherine!' the voice called. She grabbed a dressing gown and flew down the stairs, her feet barely touching the stones, opened the door, stretched out her arms, and pulled him inside. She gasped, and cried, as did he. She looked at him, dressed as he was in dishevelled civilian clothes, and caressed his poor weary face. Freddy put his arms about her and held her, simply held her.

She gathered what food she could find from the kitchen and crept upstairs with a tray. He told her everything, about his uncle, the battles, about Muller, and the intended assault in the cellar. She barely heard, so overwhelmed was she at seeing him alive again. After a hot bath, she dabbed the raw patches of skin and angry slices of scar stitching, with olive oil. She massaged his wrists, and he fell into a heavy sleep. She crept into bed beside him.

The love of her life had returned.

They woke early. She gazed at him unable to believe he was really beside her.

'My darling Catherine,' he whispered. 'I have missed you like life itself.'

'This isn't a dream, is it Freddy? You are really here, aren't you?'

She ran her finger round his face.

'I can't believe it really is you!'

He put his arms round her, and his lips found hers. Their embraces were passionate. Their hunger for each other was abandoned, intense. They laughed and cried. They had found life after death.

Freddy told her he would have to return to Dresden, but hoped he could remain at the chateau until the 23rd.

Philippe was not expected back until the 26th.

He showed her his new ID. 'I still have a conscience about it, but there was little choice. If I go back to Germany, with my own name, I could be arrested, and either put in a concentration camp or shot.'

'What will happen to Jean Louis Soulas in Germany?'

He threw the coat given him by the hospital over his shoulders. 'Arrested, and put into a concentration camp. That's why I shall have to travel at night, get into Switzerland. Friends in Zurich can get me a Swiss passport. They wouldn't arrest a Swiss national.'

Catherine found him clothes of Robert's, and told her mother.

Marianne could not have been more shocked if another war had broken out. She went into a state of catatonic paralysis. Although she embraced him, mumbling joy at seeing him, Catherine could see her mother was furious. Her plans were thrown.

'So tell me, Freddy, when do you propose to leave for Germany?'

'In a few days. In Switzerland I shall draw money out of the family Swiss account, and buy a Swiss passport.' He took a slice of baguette. 'I want to be in Dresden for my mother's birthday, the 14th of February, assuming I can get there before the Russians. I have no idea if they are still alive since my uncle's execution.' He paused briefly. 'My father always takes Mama out somewhere, to the Opera, or to a concert, the night before.'

'Seeing you will the best present she could ever have.' Marianne encouraged.

The following day while Freddy was sitting at the Bechstein and Catherine was in the village shopping, Marianne wandered into the salon.

'How lovely to hear you play again, Freddy. Look dear I must talk to you.' Beckoning him to sit beside her on the settee, she began by telling him what happened to local girls thought to be collaborators, some even being shot, so rumour had it. She quoted the new liberators next door.

'If they knew Catherine had been consorting with a German soldier she would be labelled a prostitute, and taken. That's why I'm so glad you are going back, because everyone locally knows you. Why, the war isn't over yet! You could be captured and put in a prisoner of war camp.'

Freddy looked down at his scarred wrists, and nodded wearily.

'Yes madame I know. Nothing must happen to Catherine because of me. I love her too much.' He gave a hopeless smile. 'If it weren't for my parents, I'd give myself up here and now. Just walk next door.'

'Good Heavens! You can't do that!' It was certainly not what Marianne had in mind. 'Look Freddy, if you take my advice, go back to Germany via Switzerland as planned, find your parents again, and as soon as this wretched war is over, can't be too long now, and people's memories have shortened, you can come back. That is, in a year or so, can't you?'

Freddy and Catherine spent the next few days locked away in her rooms, avoiding the new housekeeper and Jacques. Marianne went about the chateau in a highly charged state of nerves. Naturally Catherine telephoned Annabelle, who became anxious about the effect this unexpected turn of events would have. When Philippe telephoned, Catherine felt herself imperceptibly drawing away from him, and not reacting to the little intimacies that lace conversations of separated lovers.

Once again, Freddy held her heart.

He did not tell Catherine of his conversation with Marianne, but said, 'I shall probably have to wait at least a year after the war is over before I come back for you.'

'Why so long?'

'For memories to fade,' he said, quoting Marianne.

Catherine took his hand and pressed it to her cheek. 'I'll wait for you'.

He sighed. 'And I shall write, but the thought of leaving you fills me with dread.'

'Darling Freddy, let the time pass quickly.'

He left on the night of January 24th.

Catherine was distraught, and wept on Annabelle's shoulder. 'I shall have to tell Philippe. It's Freddy I want to be with.'

'Now listen. Here, dry your eyes.' Annabelle passed her deeply unhappy friend a handkerchief. 'Now let's think clearly, and sensibly. Question. If there were no Freddy, would you be content to marry Philippe?'

'Absolutely.'

'So, if you tell Philippe to get out of your life next week, and something happens to Freddy the week after, what then?'

'I don't know.'

'I do,' replied the ever-resourceful Annabelle. 'You will spend the rest of your life regretting, and possibly alone. My advice would be to say nothing to Philippe. Your four days with Freddy was a beautiful dream Catherine. Philippe doesn't want to get married yet in any case, so if you haven't heard from Freddy in a year, you will have to assume the worst, and you won't have lost Philippe.'

'But Annabelle, I - slept with Freddy - couldn't help it.'

Annabelle's face puckered for a moment as she strove to find a rationale.

'Well, if I had a lover, and suddenly, miraculously, Francois came back to me for a few days, I would too.'

Catherine sniffed and dried her tears. 'I feel so guilty.'

'You mustn't,' said Annabelle quite firmly. 'Men do it all the time, especially in war. Anyway, didn't Philippe try to make love to you, five years ago, when he already had a girl friend?'

Catherine nodded.

Annabelle beamed. 'There we are then.'

Taking Annabelle's practical advice to heart, when Philippe returned on January 25th, she tried to behave as normally as possible. If she recieved no communication from Freddy within a few months after the end of the war, she would have to assume the worst had happened.

She worked out her own modus operandi.

Catherine's period was two days late. It had to be the shock of Freddy's arrival. Immersed in study she forgot about it. On the morning of the fourteenth of February Marianne was in a curious mood as she drank her breakfast coffee. Catherine

The Girl on the Promenade

picked up the percolator. 'I hope Freddy's been able to reach Dresden. I wonder if they all went to the Opera last night?'

Marianne looked at her daughter. 'Sit down dear. You obviously haven't heard the news. Dresden is being flattened. The RAF started, what's the phrase, 'carpet bombing' from about ten o clock last night, the Americans have taken over today, and they are still bombing.'

Catherine felt she was choking. 'But - but - isn't it like Paris - an open city?'

'Not any more. Papa thought it a delightful place,' she added, almost to herself.

When the radio announced the bombing was continuing throughout the night of the fourteenth, Catherine was in despair, and thankful Philippe was in residence at Montpellier. Unable to sleep, she sat up listening to a Brahms symphony. A few days later the complete destruction of the old centre of Dresden with the Opera House and Concert Hall was announced, with an estimated loss of about 60,000 lives.

Marianne came upstairs to Catherine's room, and for a brief moment stood looking at her daughter. Without a word, she walked towards her, arms outstretched.

For Marianne it was an end, sad, but by far the best solution in the long run.

Annabelle put her arms round her friend 'I think Catherine, I think, you have now got to come to terms with - '

'Death! I know.'

When she began to feel sick in the mornings, Catherine knew without a doubt she was pregnant. She was extremely worried, and told only Annabelle.

'You have to tell Philippe, Catherine.'

'But I hate the idea of pushing him into a situation.'

Philippe was delighted. 'We'll get married right away. Don't know how it happened. Damn thing must have split, or something. Who cares? This is great. I've always wanted kids.' He laughed. 'If we like it, let's have some more.'

'But what should I do about Montpellier?'

'The baby's due in October. You can still go back to medical school. We'll get a nanny, and I get time off anyway.'

Comforted by the fact her husband-to-be approved of continuing medical studies, and was delighted with impending fatherhood, Catherine resigned herself to her new role. Marianne took the news philosophically.

'A grandchild is a grandchild, whether it comes sooner rather than later,' she beamed. Gossip-mongers would be well and truly silenced now, seeing Catherine the wife of Dr. Philippe Brincourt and mother of his child.

The marriage was a private affair in the chateau's chapel, with Annabelle in attendance. Catherine wore her mother's wedding dress, of white silk organdie, which fortunately fitted her fuller figure.

Guests were few: Simone from Vichy, and a few friends from Paris and Montpellier. In the absence of a father, Marianne walked to the altar with Catherine. The two sisters shed discreet tears, Marianne thinking how proud Georges would have been of his Catherine, and Simone thinking how proud Louis would have been of his handsome son, in the role of best man.

A reception was held in the formal dining room, and to be correct they invited the American colonel, who did not stay long because no one spoke American.

Philippe took his new bride up to the family house in Normandy,which had been left in one piece. Slowly Catherine began to appreciate her gentle caring husband more and more.

With the end of the war in May, Simone received an official letter informing her of Louis' death in Dachau so she moved permanently to the chateau.

On the evening of November 2nd, after a short easy labour, Catherine gave birth to a baby girl in the master bedroom, which Marianne had now given to the married couple, because of the adjoining nursery and bathroom. Philippe remained with her, and was ecstatically happy that they had a daughter. His excitement touched them all, waiting in the salon downstairs.

The Girl on the Promenade

Max and Annabelle whooped for joy, and Marianne danced a little jig with her adored son-in-law. Philippe ran back to Catherine, and held his new daughter washed and pink in his arms. 'Darling Catherine, she is beautiful, beautiful! Gorgeous little thing!' He cooed at the tiny bundle, stroked the miniature hands, laughing proudly, and gave her back to Catherine. 'They all want to come up. Can you bear it, darling? There are also three bottles of champagne coming up too!' Catherine was already lost in the world of new motherhood. The champagne bubbled; Simone wondered who the baby looked like. Max thought all babies looked like scrunched up centogenarians.

'So darling, surprise us! What is she to be called?'

'Sophie Annabelle,' smiled Catherine. Annabelle was overjoyed, and everyone approved.

A couple of hours later Marianne crept up to see her daughter.

Catherine was sitting in bed, fresh and happy. Sophie Annabelle sleeping peacefully in a cot, Marianne settled herself on the edge of the bed. Catherine could tell she was about to launch into something.

'Catherine', she began, 'there is something I have to tell you, and can tell you now the baby is born.' Catherine raised a bemused eyebrow.

'One morning, about the beginning of last month,' she went on 'I was near the village shops when I saw a man with a beard hovering in the alleyway across the road. He beckoned me to go to him. It was Freddy.'

For a moment the shock took Catherine's breath away.

'What? What are you saying? Why didn't you tell me? Why?'

'Listen please! Calm down. I told him you were married. I had to, and that you were about to have a baby, and that it would be unthinkable if he were to try to see you.' Marianne stopped. Her daughter's face was ashen with pain.

'Well, what else could I have done?'

Catherine put her head back on the pillow and closed her eyes.

'Go on. Tell me.'

'Well to be frank, he was - speechless really, though I can't think why. Very upset. Understandable, I suppose. Oh! By the way, his parents were both killed in Dresden, so sad, and he has returned to the family castle. He went off wishing you happiness. He should never have come back so soon. I told him, when he left last time, to wait at least a year or two. Rather silly of him not to listen.'

Her head resting on the pillow, Catherine's eyes opened wide. She looked at her mother in horror. 'You? You told him to wait a year?'

Marianne shifted uncomfortably in her chair. 'Of course!' she replied, primly defensive. 'Better than being hanged by the communists or shot, don't you think? And you needn't look as though I'd committed a crime, Catherine.'

Catherine closed her eyes, blinking back the tears.

'Please will you go. Leave me,' she whispered. ' I want to sleep.'

When Marianne had left, Catherine raised herself out of bed, picked up her little daughter, and looked at her very carefully. She saw she was long limbed, her tiny fingers slim and delicate, as indeed were Philippe's. Carrying her to the window, Catherine stroked the soft pink cheek, and for the first time saw the eyes of her newborn. She pulled up a chair, sat unsteadily, and looked again at her baby. Sophie Annabelle's pale blue irises were ringed with deep ultramarine, and as the infant mouth yawned, puckered, and pouted into a dozen mute shapes, she perceived a familiar upward curve of those rosebud lips. Her heart raced, her legs trembled. She knew without a doubt, this was Freddy's child. Holding the warm bundle close to damp cheeks, she could hear his words just before he left.

'If the worst happens, you must forget about me, you will have to, because I want you to be happy always.'

The worst had happened. Worse than death. The love of her life had come back. He had kept his promise. Kept his word. All too late.

With what dreadful irony had Fate twisted their lives.

Sophie Annabelle would remain a precious burden of guilt, a secret that Catherine alone would have to bear for the rest of her life.

War had exacted its final toll.

BIOGRAPHICAL NOTES

Throughout her professional life Elizabeth Morgan has worked in the entertainment business as an actor/writer.

She has appeared in numerous television productions which include 'The Old Devils' 'The Two of Us' 'We are Seven' numerous Dick Emery shows and 'Dad's Army', as well as performances at the National Theatre, provincial theatres and several tours in the USA with her own one woman plays.

She provides voices for animated cartoons including the voices of Destiny and Rhapsody Angels in the long running cartoon series 'Captain Scarlet'

Elizabeth has worked extensively in radio, having been under long term contract to the BBC Radio Drama Company, and recorded 'Under Milk Wood' with Sir Anthony Hopkins.

She has written 26 plays for BBC Radio 4, several short stories, two of which are in a recently published collection, and four television plays. A regular contributor to magazines and newspapers, she is now working on a sequel to her book about France, 'Can we afford the Bidet?'

A devoted Francophile she divides her time between Hastings and the South of France.

Printed in the United Kingdom
by Lightning Source UK Ltd.
118495UK00001B/250-273